Personality

ALSO BY ANDREW O'HAGAN

The Missing

Our Fathers

Andrew O'Hagan

Personality

HARCOURT, INC.

Orlando   Austin   New York   San Diego   Toronto   London

Requests for permission to make copies of any part of the work should be
mailed to the following address: Permissions Department, Harcourt, Inc.,
6277 Sea Harbor Drive, Orlando, Florida 32887-6777.

www.HarcourtBooks.com

First published in the UK by Faber and Faber Limited

"(You've Got) Personality." Words and music by Lloyd Price and Harold Logan.
Copyright © 1959 Irving Music, Inc. Copyright renewed. All rights reserved.
Used by permission. "Help Me Make It Through the Night." Words and music
by Kris Kristofferson. © 1970 (renewed 1998) Temi Combine, Inc. All rights
controlled by Combine Music Corp. and administered by EMI Blackwood
Music, Inc. All rights reserved. Used by permission.

Library of Congress Cataloging-in-Publication Data
O'Hagan, Andrew, 1968–
Personality/Andrew O'Hagan.—1st U.S. ed.
p.   cm.
ISBN 0-15-101000-5
1. Italians—Great Britain—Fiction. 2. Bute Island (Scotland)—Fiction.
3. London (England)—Fiction. 4. Women singers—Fiction.
5. Fans (Person)—Fiction. 6. Celebrities—Fiction.   I. Title.
PR6065.H18P47 2003
823'.914—dc21   2003005369

7584

Text set in Minion
Designed by Cathy Riggs

Printed in the United States of America

First U.S. edition

A C E G I K J H F D B

to India

We need applause. That's how we live.
When you don't have a lot of noise around you,
the noise inside you becomes overwhelming.
JUDY GARLAND

5 July 1940

The body of Enrico Colangelo lay on the beach. Dressed in a gabardine suit, the man had rolled for three days in the Atlantic, before the Isle of Barra came out of the dark and the tenor landed at Traig Iais. He was subject to the violence of the open sea and the awful eclipse of God's mercy. He was dead now, but in the cold chambers of Enrico's heart there remained a final certainty: he could swim to the lifeboats, he'd find her there.

He came in the night with a quantity of teacups and wreckage, and in the morning the sea was blue, the perfect blue of an Italian sea. Enrico Colangelo might have imagined the waves had brought him home again, yet the drowned man was a stranger to the Hebrides. No one knew him. His suit was foreign, so were his shoes, and he lay on the white beach with the water lapping at his legs. Some boys were playing in the marram grass over the strand. They loved it there when the wind was strong; the grass whipped at their legs and it was frightening to hear the crash of the waves and feel the rush of the sand that would sting your face and push you back to the dunes. From the top you could look across the sound to South Uist and the place where Charles Edward Stuart met Flora Macdonald at midnight.

The boys put their jumpers over their heads and ran through the spray and the sand. The wind that morning was fierce and the sand prickled their hands and made them go red as the boys ran down, still laughing, arms spread out, their voices making the noise of fighter planes as they turn and dive. Once down on the strand they pulled their jumpers from their faces, and that's when they saw Colangelo's body. None of them had seen a dead person before. One of the boys wanted to cry and without saying anything he ran back over the dunes to get somebody. There was no movement among the others, no sound from them.

What are children in the eyes of a dead man? The boys came close and stared, but there was nothing. Years later two of Neil MacInnes's brothers would be lost off Polacharra; only then, as a man of sixty-two, would Neil remember the fingers of the washed-up man at Traig Iais, the whiteness of the finger wearing a silver ring, and the fascination in Lachlin MacKinnon's eyes. The boys wished they knew the story of the man lying dead, but soon a pair of crofters came running over the sandhills and the children stood back, paying no attention to the sea and the things that happened out there, and only sorry to have lost possession of their treasure so quickly. They looked over their shoulders at Marton McDougall, the boy weeping on the dunes.

One of the crofters went through the dead man's suit, and was pleased to find his wallet; from a tight leather pocket inside the wallet he drew out a card, barely damp.

ENRICO COLANGELO
Tenor from Rome, Naples Opera Houses,
London Coliseum, BBC
Address: 15 York Road, London SE1
Telephone: Waterloo 4485

When the police came from Castlebay they put a blanket over the body and built a fence of flotsam around him, and after some questions the children had to retreat to the grass to see what would happen next. But nothing happened except it got dark and the Atlantic boomed. Neil MacInnes put his arms inside his jumper and kept spying from the dunes. He thought the sea after dark might give a clue or say something or send more dead people in with the waves. But no. Enrico Colangelo lay silent and secret on the beach, everything behind him, the black water, the world beyond.

The next day Mrs Mackenzie, the wife of the Commander of the Home Guard, came with the news that London had been on the phone. They now had permission to give Enrico Colangelo a Catholic burial. And so the adults and the Home Guard took the body away from the long beach and it was carried in a box to be prepared by some women in Castlebay and then buried in the graveyard on the other side of the island.

The three churches of St Barr's were in ruins on top of the hill at Eoligarry. The burial site wasn't large, but you could easily tell the dead generations apart in that field: the oldest gravestones were made of the same stone as the walls of the first church, and they surrounded those broken walls, whilst the other graves, more modern and flat, marking the dead of succeeding generations, were positioned sparsely on the slopes of the hill, trailing down, more sparsely still, to a part of the field where the grass seemed green and fresh. The sun shone the day Enrico Colangelo was laid to rest; from the graveside, the sea of Barra Sound glinted like the waters of Monte Cristo, and the assembled people, for whom he was nobody in particular, uttered Hail Marys to the open air.

The boys watched as the prayers were said and when the soil was put down they scrambled over the hill making the sound of aeroplanes. The sun was high over Eriskay, and you could see other beaches, giant footsteps to the mainland, across the Minch towards the skyline. In an instant, the boys were off the hill that stands over the graveyard, their sudden laughter, their quick eyes, gone now as wind comes and goes in the grass.

PART ONE

1 · Suppers

Business was slack, so the pubs closed early and the ferry came in for the night. A brown suitcase was left standing on the pier; it stood there for hours and nobody came for it and nobody complained. It was out all night, and in the morning somebody took it along to Lost Property.

The sky was pink above the school and at eight o'clock the high tide arrived and later the promenade was quiet except for the barking of a dog. From out in the bay you could see lights coming on in the windows of Rothesay, the main town on the Isle of Bute. Inside the rooms there were shadows moving and the shadows were blue from the televisions. It had been a rough winter. First the swimming baths were closed down and then a fire destroyed the railway station at Wemyss Bay. In January, the winds got up to seventy miles per hour, interrupting ferry services to the islands, and then Rothesay's assistant harbourmaster died, and then Mr McGettigan the butcher died. Two elderly men in blue blazers were standing along from the harbour talking about these and other matters, one man smoking a pipe and the other a rollup, leaning against the sea-railing, the water lapping on the pebbles beneath them, the gulls overhead.

'Good chips depends on getting a hold of the best tatties,' one said. 'It's the tatties that make the difference. They used to have them all the time. Nowadays, the chip shops are buying in rubbish tatties that should never have been planted in the first place.'

'Aye,' said the other. 'You need Ayrshires or Maris Pipers. This lot are using spuds you wouldn't feed to the pigs.'

'And the state of the lard . . .'

'Aye, the lard. Thick wi' crumbs and decrepit wi' use. Terrible mess. I wouldny go near their chips, no, I wouldny thank you for them.'

'Lard. You wouldny feed it to the pigs.'

'A good poke a chips, Wully. They wouldny know them if they came up and took a bite oot their arse.'

'Oh aye. Don't get me started. The fish they're using . . .'

'Aye.'

'They're lettin the fish lie half the week. You need to put a fish straight into the fryer—fresh as you like, nae bother.'

'That's right.'

'A good bit of fish for your tea, Wully. Oh aye. There's plenty of them oot there swimming aboot.'

'Well, good luck to them. The cafés will sell a fair few fish suppers come the morra morn. The world and its neighbour'll be oot for the Jubilee the morra.'

'Right enough. I dare say there'll be drink.'

'Oh, there'll be drink all right.'

They paused a moment.

'They were few and far between,' said the first man, 'but I'll tell you, Wully, the best chips ever seen on this island was during the war.' The men fell quiet at that, they looked over the water, and a dog came past barking and chasing seagulls along the promenade. Not for a long time had an evening on the island been so warm and so still.

MARIA TAMBINI lived at 120 Victoria Street. The family café and chip shop was downstairs, its front window filled with giant boxes of chocolates covered in reproduction Renoirs; also, here and there in the window, on satin platforms, were piles of rock that said 'Rothesay'. No matter where you broke it, that's what it said inside: 'Rothesay'. Her mother spread Maria's hair on the pillow and combed it one last time before closing the window to keep out the night. Just a minute before, she had been sitting on the edge of the bed, a silver spoon glinting in her hand, as she fed Maria from a tin of Ambrosia Creamed Rice.

'There,' Rosa said. 'Go to sleep now. Nothing will happen.'

'Tomorrow,' said the girl. Mrs Tambini straightened the edge of the Continental quilt and wiped the mirror with a yellow duster.

'It will all be great,' she said, thinking of things she still had to do. 'Try to keep your head out the quilt, it's nicer for your face.'

Maria closed her eyes. She had never known her father, and his name was never mentioned in the house, but she knew he lived somewhere in America. Sometimes, in the moments just before falling asleep, she would imagine his smiling face under the sun. All her life he remained just that: a picture in her head that appeared in the dark before sleep.

Her mother went from the room and stood for a while at the top of the stairs. Through the open window in the bathroom she could hear Frances Bone, the woman who lived at the top of the next stairwell over, listening to the shipping forecast. Mrs Bone listened to the forecast every night and often in the day too, if she caught it. Standing there, Rosa admitted to herself that it was not so annoying as she often made out: she actually liked the sound of the words coming from the radio—'Forties, Cromarty, southeast, veering south or southwest 4 or 5, occasionally 6. Rain then showers, moderate or good'—and after Maria was asleep she stood there and listened.

People were laughing down in the shop and Rosa wished someone would go and bring that dog inside. She caught the look of the Firth of Clyde through the glass over the front door. For a second the sea and the distant lights were for Rosa alone. She remembered she needed Hoover bags, and passing over the last stairs she thought of an old song belonging to her father. She remembered her father most clearly when she thought of those old Italian songs he sang, and at the same time, without much fuss or grief, she thought of him coughing blood in the hours before he died.

Giovanni was slapping fish in a tray of batter and then laying them in the fryer. He caught himself in the silver top and immediately thought about his hair; it had always been the way with Giovanni: several times an hour he would go into the backshop and take a comb through his black hair. When he smiled and showed his good teeth, the women at the tables would look up and in that moment some would consider whether they hated or pitied their husbands. Giovanni rattled a basket of chips in the fryer and went through the back with a sort of swagger.

Rosa was scouring the top of the freezer with pink detergent paste. She looked over her shoulder as Giovanni came through, and she tutted. 'This place is pure black so it is,' she said, scrubbing now in circles, her head down, the paste going under her fingernails. 'I work myself to the bone in here to keep this place clean and nobody else seems to bother their arse. It's bloody manky so it is. Why people don't clean after theirselves I don't know.'

She paused. Mention of the efforts she made in life always caused tears to come into her eyes.

'All we need now is a visit from the men, that would just suit you all fine to sit there and for the men to come in and see all this. Hell slap it into you, I say. I try my best and I just get it all thrown back at me. There's no a bugger gives a shite. I'd be as well talking to the wall. If the men come and shut down this café for dirt then hell slap it into you. I could run a mile so I could. I could just put on my coat and run a mile.'

Giovanni moved the peelings from the big sink and ran the cold water over his hands. When he'd dried them he went to put his hand on Rosa's shoulder but she pulled away. 'See what I mean,' she said, picking up the dish-towel. 'Everything's just left lying about for me to pick up.' But when Giovanni turned to go back into the shop she was shaking as she stood at the sink and she put her arm behind her and stopped him. She turned and buried her head in his chest and he sighed. 'Come on Rosa,' he said. 'You're just tired. There's that much on your mind.'

Rosa cried so often and so predictably that no one really noticed she was crying. Her eyes were always red. People seldom asked what was wrong or if they could help; she was the type, they said, who would cry at the drop of a hat. For all the years they'd known her she had been in a state of moderate distress. She cried eating her dinner and running a bath. She cried watching television. She cried at her work and even in her sleep.

When Giovanni leant back, Rosa pressed the dish-towel against her eyes in a familiar way, then put her mouth on his chin and let her lips settle and breathed with her mouth open and ran her tongue along the bristles. Then she drew her bleachy fingers down his jawline and suddenly dug her nails into him. A line of blood ran from his chin onto his white coat. He flinched a little, made no noise, but in his eyes, staring down, anger had taken him miles away. 'Rosa,' he said, lifting the towel and wiping his chin, 'I am fucking tired in here. I'm so tired of this, even if you're not. I don't know what the fuck's the matter with you.'

Just in from a meeting of the Scottish Friendly Assurance Society at the Glenburn Hotel, some customers were waiting for suppers at one of the tables. Giovanni went back and began lifting fish out the fryer and organising plates; he juggled a tub of salt and a lemonade-bottle full of vinegar. Meanwhile Rosa came through and took the duster from her pocket and climbed on a chair to clean the trays that held the cigarettes. After that she got a damp cloth and did the sweetie jars. She was quite composed and seemed quickly to lose herself in the wiping and cleaning.

There was laughter at the tables as the customers ate their fish suppers and pie suppers, their single black puddings, half-pizzas with a pickled onion. George Samson, the oldest man on the island, who drove a turquoise three-wheeler car, sat at one of the tables reading a story from *The Buteman*. He occasionally shook his head and licked his thumb. '"Although it might seem rather early in the season,"' he read, '"a swarm of bees invaded a house in Castle Street, Rothesay, at the weekend and the police had to be called in to deal with it. A swarm—whether the same or another one—was seen over Castle Street on Tuesday afternoon and appeared to come to rest at the gable walls of Messrs Bonaccorsi and Humphrey's Store Lane building, formerly the De Luxe Cinema."'

George Samson put down the paper and took a dud lighter to his roll-up. Giovanni smiled over. 'They say you'll be lighting the bonfire for the Jubilee tomorrow, George.'

'Aye,' said George, coming up to the counter to pay for his tea, 'the Marquis of Bute is otherwise *detained*—did you hear that, *detained*—it seems, at a very posh do in the grounds of Holyrood Palace.' He bowed his head as if the matter was now clear. 'So I suppose you'd better move your arse and give me a box of Swan Vestas,' he said.

2 · *Jubilee*

The next day the tables for the Queen's Silver Jubilee Party were end-to-end down Victoria Street, from the Esplanade Hotel to the doors of the Bute Amusements, and each table was decked in Union Jacks and spread with cut sandwiches, hats on paper plates, sweets of all kinds. The glossy jellies lay there in mounds, and dozens of children sat waiting for the order and the gun salute. Overnight a battleship had arrived in the bay. You could see its long strings of bunting fluttering out there, and the ship's radar turning in the heat.

'I'm sewed into this big dress. Don't make me laugh or I'll pee myself,' said Mary Queen of Scots to her friend Kalpana Jagannadham, dressed as Queen Victoria. The children were coming down Castle Street in a great procession, each child trussed in a historical costume, famous kings and queens mainly, and some whose parents couldn't think came as knights or Picts or Tudor ladies-in-waiting. None of the costumes came from a shop, they were all home-made: papier-mâché ruffs, cardboard crowns, plastic swords, cotton wool for ermine, kitchen foil for crown jewels. Holding hands, the children marched down the street two by two. Maria and Kalpana were the two oldest girls, chosen because of their 'theatricality', but the parade and all the excitement was making them feel like infants again. They walked at the front, sighing, whispering and giggling between themselves, whilst the well-rehearsed children behind them, picked out of Bute's several primary schools, marched under the nose of their sergeant major, Mrs Jean Ogilvie, the headmistress of St Andrew's Roman Catholic Primary School.

Rosa had made an early claim for Maria to go as the Scottish Queen, and got out the sewing-machine and made a flouncy dress out of net curtain material. Giovanni was brilliant: he'd made a giant collar out of polythene and coat-hangers. Mrs Bone had let Maria borrow a long red wig she had in a box of hairdressing stuff in the back bedroom, and Rosa spent a whole hour that morning patting Maria's face with white powder. Kalpana, who was Indian and Scottish and Maria's best friend, the daughter of Dr Jagannadham—everybody called him Dr Jag—wore a black gown her father had kept from his days at Glasgow University. It was gathered at the bottom over bundles of saris and held together with safety pins. Dr Jag threw his head back and laughed that morning when she was finally dressed and ready to go. Mrs Jagannadham had sprayed Kalpana's hair grey and put a line of cotton wool down the middle. She wore Wellington boots on her feet and carried a little ball and a bicycle pump covered in silver foil. Seeing her come down Castle Street, her brown face frowning over her lacy collar, Dr Jag thought she was the funniest thing he had ever seen.

'Even on a nice day you are the notice box, Fiona Wallace,' said Mrs Ogilvie, keeping the kings and queens in line with her tan-coloured handbag.

'I never said nothing, Mrs Ogilvie,' said Elizabeth I. 'I never. I always get the blame. Michael McArdle was pinging my earrings so he was.'

'Lift up your sceptre, Fiona. You're a notice box that's all you are. And you, Maria: there's no need to look so torn-faced. You'll find your pretty, half-French head is still attached to your shoulders. William Auld, I've told you before. Richard the Lionheart is in many respects a mysterious figure, but we can be almost certain that he did not suck his thumb and pick his nose at the same time.'

Queen Victoria spoke with a pure Glasgow accent. 'Your dress is that nice,' she said, marching forward in her wellies at the front of the line, 'and the neck thing really suits you so it does. I'm no joking. It's lovely. Do you think they made them wear these collary-things because of the, what do you call it . . . love bites?'

'You're terrible,' said Mary Queen of Scots, scanning the crowd in a regal way. 'Look, the Primary Ones are going daft.'

All the Primary Ones wore black sand-shoes and each child was sporting head-horns (they were meant to be Vikings).

'Oh for pity's sake,' said Mrs Ogilvie. 'Would the mothers please, oh no, good heavens, mothers, I need your assistance here!' Many of the mothers were following the procession from the pavement, walking alongside and making sure their kid's costume wasn't falling apart. Dr Jag was still laughing and taking Polaroids all the way down. Victoria Regina would occasionally look over and smile her lovely smile. 'I'm no joking, Maria,' she said, 'this is a total brass neck.'

The Primary Ones—the Vikings—had got jammed up behind a car outside Gregg's the Baker, and some of the boys were busy lifting up their tunics and peeing into the road. 'Young ladies, turn your heads please. Jesus, Mary and Joseph,' cried Mrs Ogilvie, 'please mothers, could you take your respective children in hand. This is quite appalling. No, Fergus Tully. Fergus Tully! Do not sit down! Do not take your pants down! Mrs Tully!'

The procession of kings and queens came down Castle Street and turned before the harbour. Mary of Orange had a giant beehive hairdo and one red glove (Mrs Ogilvie said to her colleagues her father wouldn't be reasoned with). The girl came up to Maria and Kalpana with jam smeared over her chin and a soda scone in her red hand. 'There's rhubarb jelly and custard as well,' she said through a mouthful of crumbs, 'and hundreds of eggs this size and chocolate and a lucky bag for everybody if they behave.' She was talking quickly and waving the scone. 'And you get a present even if you don't win a race or anything.' Kalpana took hold of Maria's blood-stained handkerchief (an object in mind of her slain lover David Rizzio) and shook it in the girl's face. 'Get lost, scabby Babby,' she said.

'Barbara!' shouted Mrs Ogilvie. 'Who gave you permission to go ahead to the dinner table? Get to the back of the line you greedy girl.' Mrs Ogilvie drew a hand across her forehead and looked as if she were now having words with some higher authority. 'Watch her,' she said, 'she's a bad article.' The children marched in their ramshackle fashion. 'Kalpana,' said Mrs Ogilvie, 'the royal procession is now about to turn into the street named in your memory. I know you are the Mourning Queen, but you will straighten your face please. This is a happy day.' Meanwhile, Robert the Bruce had climbed up on George III's back. 'This really is the height of nonsense. I promise I will have no hesitation in marching you children back up to the school if we have any more of your carry-on. Get back into your twos and holding hands. We're coming up to the corner now. Okay. Mary Queen of Scots and Victoria Regina, the elder girls, set a good example, raise your heads and walk in the royal fashion now. We must carry ourselves with the pride of the Anointed. Girls! Boys! Historians and patriots, historians and patriots!'

Maria and Kalpana giggled and linked arms and fashioned their faces for good behaviour. And down they came, the children of Bute, crêpe paper, glitter and glue, the infants trailing their rags of bin bag. Mrs Ogilvie lifted her head and nodded to the bandsmen. 'Here we are,' she called as they turned into the area of the street party, 'the Royals, in our excellent dresses, made to measure for their royal majesties by our excellent mothers of Argyll and Bute. Make way friends, countrymen, the children have arrived.'

The children rubbed their noses and darted their eyes. Local people were gathered all round the entrance to the pier, at the corner of Victoria Street, where the biggest table in Britain began. The people cheered and waved Union Jacks and Scottish flags, some shouting out names for children to turn around, others waving tumblers and cans of beer. The sun was scorching now and many of the mothers stood in bikini tops and some of the men roared out and others just stood on the putting green, looking impatient, blowing smoke-rings over the Firth of Clyde.

'Cavalier by name, cavalier by nature, David Dolan,' said Mrs Ogilvie, primping her hair and looking down the royal line. 'I'd ask you to keep with the procession, and woe betide anyone who opens that can of beer. If you must hold it, David, then keep it unopened and out of reach of the infants. Do not shake it up and down in that fashion.' David Dolan's dad had thought it a good idea to give Charles II a can of McEwan's Export to carry with him on the march. Mrs Ogilvie licked her lips. She put a Mint Imperial in her mouth as the procession came to a halt in Victoria Street. 'One at a time now,' she said. 'Find your places at the table and no pushing.'

From a flat above the sports shop a noise suddenly flooded the street as the window was raised; a couple of teenagers with spiked hair were holding a speaker out of the window, playing a record at top volume. 'Heathens!' shouted Mrs Ogilvie, letting her eye-glasses swing on their chain among her Sunday pearls. 'Close your ears children—we have barbarians in our midst!'

The two punks had only a brief triumph, for very soon a large hand came from behind their heads, and each was dragged back into the room in a flurry of slaps. The record scratched to an immediate halt, to be replaced only seconds later with Nana Mouskouri singing 'Morning Has Broken'. 'The divine right of succession,' said Mrs

Ogilvie, walking with her tribe as they found their seats at the table, 'is second only in my mind to the right of the saints to intercede on our behalf, or on behalf of the poor black babies who need God's help. Barbara Auld, put that cake down if you know what's good for you!'

Maria and Kalpana sank smirking into their ruffs. 'Please miss, what is that?' said Kalpana. She pointed to a silver airship floating over the bay. 'That is a blessing from the county council,' said Mrs Ogilvie, 'but you may feel free to comprehend it as a tear from the eye of the Baby Jesus. He weeps at behaviour such as that of those heathen boys in the window a moment ago. Now, girls, as you take your places at the Jubilee table please remember your good intentions and be in mind of the black babies who are less fortunate than ourselves. Come along the little Vikings! The feast is prepared.' Most of the children had no idea what Mrs Ogilvie was talking about, but they lost no time in pushing back their crowns and horned helmets and diving for the cakes, whilst the mothers came at their backs with tissues, cameras and special cups.

Rosa removed the red wig and took a brush to Maria's hair. 'Try to keep yourself nice for the cameras, baby,' she said, tying her daughter's hair into a short ponytail, then passing a tub of ice cream down to her from the other side of the table. Maria loved the cold feeling of the ice cream on her tongue and the sweet jelly she sucked from the spoon. Out in the bay, around the warship, the water sparkled, and on the deck the sailors stood to attention as the Union Jacks waved above them. Maria and Kalpana smiled at each other, rolling their eyes at all the antics; they looked out at the ship and filled their mouths with chocolate cake.

3 · Glorious

The old Mrs Tambini lived at 3 Morrison Terrace. Up on the headland, with the window open, she felt the breeze, and stood back for a time with the fresh wind moving over her, looking down into all the colour and all the fuss of the day.

I wonder what kind of gas is inside that balloon because they can be dangerous so they can.

For a moment her thoughts seemed to join with the breeze to tumble and fade outside the window.

Good God if this is not a day for people to bloody enjoy themselves and good for them. The church spire is bright enough good God it's nice and the weans you can hear their voices and all this happening in front of the Firth just as it is.

Her bluish hair, watery eyes and polished skin gave Lucia a look of constant freshness. Her lips were fairly tight but often she relieved them with a kiss of Avon lipstick. There was a mystery in Lucia's manner, and in repose, in her off-guard moments, a look of forgotten hopefulness would cover her face. She stood at the window only long enough to feel pleased about the Jubilee party. She could see the long table and all the flags as well as people running about and cheering on the putting green. Adults were gathered around the pier and the doors of the pubs were crowded. After she had taken it all in, she began to feel a chill in one of her eyes. She walked back across her living-room carpet and turned on a bar of the fire, then she flicked a finger at the spider plant sitting on her dining table before lifting up a pair of lace gloves and a needle. The table was covered in gloves of the same sort; she counted twelve pairs and one glove that was odd. Into the living-room with the Glade air fresheners at each corner came a smell of something like gunpowder. It must have been the bangs from the ship. She looked out the window again and the children were cheering; you could hear that much over the music. She closed the window against the smell and sat down again with the glove and the thread and the needle in her lap.

Lucia Tambini kept watch for the moments of grime in other people's lives, and her loneliness was a vigil against cruelty and vice in those around her. This one and that one—Mrs Clarty Housewife or Mr Do-As-I-Say-Not-As-I-Do—got low marks in her book, and it was a book, after all, set high on the shelf of her own experience, a life of good management and strong hopes undercut by the suddenness of grief. Inside her room Lucia kept watch: I will make a cup of tea and then go to bed at nine, she would say, and one day people will appreciate me for who I was. Good night she would say and God bless the best amongst you. All the evenings since Mario died, she went to sleep with the slowbreathing certainty that people failed to live their lives decently.

Although Mario had been good and easy-going, she now tended his memory in such a way as to make his goodness serve as a rebuke to others. Saying her prayers sometimes she asked God to make her less of a wife and more of a mother. But that was not easy. He was dead eight years—she remembered his eyes on the television the night he died, it was the night of the moon landing. She had put him into his bed and he had coughed some more and the children had looked on. 'Wait a minute,' he said in the bed, and when she looked up from her needlework his eyes were dead. Mario Tambini had died of a stroke at the age of sixty-four. And now it was her daily task to address his forgotten standards, and in this way she made her days noble for all to see, though in her heart she was simply lonely. She missed him. She missed her husband and found it hard to live with the things she had never managed to tell him.

Good night. This is my life. One day years ago he sang a song I only heard it once and I can't remember the name it was one of the old favourites and the line he sang more than once that day roughly went on to say well duty is stronger than dreaming. Good night. Good night. Forgive me Mario and duty is stronger than dreaming.

Lucia had fallen asleep in the chair. In the living-room, a picture of Mario at the fish-fryer was over the fireplace. One time he said *Take that down it's just hypocrisy,* but no, she loved the picture being there. She had slippers with zips on them and sometimes she laughed as she put them on to think how cosy they were. Next to that on a string were her rosary beads blessed by the Pope. And on the back wall above the clock was a mirror held up by a chain and next to that a standard lamp which shone on a picture of the Blessed Virgin with her eyes raised up.

The gunpowder smell was gone and only Glade perfumed the air of the living-room. When Lucia woke up she put the glove back on the table with the others. In the kitchen was a bowl of black bananas. From the top of the fridge she lifted a small box and she put on her overcoat and put the box in the pocket of the coat. She often went down to the town in her slippers. The leaves of the spider plant shuddered after she banged the door shut.

MARIA WAS halfway through a bar of Highland Toffee, and she was rushing to finish it, ready for a Sherbet Fountain. Kalpana dug her hand into her own Lucky Bag, and, with a mouth all stained with red Cola, she shouted for the men doing well in the adult sack race. Kalpana said she wished she could whistle properly like the older boys. The girls jumped up and down and stuffed their faces and rubbed off their make-up with their sticky fingers, all the while feeling hot in their royal robes.

'Come on, Dr Jag,' shouted Kalpana, using her father's forbidden nickname, 'get your arse in gear.'

'Oh-ay,' said Maria, 'you swore. You're gonnae get us into trouble.' Mrs Ogilvie was still stalking the putting green, and plucking Vikings out of the rhododendron bushes; she kept wagging her long finger, and here and there she offered impromptu lectures on some unexpected manifestations of the Holy Trinity.

Giovanni and Rosa were good the day of the Silver Jubilee. They were always somehow better when they'd had a drink. Giovanni waved over to Maria and her wee friend, and he grabbed Rosa by the waist and swung her round. She dusted herself down and shook her head as he slugged from a pint. They were with a crowd of their friends, making jokes, supervising games, and Rosa only showed her usual embarrassment when Giovanni went too far, like when he tried to kiss her too much on the mouth. Giovanni was the most handsome man on Bute. His appearance was judged to be one of the local attractions, and because the man was a stranger to the truth about himself, the scrapes he got into—all the noisy, familiar troubles and badness—only made people love him more, surmising there must be something very like themselves in the chaos that existed behind his perfect face.

Maria would sometimes put her sweets away when Rosa looked over, fearing a telling off, but all her mother did when she looked over that day was wave at her with a grand smile. One of the times she licked her hand and smoothed the side of her hair, just to tell Maria to keep herself tidy. The children rushed out from the table, and Giovanni put Maria up on his shoulders as the horn went off for the guns. They all cheered when the bangs went up and the smoke came rolling over the bay, then went quiet for a minute as the ship's band played 'Rule Britannia'. Giovanni held Maria's leg with one arm and put the other arm over Rosa's shoulder. He didn't move his eyes from the ship when Rosa tried to wipe a dirty mark off his chin, dry blood from the night before.

Another procession was soon coming down Castle Street. Giovanni put Maria on the grass and said 'For Christ's sake' and then sloped off in the direction of the Athletic Bar. Maria could hear a drum banging and hundreds of flutes playing at the same time. Kalpana came running up. 'It's the fucking Orange band,' she said. She didn't see Rosa standing on Maria's other side.

'Kalpana Jagannadham, I'm going to wash your mouth out with soap. Your language is terrible. Come on Maria, we'll away in and get ready for the concert. I hate that bloody noise. It's normal music they should be playing on a day like today.'

Kalpana rolled her eyes at Maria and ran off towards Castle Street. 'It's a good hiding that girl's needing,' said Rosa holding her daughter's hand. 'The language on her! No wonder her family don't know what to do with her. A doctor's lassie. She's like a big drunk man of sixty the way she talks. Don't let me ever hear you using them words, Maria. It's a filthy way to go on that and it'll just hold you back. Where you're headed for they don't use words like that. You'll be among nice people.'

Lucia was coming down the hill and ran into the Orange band. The noise troubled her: with her hand close to the neck of her coat she made a secret sign of the cross. The man at the front of the marching band had a big red face and was out of puff, spinning the stick round his body and throwing it into the air. Lucia could hear the coins jangling in his trouser pockets as he twisted his arms deftly to keep the stick in motion. She needed to get to the other side of the road.

Protestant rubbish I'm not kidding you on, this is really ridiculous would you look at that and such a lovely day it was meant to be and them with their flutes that lot are pure bloody rubbish God forgive me would you credit this carry-on and how am I supposed to get over there I tell

you it's a good wash they're all needing and there's women with prams
over there can't get moving for these bloody whistles oh for goodness'
sake.

She had her purse in her hand. There were young men in blue
Rangers scarves applauding the band and people and sailors on the
other side were cheering for them too. She was getting angrier by the
second.

Bloody rubbish God forgive me.

Unable to hold back, she stepped into the road in front of a row
of drummers marching under a banner saying 'Airdrie Quarter
Commemorates the Battle of the Boyne'. One of the marchers
twisted right round with his drum. 'Get back, ya old fucking cow,' he
said. 'Gone, ya fucking old pig that you are. You're no' getting across
here till we're by.' Some of the men on the pavement pulled Lucia
back by the coat. 'You better bide your time or you'll cause murder
here, Mrs,' one of them said. She just looked at him with her lip
trembling, then stared down at her slippers trying to think of other
songs.

She wondered what Alfredo would say. He always said she was a
dare-devil out on the street and now here she was, about to be
mauled by a crowd of people with drums. Alfredo always came into
Lucia's mind in times of trouble. She hadn't seen him since the day
before and that was to do with panic about the cistern in the bathroom. She decided there and then that she wouldn't wait for these
bad people to pass, she would stay on this side of the road and walk
straight down to the square, to the hairdresser's, where Alfredo would
give her a cup of tea.

'WHEN I want your opinion, I'll give it to you,' said Bill McNab,
plucking a roller from the wheely-basket and throwing a look at
Elaine, his junior, in the mirror. McNab wore a ginger toupée and big
silver glasses; he hovered about the salon as if levitating on his angrier thoughts, flicking his wrists, tutting, whipping the scissors from
the top pocket of his overalls like brandishing an axe. He had a
frightening laugh: he whinnied on a top note, and the customers
loved the sheer velocity of his bitchiness, and the staff cowered.
Alfredo was his business partner and known for his quietness.

With the crowds outside, the salon was busy and young Elaine was getting the worst of McNab. 'I don't know what your problem is, Elaine,' he said, 'but I'll bet it's hard to pronounce. Hurry over here, hotpants, and pass me up the rollers.' He spent as much time looking at himself in the mirror as he did at the heads of his customers. He touched the edges of his toupée with the tips of his fingers. 'I like you, Elaine,' he said. 'You remind me of when I was young and stupid.' The customer in the chair couldn't stop laughing.

'Bill,' said Alfredo in a low voice further along.

'Well, no wonder,' McNab said with a smile. 'What am I? A fly-paper for freaks?'

Elaine put down the rollers and papers. 'Mr Tambini, I don't have to take this. I'm only on work experience. He's a cheeky bastard and he's never off my back.'

'Tsk tsk,' said the woman in McNab's' chair.

'Don't worry about it, dear,' said Alfredo. 'Just get on with your work and ignore him. You know what he's like.'

'He's right out of order.'

'Ready when you are, Miss Hotpants,' said McNab, standing back from the chair with his hand resting on his hip. 'We're all refreshed and challenged by your unique point of view.'

'It's nice to be nice,' said the woman in the chair.

'But of course, Madame de Pompadour,' said McNab, fixing his client in the mirror with a wink. 'I'll try being nicer if you try being smarter,' he said to Elaine.

'Bill,' said Alfredo.

'Mr McNab,' said Elaine, taking off her overall and throwing it down into a chair, 'go and take a gigantic fuck to yourself.'

'Would you listen to that,' said the client.

'Oooooh!' said Bill, following Elaine with his eyes as she lifted her coat and bag from the hook.

'Bill!' said Alfredo.

'Well tatty-bye, Miss Piss. Send us a postcard.'

'You can stick your job up your arse,' said Elaine marching to the front door.

'Is that not ridiculous?' said the chair.

'We're not the brightest crayon in the box now, are we dear?' said McNab in a slightly raised voice as young Elaine pulled open the door.

'Oh,' said Lucia, bumping into Elaine at the door. 'Are you all right, hen?' Elaine, in tears, forced her way forward. 'He's a fucking bastard,' she said, disappearing into the noise outside.

'Bill,' said Alfredo, quite angry now, 'how many times?'

'Okay, okay,' said McNab quickly. 'She was useless anyway. Did you see the bloody nicotine stains on they fingers?'

'I did, actually,' said the woman in the chair. 'Not at all attractive in a young girl.'

'It was tint, Bill. That's us back to square one. Thanks very much.'

McNab pursed his lips and looked in the mirror. Alfredo shook his head and went back to clippering the man in his own chair. 'Yes,' said McNab, smiling a big smile at himself, 'I am an agent of Satan, but my duties are largely ceremonial.'

'You're unreal,' said McNab's client.

'Yes my dear, but aren't I lovely? Oh hello, Mrs Tambini. Trust you to arrive just in time for the cabaret.'

Lucia nodded shyly at McNab and the lady in the chair. She headed for the coat-rail and Alfredo helped her off with her coat. 'Hello mammo,' he said, 'are you okay? What's the matter?'

'Can I go through the back?' said Lucia.

'Of course, mammo. Come on through.' Alfredo turned to the gentleman in his chair. It was the famous George Samson, the island's oldest resident, wearing his best suit. 'I'll be with you in a second, George.'

'Oh Alfredo, I got an awful fright out there,' said Lucia, sitting down on a stool underneath the hairdressing products. 'I ran into that bloody band and I couldn't get across.'

'Mammo,' he said, 'you've got to ignore the band. You know what they're all like on a day like this. Tea?'

'Aye, put two sugars in,' she said. 'It's just they're all so loud and they've got no business being out today. It's supposed to be nice.'

'Never mind,' said Alfredo. 'It is nice. Did you see Maria all dressed up? Have you been down the green?'

'No yet,' said Lucia. 'I was on my way.'

'We've been busy,' he said. 'All those people coming in off the boat, and now we're short-handed again.' Alfredo smiled. 'That mirror shook when the guns went off.'

'Lovely day for it,' said Lucia, dusting the hair off the arm of his white coat. 'Lovely day altogether.'

Alfredo put his hand on top of the kettle. In a few seconds he could feel the heat rising steadily through the handle as he stared into some postcards Blu-tacked to the back of the kitchen cupboard, pictures of Jersey and Spain, the Italian coast.

4 · *Broadcasting*

Young Michael Aigas worked in the island's television shop and he listened to jazz all day. There were always at least a dozen televisions playing in the shop at the one time. It was an afternoon programme about the beatniks that got him into jazz; he'd watched John Coltrane's face on all the screens and decided then and there he wanted to be American. He wanted to be American and he wanted to be black. And that was the story of young Michael Aigas. He sat in Harris's shop all day listening to jazz and thinking about what he'd be doing if he lived in New York. He read the same book again and again.

'Where's the action, pops?' said Michael.

A few dozy words came down the phone. He was speaking to Gary, who was unemployed and proud of it.

'I know, man,' said Michael, 'I'm all creeped up about this Jubilee shit. The Queen is not cool, Gary. This joint is as bare as hell's backyard today man, I swear.'

Gary asked him to shut the shop. He said the pubs were swinging down at the harbour.

'I'm behind the eight ball,' said Michael. 'The old man's coming back here. It's a drag. Later on. Yeah. Let's hit that stupid concert tonight. Jim says he'll pay me extra for working the holiday. We'll go out and get heaped, man.'

Michael turned all the screens over to BBC2 and watched the test card for the next hour. He put a Furry Lewis LP on the turntable and turned the volumes down on the tellies. Then he put his chin on his hands and looked into the eyes of the girl on the test card, the girl with the clown and the faraway eyes. 'Tell it like it is, wee sister,' said Michael to the empty shop.

The phone rang. 'Hello, Mrs Bone,' said Michael. 'Yup. You just want to know what's on?' Michael unfolded a *Daily Record* on his desk and read from the television page. 'Mainly royal stuff on today. Well. *Golden Shot* at half past seven. You don't like him. Okay. *Rising Damp*? Nine o'clock. *Within These Walls*?'

A lot of the old customers phoned like this. They just wanted someone to talk to on the phone, and they thought because it was a TV shop they should know what was on the TV. They'd bought a television for company, but it wasn't enough. 'No, Mrs Bone, you don't need a new television set yet. That's right... that's just the way it should be.'

Mr Harris came in. 'Okay Mrs Bone,' said Michael, 'we'll come and check it out for you next week. Cheerio.'

'More social work?' said Mr Harris.

'As per,' said Michael.

5 · The Girl's World

Maria's best toy sat on the dressing table in front of her window. Girl's World: it was a life-size plastic head, with the hair all honey-blonde and shining and nylon. The special thing was that the hair could grow; you pressed a button on the doll's pink neck, it made a clicking sound, and then you could pull a long extension from Susie's head.

That was her name: Modern Susie. There were several versions of Girl's World; this one had Mediterranean blue eyes and raised eyebrows and a tiny nose, a nose you could hardly breathe through. She came with special make-up and brushes. You could give her earrings and spread lip gloss over her smiling mouth. Maria spent whole evenings up in her bedroom playing with her. With the record player down low and glitter on all the plastic faces, Maria would sometimes put on a show for her old dolls, and she would make it that Susie was the big star in the room. Maria would sing to her, as if she were a real person, and late at night, when even the seagulls were asleep and the seafront was quiet, the light from outside, from the street lamps, would glance off the diamonds in Susie's special tiara, causing sparkles to travel over the wallpaper.

Rosa was going up and down the banister with a duster and Mr Sheen. This was her deepest habit: not only to clean, but to make cleaning into one of life's grand and protracted gestures. Rosa hated dust—she hated its settling and gathering, as if it could only throw a terrible light on the failure to cope. In no other respect was Rosa more like her mother. Every day they went about their housework as if it were an act of violence. Rosa liked to drink tea from a cup and a saucer, and sometimes, after doing the house, she would sit herself down on the sofa, exhausted and flushed, the base of the teacup rattling on the saucer's edge.

Maria was up in her bedroom giving Modern Susie a ponytail. The Jubilee street party was loud outside the window, but she put on a record and stared at the doll. As she pulled the hair through her fingers to trap it in bobbles, the static electricity made her hands feel like somebody else's hands, and the skin along her arms began to feel fizzy, as if tiny bubbles of electricity were running up inside them. Rosa had finished her cleaning and now she stood behind Maria at a creaky ironing-board. Doris Day was on the turntable. 'You need to learn to stand on your own two feet,' Rosa said. 'You know there isn't a man in the world who isn't out for what he can get. Mark my words. Before you know it you're washing nappies and looking at the door to see if he's coming back or not. Just you watch yourself, Maria. Keep them at arm's length, hen.'

'I'm thirteen,' said Maria, rolling lip gloss back and forth over her lips and staring in the mirror.

'That's enough of that,' said Rosa. She drove the iron over the dress and then whipped the dress over. 'That's enough gloss. You don't want to make yourself look greasy. I know what age you are, Maria. I remember the day you were born as if it was yesterday. What a day that was let me tell you. I was lying up in that ward and not a bugger came to see me. Your Uncle Alfredo came right enough, and my daddy came with gritted teeth. You were such a wee thing.'

Maria's mother often talked like the songs. She didn't care that Maria was thirteen, or what age anybody was. She put down the iron. 'Don't ever think I regretted you,' she said. 'I can still see your wee face lying there. That was before I was friends with Giovanni. That man's been a good friend to me, Maria. He's not perfect, I grant you that, but I don't know how I'd have coped lifting and laying for everybody. He's been a good help about here. He's just a friend, but it's nice to have a friend. If you've got a lot on your plate you know. Men will always be men, Maria.' She propped her arm on the ironing-board and rested her chin. 'It's true what they say. When it comes down to it, hen, you've only got your mother. You remember that. There's no another bugger to care about you.' Rosa lifted the iron again and went over the creases.

'They teachers of yours are half-daft,' she said after a minute. 'I don't know what they think they can learn you, Maria. You're miles ahead of those other wee lassies and you won't be sitting around here waiting to get your books marked. You're a wee woman of the world, Maria. All the education you want has come out of that.' She pointed to the record player. She laughed to herself and took some pleasure in her thoughts. 'It's true enough, Maria,' she said. 'You and I know what we're talking about. You know your songs. Just you wait and see. I know she's no your teacher anymore but that Mrs Ogilvie out there's as old as tea anyway. What does she know about young lassies nowadays? Old thing like her. She was a waitress at the Last Supper, that one.'

Rosa winked at Maria as if to acknowledge it was a bad thing to say about a teacher. 'We love the old tunes, so we do,' she added, picking a thread off the dress she was ironing and placing it in the pocket of her overalls. She pointed a finger at Maria. 'Mark my words hen, there's nobody around here to understand a wee person like you. They're all just out for what they can get. Every one of them, and you mark my words.'

'Do you think Uncle Alfredo would curl my hair at the bottom?' said Maria, looking into the mirror, folding her hair under her small hand.

'Like Lena Martell? Aye, he'll do that no bother. You've got nicer hair than her right enough. You'll need to remember to lift your chin up though, Maria. You make your chin look that baggy when you do that. Lift it up. You need to be smarter about yourself. Nobody likes to look at a wee pudgy lassie up on a stage.'

Maria continued to stare at her face in the mirror. Rosa had taught her to sing by constantly putting the needle back to the start of the record and making her try again. She told her all the stories. Since before she could remember, it was Deanna Durbin this and Judy Garland that, Doris Day wore this, and Lulu said that to the newspaper. 'Nobody ever got to where they want to be by sitting on their backside moaning all the time,' said Rosa.

'I'm not moaning,' said Maria.

'No,' said Rosa, 'but you just need to make the effort and smile a lot more. You need to show your nice teeth. You cannae beat a big smile. There you are.' Her mother let the dress float from her hand to come down softly on the bed. It was covered in yellow polka dots and had a big bow at the throat. Maria turned around and made herself smile. She liked the look of empty clothes. She liked to imagine famous people in them and then see herself in them when she was dressed up.

'You must try to hold yourself in a wee bit when you're singing,' said Rosa, rooting in the drawer for an Alice band, 'like all the great Italian singers. Hold yourself in one place and let all the lovely sounds come out, cause you've a lovely singing voice on you, Maria. You're only letting yourself down if you slouch. You're a woman now. I can't be doing with slouchy lassies. You've got to make an impression.'

Maria lifted the dress and held it to the window. 'You've been going great guns in the dancing, Maria, but you have to lift up your chin do you hear me? There's nobody likes to look at a singer that can't do justice to herself. Are you listening to me?'

Maria had taken a box from the drawer. Inside were cardboard models with dresses and skirts and blouses you could fasten onto them: Rosa had shown her how. Maria knew the models weren't very modern. The hair on the women looked like the hair they had in photographs she'd seen of women during the War. They had long thin legs and the skirts were like wool. 'Some men have nothing but filth on their minds,' said her mother, turning a T-shirt inside-out.

'They're dirty inside themselves some men, they aren't clean and you wouldn't want them anywhere near you. Good God you can't be too careful with some men, hen, they want to ruin people that's all they want to do and you're as well keeping yourself to yourself. Hold on to your dignity, Maria.'

Maria was now up on her toes looking down into the street.

'Are you listening to me, Maria?'

'There's something happening,' Maria said, and Rosa came over to look. A lot of the children and parents were gathered at the doors of the Winter Gardens, only the older people were still sitting at the long table. A big shout came from somewhere, followed by cups and jugs of orange squash and trays of sausage rolls flying into the air. A drunk man was charging up the middle of the Jubilee table kicking things to smithereens.

'Is that not bloody terrible?' said Rosa. 'That William Rooney, look at the state of him. Drunk. Oh my God. The bloody state of him. Look, he's kicking all the nice stuff off the table.' Everyone down on the green turned round at the commotion. William Rooney was home from the oil rigs and he was running up the table in his big tackety boots causing havoc. 'Oh my God would you credit that?' said Rosa, tut-tutting. 'His poor wife'll be black affronted. All the way up that nice tablecloth as well. What did I just tell you, Maria? Men are a bloody waste of space, God forgive me.'

'Comeintaemeyafuckinbluenosebastardsthatyoozare!' shouted William Rooney as he pounded up the table, cakes flying, plumes of white spittle issuing from his mouth. 'Alltakeeverywanaeyeez— yafuckinbunchatubes!'

When Rooney got to the last few yards of the table he dived down onto his stomach and slid all the way to the end, napkins, paper plates, half-empty tumblers, abandoned hats rolling into one great ball of stuff around him as he dropped off the table, landing in a heap on the tarmac with his hands spread-eagled and a Union Jack wrapped about his head. 'Leave the bastard,' said Mrs Rooney, gathering her nephews outside Timpsons the shoe-shop and ushering them along the pavement towards the Gallowgate. 'He's a drunken, no-use pig of a man. Leave him there to rot. I don't want to know him, the bampot that he is.'

The last ferry left for Wemyss Bay and the sun went down behind the Argyll Hills, over in the direction of Tighnabruaich. The neon signs above the doors of the pubs flicked on as the sea went pink for half an hour, the darkness seemed to come quickly after that, then just as quickly came to life as music started pouring from the pubs. Giggling, holiday-minded children took the last of the Empire biscuits from the table and groups of sailors came walking up the seafront in their uniforms. Old George Samson, with medals, three-piece suit, and a new haircut, lit the bonfire on the rocks with a torch handed to him by the local MP. Everybody roared. Then fireworks exploded above the bay and the colours swam over the water.

6 · Sugar

The Winter Gardens opened its doors. In no time at all the place was mad with the scraping of chairs and the ringing of the bar till. A woman quite drunk on lagers and lime won a bottle of Bacardi at the raffle and was too embarrassed to go up and get it. Her son was famous for his cheek, and when she sent him up he took the microphone from the bandleader, Davie Devine, and gave a speech about how much he wanted to thank his agent and his hairdresser. Everybody laughed and clapped him through the cigarette smoke and said to each other he was an awful boy. Some of the younger kids were winding themselves up in the velvet curtain and the caretaker chased them. The tables were covered in pint jugs and they all had foam sliding down their insides and the dancefloor smelled of Brylcreem and Old Spice.

Kalpana Jagannadham, still in her Queen Victoria costume, was sitting in a plastic chair covered in coats. Nobody was wearing a coat because it was too hot, and now and then she would duck under a mackintosh and take a slug of shandy. When Maria had gone in to get ready for the concert, Kalpana had hung around inside the venue, staring into space and stealing drinks from the tables. 'And how's the wee lassie doing then?' said a drunk man leaning over with his tongue sliding along the edge of a cigarette paper. He could hardly stand up and his wife was all ruby-cheeked and creasing with laughter at his side.

'I'm all right, I'm counting my fingers, shush,' she said. The man was insinuating something with his drunk finger in the air.

'You just look like a wee monkey,' he said. 'Hey Ella. How about a wee banana for the lovely wee monkey sitting here?'

Ella laughed at the top of her voice and spilled some of her vodka. 'Never mind him,' she said to Kalpana, 'he's daft as a brush.'

'Wee Pakistani monkey. Geez a kiss,' he said.

'I'm Indian,' said Kalpana, 'so fuck off, you fat prick.' Ella immediately stopped laughing.

'I'll tell you, lady,' she said, 'you have a right dirty mouth on you. If that father of yours was here. Such a nice man as well. He gives your people a good name. Come on, Freddie. She's a right wee tearaway, that one.'

'Byzee bye,' said Freddie, 'my wee spicy monkey.'

Kalpana just stared at him. She was used to this. On the sly she drank the rest of the shandy and slid the tumbler inside the arm of somebody's fur coat and it hit the floor with a clunk, but nobody noticed because the band had started and the compere was already reading out the names of the acts.

Over in the café, Maria was sitting on top of the counter with Alfredo fixing her hair. Lucia was at one of the tables with a hot orangeade and an Askit Powder. 'I heard you were a royal personage today,' said Alfredo, moving a fat jar of beetroot out of the way so he could lay down his brushes. 'They were all talking about it in the salon. I saw you coming down Castle Street in the procession,' he said, 'you and Kalpana. The two of you looked smashing.'

'Were we the best?' Maria asked.

'No doubt about it,' said Alfredo.

The jukebox was playing Abba. There hadn't been a single place where music wasn't playing that day. There had been a band on the royal procession, there was music coming from the pubs and down from people's windows, and Maria remembered there had been music on the putting green. Even the ship had had music: the music for the Queen and that other music. There was music in every room of her mother's house: the transistor radios, the record player in the bedroom, the jukebox here in the café.

Sitting on the counter, Maria looked along the jars of sweets up on the shelf. She knew the look and the taste of each one. As Alfredo teased her hair, Maria mouthed the names of all the sweeties you bought by weight and thought of the way they tasted and the way they felt on her tongue.

'Sweet peanuts,' she mouthed.

Caramelly in your mouth a bit tough and then sugary then you cracked them open and gritty inside.

'Midget Gems,' she said out loud.

Nice and rubbery and millions in your mouth at once and the black ones are best you can make a ball in your mouth and swallow them in one go at the end.

She said: 'Cola Cubes'.

Fizzy sugar and rub them down smooth with your tongue and crack them with your teeth and goo comes out.

'Edinburgh Rock.'

Crush like powder and it sticks inside your mouth.

'Parma Violets.'

Only flowers.

'Soor Plooms.'

Like marbles and lemons and sour they make you pull your cheeks in like sherbet does.

Maria looked down to see if she could see her face in the shop window. 'Uncle Alfredo, do you like Cough Candy?'

Alfredo, smiling, twisted one of her curls round his index finger and lifted a can of lacquer from under his arm to spray it into place. 'I like all of them,' he said, 'except chocolate mice. They're rotten.'

'Can I have a sweetie for after?' asked Maria.

'Okay,' said Alfredo. He put his hand over the glass counter and got a packet of Munchies. He broke the tube in two and put both pieces into her sequined purse, then he lifted her down onto the floor and stood back. 'That's you done, Maria. Look at our famous kidlet, mammo. *Ma che carina—è veramente bellissima, no?*'

Maria jumped down and smiled into the silver of the counter. A brace of blonde curls rolled from her head. Lucia looked up and smiled. Her granddaughter's lips were Candy Super-Pink and glossy as all get-out. The lids of her eyes were Frosted Summer Jade with an ivory highlighter from Boots, the No. 4 Rimmel blusher, and mascara: Lady Night-Time Blue. Maria looked into her own eyes in the counter and used her hands to smooth the creases at her waist. At the top of the yellow dress she straightened the bow. She had Woolworths doily-patterned white socks up to the knee and black, single-strap shoes, shiny enough to capture the movement of shadows around her.

She stood in front of her grandmother, who put down her long spoon and gave her a look of concentration. It was very often that way with Lucia: she looked into the eyes of the people close to her and she stayed looking for a long time. 'You are a perfect and lovely young woman,' she said. Her eyes filling up, she put the ends of her fingers on Maria's face. 'In the name of the Father, the Son, and the Holy Ghost,' she said, touching Maria's forehead and stomach, one shoulder and the other. 'God bless you and keep you, my lovely wee lassie.' Lucia looked up at Alfredo and something passed between them and she placed her hands on Maria's small shoulders. '*Brava, brava, bellissima,*' she said.

Maria turned round and looked through the greasy window of the fish fryer. Giovanni was crouching on the other side with his white teeth all smiling and a handkerchief pouring from the top pocket of his brown suit. 'Aaahaa,' he said, tapping on his side of the glass, an array of battered hamburgers, black puddings and fish between his face and Maria's. 'And who is this lovely person I see on my television screen tonight? Is it not the world-famous Maria Tambini? Everybody give a big hand for the most talented and lovely-looking little friend of mine—Maria Tambini!'

Maria pulled herself up on the counter and hung there for a kiss. 'Mmmwa!' said Giovanni loudly. 'And anybody who says any different will be getting that.' He showed a fist and round eyes to Maria and when she giggled he clipped her nose.

Lucia produced a small box from her pocket and turned to Maria. 'This is for you,' she said.

'What is it?' asked Maria. 'Is it jewels, mammo?'

'No, it's not jewellery but it is treasure.'

Maria opened the box and picked out the coin. It was shiny in the chip shop and Maria stared at it. She spoke as she read what it said: 'Queen Elizabeth II Silver Jubilee Nineteen Seventy-Seven.'

'Now is that not special?' said Alfredo.

'Thank you, mammo,' said Maria.

Looking at Maria's pleased expression, Lucia unconsciously fingered the chain around her own neck, its silver crucifix and miraculous medal. 'I'll go over the road and find my seat,' she said, getting up and putting her hands into her coat pockets.

'You're still wearing your slippers, mammo,' said Maria.

'There's no need for me to be dressed up at my age. Now do your best, Maria. And remember that no matter what happens you are the best one. Do you hear me?'

'Thanks, mammo, and thank you for my coin.'

Lucia took the coin from Maria and turned it over in her fingers. They all watched as the strip lights glinted off the coin and made it look like the centre of the chippy and the centre of the turning world. 'You know they were not always good to us, these people, the English,' she said, and Maria noticed that mammo's hand was trembling. 'They did bad things and we mustn't forget the bad things.'

'Oh Lucia,' said Giovanni, walking over to the till. 'This is a happy day.'

Lucia threw Giovanni a look. 'This has nothing to do with you, what I say to my family,' she said. However, Giovanni's remark had brought her up short. The adults would speak Italian only seldom, usually when there was something they didn't want the little one to hear. 'It's not worth the effort,' said Alfredo. '*Non vale la pena.*'

'He only pays attention to his good looks,' said Lucia. '*Si dedica soto soltanto al suo bell' aspetto.* Just remember,' she said as she kissed Maria's cheek and turned to lay two kisses on Alfredo, 'you come from proud people who are clean and tidy and have morals. Nobody can take away what we have worked hard for, Maria. I'll get across the road now.'

The bell rang over the door as she left, then two small boys came in carrying armfuls of empty lemonade bottles. Maria was still standing next to the fryer, but she was in a world of her own, going 'step ball-change, step ball-change' and moving her lips to remember the words of a song.

'You better hurry up,' one of the boys said as Giovanni leaned over and took the bottles from him. 'It's starting over there.'

Just then Rosa was hurrying down the stairs into the shop pulling at the straps of her dress. 'Come on, miss,' she said. 'Are you ready, Maria? Is she ready, Alfredo? Pull your socks up for goodness' sake, Maria, you're not a baby and that's us ready.' Rosa looked at Giovanni who looked back and smiled over the counter. 'You'd think it was you that was going onstage, Mr Universe,' she said, taking Maria's hand. 'Give me the pink ones,' said Rosa. Giovanni handed her a jar of sweets labelled 'Plantation's Sugar Bonbons'. She took two out and turned to Maria. 'Open wide,' she said, and she put the two sweets into Maria's mouth.

'Yes!' said Maria.

'Elaine will take over,' said Rosa, gathering last-minute things. 'It's time for us to get over there. I can hear the band.'

'You all right, Elaine?' Alfredo said, giving her a nod.

Elaine was wearing black lipstick, and seemed no happier than usual; but she was glad to be free of McNab and the hairdresser's, so she teased her spiky helmet and tried to smile gratefully at Alfredo. 'No bother, Mr Tambini.'

The bell rang again and the door closed and the shop was quiet. Elaine looked bored chewing a mouthful of gum as she rattled a basket of chips in the fryer.

'Can we get the money for these?' asked one of the boys standing the empties on the counter.

'No,' said Elaine. 'You can get chews or anything from the sweetie jars up there or else chips.'

'Can we no get the money?'

'I said no didn't I? What do you want?'

'Can we no have ten Bensons?' The boys looked at each other.

Elaine blew out her breath, still chewing, then, staring at the two boys, she reached under the counter and took the lid off a tin of Hamlet cigars. 'You can have two singles and the rest in chips,' she said, 'but if you tell Rosa yous are dead, right, and I'm no kidding.'

The night-time glow of the street spread over the window and passed through the glass, lighting on the chip shop's silver counter, and the smiling boys, the empty bottles, and the boxes of chocolates up on the shelf.

'WHAT DO you call a Glasgow bloke in a shirt and tie?'

'The accused!' shouted Ella from the table.

'And what do you call his lady wife?'

'The witness for the prosecution,' shouted the barman.

The comedian was using darts as part of his act. 'Okay,' he said, aiming for the board at the back of the stage, 'for the double top. Oh Jesus, that's a left-handed screwdriver.' The dart had stuck on number 5. A few spare laughs came from the crowd and the comedian plucked the dart and slugged from a pint.

Dr Jag had found Kalpana and he decided to be lenient and let her stay to see Maria sing. They stood up the back. Maria waved to her friend when she came in and Kalpana smiled back and chewed her bottom lip. The doctor gave Maria the thumbs-up, and when she saw him she too began to bite her lip.

Lucia was sitting on a chair next to the cloakroom. She wasn't drinking or talking to anyone; she just sat with her hands clasped on her lap. Meanwhile Bill McNab the hairdresser was howling with laughter at the bar and downing vodkas. He was wearing a purple shirt open all the way down with a gold sovereign on a chain. 'Alfredo,' he said when the Tambinis arrived, grabbing Alfredo by the arm, 'somebody's looking for you. A flashy young lady, Alfredo, not from round here. She's done up to the nines.' He looked round the room then drew close to Alfredo's ear. 'She said she's from the London television.'

Alfredo led Maria and Rosa to the soft seats that ran along the side. Rosa was staring at the band and occasionally primping Maria's hair, and Maria was miles away. She always got like that when she was about to sing. She went into herself. Giovanni came in behind them and went straight away to the bar. He brought over a gin and bitter lemon for Rosa and took a drink over to Lucia but she just nodded for him to sit it on the floor next to her.

Cigarette smoke billowed over the tables. Glasses rattled on trays. People were chatting and laughing even when the acts were on, then

the band made a flourish and the compere was back onstage. 'La
and gentlemen, please put your hands together for an amazing I
talent from Ardrossan, Tony McFarlane. A round of applause, ladies
and gentleman, that's the stuff. Now it's been a grand day today with
the festivities and the like and I know that every one of you will
be ready for a wee song. So please give a big Rothesay welcome to our
ain wee bit of Highland fling—down from Oban, please welcome
Hamish and Hazel Watson with a personal tribute to Jimmy Shand.'

Alfredo found the woman from London at one of the faraway
tables. He shook her hand and sat down. He had spoken to her several times before—in fact that morning, to give her directions from
Glasgow. She was Miss Black, a young talent scout from London
Weekend Television, wearing a short skirt, enjoying her drink and
smiling as she looked about the place. She was posh but up for a
laugh, Alfredo reckoned.

'I'm sorry it's all a bit, you know...maybe a bit rough,' he said.

'Not at all,' she said. 'I spend a vast proportion of my time in
these places.'

'And how did you get on in Glasgow?'

'Oh, remarkably well. It was something called the Clyde Show-
boat. They have it every summer. It's a good place to sample some of
the new talent. So it worked out well—receiving your letter. And the
tape! She has such a great voice. You're her uncle, is that right?'

'Yes,' said Alfredo. 'Everybody loves her and she's always been
really serious about her singing.'

'Absolutely,' said Miss Black. 'How did you know me, by the way?'

'We don't get many of you to the pound round here,' said Alfredo, and then he blushed, looking over his glass.

'I'll take that as a compliment,' she said.

'Do you want to meet her?'

'Not just now, Fred. I find that children get over-excited if they
think...well. As I said on the phone, it's always better for them to be
surprised if there's to be any good news...and...you know? I just
arrange the auditions for Mr Green and the production team. I don't
have the power to do anything more than bring her to the auditions.
It's quite bizarre, Fred, you know: everybody wants to be on television nowadays. But only a few turn out to be good enough.'

'Don't worry. I kept it quiet,' said Alfredo.

'Who's that woman Alfredo's talking to?' said Rosa. She screwed up her eyes and fiddled with her chain. But Maria wasn't listening. Noiselessly, she was moving her lips, thinking of words, and she kept her eyes fixed to the tiles on the floor.

Hamish Watson was wearing a kilt and had an accordion. His wife Hazel wore a long tartan skirt, a ruffled blouse, and a pair of blue National Health spectacles. A giant theatrical laugh came from the bar as Bill McNab spat his drink out and tried to cover his mouth with the collar of his shirt. 'Shush you,' said the girl next to him. 'A wee bit of respect for the performers.' The people at the tables held up their glasses and swayed to 'Flower of Scotland'.

'Are you all right now?' asked Rosa, looking at Maria. 'Remember to hold yourself up. Smile and give it everything, eh? I don't need to tell you anything, hen, you've done it all before, but just sparkle, that's all. Lift your head up and sparkle. Hold your stomach in when you go up there. I'll make you one of my specials later on.' Maria felt she had to smile at her mother so she did that and then she stared out, thinking only of the words.

'All right, ladies and gentlemen, a big round of applause please for Hamish Watson and his lovely wife Hazel. I can tell you these two have won many talent contests all over Scotland and they have a big future ahead of them. Rothesay people are famous for liking a good laugh—a fact I've often relied on when it comes to asking my mother-in-law to buy me a drink—so our next act is down from Glasgow, a comedian again, he's done one or two bits on Radio Clyde and he tells me he'll be turning professional at the end of the year. We're lucky to have him here tonight, ladies and gentlemen, please give a big welcome for *Crazy Davie from Tollcross!*'

Crazy Davie came on wearing a cloth cap, with jagged spears of ginger hair poking out the back. 'Hello, hello, hello,' he said. 'Isn't it nice to be in sunny Rothesay on a day like today?'

The crowd cheered.

'My father was a shipbuilder you know. Oh yes. The great ships of the Clyde. We used to come doon the watter to Rothesay as a way of avoiding the bathhouse. That's right, the soap-dodgers can mingle in no bother in Rothesay. Yous are that black-enamelled in this town, nobody would notice if you had rabies never mind a bit of dirt behind your lugs.'

There were a few sniggers, then a few boos.

'Oh away and give us peace,' he said, looking over the crowd. 'I'll tell you what, it's nice to be here right enough. Usually I would go to Italy for my holidays but the cost of the disinfectant's become too much for me.' The band's drummer struck his snare drum.

'You're shite!' shouted a man over the edge of his tumbler.

Crazy Davie leaned into the microphone and lit a cigarette and he stared at the audience with a crooked smile on his face. 'We all love Italians, don't we?' he said. 'But it's a good job half of them are living in Scotland. Have you ever wondered why Italy's shaped like a boot? Well, think about it, fun-seekers, you could hardly fit that amount of shite into a tennis shoe. No. It's true. When I was a kid I used to wonder why Italians didn't have freckles, well, it's obvious when you think about it: they would slide off, wouldn't they?'

Laughter started to come up from the tables.

'It's all true,' he said, 'but my father, he fought at Anzio you know, and he came back with a few funny observations about the Tallies. He used to say, he used to say, Davie, how do they advertise World War Two Italian rifles for sale? Never fired, and only dropped once. Ha ha. Oh we love the Italians. And they say there's a lot of life in their culture, which reminds me, what's the tiniest book in the world? Well, it's the *Italian Book of War Heroes*. It's got four pages of instructions on how to run backwards dressed in opera costume.'

The audience were really laughing now. Some of the men were dead silent and groups of women tutted and shook their heads but the crowd was listening, and the comedian came into his own. 'But honestly folk, the Italians are good with their families, they could certainly show the British how to look after their own. I mean, look at the Mafia. The last time I was in Italy I heard a barber asking one of the godfathers if he wanted his hair cut or just a change of oil.'

Giovanni was standing at the urinals when Alfredo came in to splash water on his face. Giovanni caught his eye in the mirror. 'All right?' said Giovanni. 'It's starting to get a wee bit stuffy in there eh?'

'Same old tripe,' said Alfredo. 'Heard it all before.' The trough of the urinals was filled up with white deodorant cubes and the smell of them seemed to claw at the tiles. Giovanni stepped away and patted Alfredo on the back.

'Who's the woman you're sitting with?' said Giovanni.

'Don't say anything, Gio,' he said, 'but she's a talent spotter. She's from *Opportunity Knocks*, you know, the thing on the telly. I wrote to her a while ago and it turned out she was going to be up here this weekend, so she's come over specially to hear Maria.'

'You're kidding, man.'

'No, I'm not. But shush about it. I didn't even tell Rosa.'

The Gents door swung open and they heard clapping.

Michael Aigas from the TV shop had just come into the Winter Gardens with his pal Gary. They walked up to the bar. 'Let's crack some suds,' said Michael.

'Are you old enough for drink?' said the barman. Michael raised an eyebrow and shook a beaded wrist in the barman's direction. 'Cool your jets,' he said, 'the twenty-fifth of the first '59. I was eighteen last month.' The barman knew this wasn't true, but he said nothing more and put two pints of lager on the bar and drew them a look, taking the money.

'Here's how,' said Michael. Gary looked around and swallowed his lager and felt he was disappearing into his anorak. Michael always made him feel like a tramp. Gary felt spottier next to Michael, and he felt more stupid—Michael was cool and he watched TV all day and made out like nothing ever bothered him. 'Check all these oldsters digging their time,' said Michael.

'I know,' said Gary. 'They really fry my wig.'

Michael scanned the crowd until he saw Maria. When he caught sight of her he went over and said hello. 'You look amazing, kiddo,' he said. Maria blushed. Michael was always nice to her. Then she smiled and he raised his tumbler and wished her luck.

'How come you know that big no-user?' asked Rosa when he'd walked off. 'He's a complete weirdo, that boy.'

'I like his shop,' said Maria.

'Who's the wee chick?' said Gary.

'She's just a nice girl,' said Michael. 'She's just a girl but there's something amazing about her.'

'Hey-hey.'

'You're a half-wit, man,' said Michael. 'She's just an amazing little kid that's all. She's awake. Check her out when she sings. She always does those onion ballads, but wait till you see the way she burns them up. Look. There's all these deadbeats in here, and there she is in the middle—totally switched on.'

Gary turned to the bar. 'Let's get mashed,' he said.

The compere skipped back onto the stage.

'Thank you very much, ladies and gentlemen. It's been a couple of years since we first heard the sound of Rothesay's very own little queen of song, Maria Tambini. She was knee-high to a grasshopper then, and she's only a wee bit bigger now. Under the guidance of her mother Rosa and Madame Esposito's Dance Class here in Rothesay, Maria has gone from strength to strength. She's won every competition going and I'm sure you're in for a big treat tonight. Please give a big hand for Rothesay's very own wee darlin' starlin'—a smashing lassie we're all proud of her—Maria Tambini.'

Rosa put her hand on the small of Maria's back and gently pressed her forward. Maria walked between the tables thinking of the words and keeping her hands tidy.

I don't care what's right or wrong I don't try to understand let the devil take tomorrow cause tonight I need a friend yesterday is dead and gone and tomorrow's out of sight all I needed now is gone.

'Hello everybody,' Maria said. Now her eyes were shining and she was smiling every second. 'With the help of Jack Clark and the band I'm going to sing a song. It's called "Help Me Make it through the Night". Take it away boys.'

'Mow them down, Maria!' shouted McNab from the bar. The women at the tables turned round saying shush.

Lips teeth tip of the tongue lips teeth tip of the tongue.

Maria looked over the faces.

All I needed now is gone.

She didn't see her mother or Alfredo or anyone. Everyone disappeared as the music started. All the eyes out there were becoming one eye—one great eye and a single beam of light—and the sound she could hear was the sound of her own thoughts in time with the band as it opened up the verse.

Let me lay down by your lay down by your let me lay down by your side . . .

She opened her mouth.

'Go on, sugar,' said Michael Aigas to himself.

Nobody ever heard a little girl sing like that before. The sound came from somewhere else. She gripped the microphone and swayed into every note; she bent her knees and clambered up for the feeling in the words; her eyes grew wide and then suddenly narrow: she couldn't be without the song. She spread out her fingers and beamed and her eyes filled up with tears. She pulled back the wire of the microphone, throwing her head back, hugging herself, raising herself, stopping dead.

'Daddy,' said Kalpana.

'Oh my God,' said Miss Black from London.

McNab was quiet. Giovanni shook his head. Michael Aigas was lost in the dense sparkle of her performance. 'Now that is what you call talent,' said Alfredo. Lucia Tambini sneaked out of the door and cried quietly to herself as she walked up the road.

Maria finished the number with her eyes closed. When she opened them and put down the microphone the whole room was up on its feet.

Watch there are cameras there and smile yes keep smiling and walk to the side oh listen to all these people don't forget to hold yourself the nice way, oh this is a happy day.

She reached the bench and sat down. Her mother was staring forward and didn't move. She put a hand on her daughter's knee, and spoke so no one would notice. 'Pull your socks up,' she said.

7 · Migration

Walking back to their house in Craigmore, Dr Jagannadham said what a beautiful evening it was, and told Kalpana about the huge orange sunsets he remembered from his boyhood in Madras. Kalpana was always at her best alone with her father. She walked along the promenade in her Queen Victoria costume and she held on tight to his hand.

'Somebody at the concert called me a monkey,' she said.

'There are very ignorant people in the world, Kalpana,' he said calmly. 'We must learn to forgive their ignorance, if not to forget.' Then he changed the subject. 'We have been eating very badly today,' he said, 'and we have been speaking badly. Tomorrow we will show an interest again in clean living and go down to the beach. How does that sound, my little Scottish friend?' Kalpana smiled and put her head on her father's arm.

The doctor was interested in the world. He thought it was joyous that Maria had such a talent for singing, but he did not, like other people, enquire about how the world would reward her talent. Indeed he thought talent was its own reward. He was a moderate man and a good doctor: he seemed to comprehend the value of human gifts, but his real interests were scientific and historical. He was a good father. He brought Kalpana a sense of the past and a sense of the wonder of her own future.

The sea was oily now and dark, and the beam from the Cowal lighthouse moved across the water while a group of pigeons walked on the roof of a bus shelter at Craigmore. 'Do you know,' he said, 'what happened to the passenger pigeon?'

'Did they carry messages?'

'Yes. Once the most numerous birds in the world. In America, when they flew in number they blackened the skies, millions of them, a giant shadow, they could block out the sun. Yes, I think they were probably the most numerous. When they came in great numbers it must have been like an eclipse.'

'What were they like?'

'Well. They had blue heads. Behind the neck they were green or purple or bronze, according to the light. The breast I think was rust-coloured and then white. They moved, you know, at a very good speed. Very beautiful, Kalpana, and I read that when the birds at the front moved or dipped in the sky—all the others, sometimes going back three miles in the air—the others would move in precisely that way.'

Mrs Jagannadham whistled at their lateness when she opened the door. In two minutes, Kalpana was sitting on a large cushion, her mother wiping her face with tissues and cold cream. 'You were very very good today,' said her mother. 'They were all saying such things.'

The doctor had taken a book down from his study and opened it on his lap.

'Here,' he said. 'Listen, Kalpana. "In the early years of your reign . . ."'

He looked up and laughed, and Mrs Jagannadham also laughed.

'This writer saw one of the great flocks of passenger pigeons at a river in . . .' He drew his finger across the page. 'Kentucky.' Then Kalpana's father began to read from the page. '"Here they come!"' he read. '"The noise which they made, though yet distant, reminded me of a hard gale at sea passing through the rigging of a close-reefed vessel. As the birds arrived, and passed over me, I felt a current of air that surprised me."' He turned the page. '"The pigeons, arriving in their thousands, alighted everywhere, one above another, until solid masses were formed on the branches. Even the reports of the guns were seldom heard, and I was made aware of the firing only by seeing the shooters reloading."'

'What happened to them?' said Kalpana, peeling a tangerine her mother had given her.

'Well, it was the hunters. The birds were shot in great numbers by hunters in America.'

'But I thought there were millions.'

'Yes. That's what I'm telling you Kalpana. They shot millions of them. It says here there was one competition where to win the prize you had to bring 30,000 dead pigeons to the judges.'

'No.'

'Yes, it says so here. And by the year 1910 there was only one passenger pigeon left. Only one. Look here, there is a picture of the last one. She was called Martha.'

'Martha,' said Kalpana, showing her white teeth.

'Martha. The very last one.'

'And what then?' asked Kalpana.

'Extinct,' said Dr Jagannadham.

'All right . . . bedtime,' said Mrs Jagannadham getting up from the matting and stroking Kalpana's hair. Kalpana looked up at her mother. 'Bloody hell,' she said, 'all of them gone. That's amazing.'

They stood beside the door and looked at the doctor. '"When an individual is seen gliding through the woods,"' he read before closing the book, '"it passes like a thought, and on trying to see it again, the eye searches in vain; the bird is gone."'

8 · The Athletic Bar

Maria was on a piano stool at the back of the Athletic Bar, and people were closing in from all over the pub, some to say nice things to her about her singing, some to kiss her cheek or pat her head or just to look at her with memories of themselves at that age.

Alfredo was playing new Scottish tunes on a piano, then old Italian ones, Hamish the accordionist joining in between single malts, while Hazel was trying to find her specs under one of the tables. It was four-deep at the bar, and there were clusters of pint glasses on the wooden top, overflowing with lager or heavy or McEwans Export. It was so hot that the cubes of ice melted as soon as they were dropped into the glasses. Big Jack the barman had put a barrel against the door to keep it open, and the music and the shouting poured into the street.

The Athletic Bar smelled of sweat, thought Maria. Although there was noise and a lot of smoke, and although she smiled a big and constant smile, she was in fact sitting there in complete silence. On her low stool she was dwarfed by all the bodies standing around her. She sipped a glass of Irn Bru, and sitting there, with the loudness of the pub, the music, the faces bobbing and weaving in front of her, she felt she had retreated to somewhere else. She liked the feeling, liked to imagine herself here but not here, the sweetness of the Irn Bru and its bubbles nice in her mouth.

'Hello superstar,' said Michael Aigas. Maria shrugged her shoulders and giggled down her straw.

'Hiya,' she said.

'Christ, little sister. You certainly go the whole bundle.'

'Did you like me?'

'What? Too righteous. Too righteous I liked you. In my book you're way upstairs.'

'You're daft, Michael.' Maria giggled.

'No kidding,' he said. 'Maria. You're gonnae have to get yourself a manager or something.'

'I know,' she said. 'My mum and Alfredo were talking to a woman who works on the telly. She came tonight. I might get a chance to sing on the telly.'

'That's jake,' he said. 'That is totally jake.'

She giggled again, and she looked up at him. 'You're daft, Michael,' she said.

'Take it easy, kiddo,' he said. She looked at him but she wasn't quite looking at him. People surged in and he was squeezed behind them. Though she continued sitting on the piano stool, something in Maria—he saw it—stepped right out to meet the strangers' handshakes and the enthusiasm in their voices, and she rushed into their feeling for her, instantly smiling and blushing for them.

'Look after yourself, do you hear?' he said. But she couldn't catch him from where she was, and Michael Aigas, young Michael Aigas, just sixteen, who thought she was great, disappeared into the noise.

Around the walls of the Athletic Bar hung framed photographs of Rothesay: they showed Edwardian ladies under parasols on the promenade, crowds of 1950s holiday-makers at the pier, wooden gangways being rolled into place, Glaswegians laughing, and bands striking up before the Winter Gardens. The photographs were dry and uninvolved behind the glass, but the glass itself was clouded with condensation, the small, hot breaths of the living running like strangers before the cold windows of the past.

ROSA WAS at the back of the café. She could hear some late punters at the tables talking about baptism, of all things. Mrs Bone was sipping a Russian tea. 'Only if you're then going to get up on a Sunday morning and take them yourself,' someone said, 'because if you don't the whole thing's hypocritical. You get them baptised then you live the life. You go and do all the stuff. Get up on a Sunday and take them yourself.'

Frances Bone didn't look round. She just blew on the tea and stirred it with a spoon.

Rosa was throwing things out of the fridge. Alfredo had introduced her to a well-spoken woman after the concert and that was nice, that was good, that was right, she was wearing a fine blouse and they'd be hearing from her soon, so Rosa came straight over the road, went upstairs and cleaned her teeth, and now she was doing the fridge.

Just go off their heads and don't give a bugger at that Cash and Carry and come in here with more and more stuff and half of it's bloody rubbish anyway and we're left with all this food the bloody waste is diabolical.

Rosa smiled at the tables as she went through the front to find more bin-bags. 'It's been a nice day, hasn't it?' she said to the group.

'Oh aye,' one of the women said, 'but you must've been run off your feet, Rosa.'

Rosa smiled and narrowed her eyes as she walked back to the kitchen, but when she focused them again next to the fridge they were filled with tears. She had enjoyed the afternoon. It was a good party and she was happy it went well. Drinking with Giovanni had been a lovely thing to do; so handsome, Giovanni, in a nice clean white shirt there was nobody like him, he could charm the birds off the trees. But nobody, not even Rosa, could explain how one thing could quickly turn into another. Today was all out of sorts, she thought. Holidays and special days were always like that: drinking since early, eating at the wrong times, some shops shut all day, pubs open half the night. 'I'm just tired,' she said to herself. When she got like this nobody could do anything. 'It's just me,' she said.

She put a pan of water on the cooker. She had a basin of chopped vegetables—onions, celery, carrot and garlic—and she put them in a pan. There was mince in the fridge she was going to throw out, but she browned it and then put it in with the vegetables, then added salt and tomato and let it simmer. Rosa never really sat down to a meal herself. She always picked little bits of the ingredients along the way. She liked to be busy making dinners for the men and the customers and she didn't bother for herself. She picked. She always said to Maria the men should get the biggest bits of fish. Make sure they are fed well and see to yourself later.

Rosa could make all the dishes in her sleep. She knew them by heart, and on the shelf there was a book of scribbled recipes—the *Book of Stuff*—a loose-leaf compendium of notes Lucia and her father had put together over the years. Most of them came from the days of the first café. As she stirred the pan and gazed at the deep red of the sauce Rosa began to think of the book, but then the thought of the book and the redness and all the events of the day somehow merged in her mind and she began to think of the night the old Academy went on fire.

She took the book down. Over time, Lucia had put scraps of paper between the pages—boat tickets, goods receipts, articles ripped from the *Rothesay Academy Magazine,* sometimes prayers brought home from the chapel, cuttings of one kind or another. Rosa remembered the night of the fire. It was the year of the Coronation and Rosa was eleven. Her mother came to her room in the night and shook her. 'The Academy's on fire!' she said. Through the window they could see the sky all red, and up on the hill the school was blazing: you could see crimson sparks flying into the air for miles. The whole of Rothesay Bay was lit up. In the morning the arches of the old school stood empty in a black ruin with the smoke still rising.

She leafed through the pages. She passed lasagne al forno and cannelloni, passed her father's secret, the recipe for Tambini ice cream, and stopped at *fetuccine* sauce. They didn't make these dishes so much now. They ate rubbish now. Folded over and stuck in the spine was a tea-brown cutting. She opened it and right away recognised it as something from the *Academy Magazine.* It was something of Alfredo's.

What I Should Like to Make of My Life

I should like to dedicate my life to the service of God. I do not believe that there is any other way of life which is more satisfying than working for Christ. When I see and hear those people whom God has chosen to work for Him, when I see how fully satisfied they are, how happy and content whatever their lot, I long to be like them.

I should like to serve the Lord with humility and understanding and not to seek after the pleasures of this life. What greater joy can this world hold than to bring some heathen to believe in God?

I should work in darkest Africa or in the darkest slums. I should go willingly without a grumble and work till I could work no more. Discomfort and disease would not hinder me. The worst loneliness and persecution would not dissuade me. What a gladdening thing it would be to be loved, to be sought after for advice by some community which had come to know and love the Lord! And then, when I am old, all would come to me for sympathy and advice. I would not be lazy nor selfish or cross.

Alfredo Tambini, Form IV

There were other articles of Alfredo's, several short notes from the Drama Club, paragraphs about signal boxes, a dissertation on fish and chips, and other ones about school dinners, teachers, and the Isle of Arran. Later on in the book, against a recipe for spaghetti carbonara, written in ball-point pen with wiggly lines underneath and things scored out, was lodged another small square of yellowed paper.

EDINBURGH

The first place we went to in Edinburgh was the castle. It was very interesting. We saw the famous cannon, Mons Meg. Beside it is a telescope through which we could see nearly all of Edinburgh. After that we went to the Shrine, which I think is one of the most beautiful places in the castle. We went to the Crown Room, where the Honours of Scotland are kept. After that we went to Cannon Ball House for lunch and from there to Holyrood Palace. We saw the place where Rizzio was murdered and Queen Mary's rooms. Lastly, we went to the zoo and saw the lions and tigers, bears, birds and fishes. We had tea at the Ice Rink, and were lucky enough to see some skaters practising. All too soon it was time to go home. We arrived at the pier soon after nine o'clock.

Sofia Tambini, Primary 5

The sauce was bubbling and Rosa stirred. She put spaghetti into the pan. 'Sofia,' she said, 'my big sister.' She knew most of the stuff in the cookbook but she had forgotten Sofia's trip to Edinburgh. She'd never met Sofia. Her big sister was dead before Rosa was born. Lucia always said she had died of leukaemia, but Rosa thought she knew better. Poor young Sofia had drowned on a ship at sea. It was during the war. Lucia would never speak of it. She never told the truth.

'Forgets everything it suits her to forget,' thought Rosa. 'The story of her life.'

Then she found a clipping from the *Academy Magazine* about herself. There was a photograph too, from 1955. She remembered the year. It was just before the new school was built, and they were saying it was like a nuclear power station, the new Academy, or like something that had dropped from outer space.

HIGHLAND FLINGS

A Rothesay Academy pupil, Rosa Tambini, Form 3L, has won top honours at the the Annual Scottish Inter-Schools Highland Dancing Gala held at Dundee Central Halls. Rosa won the finals for Individual Highland Dancing for Rothesay Academy, and the formation finals were won by Blane House. Rosa says she is serious about her dancing and will be performing displays in various venues, some as far north as Aberdeen. The picture shows Rosa holding the Championship Bowl.

The spaghetti swirled in the pan. With the pad of her finger Rosa picked up chopped pieces of onion lying on the table and put them in her mouth. When she was tidying up she would do that all the time. Maria always saw her picking up stray morsels like this, and couldn't decide whether her mother was hungry or whether she was just tidying. Anyway, the bits of food she couldn't get hold of with a cloth and shake into the bin she ate, and the pasta was bubbling when Alfredo arrived.

'Thank you,' Maria was saying at the end of his arm, looking back towards the customers.

'Here's our wee star,' he said. 'She's absolutely knackered, Rosa.' Rosa looked at her daughter.

Oh rubbish you've got to have stamina if you want to make it in this business Maria oh look at you you're that well turned out and an absolute picture that's all, did you see the nice woman from London now this really has been a successful day for us Maria and I don't have to tell you hen the way you sang in there tonight you could've heard a pin drop.

'I want you to eat something,' she said.

'It's pyjamas time,' said Alfredo. Rosa scooped the hot sauce into the drained spaghetti. Maria looked through the steam rising off the table and saw into her mother's eyes.

'Don't forget the big curlers tomorrow, Uncle Alfredo,' said Maria with a yawn. And they all said goodnight. Maria sat down at the kitchen table.

'Eat it clean,' said Rosa.

Maria swallowed the steam. 'It's really nice, mum,' she said.

IN THE Athletic Bar the floor was sticky and Big Jack was hitting the bell for last orders. Mrs Ross who worked in the Amusement Arcade sang a song beside the organ, 'I Left My Heart in San Francisco.'

Rosa and Mrs Bone and other women from the shorefront flats were out sweeping Victoria Street. They had each brought down their brushes. There were streamers and forgotten Union Jacks lying about. The women swept all the rubbish together and made a pile outside the Winter Gardens, and as they swept they spoke of old singers and dance halls they used to go to years ago. 'Your Maria was something else in there tonight, Rosa,' said Mrs Bone. 'Never heard her so good as that.'

'She's got a chance at singing on the television,' said Rosa, leaning on the end of her brush. The music was coming down from the Athletic and a small wind began to rustle through the palm trees over the putting green.

'Well, if that's not cause for celebration I don't know what is,' said Mrs Bone. 'Wait here a minute.' By now there was a great pile of paper hats and half-eaten biscuits and everything lying heaped in the road.

'Here you go,' said Mrs Bone coming back. She handed out five small glasses and brandished a bottle of sherry.

'Oh to hell,' said Rosa, laughing and putting her glass out.

Mrs Bone poured a measure into each one. 'Whau's like us?' said Mrs Bone, putting the bottle under her arm and sipping her own.

Maria looked down from her window at her mother and the women laughing in the road. She could see the lights towards Port Bannatyne and hear the music from the Athletic Bar and it was nice to look out. She curled up on her bed and gazed at the luminous stars on the ceiling but in minutes she was fast asleep. Sitting on the dressing table next to the window was the blonde head of her Girl's World; it looked out with plastic eyes at the dark of the room and the girl asleep.

When the sweeping was done and the women had gone inside, Rosa propped her brush against the window of the café and went over to the seafront. She put her hands on the iron railing of the promenade and felt the cold in the metal coming up through her. The water was calm and a beam from the Cowal lighthouse reached over. She heard giggling. Though nobody could see her, she had a clear view of the covered benches further down the front, where Giovanni, the man she had decided never to marry, was kissing and licking the naked breasts of the television woman from London. Rosa watched them for a moment. She looked at them, listening to her own breath and feeling the cold off the water, then took off her shoes and walked back to the café in perfect silence.

9 · Rosa

It's funny how things come back to you. I loved games when I was young—dancing, uh, the dancing bug—and my daddy used to watch me from his chair and say I had two left feet. He was only kidding but I used to pretend it bothered me just so's he would feel bad and go down the shop and bring me up a bag of chips. He said he had to put fresh fat in the fryer for me but that was just pretending. You didn't believe half the things. My only regret when I look back is I wish I had spent more time with my daddy on my own. They never allowed you much time for that to happen but I wish it had you know.

Funny when you look back on it. It was her that made all the fuss but it was really my daddy who looked after us. Me and Alfredo learned all the songs from my daddy and God knows who the man really was because he looked after us but he never really said much. I mean you couldny really say you got to know him. He wasn't like that. Half the time you wondered if he was even there. But he was there. When it came to the things that counted, the truth to be told, my daddy was like an old man from as far back as I can remember. He just worked all the time.

I only saw him lose his temper the once. We were up the meadows and it was an autumn day; leaves everywhere, and me and Alfredo and my daddy, we could see our breaths, and we ran through the meadows wearing balaclavas and gloves on our hands. She had told us so many fairy tales when we were weans I'm telling you we were frightened of trees, but we dodged round them and me and Alfredo chased each other in circles up the meadows and my daddy just whistled the dog.

We had a leaf fight that day. I can still see them giant brown leaves, some of them wet, other ones dry and crackly and when you threw them up in the air in a bundle the dry ones came down slower. We had a leaf fight, and my daddy was up ahead of us. Alfredo hit me with a branch so I started burying him with leaves, giant bundles of them; more and more leaves, and I remember, I remember getting carried away with it, and Alfredo was shouting but I just put more and more leaves on top of him. He said his leg was trapped in the fence and I just ignored him and put more leaves and more leaves until he was buried.

I ran away and left Alfredo there. My daddy said where is Alfredo and he turned round but I just didn't say anything and we had to walk back and Alfredo was crying where he was buried under the leaves. He said that was a horrible thing to do to your brother and he told her and I got kept in for two days and she said that's just the measure of you, to make your brother suffer and bury him with leaves. It didn't bother me that she was angry but I hated it that my daddy wouldn't talk to me and said I was a bad article and he wasn't nice to me.

When I got pregnant with Maria it was my daddy who took me to one side and said not to worry. I fell pregnant in the summer and all he said was it's best not to wear them short skirts so often hen. She wouldn't speak to me and said she saw trouble coming as soon as I met the guy—Alan, that was his name, he worked at the submarine base on the Holy Loch and when he said he would go back to America no matter what, my daddy just said let him go. 'Good riddance to bad rubbish,' he said. She put on the waterworks of course. 'There's no use greetin' about it now,' my daddy said. 'She's still our wee lassie and that's that.'

She always kept a clean house, my mother. She watched me and Alfredo all the time as if she was scared she might lose us, but she did lose us, me in my way, Alfredo in his, good God, though she wouldny choose to see it that way herself. I feel sorry for her so I do when I think of her up in that house with all the lies she's told everybody. It's terrible if you get to an age when you realise you can't talk to your mother. Things would've been different if my daddy was alive. That's what I say to myself all the time. Right enough: he let her go for years telling lies and covering things up.

When she wants to get at me she says I'm selfish and tells me about the time I covered Alfredo with leaves up in the meadow. I was only playing, I say. 'You weren't only playing, you made him stop breathing,' she said.

'You stop me breathing,' I said once.

'That's just an evil thing to say to your mother.'

One day—Maria was just a wean—she came into the house and said she would love a new pair of gloves to go with her new suit. 'I won't spend the money,' she said. And what she did, she went out and bought some chamois leather; it's soft and easy to sew, she said. She bought a pattern and she sat there all winter making the gloves. Messing about with scissors and pencils and pins: oh, the fuss she made, how she was going to have embroidery on them, and sew elastic in at the wrists, or change from chamois to doeskin, make them suede on the hands, or start over again and make them gauntlet-style. She made us sit and watch her at night with the gloves. My father was dead. 'I will do without the gloves if I can't make them myself,' she said.

'I'm a grown woman,' I said. 'I can't sit here and watch you making these gloves. I'm going up the road.'

'You blame me for everything,' she said.

'Live your own bloody life.'

'Huh,' she said. '*Life.*'

And she never made the gloves. She wouldn't buy new gloves and she couldn't make them and we wouldn't take the blame so everything ended in nobody saying a word. 'Laugh at me,' she'd say if I ever brought it up, 'but if you knew the sacrifices I had made you would smile on the other side of your face.'

If it was up to her my Giovanni would never have looked twice at me. He would be somebody else's and that would suit her just fine. That would please her no end. Poor Rosa, who could never get a man worth holding on to. Poor Rosa, she just sits up there surrounded by dirty nappies. She doesn't have a life at all. Poor Rosa. Men. She hasn't had much luck there. Trouble is she's got too much anger in her, Rosa. She'd frighten a man away so she would, with her carry-on. Wouldny listen to my advice years ago when I said watch yourself hen you're going places in the world. Italian men are good so far as it goes but remember you've got to have a wee bit of ambition for yourself, Rosa. You don't just sit down and take life on the chin. The Tambinis were meant for better things, Rosa, just look at your father.

I can remember the huge piles of leaves I put over Alfredo and even yet I remember the smell of them for God's sake. It was a cold Rothesay day and the leaves were rotting. We were only playing up there in the meadow so we were. You don't think I would hurt Alfredo? He's my twin. We started off laughing and Alfredo just disappeared under the leaves and when I looked up it was foggy in the meadow and my daddy was up ahead and I just stopped for a second to see what it was like with the smell of the leaves and nobody there but me. When I ran away I thought Alfredo would come, I promise you I thought he would come. Thought he was right behind me.

Just the other day Maria was talking on the phone to one of the people from London—a producer, they wanted to hear her speaking voice. I was standing in the hall and there was nothing left of my nails I'm telling you. You just can't argue with talent is what I say. Sometimes I wish I had her confidence I'm no kidding. For a wee girl that size she can hold her own with anybody. I'll say that for Giovanni, he's good to Maria; he never passes that wee lassie but he's got a joke for her or a smile. I would definitely say that kind of thing has boosted her confidence no end. I hope and pray I'm not like my mother, that's all.

Maria and I do wee things together. Sometimes it's like we're more like sisters than anything else. I think she knows sometimes my nerves get the better of me, right, but she just gets on with it. You know that way, even with somebody young like that, sometimes if they're calm then they sort of calm you down as well just the same. Never mind. I'm good to Maria and I don't need to tell her that, she knows that. We're more like sisters that's the thing.

We made a cake the other day. I'll tell you it's a good job it's singing Maria's good at because I'm not kidding you she is definitely not one for the cooking. All the old Italian dishes are in the scrapbook but no, Maria looks at them as if they were written in Latin. No way. She would not thank you for cooking lessons either. The thing is but you've got to learn a wee bit; a lassie can't go through life not knowing how to boil an egg. I mean men would run a mile from the like of that. Not that she'll be looking for a man, she's got all that in front of her, but you know what I mean. Even just to be independent a woman should be able to turn her hand in the kitchen.

I must admit I was never one for reading. I'll give my mother her due on that one, she was a reader; me and Alfredo had our heads full of fairies and Rapunzel and all that palaver and it was her that read them out to us. Alfredo absolutely loved it, but not me—give me an old movie or a record any day, but I wouldny thank you for a book. But making the cake I brought down a book from years ago—an old pink book, old as tea—it had been in the house for as long as I can remember. It was daft I suppose but there were some good things in it. *The Modern Girl's Guide to Charm and Personality.*

Maria sat at the kitchen table looking at a *TV Times* as usual and moving her lips to a song. I put all the stuff out on the table and got her attention. 'So let's get on with this cake, Maria. Look here.' And then I read a bit from the book. Maria probably thought I was going off my head.

Here's the book and here's the bit:

Admittedly, some household chores are rather deadly. You dust a room, and it looks much the same after you've finished; you sweep the carpet, and who can see any difference? But with baking it's another story. You do see something for your labours, even if a greedy family do not allow you to see it for very long. Indeed, that is one of the snags of home baking. The cakes and buns made at home are so much more popular than the shop varieties that they disappear with depressing rapidity, but that is quite a cheap price to pay for the reputation of turning out good 'eats'.

And Maria said right away, Oh boring, we've already done stuff like this in Home Economics, can I go up the Amusements with Kalpana? No you will not, lady, I said. You will sit right here and spend a wee bit of time with your mother if you know what's good for you. I mean it's not as if I crack the whip around Maria and her friends. I would just like a wee bit of input now and then. I mean that's all you hear from them—amusements, films, running here and there, and busy all the time with rubbish. It's not all just fun and games I told her. They get away with holy murder the lassies nowadays I'm telling you, and so I said just you sit there lady.

'Sultana cake is made by the creaming method,' it said, and as I read it out I pointed to the stuff and Maria started lifting and laying. There it was: three cups of flour, a half pound butter, half pound sugar, half cup sour milk, three eggs, three-quarters pound sultanas, one and a half teaspoonfuls baking powder. Method: cream the butter and sugar and add the sour milk. Break the eggs separately in a saucer, then drop each in singly, and beat them well. Sift the flour and the baking powder and add, then put in the fruit, and beat to your heart's content.

We fairly enjoyed ourselves by the end. Maria was mixing and filling the tins and she hardly looked up I swear to God. It was like sisters the two of us laughing and her licking the stuff off the spoon and me saying that's enough you'll give yourself a tummy ache. That's what it's all about, I thought. You know. Learning how to cope is the best thing in the world I said and I could tell Maria was happy because we were doing something together. It's good for the two of us to spend a bit of time like that.

When she got back in from seeing Kalpana the smell was everywhere and we opened the oven and it was ready. 'It looks just like the picture,' Maria said, and I said, 'That's right, it's not very hard when you know how, Maria.' I took up the book and said to her, but listen, it says in the book:

When you've finished your baking and the cake is safely done,
there is still another job waiting for you. I expect you know what
it is. Yes. The bowls and spoons and knives that you have used
must all be washed up and put away, *and the kitchen left as tidy*
as when you began. 'A good cook tidies as she goes,' as I used to
be told when I was learning to bake. There's something very sat-
isfactory indeed in a happy ending.

I read this last bit out of the book and then slammed the book
shut and laid it in front of her. 'This is yours now, keep it good,'
I said.

'Oh mum,' Maria said.

'Mum nothing,' I said. 'Don't mum me. We've all got to do our
wee bit and that's a book you should know off by heart.'

I'm tired telling Maria. You don't get anywhere in this world just
sitting on your backside. Half the time she just looks at me. I say to
her don't think I'm getting onto you Maria—I just want you to
stand on your own two feet, that's all. But we certainly enjoyed ourselves that day. It's worth spending a wee bit of time. I said to her, I
said, 'Maria, you've got your whole life in front of you hen.' At the
end of the night we just sat looking at the cake in the middle of the
kitchen table. 'Goodnight mum,' she said. And she went away to her
bed as happy as Larry.

I'm not much of a cake-eater myself and neither is Maria thank
God, but it was a good day that, a nice wee lesson for the two of us.
When Giovanni came in he put his hand on the cake. 'This cake's
still warm,' he said.

'It's brand new,' I said. 'Maria made it.'

10 · Devotions

In October, Lucia felt the very first of the winter cold. She was walking along the seafront one morning on her way to St Andrew's, and
as she passed the West End Café, sausage rolls and bridies out on
trays, she realised she was hungry, and licked her lips. The rain

poured down and the seagulls scattered before the shops. On days like these, Lucia felt she was really on an island, she felt the distance in herself, but then she grew comfortable as she realised this was her ground and she had known it for the longest time. Looking down the promenade with its curtain of drizzle, she thought of seafronts the world over, places that held you back before the great currents, where one day, looking out, you could find you were not just looking but waiting.

She never ate breakfast before Communion. In this respect, as in others, she deferred to Saint Catherine of Siena, who featured in the stained glass of St Andrew's. The window showed the devils trying to tempt Catherine from the rigours of her fasting. When Lucia arrived at the chapel she took off her coat and looked up: the light of Argyll was passing through the glass, falling on the pews, where her son sat waiting.

'Mammo,' said Alfredo, 'it's yourself.'

'Aye. Lucky you've got your good coat. That's the rain started.'

'Thought as much. You couldn't see the hills for fog this morning.' Lucia placed her missal and beads on the wooden shelf and pulled down the kneeling-cushion. She crossed herself.

'She's been at me again,' said Lucia, kneeling down. 'I don't mind telling you, Alfredo, I've had it up to here. I hardly dare go into that café the way she is. Determined to be unhappy that lassie when she's got everything going for her as well. I only go in there to see Maria, but that's her weapon you see—she wants to turn that wee lassie against me.'

'Don't be daft, mammo,' said Alfredo. 'She's just going through a bad patch.'

'And how long's the bad patch supposed to go on, Alfredo? I don't know, the way she is, she must give that poor lassie a hell of a time. I feel sorry for Maria. It's a blessing for her she's not sticking around here I'm not kidding you. As for him—the boyfriend—he's worse than useless.'

Alfredo breathed out. He looked at the altar. He was always overwhelmed by the physicality of the statues, the hands and the eyes, the bones of the arms, the arrangement of legs and the beautiful feet of the saints in their sandals. Over the hours and over the years he had examined every curve and every fingernail on those statues.

'Why can't people just live their lives?' Lucia said. 'Don't know why people can't just be happy and get on with it.'

'Are you happy, mammo?'

'What are you asking me that for?'

'Are you?'

'There's nothing the matter with me. She's taking pills. The girl who works in Hick's said she's never out of there. She's taking tablets.'

Alfredo kept his eyes forward. 'She'll be all right,' he said.

Lucia sighed and stood up and walked over to the candles at the side. She dropped some coins into the box and lit three candles.

'Why do you always do three, mammo?' he asked when she came back.

'Don't have the energy I used to,' she said. 'I can't do as much any more. I always light one for Mario and one for Sofia, God bless them.'

'And who's the third?' asked Alfredo.

'I'm too old to hide things now,' she said.

'I know, mammo. Who's the third?'

'There was a man on the *Arandora Star*. You know what happened and God bless us, it was a long time ago. Thought it was all well and gone. But some things that happen to you are there all your life, Alfredo. That's what people don't understand when they're young. Just have to close your mind to it, son, and get on with the day. You think things are past but they never are. I think of that boat.'

She stopped herself. She didn't want to remember.

'It doesn't matter,' said Alfredo. 'As you say it was all another time and what's the point?'

'You won't speak to them about it, Alfredo, so you won't?' said Lucia.

'No no,' he said, 'I never have.'

But he knew that Rosa had been told about the *Arandora Star* and what really happened to Sofia. Their father had told them before he died. They didn't know why he decided to tell them, but he made them promise never to speak about their sister to Lucia. And then one day Lucia told Alfredo over a cup of tea.

'Your sister didn't die of leukaemia,' she said. 'She died on the *Arandora Star.*'

'No, mammo,' he said. 'Only men were on the *Arandora Star.* The women didn't get interned. You're getting mixed up now.'

'Your sister Sofia was on the ship the night it sank, and so was I, Alfredo. That's all I can tell you now. Your sister died on the *Arandora Star* and your father never really forgave me. That's about the measure of it. That's what happened in my life.'

Alfredo recalled the day she told him. The chapel seemed to grow darker in the minutes of their conversation and the following silence. He stared into the pews and felt his thoughts descend into the grain of the wood. Lucia's great secret would always be safe with him. Rosa thought she was a hypocrite, but even she held back; she never told Maria, never told Giovanni, and quietly kept her mother's great mistake to herself, the invisible source of an unending grudge.

'Some day if I can ever remember I'll tell you it all,' said Lucia. 'There was a man.'

She looked at her son to see what he would say. He felt she was struggling to go on and say something else but then retreating. 'A couple of months ago I got a suitcase delivered from the pier. The post office put it on the ferry at Wemyss Bay but then there was some mix-up and they didn't know who it was meant for and it was taken to Lost Property. They sorted it out and then a young fella brought it up and I had to sign for it. You remember that thing in the paper about all the stuff that was kept in storage in Glasgow at the post office? That suitcase has been sitting good God in the basement of the post office at George Square for over thirty years. It's a giant place, they never went down there. They said they found it at the back of an old storeroom. A brown suitcase.'

'What is it?' asked Alfredo.

'I put it in the cupboard. I don't know.'

'So you don't know what's inside?'

'Can't remember. Old clothes and things I suppose. I'll sit down with it eventually,' she said.

Then she lifted up her rosary beads and joined her hands around them and looked out at the altar. There were only seven or eight people in St Andrew's, and when the bell rang they all stood up. 'The future is all Maria now, isn't it? The past is the past.'

Alfredo put his hand over his mother's and unfolded his distant Italian smile. 'That's right, mammo,' he said.

MARIA WAS always up in the living-room dancing with a hairbrush in front of the mirror. She was going to Madame Esposito's dance-class ('Modern, Tap, and Ballet') every other night after school, and all day Saturday, but she worked out her best routines in front of the mirror at home. That was the thing about Maria: she sang every-where, her voice shouted out in pubs, cafés, down on the seafront, from time to time in the neighbours' houses. And she didn't dwell in rooms as other children did—rather, she placed herself in the middle of them as if every room was a stage, an echo-chamber, built for pro-jection and confidence.

But her mother's living-room would remain in her mind as a world apart. Years later she could still provide a list of every orna-ment and piece of furniture. She spent her first few bedtimes in Lon-don counting through them to get to sleep:

1. The television. An ITT 24-inch. It was rented from Har-ris's but bought later as a reconditioned. On top of the TV was a large bowl of fake flowers stuck in green sponge. There was also a brass 'picture-tree' featuring cut-out photographs of relatives in the 'leaves'. Standing on the floor next to the TV was a giant gold-coloured Chinese lady.

2. The fireplace. A brown surround with plenty of shelves for ornaments and an oyster pattern round the edge. The fire it-self had two bars, fake coal, and a little whirligig which made 'flames' appear on a plastic screen behind the coal. Above the fire was a picture of an Amazonian lady in a white frame. Her dress was more off than on. Above the fireplace in the middle was a carriage clock. On either side were several porcelain-effect ornaments, usually scenes of a rustic nature, with rosy-cheeked maids and farmers sitting on country stiles. On the row below

this were many clear glass fish with a dash of paint trapped inside. Mixed in with these were ceramic rabbits and curled-up cats and carved wooden ornaments featuring deer leaping. The base of the fireplace held a number of more expensive ornaments: glimmering crystals in the shape of pineapples or mice, a bottle of sangria wrapped in black and red leather. This was a present from Spain. On the other side of the fireplace a porcelain Clydesdale horse pulled a cart full of wooden barrels.

3. The room divider. A wooden item on short legs which offered a series of shelves on which to place more ornaments. Rosa had placed a bowl of ceramic fruit she was fond of in the middle of this. On another shelf was a collection of tiny brass ornaments: a phonograph, a boot, a tortoise, a miniature grand piano, Big Ben, and a racing car. Most of these were bought from a shop in Montague Street called Bojangles. One of the other shelves on the room divider held a digital clock radio. The bottom part with sliding doors had booze inside, mostly cans of McEwans Export and Tennant's Lager, the odd bottle of stout, and a half-empty bottle of Bell's. At the back there was usually something like Advocaat, Midori or Martini Bianco, booze for women who didn't like booze. The tumblers were also kept in here.

4. The sofa. A green cord three-seater which had been Maria's entire planet for the first three years of her life. If you put your hand down the back there were masses of biscuit crumbs, a child's debris, stuff that had somehow missed Rosa's vacuum cleaner and her damp cloth. Now and then a brown coin would turn up too: Maria would scrub any coin she found with ketchup, making it shine like a gold button. The knots of nylon on the sofa's surface were coming undone. It was like a giant dog and even in adulthood Maria would think of its comforts.

5. The coffee table. Smoked glass with a bit underneath for the *TV Times*. Rosa kept several small ceramic baskets of flowers on top of this, and at the centre was an alabaster ashtray and a matching alabaster lighter shaped like a cube.

6. The dining table. At the back of the living-room was a table bought at some expense for family dinners that never happened. It was always covered with ironing.

One of the nights before Maria went to London her mother gave an Avon party in the house. It wasn't meant as a send-off party or anything, but it turned into a night she would often think of when she thought of her last days on the island.

Kalpana was allowed to stay overnight. Rosa had placed bowls of crisps and nuts around the living-room—on the coffee table, the room divider—and she took the chairs from the dining table so all the women could sit. The living-room was filled with laughter and coughing. Everyone had a drink, the Avon catalogues were spread over the carpet, and to do her job Rosa was going round squirting perfume on people's wrists and shaking out her own wrist to let them smell. Kalpana and Maria sat on the stairs in their nightdresses. They could watch everything that was happening and people passed them up crisps and then gave them chocolates too and they were watching all the events and feeling great.

Maria had noticed that something nice happened to Rosa when she was surrounded only by women. Sometimes, the years fell away from her, she laughed more and drank more, was more girlish, and the weight she perpetually carried around seemed to drop off her. Maria had only seen her like that with men a few times in her life. Wearing her carpet-slippers, a bottle under her arm, distributing glass tumblers to the women, Rosa seemed happy to be herself for that time. She never cried so much in front of other women, the way she did with men.

All the Avon perfumes that season were named after Greeks. One that Kalpana thought smelled of oranges was called Ariadne. One in a round blue bottle was called Pandora. Mrs Bone liked the smell of Medea. Doing her saleswoman act, Rosa liked them all but her favourites were Jocasta, Leda and Penelope. She went from chair to chair spraying wrists and giving out little glass tubes of free samples. Maria had not seen her mother so happy in a long time. That was the thing about Rosa that took years to understand: beneath the everyday buzz of unhappiness and self-pity, she had the most amazing resources, no matter what—they fuelled her bid to survive her troubles, and she liked to be among people, until she felt they had let her down.

The girls got to stay up late, and when the women had all filled in their order forms Rosa put on a record and brought the girls downstairs. Kalpana loved the party. Rosa turned the music up and put a curtain across the kitchen door. Maria was behind it. Then Rosa put on a new record. 'Ladies,' she said, 'a wee bit of hush. For your own pleasure. Wee bit of hush for the proud mother. In a special command performance, for one night only, I am delighted to introduce my own daughter—Maria Tambini!'

The record started and Maria jumped through the curtain. All the women clapped and Maria was holding a hairbrush and immediately began swaying and popping her eyes. 'Would You Like to Swing on a Star'. All the women cheered and Kalpana clapped. Rosa swigged from her glass and handed out ashtrays; she kept time to the music and didn't seem to care if things got spilt or if anything went on too long. 'What the hell,' she said, 'it's only us having a nice time for a change.' Maria would sing her song three times that night and the phone rang out in the hall, but they ignored it, going on with the song, and then other songs and drinks from the back of the cabinet.

In the morning the records were spread over the living-room carpet, and the Rosa who put them back in their sleeves was not the same person who'd taken them out. The mother Maria adored came out when Rosa forgot herself. But that didn't happen often. Maria was still lying in bed, smiling and singing, when she heard the Hoover scrape over the landing and knew her mother had become herself again.

11 · Giovanni

I used to work on the trawlers, that's what I did before I met her, so the work just carried on out there but I hated it, and during a bad night I'd think about her lying in bed, and sometimes in the middle of fucking nowhere I would say her name, standing on the deck it was bloody freezing and I'd just say her name.

Rosa.

Miles from anywhere. Fucked. That's when you know you love somebody when their name comes into your head and everything else just fades away, nothing else matters but her name and her face on the pillow. Listen to yourself, you're pathetic. A woman like her and she is always sad I swear to Christ you could have a happy life just doing the right things I've told myself a million times. When the boat came back into the bay and you could see the lights you just loved her and when you got in the door she would wash your hair and say you're daft go to sleep. You're daft, so you are.

There's no need. You don't know it sometimes but you're just letting yourself right fucking down aren't you? She's unhappy. That is a fact. I just touch her head sometimes and hold it in my hands and when she moves my overalls are wet where her eyes were. There's no need for that in this day and age. We should be happy and that's my job is it no to make her happy? That's what I want as well. I'm telling you. I should fucking run away and leave them all in peace so I should. Sometimes when I'm out I can hear her voice talking to me. She's not there. I've gone to the phone and rung her and she comes to the phone sleepy and says leave us alone you're no good. You're not a good man. Leave us alone she fucking says to me.

She already had Maria when I met her. There was never any problem. Even in her cot the wee lassie was special I'm telling you straight. I really took to her, and me and Rosa used to tuck her in at night. I never met her real father and neither did the wee lassie and that didnae matter. He worked up at the Polaris base on the Holy Loch once upon a time and he was back living in America years ago as far as I know. I hate it when Rosa says I'm just like him, we're all tarred with the same brush—it makes me feel like fucking nothing. I'm not like him. Just sometimes it seems there's nowhere to go and you know you could do everything right if you wised-up.

I don't want this I'm telling you straight. She calls me a people-pleaser and she's right all I do is laugh and joke in the pub, as if those people mattered. Have another drink boys. Go on eh. Live it up. Live it up eh the big fucking diddy's getting the drinks. You don't just stand back and watch things go to hell, go to fucking pot. That's some bloody way to go ahead being the big man right enough. You need to have a word with yourself and sort the thing out for Christ's sake. Here you are fucking pathetic and feeling sorry for yourself again, away and do something about it then. You've got to put an end to all this and make things right. She deserves a better kick of the ball than this.

On nice days I used to drive them around the lochs and across to Dunoon or else over to Largs. What a good carry on and a good laugh. Like a proper family. That's the way it should be. The windows down and racing up the Electric Brae. Getting the stuff in at the ice-cream van. Have whatever yous want. Life is what you make it eh? I love to say her name. You'll see a change Rosa. Believe you me you can bet your life.

I found a pack of old radio cards. I gave them to the wee lassie as a present and she loved them so she did. Pictures of all the old stars that used to sing on the radio. I think they were American. They had people like Mario Lanza and Judy Garland on them. All that. And then sometimes we'd have wee concerts in the café. What the hell I'd say. A rainy day. Hand sweeties out to the weans and let them sit at the tables and be the audience. And wee Maria would come down-stairs all done up and a right lady. She always sang that wee lassie as if the whole world was watching her. Would hardly credit it now: London. They're working it all out for her down there now and I'm telling you she fucking deserves it that wee lassie, deserves the lot. There's people belong in a place like London and she'll have all the chances in the world down there.

Life is what you make it. The weans would all clap and shout for ice cream and Maria would sing her wee heart out. What the hell I would say. Give them the lot. Give them the whole bloody lot. I would empty the shop for them so I would. There was a television mast up on the meadows and Maria and her wee pal Kalpana used to go up there with their dolls and have concerts. Right underneath the mast with a force ten gale blowing half the time. She has some fuck-ing guts on her that wee lassie. It's frightening so it is, frightening to watch.

You should see her watching the telly. If it's one of they singing programmes she fidgets on the sofa in time to what they're singing and mouths the words, you know? She's totally into it. The other night I came in the door of the living-room and she didn't see me. She was right up against the telly screen. She was putting her hands on the glass the way kids do to feel the interference. Then she sat back on the pouffe and watched. The Miss World competition was on and she just stared into the faces of the lassies and giggled when they said what they'd do if they won. She's a treasure I'm not kidding. I watched her from the door and she didn't even turn round, it was as if she was just sleepwalking or something, just her wee hand stroking the telly screen as if she could actually touch the hair on the lassies. Maria watches the TV the way other people look at people they love. She just pulled her knees up to her chin on the carpet and then the commercials came on and she still stared. It was only a lot of commercials but you should see the way she watches them. Six inches from the screen.

Beanz Meanz Heinz.

Rosa's never been a laugh a minute. She's just got too much on her mind half the time but she can be a great woman when she wants to be. I was shaving this morning and I looked at myself in the mirror and said, this is up to you. If you want to fucking mess up your life then it's up to you. It's in your hands. Control yourself man and get your house in order. There's no excuse. There's a lot of things I'd like to say to Rosa. Remember that time at Saltcoats we rolled down the beach having a kiss? We couldn't stop laughing and we got sand in our mouths and everything. 'This didn't happen in *From Here to Eternity*,' you said. Back in the car I said I loved you and you cried and we went to the Melbourne Café and had knickerbocker glories leaning against the Vitrolite. Perry Como was playing on the jukebox.

I'm back on the boats for money. Out here at night the men are rolling drunk and talking rubbish and I just walk to the stove and above it the radio crackles and I think 'land'—oh, for Christ's sake, dry land—and I think about you, the moon over Arran and here's the ropes dragging over the good boots you bought me, and the big horn sounding out: I think to myself, holy fuck, I'll never be a good man in your eyes. Up on the deck it's a bunch of bams—fucking diddies talking about fighting and all sorts of shite. Some prick from Brodick's going on about how he fell out with his sister over a pot of soup. The sister says to him, 'Oor mother made a rare pot of soup,' and he says, 'Don't talk fucking shite, it was like tar thon soup.' 'Away,' she says, 'it was the best soup on the west of Scotland, pea and ham, ham thick as the walls at Barlinnie, you loved it.' 'Away and geez peace, and stop telling me what I loved,' he says, and he's telling us the full story. 'You could've danced on thon soup and it was bloody horrible and I'm fed up listening to you bumming it up. Soup, soup, the fucking soup was boiling hot and it near melted the fucking spoon. Jesus, it was molten lava, would you no geez peace about the soup!' That's the kind of thing you have to listen to, that's the fucking level of conversation out here.

The times me and you had in the car. We could talk to one another about things, you and me and the wee lassie out in the car with pokes of chips, we know how to live, sitting parked at Portencross and the rain battering down, remember, the windows of the car clouded up and wee Maria in the back making footprints on the window with the heel of her hand and her fingers. You Rosa and me and the wee lassie out there ourselves: the smell of air-freshener and the rain pelting outside. We know how to live hen. I want to be good in your eyes. If God should strike me down. Starting from today I swear to God, no more rubbish from me. Don't turn the light off I'm asking you, don't forget me Rosa in your green eyes.

12 · Kelvinator

Lucia was down in the café. She was looking for some tape in a drawer through the back; the drawer was full of tacks and labels and batteries and old peelers. 'This is some state to keep a drawer in,' she said. 'Bloody ridiculous. No like you at all.'

'We're trying to run a bloody business in here,' said Rosa, 'and there's a family as well. I'm run off my feet here. I've only got one pair of hands. And you want me to bloody stop and tidy the drawer into the bargain.'

'I'm just saying,' Lucia said. 'I'm just saying it doesn't do to let things go. You need to keep on top of these things.'

'And you're so organised about everything aren't you mammo?'

'Well. When you've no choice you just have to cope.'

'And you're so good at coping aren't you?' Rosa had now put down the knife she was cutting with and was looking straight at Lucia. 'You always do the right thing don't you mammo?'

Lucia was stirred by the way Rosa spoke to her, but she was frightened to go further. 'I was just saying.'

'Well don't say!' said Rosa. 'I've got fish to prepare here and you're just getting in my road.' She squeezed herself in front of the drawer and found the tape right away. She dropped it into Lucia's hand and went back to the table.

'I just want to pin up a sign about the jumble sale,' said Lucia, but she walked through to the front shop with her bottom lip trembling. She put the notice up and left. When Rosa looked into the café she could see the prints of Lucia's slippered feet all the way to the door. All the time she was through the back her mother had been standing in a puddle of dirty potato skins. 'Well done, Mrs Mop,' Rosa said to herself.

Maria was up in the living-room watching *Opportunity Knocks*. A man-and-wife act from Torquay were doing a routine about clowns. Maria sat on the sofa biting her nails. The woman leapfrogged over the man and they knocked each other over then returned to the microphone for the finale, and Hughie Green the compere came back. He had grey hair slicked back and his voice was half-American. There were lines across his forehead and he only smiled on one side of his face. 'I mean that most sincerely, folks,' he said.

Maria wondered if Hughie Green had been to all the places in America. He talked as if he knew everyone and had seen everything. He always used the word 'talent'. He said this one had talent and that one had talent and what a lot of talent there is packed into the next act. Maria tried to picture the studio in London. She was going there in two weeks. After her big night at the Jubilee she had gone to another audition at the Barrafield Halls in Largs and the letter had come soon after saying she had made it onto the show. She watched Mr Green on *Opportunity Knocks* and wondered if he would like her. He was nice with his grey hair, and she felt he looked like someone she had known all her life.

'What talent is, how you find it, is what *Opportunity Knocks* is all about,' said Hughie Green, 'and we like the public to make the decisions for us. Not just the public here in the studio, but the mums and dads sitting in front of their television sets at home. One thing I've learned, ladies and gentlemen, is you can't beat the opinion of the great British public.'

You saw each of the acts on the screen and the clapometer recorded what the studio audience thought of each one. When she was only a baby, Alfredo had told Maria the clapometer could hear the claps in Rothesay and all over Britain. She knew that wasn't true, but she still clapped for the act she thought was best, feeling glad when the needle went up. 'I can't believe it, that will be you soon, Maria,' said Rosa coming in with the Hoover. 'Don't bite your nails.'

'Oh mum,' said Maria, 'what will I wear?'

'Mrs Gaskell the agent,' said Rosa, 'remember she came to Largs to see you the other week? We went to Nardini's?'

'Uh-huh.'

'Well London Weekend Television gave her your tape and that's why she came up. We signed the paper. You're going to stay with her and her husband in London for a wee while. She's talking to a stage school. She's got people working out a costume and everything.'

'Oh mum,' said Maria.

'I know, soon we won't know you.' The credits were rolling on the television and the rain was driving against the living-room window. 'Mrs Gaskell said the show is just the beginning. She said people who don't win can still make it if they're as good as you.'

Maria was wide-eyed. She put her arms around Rosa's neck. 'Do you think I will get to be on the programme for real? Will you all watch me?'

'Yes. We hope so.'

Maria pressed her cheek against her mother's and giggled.

'Pyjamas,' said Rosa.

Maria jumped up and made for the door. On the way she grabbed the Hoover. She pressed the release button with her foot and freed the arm, and then, beaming, she sang the first few lines of a song, 'Rockaby'. The thing about Maria was that she always sang at full pelt; even when she was nine or ten she had all that power in her voice; it seemed to rear up from nowhere in her tiny frame wherever she was. Even for thirteen she was small, but her singing voice never was.

> *Rockaby your baby with a Dixie melody*
> *When you croon, croon a tune*
> *From the heart of Dixie.*

Rosa turned and plumped the cushions on the sofa and smirked with pleasure towards the dusky window. 'You're off your head,' she said to Maria and then said the same to the empty room. When Maria had gone upstairs her mother stared at the television screen for ages without blinking.

As Dr Jagannadham never tired of telling his patients, the range of the temperature on Bute is narrower than in any other place in Scotland; the hydros and spas so favoured by earlier holidaymakers had honoured the fact, and people travelled on steamers to enjoy the soft air and to eat ices. Once it was called the Montpellier of the North. There are palm trees on the seafront, and, though the people have gone, though the seafront is quiet, a stream of soft air still comes down from the lochs.

Maria often kept her window open at night. She lay on top of her quilt with a record down low on the dansette. Mrs Bone was going deaf and was playing the shipping forecast louder and louder; you could hear it at all hours through the wall. When Maria had been in bed for ages and she heard those strange words—Dogger, German Bight—she knew it had to be around one o'clock. Lying in her bed, the radio's London voice coming through the wall, the lights of Ardbeg glowing orange, her imagination would dance on the windowledge, and she clenched her fists as she thought of different singers and the way they sang. She said her prayers, often more than once over the course of the night, and would open her fist to find sugarlumps she'd stolen from one of the tables in the café, and she'd eat them.

She had thought the same things at night for as long as she could remember. She imagined there was a camera way out there. It had wings and she knew it was looking for her. It took photographs as it flew overhead but really what it wanted was her. It came from Glasgow and tore down the River Clyde. It passed hotels and shipyards and the Erskine Bridge and Dumbarton Rock. It came low out of the mouth of the Clyde and then skirted the tops of the churches and the new computer factories at Greenock. It almost skipped over the water of the Firth of Clyde to Dunoon. It rose over the roofs of the houses there and skirted the cinema, then plunged sharply into Innellan and past the craft shops and over the Cowal Hills. The camera could see in the dark. It took pictures of Cumbrae in the distance. Then it swept in low over the sea, clicking all the while: a fishing boat out in the bay trailing foam and seagulls. Now the lights of Rothesay were obvious and the camera raced ahead. It passed over the pebbles on the narrow beach. It passed over the promenade and the putting green. It crossed Victoria Street above the cars and then the strange camera-bird stopped and hovered at Maria's window. It just hovered there. She created a look on her face and turned her head on the pillow once again to the open window.

Maria knew the boards that squeaked on the landing; she stepped over them and carefully began to descend the stairs. Part of the way down she noticed a strange blue light coming through the window over the front door. It was very blue and fell on the staircase; it made her feel alone and bright in the dark. A trace of the blue light was picked up by the gloss-painted banister, yet looking up at the wall she saw the light was hopelessly faint, though it began to illuminate a photograph hanging there, an old one of granny Lucia and dead Mario. She leaned in closer to look at their faces. They were barely smiling. Lucia wore a ruffled blouse and her dimpled face was pretty. Grandad Mario had sticky-up hair. The photograph was in a round frame and at the bottom it said 'Lucca'.

Maria walked to the kitchen at the back of the café. A pile of newspapers sat on the table, fish-and-chip paper; she put her hand on top of the pile and noticed how small her hand was and how cold the papers. The headline said, 'Heart Broken: Maria Callas Died Yesterday of a Broken Heart'. Bending the papers back she found one for Friday 19 August 1977: 'The Heartbreak Farewell: Thousands Turn Out to Bury Elvis'.

She stood in her nightie and felt sleepy. The kitchen was dark but when she felt the top of the fridge with her fingers she found the grooves Giovanni's cigarettes had burned into the plastic rim. He was always balancing cigarettes there when he was peeling potatoes or stirring the broth. She opened the fridge door. Yellow light beamed out. She sat on the linoleum with her knees pulled up and enjoyed the light that flooded from the fridge. Inside it was white and the brightness went on for ever.

She reached forward with a finger and touched the cold glass of a milk bottle. There was a plate with butter on it; she drew two fingers over the top and brought them to her mouth. She tasted the salt and then leaned back on her hands, looking at the chicken and lettuces and tins of peas that were stored in the fridge for no good reason. She took out a cold egg and licked the shell.

The light from the open fridge was fantastic. Maria spoke a few words to the audience under her breath.

13 · Alfredo

One of the first things I remember is my mother drawing back the red blanket on my bed and lifting me out. She said I always spoke of a bad dream, the same dream over and over: a bird had come in the night and was flicking my lips with the feathers of its tail. My mother said there was no bird on the island to do such a thing as that, but I remember waking up and thinking the bird was real.

She was always there when I opened my eyes. My mother would stand at the end of the bed with a bottle or a towel for me. Rosa and I are twins, but years ago my mother would never leave us by ourselves in a room. If we sat on the stairs or lay on the landing she would sit beside us. Before I went up to the Academy there wasn't a day I can think of when my mother wasn't there: she watched over us; all the time she watched over us, and when it was time to say goodnight my father would have to come and take her from the room.

She had no rings on her fingers. Not even a wedding ring. As time passed my father would say things out of the blue. He just spoke up and then went quiet again. Once he had a few bottles of beer and he told me—I was about twenty then—that my mother had given up her rings for the Fascists. At one time, he said, she was involved with St Peter's Italian Church in London—the church supported the Fascists in the 1930s and my mother was involved. She went there for the Fiornata delle Fedi, when Italian women gave their rings. 'It is our job,' my mother said, much later, speaking of other matters, 'to make people believe things are possible. Do you know that? The power of belief. You have it, Alfredo. We all do.'

My father wasn't good-looking and he just worked in the ice-cream parlour and never said much. She adores him very much now he is gone, but I remember my mother, the way she looked at him, the disappointment on her face when he spoke to her of things he didn't understand. He told me she had loved him for a night in Lucca. He could always remember the evening and the look of the town from the walls. She did love him that night he said, and afterwards she merely spoke well of him to others. But all these years in Scotland she mostly lived alone in her own head. My father said she should have married Beniamino Gigli.

My mother can't tell the truth. She spends her days making up stories about the past. Speaks of a time she never really lived through, or not in the way she claims. She knows I know. She always said my face was a clock. 'You're neither use nor ornament, Alfredo,' she'd say back then, 'but your face is a clock. You better buck your ideas up, Alfredo, or you'll spend your days just ticking away up there on the shelf.' These were my mother's words to me. I suppose I have disappointed her as my father did, but even the unblessed have their blessings. She knows I know her true story and will guard her against it.

In the chapel the other day she told me a suitcase had come on the ferry and she hadn't opened it. An old suitcase. It might be a lie. I wouldn't put it past her to make up such a lie. But there was pain in her voice as she spoke in the church. She thinks it all matters now and it doesn't matter, except that the rest of them get it into their heads that she's punishing them. Not Maria though. She looks at our lovely Maria and she sees a wee bit of the Gigli magic—she hears music and she hears applause. When she looks at Maria she thinks everything was for a purpose.

'You gave me a fright.'

My mother falls asleep sometimes when I'm doing her hair. I put down the scissors and comb and feel the shape of her head and look into the mirror standing on the sideboard against the wall opposite. I run my fingers over her head and can hardly believe the hardness of her skull, and yet it's fragile and her shoulders slope away so weak underneath. She continues to sleep in her chair. My fingers travel over my mother's scalp and I put the palm of my hand on her forehead. I say to myself: this is where she lives; this is where my mother lives her life, and where she knows more than she admits.

'You gave me a fright,' she says. My hands are on my mother's head and my fingers are meshed in her hair and I know it must seem to her an affectionate thing to be caught doing. And that is true also. She peers into the mirror and I begin to tease the curls and look back at her. 'You've always been good at making people look nice,' she says.

My mother told us that famous people are different from other people. 'They glow in the dark,' she said. It was no ordinary life she wanted for us: Sofia, so I gather, was meant to sing for the world and live larger. In the end she didn't get to live larger or even to live at all. She died, didn't she, mammo? Holy Jesus and Mary the Mother of God and all the Saints. She didn't sing for all the world, mammo, did she now? My wee sister didn't do that. She heard your stories of Mr Gigli. She sang at the end of the pier down there. But no, no, Sofia, bless her soul. She drowned, mammo. She drowned on a ship filled with men. How was that, mammo? How did a wee lassie of nine get to be on that boat?

Make a straight way for the Lord. The Lamb of God that takes away the sins of the world. All my life I have kept watch for openness and love. We can live, mammo, with our disasters, is that not right and is that not true? You smiled from your seat when I was only ten and reading from John's Gospel. My hair was wetted with water and slicked down. 'Take all this out of here and stop turning my Father's house into a market. Then his disciples remembered the words of scripture, words which confirm the faith of the son: "Zeal for your house will devour me."' Jesus never needed evidence about any man's life mammo. You know that. He could tell what a man had in him. Be at peace with yourself. Our secrets are nothing much. Make a straight way for the Lord.

My father's café was open every day of the year except Christmas Day. He worked into the night: peeling potatoes, talking to himself, sweeping up, frying, mixing, forever working to hold on to the life he had made. He never went on holiday my father and he never missed a delivery. A clean white overall every day. He came from La Spezia with a hundred pounds and two pairs of shoes. My mother was much more interested in the world than my father. It wasn't just the politics: she wanted to play a larger part in everything, in the daily affairs of Rothesay and in the café, and, just as much, in her husband's thoughts. My father's greatest extravagance was always his devotion to my mother; he forgave her everything. He silenced himself on her behalf. Glad to be alive, my father. Glad to have survived.

The shop was nice then. There was no Formica: it was porcelain barrels and glass sweet jars in those days. Competition came from Vittorio Gazzi's West End Café and Coia's Fish and Chips. But they all got along. My father had sweets and chocolates that people had never heard of. They would queue up to taste the new things: twisted sugars, printed rock. My father was Italian to the ends of his fingertips, but he loved Scotland, he thought the country had been good to him, and he had a gift for inventing comestibles that chimed with Scotland. Nobody had a bad time at Mario's café in Rothesay. Ice drinks. Music. Give them the good food and the nice time and they come back, my father said. They always come back. The people love it here.

God bless you where you are.

My father would stand at the door of his café and feel the sea breeze. 'It will be a busy day today,' he said. 'You smile on a day like today. The weather it is so beautiful and the hills they are beautiful, Alfredo. Come and breathe all the good air before you work. Business is good, Alfredo, and soon you will make money over the road. People want to be having the nice hair and the smart cut. You are a clever man. Have to smile on a day like today, Alfredo.'

God bless you where you are, Mario.

In those days Rothesay was popular and the excursion steamers brought more customers than you could serve; he fought not to turn them away. The promenade was full of people. Men would go into the water there with their trousers rolled up and children would shout their heads off running about on the putting green. For years we rushed back and forth to the café tables with ices and pies and plates of chips. Giant glasses of ginger. That was before the island went quiet, before the days of jet engines, Thomson Holidays and Lloret de Mar.

We wanted to be famous pop singers, so we did. We wanted to be actors with champagne and the world at our feet. My father's café was a meeting place in the 1950s; even when I wasn't working there I'd go with my friends and smoke cigarettes and listen all night to the jukebox. For a while I was in charge of the jukebox. We had good shoes and suits. Nothing but the best. All the Italian boys at Mario's—there we were, the wind at our back, and thinking of the big break that was sure to come, of being the new Victor Spinetti, the new Dean Martin. My father put pictures of the great modern Italians around the walls of the café. There was blue neon running round the window and it shone at night time. If you were out in the bay it was the first thing you saw.

Mario's café. We always thought it would be one of the Italian men who would make it. It would be me, singing or driving a big car, or it would be Eduardo Gazzi, Eduardo down the road, whose father had made ceramic figurines in Manchester before coming to Bute and opening the café. Eduardo, bright, smart, was becoming a sculptor and would surely light up the world soon enough. One of us would be famous like Frank Sinatra. But soon we just worked and some had families and we forgot. Rosa didn't forget though and neither did my mother. Right up to today—this very second—they want the whole world to listen.

My father always combed his hair at the mirror in the back shop and he covered his grey with black dyeing cream. I used to buy it for him in Glasgow at Salon Services: he would take the box and put his finger to his smiling lips saying *sshh*. I never once heard my father say the word Mussolini. The man was never mentioned in the house or in the shop, only sometimes you'd hear my father tell my mother to be quiet, usually when she tried to speak about some terrible family on the island or some old event. He would tell her to stop. Somehow my parents' experience of the war coloured every day of our lives. But it wasn't mentioned, no, it wasn't mentioned in front of us.

I was upstairs in their house one day. In my mother and father's bedroom I was looking for a needle and thread. (She always stuck used needles into the wallpaper. It was the only way to keep them from getting lost, she said.) On my father's side of the bed the pillows were cloudy. She was always washing them, but they were cloudy still, the black hair cream coming off in the night and staining the fabric. I tell you something about families, always there are things never spoken of and never mentioned, like my father's head turning on the pillow slips and leaving them dark, and my mother, every once in a while, taking them away to be washed.

Mussolini was a dead word, banned. But, yes, in the last few days of my father's life he finally did speak about it. Il Duce. With some clarity at the end he spoke of the Fasci. In June 1940 people my father and mother had known for years came running down the seafront smashing the windows of the Italian cafés and raising their voices. A group of men took all the records from the cafés and broke them one by one on the front step. My father remembered the black vinyl lying smashed on the pavement. Carlo Buti. Caruso. Beniamino Gigli. He could see them as he spoke. A torn label on a record, 'Porta un Bacione a Firenze', lay on the pavement and was picked up by the wind and blown to the Firth of Clyde.

Sofia was the only child then. When the smashing of the cafés began my father just sat in the parlour with my mother and my sister and he said a prayer and kept still. 'Not until you've lived through something like that can you know what the world is all about,' he said to me. 'All the jars were smashed. Down there in the old café the floor was thick with sweets. All kinds of sweets and the bottles were broken. Alfredo, it was a very bad day to see all the good things lying on the floor. Your mother shouted out the window but I took her back from there. It was the only time I had to slap your mother, Alfredo, and it made me vomit at the sink to be the one to do that.'

'Did you forgive them?' I asked. And my father coughed and creased his mouth and shook his head.

'No,' he said. 'None of them.'

In those last days I spent hours alone with my father. He took out an old cigar box from his bedside cabinet; among receipts and Mass cards it contained a ripped-out newspaper advertisement. It was from *The Buteman* in 1940.

Mrs A. Viccari
of the West End Café
17 Gallowgate, Rothesay
wishes to inform the public
that she is a
BRITISH SUBJECT
and has a brother now serving
in the British Army and also a
brother now serving with the British Navy

They came and took my father out of his bed one night. 'This same bed,' he said. There was a ship in the bay and he was made to join it and taken to the mainland to board a train for England. 'I don't know whose fault it was,' he said. 'Anyway I had to leave your mother and Sofia.' When he said this I remember it was the afternoon of the moon landing. I remember going back and forth that evening from the television and whenever I came back to his bed he would tell me something new.

'Are you comfortable, Dad?'

'They came in the night,' he said, 'and I walked over the glass. I can hear the crunch of the glass in the shop, Alfredo, and not long after that I was away. That was me away.'

He fell asleep. His pillow rolled onto the floor. What I remember now is combing my father's hair and then lifting the pillow off the floor. I went to the linen cupboard and found a white pillowcase and slipped it on and when I came back I lifted up his head and put the clean pillow underneath. He breathed so quietly that you could barely hear anything but the clock.

'That was me away,' he had said.

My father eventually made it home again and built the business back up. But he never spoke of those war years and he banned Mussolini. My mother gave birth to us a year after his return, in 1942: Rosa and me. Like Mussolini, the word for our sister, Sofia, was something my mother would only whisper. The little girl with the big voice was one of the mysteries of the war we had missed.

Lamb of God that takes away the sins of the world.

Grant us peace.

There was so much water keeping my side-parting in place I could feel it running down the back of my neck under my school blazer. It was freezing running down my back I swear to God. I looked up and saw the faces of my mother and father sitting in the front row. It was the old Academy up on the hill before it burned down.

I said I will read from the Gospel according to John. Chapter 2, verse 17. The Cleansing of the Temple. 'Zeal for your house will devour me. Destroy this sanctuary and in three days I will raise you up. But he was speaking of the sanctuary that was his body, and when Jesus rose from the dead, his disciples remembered that he had said this, and they believed the scripture and the words he had said.'

Dying on that old bed, my father must have been dreaming about my missing sister, I feel certain he must have thought of her as he slept on his white pillow.

Zeal for your house will devour me.

14 · Tales

OPPORTUNITY KNOCKING
FOR ROTHESAY TEENAGER

Pint-sized Scottish singing sensation Maria Tambini is on the road to stardom after landing a spot on LWT's talent show *Opportunity Knocks.*

Maria, 13, who hails from Rothesay on the Isle of Bute, is due to appear on the top-rated show in two weeks' time. But no matter what the outcome, Maria has already attracted the attention of a top London agent and has secured a place at the Italia Conti stage school.

Excited

Maria's mother, chip-shop owner Rosa Tambini, 35, says everyone on the island is really proud of her. 'She's been performing at different places on the West Coast for a few years now,' said Mrs Tambini, 'and we've been holding her back just to let her grow up a bit. Now she wants a chance at the big time and we've got to let her go. I've told her not to get too excited, but all her family are rooting for her and so are her friends.'

Maturity

A spokesman for LWT said the producers of the show are keen to bring on new talent regardless of age. 'We were very struck by Maria's maturity as a performer,' he said, 'and wish her the best of luck on the night.'

Tambini is the latest in a long line of Scottish performers who have enjoyed an early boost to their careers through television. Maria counts Lena Martell and Lulu among her favourites.

Family

'It's more like we're talking Streisand and Judy Garland,' said an excited Marion Gaskell, Maria's new agent, speaking from London.

But rest assured, win or lose in two weeks' time, we'll be hearing a lot more from sweet little Maria Tambini. She's a lovely girl from a lovely family. In a fortnight she's not only singing for Rothesay but for the whole of Scotland.

Maria put down the *Daily Record* and smiled at Kalpana and Dr Jagannadham. 'Do you like the picture?' she asked.

'It's very pretty indeed,' said Dr Jag.

'It's soooo amazing,' said Kalpana.

'They took it in the café,' said Maria. 'Alfredo did my hair with those new rollers and that's Giovanni's hand poking the lollipops in from the side.'

Mrs Jagannadham was smiling by the door of the Civic Centre. 'Everyone is talking about you, Maria.'

'Down with lollipops!' said Dr Jag. His wife ignored him and continued looking at Maria.

'I think your dress is lovely Mrs Jag,' said Maria.

'Do you like it? It's a sari. But thank you for noticing. It is made of old material which I like.'

'Down with candy floss!'

'Oh stop it, Daddy,' said Kalpana. She looked at Maria and then at her mother. 'He's such a lunatic,' she said. 'I get a pure beamer standing next to him.'

Dr Jagannadham was leaning against the glass door of the Civic Centre laughing. He held a folder to his chest and every time he made an exclamation he pointed to the heavens. 'Down with Mars Bars!' he shouted. 'Rebel! Rebel! You have nothing to lose but your teeth.'

Maria and Kalpana looked at each other and snorted. 'Just ignore him,' said Kalpana. 'He's not playing with a full deck. Such a knob.'

'Language!' said Mrs Jag. 'What have I told you, Kalpana? I won't have you speaking these words.'

'She's a native speaker,' said the doctor, laughing. 'My lecture may embarrass you but it should educate you also, Kalpana. Stay and listen, you two. May do you some good.'

It was already dark and rain was blowing over the harbour and a bell was sounding out in the water. It was the ferry tied up for the night; the swell of the water made the bell ring and the sound was clear over the bay. Maria and Kalpana were still in their school uniforms. They had stayed on after school to help with the rehearsals for the Halloween play: they were doing the make-up but really there wasn't much to do, so they had wandered the corridors of the school for an hour and poked their heads into the dark classrooms.

It was Mrs Beezley the Modern Studies teacher who had given Maria the copy of the *Daily Record*. She gave it to her and said everyone was looking forward to seeing her on the telly. Kalpana noticed that Maria took the paper and said thank you as if she was giving a speech and was being photographed all over again. Then they had gone to the stacked-up chairs at the back of the dining hall and read the article over and over again.

Maria's eyes were glassy. 'Oh my God Maria that is just brilliant. It's such a gallus picture,' Kalpana said.

'You don't think I look a bit cross-eyed?'

'Don't be daft, Maria, you look like a film star.'

'King Kong.'

'Don't be daft. Princess Leia.'

'Chewbacca more like.'

'It's a brilliant picture, Maria. Just think, everybody will be looking at your picture and saying "I know her."'

They walked the corridors of the Academy and sometimes ran giggling. They looked into Mr Scullion's Maths room. It was dark and all the chairs were up on the desks. In Miss Marshall's Biology class they sat in the light of the aquarium. They put their fingers up to the glass. There was pond life there, ribbons of algae and frogs swimming through; a lamp hung over the water and made the classroom blue.

'I think there's something wrong with my mum,' said Maria out of nowhere. Kalpana looked at her.

'Don't be daft. What you saying that for?'

'I don't know. Just...' Maria shrugged. 'Just things.'

'Because of Giovanni?' said Kalpana.

'Sometimes,' said Maria, 'but not just him. She cries and throws eppies for nothing. I think she hates my granny. The other night I looked into the living-room and she was staring at the telly and there was nothing on. It was just... what do you call it... interference? It was after *Late Call*. There was nothing to watch on the telly and she just sat there watching the fuzzy picture.'

'She was probably asleep, Maria.'

'No she wasnae.'

'Probably thinking about stuff then. Like things on her mind and that. You shouldny worry about it cause you'll be going away soon won't you?' Kalpana jumped off the desk. 'She totally loves it that you're going to London and everything, doesn't she Maria? I mean she's dead proud and all that. Who wouldny be?'

'Aye,' said Maria.

'It'll be brilliant.'

'I know.'

Kalpana went to the blackboard and picked up the chalk.

MISS MARSHALL FANCIES SENORITA DOBLAS THE
SPANISH TEACHING ASSISTANT. THEY WERE KISSING
IN THE BIOLOGY CUPBOARD WE SAW THEM AND THEY
WERE DRINKING THE WINE FOR FERMENTATION
STUDY. THEY WERE PLASTERED. SIGNED R2-D2 AND
C3PO

The girls tussled over the duster then ran from the classroom
screaming with laughter. Kalpana ran as fast as she could down the
corridor and slid on the tiles with her hands raised. The smell of disinfectant was still strong from the mopping. 'Just remember me
when you're famous Maria Tambini or I'll grass you in for what you
did!' Kalapana's voice echoed down the corridor.

But Maria had gone silent. Halfway down she started walking
backwards towards her friend. She walked backwards and slowly,
looking at the labels on the doors she was passing: English, Home
Economics, Classical Studies, History. She stopped in the dark of the
corridor and looked down to the end. 'Goodbye,' she said.

Under the orange street lamps lighting the rain the girls ran
down the hill to the Civic Centre. Kalpana wondered if anyone
would show up to listen to her father's talk. They ran down, pulling
their blazers over their heads, the taste of sea-salt arriving on their
lips, the rubber soles of their shoes chewing on the wet pavement.

THE HALL in the Civic Centre was freezing. There were only nine
people there, including Mrs Jagannadham. Kalpana and Maria were
told by the caretaker that they couldn't hang about the door, so they
took a couple of plastic cups of orange squash from the ping-pong
table, drank them, and sat in the back row laughing and making
beaks out of the empty cups.

Dr Jagannadham stood at a lectern on the stage. Behind him was
a banner saying 'Bute Boy Scouts'. The people ready to listen to the
doctor's lecture were spread over the first eight rows or so; several

were old men, like Mr Samson, or familiar people who weren't old but had always seemed so, and then there was Mrs Bone, who had always professed an interest in knowledge. 'There's that guy from the TV shop,' said Kalpana.

'I haven't seen him for ages,' Maria said. 'Does he still work there?'

'My dad says he's going to university,' said Kalpana.

'Shh. They're looking at us.'

'Thank you, thank you,' said Dr Jag. 'Thank you for coming out on such a wild night for my talk on sugar, a subject that is very much of importance in Scotland, as it must be everywhere. But here, ladies and gentlemen, you might say it is a subject close to our hearts—closer, indeed, to our hearts than we might care for it to be. It will be no secret to this audience that sugar intake in this country far exceeds that of most places.'

'Here we go,' said Kalpana.

'As a GP I can attest to the fact that excessive sugar intake has a direct relation to heart disease and to other known killers such as diabetes. But I should hasten to say, ladies and gentlemen, that this is not intended to be chiefly a medical talk. Indeed it is intended that it be interesting on the subject of the sugar industry itself. The history of sugar's production and refinement is a tale of glorious ingenuity and also, you might say, of hazardous profiteering, showing both the brilliance of modern entrepreneurial methods, as well, I'm afraid, as what we can only describe as the shortcomings of the colonial experiment.'

'Why is he talking like that?' asked Maria.

'Oh, he has to,' said Kalpana. 'Whenever he gets onto one of his thinking subjects he starts talking like a book.'

'All the words.'

'Listen to his accent and all. When he's having a carry-on he sounds like an Indian but when he stands up to say those ginormous words he sounds like a man on the radio or reading the news or something.'

'Weird.'

'He says it's normal. Everybody goes on like that. He says it's all part of the performance.'

'But nobody'll get it.'

'It doesn't matter. That's what they come for, they come to enjoy the big words.'

'Weird.'

'He talks like a book when he's angry as well.'

'When the Indian sub-continent was overrun by the Persians in 510 BC they described sugar as "the reed which gives honey without bees".'

'It's gonna to be a long night,' said Kalpana.

'Do you think he'll talk about Munchies or Mint Cracknel?' said Maria. The girls laughed again into their cups.

'Only if they scoffed them in Ancient Egypt,' said Kalpana under her breath. After fifteen minutes the girls were sucking the cups onto their faces and staring at the floor.

'The West Indies became the world's main sugar producing region,' said Dr Jagannadham. 'In 1493 Christopher Columbus established a crop on the fertile Caribbean island of San Domingo. Sugar cane grew faster there than anywhere else in the world and by 1530 the island boasted twenty-eight sugar mills. Cane sugar farming was so lucrative that plantation owners referred to sugar as white gold. By the eighteenth century the West Indian sugar industry was supplying the whole of the Western world and fabulous fortunes were made. By 1750 there were 150 cane refineries in Britain...'

'Have you ever seen him naked?' asked Maria.

'Loads of times,' said Kalpana. 'You know what he's like. We used to go swimming in Loch Fyne and he'd say he would only swim as God intended.'

'Like a fish.'

'Naked as a cod.'

'A God cod.'

'A cod bod.' The girls fell about laughing. Mrs Jagannadham looked round with an annoyed face and told them to shush.

'Gads,' said Maria. 'I am never kissing anybody.'

'Don't be daft,' said Kalpana. 'There's nothing wrong with that. Depends who.' She looked round at Maria. 'You're just a baby.'

Maria shrugged. 'Shut your face,' she said, then stared down the empty rows again.

Mr Samson was snoring in his chair. Michael Aigas from the TV shop looked up at the windows and thought it was like the whole of the Civic Centre was going through a car wash. 'Man,' he said to himself, 'the rain god is certainly tossing his cookies tonight.' Off to the side of the stage there was a bingo machine and a gymnastics horse. Against the back wall was a large piece of scenery, a luxurious garden; Maria could make out green painted bushes and giant yellow flowers. It was an enchanted garden, with butterflies and birds, and a broken castle in the distance. As the doctor went on speaking, her eyes focused on the piece of scenery, and the doctor's words began to mingle with her thoughts, the things she and Kalpana had spoken of that night.

The scenery reminded Maria of stories Granny Lucia had told her when she was a baby. They were stories from Florence and Bologna and Abruzzo, stories of beautiful princesses born from pomegranates, apples and rosemary bushes, and many of the details began to float in front of Maria again as she sat in the cold hall.

'My father and mother worked in the sugar factory in Aska outside Madras,' said Dr Jagannadham, 'and if you go there now you see that the waste waters coming from the factory have changed the plant life of the area. My family have told me all they can remember of the Aska sugar factory. At one time it was a famous place. A hundred years ago the factory was among those which met the increasing demand for granulated sugar around the world.'

A man and a woman once lived over the fairies' garden. The woman was expecting her first baby and she had a craving for parsley, so every day she ate the parsley from the garden. One day the fairies noticed all their parsley was gone and they caught the woman eating it and made her promise to call her baby Prezzemolina. The fairies said they would take the baby when she was grown up. The woman was in tears as she told her husband. 'You awful glutton,' he said, 'don't you see you have brought this upon yourself?'

'Here in Rothesay we are close to the heart of the old Scottish sugar industry,' said Dr Jagannadham. 'Outside London, the largest centre for sugar refining was in Greenock. In 1860, there were about thirteen refineries, with four more in Glasgow and one in Leith. In 1866, a total of 162,368 tons of sugar were produced on the Clyde.

They supplied the whole of Britain with white sugar crystals and white and yellow "crushed" sugars.'

The fairies took Prezzemolina, put her in a dungeon, and said they would eat her if she did not paint pretty birds on the white wall. 'I would rather let the fairies eat me than allow a man to kiss me,' said Prezzemolina when a man, Meme, the fairies' cousin, offered to help her in exchange for a kiss. 'The fairies can eat me before that.'

'There were two major changes in sugar production during this period. The first was the adoption of the centrifugal machine, by which the sugar in the boiled crystalline mass is separated from the syrup in a few minutes. The second was the boiling of yellow sugars at a low temperature, causing the sugar to be turned out in a uniformly moist state, and with a pale and delicate primrose colour.'

'This is sooooo boring,' said Kalpana. 'Shall we go down to the café?'

'In a wee minute,' said Maria. Her eyes were still lost in the scenery and she didn't look round.

'Are you actually interested in this guff?' said Kalpana. She blew out her lips. 'It's bloody well freezing in here.'

'What time's it?' said Maria.

'Quarter to seven,' said Kalpana. 'I'm starving.'

Maria looked along the empty rows of chairs.

Tomorrow, when Prezzemolina has finished all the housework, we'll have her put in a large laundry tub full of boiling water, said the fairies.

'The Clyde yields were brought to a summit of 250,000 tons in 1881. But the influx of cheap European sugar brought this down by more than half by the year 1900.'

But Meme showed her how to kill the fairies and save herself—by blowing candles out. One by one Prezzemolina and Meme blew out candles until the largest one, which stood for the chief fairy, was blown out and the danger passed. They did this together, and then Prezzemolina kissed him, and they lived happily ever after.

Dr Jagannadham placed his hands on the sides of the lectern. He smiled over the audience as if he'd been addressing a capacity crowd at the Albert Hall. 'So, ladies and gentleman, the story of sugar is for me a personal story and a historical one and a local one too. Sugar cane is gathered in India in December. It will soon be time for the harvest and for the process to begin again. The consumption of sugar is also fascinating, and perhaps there will be some future opportunity to discuss this aspect in relation to our customs and our health.'

There were twelve pairs of hands clapping if you included the caretaker's. 'Thank God,' said Kalpana. Maria was clapping but she was still thinking about Lucia's old stories.

'HELLO MARIA.' It was Michael Aigas.

'Hiya Michael. How are the the tellies going?'

'We're doing some cool business because of you,' he said. 'Even the seagulls are taking out rentals with you coming on.' Maria blushed and flicked her hair from her mouth.

'Away ye go,' she said.

'No kidding. You're cooking by gas now, Maria.'

'She's in the paper,' said Kalpana.

'You bet. We saw it in the shop. Come clean then. I hope you're thinking about driving lessons cause it'll be a Rolls Royce next. Are you going to forget all about us or what?'

'She won't forget me but she'll forget you,' said Kalpana, placing a piece of chewing gum in her mouth. 'That's true intit, Maria?' Maria's face was warm.

'Did you like the talk?' she asked.

'Really cool,' said Michael. 'Dr Jag's a top man. I loved his evening rig as well, dressed up nice for the occasion.'

'You what?' said Kalpana.

'I better go,' said Michael. 'Listen Maria, you mow them down, do you hear me? Down in London, give it loads.' Maria just nodded and made an embarrassed laugh. 'See you around, Kalpana,' he said.

'Not if I see you first,' she answered without looking. Michael walked towards the door. Maria stood up, turned round and put one of her knees on the seat.

'Michael,' she said.

He turned round and there was a smile on his face as he zipped up his jacket. 'Yup.'

She paused. She wasn't sure what she wanted to say to Michael Aigas but she was sure she could say a thousand things to him and he'd be okay.

'Good luck, Michael.'

He took his hand out of his pocket and pointed at her before turning. 'You,' he said, 'are going to be great because you're great already.'

'Get a load of him,' said Kalpana. But Maria just stood with her knee on the chair and looked back at the slow-closing door with the shape of Michael Aigas fading behind the frosted glass.

'Don't,' she said under her breath.

15 · All That Move in the Waters

Coming down Columshill Road, Giovanni looked up and noticed the dirty whiteness of the sky and he threw his cigarette into the grass and felt sick.

It was early morning and the shops were closed. In the Amusements Arcade the heaps of coins were motionless in their glass cabinets; one on top of the other, the coins hung from the silver ledges of the Cash Rivers, and the pale light from outside crept like an illness over the carpet with its smell of spilled orangeade.

It was the day of the flood. Before the sun was properly up, seawater was pouring over the sleepers of the pier and rolling across the road. There were sandbags at the doors of the seafront shops and tenements but the water was strong and they didn't hold. By 7 a.m. the Amusements had flooded right up to the change kiosk; paper cups floated in brown water under the rows of toy-grabbing machines, and the stuffed animals looked down from the walls with expressions of surprise.

The flood's power seemed to grow, as if there were no carpets and floorboards underneath it, or concrete, or landscaped gardens, but instead the flood moved over Rothesay as if it had always been there, or had meant to be there, moving normally, like over barnacled rocks and swimming fish and sea caverns, the stuff of the ocean. At last one of the waves burst through the glass doors of the Amusements and struck the Cash Rivers; coins could be heard falling in the early morning and then cascading into the metal trays at the base of the machines.

Rosa was standing in the bathroom. In the night she had turned in the bed and grasped that she was alone. The wind was bad outside, she could hear it rattling the window-frame, and falling back to sleep she had noticed the weather's shadows leaping over the bedclothes and she sank down wondering where he was. At the bathroom mirror she wiped her face with cotton-wool and cleanser. She wanted to free herself of the night's grime, and after she had put the cotton-wool in the bin and splashed her face with cold water, she looked at herself in the mirror and stood there until the mirror clouded over.

Giovanni came walking up Victoria Street with the pressure of water holding him back. It was halfway up to his knees, seawater, drainwater, with clods of dirt and broken plants rushing past him. He spread his arms to steady himself: the flood seemed to be rising quickly and he moved slowly against the driving wind, thinking as the water lapped up his legs about rough times out on the boat.

Boxes of crisps were floating inside the door of the café. As he turned the handle, more water flooded in, and he saw that the sugar bowls and sauce bottles were still upright and untouched on the tables. The ashtrays were emptied and cleaned and the tables wiped. Morning light settled on the sweetie jars up on the shelves and the famous Italians looked down at him with their prosperous smiles and placid cardigans. One of the shelves collapsed after he entered: jars crashed on the serving counter, and in seconds there were mint imperials and cola cubes floating in the water around his shins like doused confetti.

'Where have you been?' she said. Giovanni steadied himself on the counter and looked up to the back kitchen where Rosa was standing. Her hair was tied back and her eyes glistened; she stood in the water and he could see cartons and empty bottles floating around her.

'Just a wee party,' he said.

'Who with?'

'Och Rosa never mind. It was just a wee party and it went on a bit long.' Giovanni's hair was full of old Brylcreem and was now sticking to his forehead. Even in the greyness of the room and with the door wide open and the wind blowing through, he smiled, his white teeth showing, and he waved his hand unsteadily over all the things that didn't matter. 'Look at the state of this place,' he said. 'They said it wouldn't happen this time.'

'Look at you,' she said.

'Come on hen.'

'Look at you and look at this place. Stinking. Stinking and bloody disgusting.' She breathed heavily. He stepped forward in the water to try and meet her where she was. 'I'll say it one more time. Where have you been?'

'I've been out!' he said. 'I've been out getting fucking rotten.' He lifted the jars from the water and tried to place them on the counter. He bent over and took a dishcloth and started to wipe the counter. 'I'll clean this up before you know it,' he said. 'We'll have it tidy and back to normal soon as you like. We want to keep things nice in here, don't we? You never know the time of day around here; it's just an act of God.' He picked up some of the sodden crisp boxes and stacked them on the tables; he scooped sweets and debris out of the water. 'It's a struggle intit darling?' he said. 'Trying to keep everything in good order. I'll get a pump and we'll have this place fixed.'

'You're a bastard.' She almost whispered.

'A wee bit of bleach will take the scum off these chairs . . . before you know it, we—'

'You filthy bastard,' she said. It was as if Giovanni was talking to himself.

'This has happened before. I don't know why the Council can't be ready for this kind of thing. I'll work hard to clean here . . .'

Rosa cried and the tears stood out on her bleached face. 'You're drunk as a pig,' she said. She looked at him and didn't know whether to tidy him up, or run out, or slap him, slap his dirty face and push him down into the water where he belonged and drown him there. 'You lie to me and my daughter, Giovanni. The bastard that you are. You are bringing evil into this house. You rotten bastard you are killing us. You won't be content until everything's wasted.' She moved forward in the water and gritted her teeth as she spoke. 'You're not a man,' she said. 'You haven't a decent bone in your body you fucking bastard you're bringing fucking badness into this house.' She drew level with him, swung her arm and slapped him. The towel fell into the dirty water. 'You're all the same,' she said. 'You selfish fucking bastard I wish you were dead.' When he straightened up, holding his jaw, she spat in his face.

'I can clean it,' he said.

Rosa stood staring at him, her lips trembling. She lunged and grabbed his hair and shook his head from side to side. There was lustre in his hair and she could feel the heat from his head and she almost stroked him, but her anger took over and she threw him down into the water.

'We were meant to have a different life ya fucking bastard you. You're bringing us all down ya useless bastard, not a man. Not a man at all. Look at you.' Giovanni pulled away from her hand and jumped back. By now she was ranting in his face and her mouth was white with spit. 'Go back to your fucking tarts,' she shouted. 'Away you go and give us peace. We don't want you here. Think we won't manage without you? You're fucking wrong ya dirty messing bastard. We don't need any of yous. You're no use. None of yous are any use to us. All we want is peace and quiet ya filthy no-use pig of a man. That wee lassie upstairs disnae need you either. You're no good to anybody. You're no even her father and we were fine before you ya fucking lowlife. Get out of my shop.'

Giovanni leaned forward. His jaw was loose and his eyes were red with tears and drink and he breathed hard. 'That's right,' he said, 'I'm standing in all this filth, Rosa, and I fucking love it. I love it. Fucking shite and dirt everywhere and I fucking love it. I'm no her father and I'm no your man. Aye. I'm filthy. I've worked here every day for ten fucking years. I've put everything into this shop and your own wee lassie. Big Giovanni. The fucking smiling Giovanni, eh. Always here. Always here and shutting his fucking mouth. Well I love it here this filthy bastarding place. Fucking clean clean. When was the last time any of you were fucking natural? When was the last time you were just yourself Rosa? Clean fucking clean, that's all you ever hear.'

He tore at the buttons on his shirt and swiped his hand over the boxes and scooped dirty water into his hands and threw it over himself. 'Fucking filth!' he shouted. 'I love it, Rosa. Love it. Can you see me? Have a good look, Rosa, it's miserable intit? Well have a good look. It's a bad light, do you want me to come closer? At last Rosa, at last, this place is fucking bogging and so am I and you can just get your fucking cloth and wipe it all away, Rosa. Just get your fucking cloth. Wait a minute.' He lifted the lemonade bottle with the punctured cap they used for vinegar off the counter. Then he turned in one quick move and hurled the bottle at the front window. It cracked the glass and fell heavily among the cakes. 'There's your window,' he said.

She stood without moving. She could've been a girl herself watching some terrible adult conflagration and not knowing where to run for cover or where to apply for understanding. She just trembled standing in front of him and her face was blank. At her knees a tray of shortbread came floating past like a framed picture. She turned to look at the back kitchen and could see water bubbling out of the toilet. Food bobbed up to her and past her: potatoes, rolls of wine gums, and then several tins of Vim, old playing cards with pictures of radio personalities on them, Fry's Turkish Delight, and hairbrushes, clasps, a bottle of Domestos, packets of soap.

His face was crumpled. 'This can all be cleaned up,' he said. He seemed to grow calm or resigned. 'Give me a towel and I'll dry this counter.' He rubbed his head and stared into the mucky water. He turned with a rag and wiped the counter in circles while he trembled. 'When the ferry stops we can all get away,' he said.

'No we can't, Giovanni,' she said. 'There's no a boat that will take us far enough.' He looked at her. 'But Maria's leaving and she will have a life,' she said. When she said this something caught in her voice and it was a different kind of weeping that came. She cried softly as he had seen her do so many times, but it was not the same crying as before, and if there was accusation in her eyes it was a different kind too, an accusation directed as much now at herself and the unfairness of words and the remoteness of the world as she found it.

He walked forward and put his hand on the shoulder of her housecoat. 'Get out of my sight,' she said.

'I'm sorry.'

'I don't feel anything,' she said.

He dropped his hand and walked round her in the water and disappeared through the back. She heard his footfalls up the stairs. Around her in the shop the smell was bad; she looked into the white light and the cracked window and the flotsam at her feet. Spreading out her hands she saw his hair tangled in her fingers. Hating him, she thought of his hand stroking her face; she thought of him running his hands up to the top of her legs and him leaning in to kiss and lick her throat. She wished he were dead. She thought like this for a moment standing there, then she put a hand on one of the tables, bent over, and vomited into the floodwater.

Maria had come down the stairs and was standing in silence behind her mother. She saw her crying and being sick and she stood watching as the stock floated into the kitchen. She didn't move forward in the water or approach her mother and while she stood there she realised there was only a song in her head. Maria lifted the bottom of her nightdress out of the water with both hands and without making a sound crept back up the stairs to bed.

16 · Kalpana

Hello Diary,

This is Maria's last day on Rothesay. It's dead sad and now it's like I'm losing my best pal but Maria says you can't stay in one place for ever can you and that is true. All this week it's been cheerio to this person and cheerio to somebody else but I want to say wait a minute what am I going to do with my free time but I don't say it out loud because it's a bit selfish. My mum says we can still get together on the holidays and I told her it would be pure brilliant if I could go to London for a visit. Mrs Tambini is going to keep Maria's room just the same and Maria asked her if I could borrow Maria's spare brushes and that but she said no because she'll be too busy. I'm not bothered I've got too much stuff anyway and Alfredo said I can maybe get spare brushes if there's any at the shop. Maria is not taking that much stuff considering it's all the way to London, but she doesn't know yet how much space there will be for her things but she said none of it was wasted in the flood anyhow and that's good.

Bloody hell!!! I still can't believe she's going to London. My mum was pure cracking up because she said I have to stop going on about it and start thinking about the work at school and I say BORING. Why does exciting stuff never happen to me?? Maria says the people she will miss most are me, her mum, Alfredo and Giovanni and her granny, old Mrs Tambini who lives up on the hill. I went into the shop this morning and gave Maria a shiny penny to keep in her pocket for good luck. There's a typewriter up in the library and I can use it after school to write letters with all the news. Mrs Bone is really nice, she came in and gave her a Collins dictionary brand new and a tiny radio that says Radio Luxembourg on the front. At the special school Maria's going to it's dead lucky cause you only have to do proper lessons in the morning and the rest of the time it's dancing and stuff.

Remember remember remember. Just because somebody is far away it doesn't mean they have to stop being your best friend. Alfredo and her are getting the overnight bus from Glasgow and you can sleep on it or have sandwiches and drinks and stuff, her mum put on a red dress for specialness this morning because it was Maria's big day. I helped Maria pack the bag it was full of dresses and two leotards and another bag is all shampoo and talcum and stuff you might need in a strange house and shoes. I'm waving her off and we said we would keep looking until the boat is out of sight and oh God it's not fair she will have a great time but it's true we can still talk about everything and write loads of letters being silly and that.

17 · Chorus

Lucia was married to quiet and patient industry. She could spend hours over her torn gloves with a needle, mending holes and tears. In the late afternoon of the day Maria and Alfredo were leaving for London she sat at her living-room table, the secondhand gloves spread out and almost done, content in her solitude. Her pension book sat on the table's edge with a sheaf of banknotes fanned across the top, and next to it, wrapped in wallpaper, was her Mass Missal.

She was working on a pair of mittens, then put them down, checked the clock, lifted the notes and walked through to the kitchenette, where the whiteness of everything startled her. The silver of the draining board glinted under the window; a single, half-pink Brillo pad lay on the corner, and a cloth was neatly folded in two and hung on the arc of the high tap. The cooker was never on: it gleamed, and the door of the grill was permanently down, a shelf now for pots that were dusted but never scoured. Lucia lifted the lid off a red casserole dish and placed the notes among rolls of other notes. She wasn't rich. She owned the café but never took anything out of there. She found she had got to the age where she hardly ever spent money, and most of what came to her, this way and that, ended up in the pots and covered dishes of her old kitchen. She no longer believed in banks.

She took a few steps out of the kitchenette and turned back again. She put her hand inside the red dish and took out a roll of money, and for no reason in particular rolled the rubber band back and forth with her thumb, and then she put the roll of money up to her nose and sniffed. Dead, she thought.

There used to be what is now called a nursing home at Lochgilphead, in its heyday called a home, and at the time of its opening called an asylum, which was meant for people who didn't know where they were. It was once filled with people from all over the world, people with uncertain nationalities, Scots, Poles, Italians, Germans, people who had somehow landed among the mountains and trees at the head of Loch Fyne, people who found they were both Scottish and nothing, lost people, mute people, and those whose minds, according to their ailments, coagulated the waking hours and dampened all memory, and so they had existed for years, strangers in that house at Lochgilphead with the many windows.

A boat with red funnels used to leave Rothesay for the port of Ardrishaig, a pier at the head of the Crinan Canal, the nearest to Lochgilphead, and people in Rothesay would often say, if a person's mind wasn't right and the person wasn't listening, that he was 'away on the red-funnelled boat to Lochgilphead'. By the 1970s the old house had closed and the council moved the remaining occupants to Bute, and new people joined them, in what was now called a residential care centre for the deaf and the speechless. It was often said, and was always true, that all the important events of Rothesay life were retold, somehow, in that new place at Ardbeg Point, and the house was famous as a hotbed of local gossip, passed from one to another, in a semi-circle of high-backed chairs, rain, hail, or shine, in the afternoon atmosphere of the television room. Some of the people could lipread but most of them signed with their hands. Their heads were full of vernacular, and somehow, over the years of their acquaintance, that too was communicated by the hands.

Lucia arrived with her bag of mittens. For years she had been coming down to the house at Ardbeg Point with her sewing or with cakes: she sold them to the deaf and dumb for a few pence, and she collected the money in a whisky bottle clad in sea-shells, to be handed over every Christmas to the Lifeboat Appeal.

MARY NUGENT (*with hands*): God love her. There she's. Old Tambini with her bag of stuff. Better buy a pair of mittens Ina the nights are fair drawing in and you feel the cold, you know that.

INA STRANG (*mouthing*): Hello hen.

LUCIA: Hello Ina. I'm just leaving this bag here right hen and I'll away and get a cup of tea. See what yous want and I'll get yous in a wee minute all right?

THOMAS GEDDES (*standing up and pointing*): Gloves!

LUCIA: Aye Thomas, how you doing son? That's gloves in there, right? Have a wee poke through. Aye, on ye go. There's men's ones as well. See if there's anything you want in there.

INA (*with hands*): That pair's braw Thomas. You suit the blue. It's no everybody can get away wi' blue. Look at him. He fair fancies his-self God love him. That's a wee man that loves a bargain tae. Oor Jimmy was the same. He'd wander all the way from Buchanan Street to Wester Ross to save he's-self the trouble of paying for anything. Them's nice as well, Thomas. Try them on, son. Fawn's a nice colour for a man.

MARY (*nodding towards the kitchen*): That wee lassie's away the day. She's away to London for that talent thing. They need to watch they don't push that wee lassie too hard I'm telling you. It's a big place London.

INA (*signing back*): But that house Mary. You've got Rosa running that business and about half-daft with that man. Don't get me wrong he's a lovely fella but Christ he's got her heart roasted.

Been with every lassie on this island and half the mainland and a'. Her heart must be roastit wi' him.

MARY: I know. Mind you, she's a handful that lassie nae doubt. I've never seen such a greetin-faced woman in all my life. I know it's a terrible thing to say, but no wonder that man's away half the time. She'd put years on you. I remember we used to bring her things for the wean when she was born. Hats and wee dresses, good stuff. Oh aye, she would thank you right enough, but you'd never see the wee lassie wearing any of the stuff. Wasnae good enough for her.

INA: A lot of pressure for a young one to be going to London like that. London's that far away. It's a far away place London and if you don't know people. I mean, who's going to talk to you away in London? It's the world's worst.

MARY: People go away there and never come back.

INA: Oh aye, and even badder. That's what I mean. That wee lassie's got a lot going for her right enough. And she's probably just as pleased bless her to get away from all the carry-on. It cannae be good for a wee yin to have that all the time. They argue the bit out. Too much pressure. Mark me. That wee yin's got a talent, and she should just say to hell wi' the lot of them and get on wi' it.

MARY: Doesny say much. She's a quiet wee thing.

INA: What a singer though. I can just feel it. She could definitely go places that wee one. Even at her age she's better than half the ones. I cannae really hear her right enough but you can tell all the same.

IRENE BUTTERLY (*leaning in from another chair, and signing*): Everything's sorted up for her in London. She's going to a special school and everything. You can make a lot of money at that thing nowadays. If you know the right ones.

INA: Oh I know Irene. Our Stephen was in a band. He went about the halls, weddings and that. He made a fortune. I mean years ago you had to have money to begin wi'. These young ones just lift a guitar and the next minute they're away to America and all sorts. They all like to dance.

MARY: Well, they say all those London ones have been up and down to see them. Managers and all them. She's got a fair crack at it right enough. But, *oaff,* that wee Tambini lassie'll have it rough down there. She'll have to work like a dog and tummle her wilkies into the bargain for they people. They people don't just take anybody, Ina. One false move and you're out, that's what your Stephen always says.

IRENE: Aye Mary, he's right enough. But you wonder if that auld one will be able to cope without her. I tell you she'll miss that wee lassie.

INA: Oh definitely.

IRENE: You know I think half the time she mixes her up with that other one. Bless her heart. She speaks about Maria as if she was the other one.

INA: Is that the one that died?

IRENE: Oh aye, she drowned it seems. But nobody can talk to her about it. She's never talked about that. It's as if, you know, it was a secret, but half the island knows. There was some weird business there, I don't know what. There's definitely a story but she'll ... she'll probably take it to the grave with her.

INA: I've heard that before right enough.

MARY: Oh, they say it was terrible, really bad. But she's a good old soul bless her. She never passes the door here, I'll say that for her.

INA: And was she with the wee lassie when she drowned?

IRENE: I couldny tell you Ina. I really don't know. I don't think anybody knows what actually happened there.

INA: It's a shame all the same it really is.

MARY: Sofia was her name.

IRENE: That's right. They say she was a lovely wee thing but you're talking years ago now.

MARY: But it's true enough Irene. Even after all this time she gets her mixed up with that wee singer.

IRENE: Aye.

MARY: She's used her name a few times when she means the other one. As I say she'll be lost when that wee one goes to London because ...

IRENE: Oh aye, she's a great wee thing. Just looking at her you can tell. The talent in her is no real. Did you see her Ina?

INA: Oh aye. Well she's got that much confidence. That is ...

MARY: Oh that's half the battle Ina. If you've got the confidence you can do anything.

IRENE: You can feel the beat of it coming right through the floor. And...

THOMAS (*offering gloves*): You.

MARY (*signing*): No you're all right son, we'll see them in a minute. He's no the full shilling that one.

IRENE: What a family right enough. They used to be that wellknown the Tambinis. We used to go down to that café years ago and it was something I'm telling you. All the fine boys used to meet in there. That was a different Rothesay in them days.

MARY: Do you remember Mario, her man? Oh he was a lovely fella him Irene. Never passed you. Dressed like a lord. Worked like a dog that man. He was never out of that café and what a beautiful white apron he had. Beautiful. On a summer's day out there. Oh he would always stick in an extra snowball when you went for cakes. What a gentleman. Never said much. Quiet.

IRENE: They say he'd a lot to put up with.

MARY: So they say.

IRENE: The town was busy then. He was just a pure gentleman that man. Never passed you. Always had a smile so he did and never looked at anybody apart from her.

INA: Other women?

IRENE (*shaking her head*): Not at all. Not at all. She's never been right since he died you know. He was a right gentleman. He never looked at another woman. I mean that café was busy at one time, but no, he was daft for her. You could see it on him. He was the one that did all the running after her.

MARY: Aye, it's a changed place noo.

IRENE: You're no kidding there Mary. It's dead out there. You think they would do something to gee it up a wee bit wouldn't ye? A swing park or something. It's a shame for the young yins. I don't know. There's nothing for them.

INA: That's the swimming baths shut doon.

IRENE: Is 'at right?

INA: Aye. They didnae have the money. 'S always the same. They've got plenty of money tae gi' themselves wage rises right enough but there isnae a bloody bingo hall left in the place.

MARY (*staring forward*): At her time of life, Lucia should be sitting back and letting them all get on with it. They're all the men and women they'll ever be noo. But they're all still at it. She runs the bit out for that family. Nae wonder she's depressed.

IRENE: Has she got the depression an' a'?

MARY: So they say. Lassie that works in the chemist says she's been in for tablets.

IRENE (*accepting gloves off Thomas*): They're a nice family right enough Mary. I mean, you've got to admit they've done a lot for this place wi' the cafés and that.

MARY: Oh but I could tell you a few stories.

IRENE: They say that Alfredo's got a boyfriend.

INA: Away ye go!

IRENE: Aye. So they say. He was always the odd one out that fella. Nice enough. But *oaff*... You wouldny credit the half of it.

INA: Good God, I wouldny have thought it. Our Carol's been getting her hair done there for years.

IRENE: Well there you go. Who would have thought it? A nice fella all the same. But they say he's like that.

MARY: They've said that for years.

IRENE: Oh I know.

MARY: Me, I don't think there's anything the matter with the fella. I think he's just quiet.

IRENE: Well, you never know the time of day round here right enough.

MARY (*coming to the edge of her chair*): Okay Thomas. What ones do you think I should go for the day? Do these ones suit me? Well, do you think they'll get me a dance at the Pavilion? Eh Thomas. Will they get me a lad?

Lucia was always amazed at how peaceful and quiet it was in the home at Ardbeg Point. She said hello to the nice young man, the warden, and made herself a cup of tea in the spartan kitchen. There was hardly a sound coming from the dayroom, just the odd bark or moan, and a creaking sound from the chairs as the deaf and dumbs shifted, and the same as they moved their hands in silent conversation. You could hear the fingers beating together as they did their sign language.

She could hardly believe how composed Maria had been, the wee thing, standing downstairs in the café with her scarf on and her suitcases up on one of the tables, and Alfredo that nice in his dark suit, the two of them ready for the long journey to London. Thinking about the overnight train made Lucia think of journeys she'd taken a long time ago when the trains were clean and tidy. They weren't always happy right enough those journeys. When they first came to Scotland from Italy they passed Greenock on the train and all the smoke was coming out the chimneys and she remembered thinking all the people sitting on the train had eyes that looked like animals' eyes.

But, bless her, Maria stood ready to go. In the white formica of the kitchen Lucia thought of Maria and Alfredo going to London. When Lucia stopped by the shop they were all ready to go and Rosa was combing Maria's hair and panicking about them missing the boat although the boat wasn't even in yet. Lucia had kissed her only granddaughter in the middle of her forehead. She had drawn close to Alfredo and pressed the roll of money into his hand and shushed him and that was that. There had been so much fuss in Lucia's life that now she just wanted to let events happen as they might. She had said goodbye and walked towards the glass door of the shop. Maria came up and hugged her grandmother again. Just at that moment Lucia was filled with grief for a thousand particulars in her life. Somehow, over time, she had moved the small things to the centre, but here, standing at the door and feeling the draught, she was instantly aware of the larger forces in her life, and was moved by them, and tears came into her eyes. For a moment she stared into Maria's lovely clear face. 'I'll come if you ever need me,' she said, and then she closed the door behind her.

Oh it was lovely and quiet in that kitchen. Ardbeg Point was a place without noise or fuss of any kind. When she walked back into the dayroom Lucia saw that Thomas was standing between the women and a large vase of imitation flowers. The mended gloves were spread out on the carpet. He was laughing and signing with a pair of them on. The women's faces shaped themselves to laugh but only moans came out. It sounded like the noises children make, but there was experience in the women's eyes. Lucia stood in the gloaming of her own thoughts. Her green-coloured eyes, her old eyes, gathered the remaining light from the windows and drew it to themselves, and as she stood there the sky became dark, and still she stared out, peering into the world from the centre of her deepest privacies. The deaf-and-dumbs were putting on the gloves and making sounds in their throats.

The television was on low. Lucia put her hands on the glass and the glass was cloudy from the breathing of the women and from her own breaths too. Her mind had come back to where she was in front of the window; looking at the darkness outside she told herself the stars had come into the water. But it wasn't that; it wasn't stars: what she saw in the water were the lights of the last ferry as it passed on its way from Bute to the mainland.

PART TWO

1 · *Mr Green*

Every time I drink a glass of claret it goes straight to my face. I'm not kidding. And when I pass a mirror and check out my chops I know I'll be dead in no time. Don't worry, viewers: don't write in. I'm a hundred and one times happier than the version of myself the doctor's been recommending to me all these years. You can bet your life on that. So just sit back, put your feet up, relax a little, and stay tuned for the old conversation, for what ails us is present in the world before we are.

Showbusiness. Before you call it an illness you want to think what it does for people. I've met everybody, and I'm telling you there ain't a single soul who couldn't use a little more shine on their shoes. Who can't love a person whose purpose in life is to offer a purpose to life? Showbusiness is glory in the afternoon and sunshine after dark. There you go. I'm a man of definitions, you can ask anybody. Showbusiness is tearing life down and putting it all back together again, funnier, larger, shinier, more harmonious, Goddamit, purer, more special. Don't tell me after all this time the world don't want special. I know it does, I'm telling you straight. I've watched it for fifty-odd years and I know.

You just sit there, citizen, and laugh yourself silly and scratch your beard, I was here before you were, me and the dawn, me and the bigwigs, me and the professors, me and the great British public at large. My show on television is called *Opportunity Knocks*. You all know it, I'm sure. We sit here and wait for talent to show up and you know why? It's easy to know when you've sat waiting. For life. Waiting for something to remind us we're all alive out here. Vocation is the heavenly thing on earth, not opportunity for Chrissakes. We wait here. We have always waited here. Somebody said it: vocation acts like a law of God from which there is no escape. Goddamit. That's what we believe around here. Listen. Do you want to know what vocation means? It means 'addressed by a voice'. I learned that when I was in short pants. I Hughie Green believe talent will save us all. There. I've said it now.

I've spent my whole life loving talented people and waiting for talent and taking it like drink when it turns up. There's always somebody new somewhere. There's always that new constellation that makes the night. Napoleon once said he felt like he was going mad when he heard Crescentini sing. Good God. What a thing to say. The world has seen its share of men who love the larger-than-life more than they love life itself: I know that town, yes I do, and I know all the roads that lead there.

When I look down the years and think of all the stars we've made on this show I could cry—and I see them out making the decade fit to move in and the air fit to breathe. Good Lord, you wouldn't stand in the way of goodness. Those people were fine. Those people woke up in the morning and they got out there and worked hard and when they saw the bright lights they knew they hadn't bungled their lives. That is what they knew. And our ratings go up and up and people just love it on a Monday night. That's what we're here for. What talent is, how you find it, is what *Opportunity Knocks* is all about. I found the secret, I think, of making sure that we never made a mistake—by asking the public to make the decisions for us. Not just the folks in the studio, but the mums and dads sitting in front of their television sets at home. And believe me when I say the public is always right. They see talent coming: it might be a born star like my old friend Liz Taylor, it might be a Cockney with a personality as bouncy as a beach ball. But the public know. They always know. They won't be fooled any more than they want to be. Talent is a demonstration of the fact that there are people in the world—special people, mind you, some of them dear, dear friends of mine—who really believe they are what they pretend to be. I used to say that to my old mother bless her heart. She'd say: 'Stop talking rubbish, Hughie.' But it ain't rubbish. Talent is the heart's bid for freedom my friends. And I mean that most sincerely, folks.

Stay in showbusiness long enough it begins to seem like philosophy. Who came up with that one? You scratch the silver on a little bit of talent and a whole world begins to show through. You take it from me. Growing up in Ottawa back then we wanted to be good, my friends. We wanted to be the best. Nowadays the kids don't want to be good and they don't care about being the best: they want fame. People nowadays don't think they're alive until they're on the television screen. That's true. There it is ladies and gents: the biggest known intimacy in the modern world, right there in your living-room. The true stars are out there for sure. They know who I am and I want to take their lives and make them personalities people will never forget. I'm telling you I want to take those kids and give them the world. When the sun climbs down at the end of the day, that is what they deserve, that is what the best deserve and what they will get from me and what they will find reasonable, and surely viewers, surely my good customers, this is what we all must enjoy if life is to be sincere.

MY FATHER was famous for a reason you know. Hugh Aitcheson Green. They called him the Fishmonger General of Canada. That man had a serious face for work I'm telling you. Sometimes when I'm presenting the show and I step up to the microphone my father's seriousness comes and pats me on the shoulder. Still does. I'm not kidding, I feel him looking right down at me, but I just nod to him you know and go on as before and the old smile takes over.

'You're an educated man like your father,' my mother said all those times, 'you've read books, and I don't know what you're doing messing around in costumes and singing crazy songs. A man has to understand the world Hughie and go about his business there in an orderly fashion. But I suppose you're a different story, Hughie Green.'

She came into the house when I was young with armfuls of flowers and my father with armfuls of cod. She would push her hair away from her face and smile over the petals as if she were already in an old photograph. She was a good one for whispering caution, my mother, but don't you know she'd a great head for heights herself. She liked the ordinary hours of the day, and no one had a knowledge of how to live that was quite so certain as my mother's. She was a middle-class Canadian in love with her married name and in thrall to a well-stocked kitchen closet. *Look at our Hughie's face when he sees us kissing. You'd think he was watching a picture show.*

My parents knew how to make life float while it was happening. We used to go ice-skating on the Rideau Canal and I can still see that stretch downtown, in the iciest winter, right through the centre of Ottawa, the fairy-lights twinkling on the bank of the canal with all the skaters going round on a cold night like the last night on earth.

One time my mother and father stopped holding hands and watched me skating off on my own: looking back I could see the amazement on their faces as they tugged at their gloves and stood transfixed. I was twirling and dancing on the ice, miles away from the hockey boys chasing one another. The wind rushed round my ears as I spread my arms and glided over the frozen water and it all felt true. Under the lights on the Rideau Canal I saw the moment my parents recognised me at the centre of my own propulsion: I had a life of my own, friends who really knew me, evenings spent skating to music they knew nothing about, putting my tongue into girls' mouths, yes indeed, and now, with my parents twenty yards away but dwindling there in front of my eyes, I had a place in this city, places to go, conversations, secrets, haircuts.

People stopped skating and stood together in a circle watching me as I danced on the ice. I remember the Rideau Canal. At the end of that night the three of us walked over the Pont Laurier Bridge and down O'Connor Street lined with trees and past those 1930s windows bright now in the dark when I think of them. My face was flushed and I could see the tears in my mother's eyes as we walked and all our white breaths billowed in front of us. We walked right through the breaths in the cold night as if we couldn't be moved by the miracle of expiration or the wonders of the weather and with every step I thought only of the breaths to come, the great gulps of air to be taken again and again out there in the world.

Oh, that night going home from the Rideau Canal was for me the very beginning of life. We walked past the houses in silence and I felt for the first time that silence with my parents was my best announcement. God yes. I was a good skater and I knew it then with all the bothersome things unsaid beneath the frozen trees on O'Connor

Street. My heart drummed that night with those people applauding on the ice and traces coming from the lights on the bank. When I stopped skating I was panting there with my chest heaving and my parents across from me fixed to the spot.

My father loved to read old books when he'd had enough of the day. He read me parts of *The Old Curiosity Shop* and told me it was good to memorise the look of the rooms in the house you grew up in. 'You have to belong somewhere,' he said, 'and you'll see one day a happy home is a constant project.'

'I guess so,' I said.

'Yes, you would guess, Hugh,' he said. 'You don't care about life the way we do,' he said, 'you're only a show-off.'

There's a certain passage from that Dickens book he copied out for me. 'It always grieves me,' the book said, 'to contemplate the initiation of children into the ways of life, when they are scarcely more than infants. It checks their confidence and simplicity—two of the best qualities that Heaven gives them—and demands that they share our sorrows before they are capable of entering into our enjoyments.'

That was the thing with my old man: he read books, we read them together, philosophy, poetry, good God, the very best books you could lay your hands on, Plato for goodness sake, Walt Whitman, and we'd sit down at the card table and my father would mark the pages with a pencil he stored behind his ear for safety. Ha! The hours we spent with books. He loved the way they slowed life down to a heartbeat, and he'd say, 'Hugh, whatever you put into these books you'll get it right back a hundred to one. Here's words to change the shape of your mouth.' And we'd read about honour and duty, justice and freedom, the kind of stuff to set your hair on fire, and we were really by ourselves in those hours being curious and willing and uncertain, my God.

'Here's words to change the shape of your mouth.'

Trouble is my mouth was setting otherwise, into a perpetual smile, into a great big howdydoody for the audience. I wonder if he was ashamed. I guess people will always think of me as Hughie Green, television's travelling salesman, the guy with the cheap show-business banter, and the rest has been closed down for good. But heavens above, if God should be my witness, my father and I read all the stuff. You have to make choices in this world. He's dead now. Reading was our secret. And when I sit down like this to have a wee drink by myself, goodness, I remember the old conversation, his eyeglasses, the 40-watt bulb. 'You're a goddamn split personality,' he would say. And that's the way it goes. The books are up on the shelf sure enough, and I'll take one down, but I'd say this to him, talent and entertainment are out there, making the world fit to live in, changing the lives of billions of people. You won't find that in books. No sir.

My mother ran a wedding shop: she liked to be near impending domestic crises. Running in and out of living-rooms where young people were seated, foretelling bliss, bearing flowers and cloth samples and brochures, gave her a direct line to the wishes of others, just as it afforded her a constant reckoning of her own happiness. Her afternoons were spent with a teacup balanced on her knee, her painted fingernails pushing back her red hair, as she went on smiling to hide her thoughts, expressing surprise at previously hidden pasts, confirming suspicions about 'bad husband material'. She was like an undertaker who took all the prizes for conviviality, my mother; every day she came home from her encounters with the nervous and the dreamy, and there we would be.

I got the OBE two months before my father died. By then all his stories were of how charming I had been as a boy. But don't mind me about my father I'm telling you: I had a happy childhood; I only say my memory of the happy bits did not entirely coincide with his. My father understood the enactment of happy days as a matter of uniformity in the Green household. Like most mothers years ago, my mother liked me best when I was most dependent on her, and naturally, almost lightheartedly, she held my independence to be a filthy mark on a nice boy.

I wanted to dance and sing. I knew I would be a performer. I don't recall a moment of the 1940s when I wasn't laying plans for the most profound success in Light Entertainment. Yet the pressures of a good family can make mincemeat of the best intentions: I became a pilot first. The OBE came thirty years later and was nothing to my mother compared to me coming down the path in Rockingham with a crease all the way down my Air Force pants. The neighbours were beckoned from their high teas and a cinecamera was brought in: my mother drew her red hair out of her eyes and cried on the lawn out there, setting me up, with my cap under my arm and my borrowed smile, setting me up, high and sweet I'm telling you, at the top of a wedding cake she fashioned in secret for the Lord Jesus Christ.

The Royal Canadian Air Force. At seventeen I was one of the youngest pilots they ever had. At the same age my father had been in Ottawa pestering battalions of civil servants with his idea of 'fish for the fighting forces'. I often returned to flying over the years; between dates in showbusiness, while other actors were tramping around Camden Town with nothing to do, I was up in the air, watching Great Britain below like an old song, all those fields and rivers and lochs and the little towns at the coast.

Those guys in the business who complain about bad notices: they ought to put their gas on a peep. Should try piloting a brandnew flying boat over 3,277 nautical miles from Bermuda to Largs on the Clyde. We did it in the most treacherous winter weather, storms over the North Atlantic, and it was the world's longest hop back then for a twin-engined aircraft. With ice forming on the aeroplane I thought the weight would finish us; I remember thinking we were just about to drop into the drink, and I had to climb to 17,000 feet and we had one bottle of oxygen between three of us. Even a rough night at the Glasgow Empire is a cakewalk after a nightmare flight like that I'm telling you.

The British can't tap-dance. They move on the balls of their feet and shuffle in that slightly elegant way, but they can't use their heels like American tappers, and there's no ease in the syncopation, and it's all wrong. In the early Fifties I got some work flying commercial planes—London to Moscow, or the Atlantic run, and banking over the Isle of Man or the foothills of Galloway in Scotland you come to feel there's a kind of loneliness that nearly counts as an accomplishment. I used to manipulate my feet in the cockpit until they were sore; tapping my feet, thinking of jobs that might come along. Was I free up there? Or was there never a moment in my life when my nerves didn't scream out for the remedy of applause?

What is freedom in the end anyhow? You're up in the sky and Britain down there is covered in ration books and flags and all those tiny towns full of houses and you see the clouds dissolving over the cockpit in front of you and your mother and father are somewhere behind the horizon, out there in back of all the quietness. You think you might just keep flying on and on and never see a crowd again. You think you might get up a head of steam and just keep going until you run out of gas or run out of sky. Up in the air you feel free for seconds at a time. Like standing in a line-up at the Royal Variety Performance and Her Majesty the Queen is coming down. 'This is what life is all about,' you say. 'I'm my own man for ever.'

Talent is the fight against quietness. And yet quietness is always waiting. It waits for each of us—the blood moves round, redder than claret, silent as the frozen air—and one day that quiet circulation gives way to the most perfect silence in the world. I'm telling you. You know it. You can weep for applause but silence is your destiny.

The ease of the ice on the Rideau Canal? Sugared almonds distributed at weddings and my mother floating between the tables and shuffling name-cards? And there I was crossing the miles of sky with a rush of clouds coming on and the blueness breaking up. I look back on everything and see that in my own head I was always moving and never arriving. Something inevitable checks your course. Always does and always will. I'm telling you. Freedom may turn out to be the flattest gag in the business. You die and then it's somebody else's turn.

Shall I tell you the best? *Lassie.* The popular Hollywood movie serial starring the dog of the same name? That was my first time in front of the camera and oh my God even today I can't speak about the sickness I felt walking onto that set and totally blank. They were filming at Shepperton Studios and this big man somebody or other walks in and everybody freezes. The dog pees from one end of the soundstage to the other and the big man shouts what he wants. The boy beside me had been a child star called Baby Sunshine. We played a couple of young crofters who spend their time chasing that damn dog through the heather, later attesting to its intelligence and bravery in the High Court at Edinburgh. And it was of course Lassie that got the star treatment; Jim Copeland (Baby Sunshine) and I had to shine shoes and lick stamps between takes. They say Jim disappeared completely a few years later. He left for Southport and was never seen again. I can still see his eyes all eager for the cameras. Once upon a time his father and his grandfather did a show in Southend that involved Jim being a baby who lived in a bass drum. On the *Lassie* film Jim just chatted up the girls and cried on cue.

'My father knew Pavlova,' he would say, 'and he knew Sarah Bernhardt and Stan Laurel and Sir Harry Lauder and... you know what? George Robey used to borrow his nail-clippers.'

Hughie Green, that's me, came down out of the clouds and hit paydirt in the spring of 1956. That's when I brought *Opportunity Knocks* to ITV. It quickly became the most popular TV show in the country and I guess I was what you call famous overnight. Like a lot of the old-time entertainers who ended up on the box, I never really danced again, though I have sung sometimes, and I found after a while I wasn't looking out for acting parts. It was a new life. Suddenly I was spinning, popular, and taken everywhere, and in no time it was command performances, and the age of television, my God, and in the middle of all that, in the sweetness of England then, you got the feeling people were rushing at you with hopes. People want you to absorb them, to make them successful too, and in no time you see it, you see your public face emerging, you see it recognised everywhere, and there you are, a personality, smiling, waving, passing into the moment when the slickness of your public face dries into a mask.

Deep down, my father reckoned I was a phony, and in his last year, a long time ago now, the disdain he had nearly always felt for me softened into an admiring sort of pity. 'You carry your own climate wherever you go, Sonny Jim. I'll say that for you.' And then he was gone, the old bastard. He was gone and the very next day it was the last in the series of *Double Your Money,* and who do you think was up and into the studio early, ironing his own tie, making up, rubbing chalk over his teeth and smiling like a skull? Well yes, the oldest clichés in showbusiness are like the oldest clichés in life, not only true, but truer by the day. The show must go on. Harry upstairs said it was the best *Double Your Money* I'd presented in the whole run.

Never mind all that. You pay the price for being good and being on time. I'm past the point now where I worry about being misunderstood, even by myself. Never mind. There are no prizes in this business for knowing yourself. None. I have worked in showbusiness all my life. That is all I know and that is all I need to know. I love talented people and as I've told you they sure make the world go round.

A girl came in here the other month. I swear she's thirteen years old, and she doesn't even look thirteen. She is tiny. They found her in Scotland, and I said, 'Where from?', and they said, 'Isle of Bute'. Chrissakes, I remember that place from the air, I said, I remember flying over there and the green on the hills you wouldn't believe it, 1943, and the water around the Clyde there, my God it's a boom from the tomb that one. And this little girl comes in, she sings like Barbra Streisand. We bring her into the studio and she sings out of that little body like Ethel Merman, Jesus, the beautiful voice on her, and the feeling in her movements. She's full of fun too. All that fun the good ones always have, the confidence, she reminds me of myself, working hard, keeping time, rolling her blue eyes and giving it a bit of razzmattaz. She's got the nature. She's got the liveliness, God bless her heart, the maturity.

Well, she just might be the best I've ever heard. Talent is a matter of guts and that girl has guts to spare, you should see her rehearse, unfailing, tireless, God she goes the whole bundle, and we know nothing about her except she's a little Scottish-Italian girl. Well we don't need to know anything about her.

It's snowing outside.

Every time I drink a glass of claret it goes straight to my face. Quiet now. I get tired in the afternoons.

Talent is the fight against silence. I mean that most sincerely, folks.

2 · Primrose Hill

Marion Gaskell Associates was situated in a small office above one of the guitar shops in Denmark Street, but the lady herself, one of the best light entertainment agents in the business, was able to do a lot of work from her house in Primrose Hill, where she kept a room of her own at the very top. The room mattered to her, and it contained the oldest and most beautiful rug in the house, as well as a desk and two red telephones, one of which, the more used, had its own line, as well as its own callers.

She clipped on a second cameo earring and then pulled a string which made the wooden blinds open. 'Oh shoot,' she said under her breath, 'no more snow.' The trees on the hill were forlornlooking, and up at the top a group of children in coloured mittens were struggling with a sled that wouldn't move. 'Poor little things,' said Marion. When she poked a finger through the blinds and looked down the other end of St George's Terrace, she noticed a couple of men in hard hats inspecting a building next to the Queen's Arms. She watched them for a minute then went to her desk to look for a lozenge. 'All architects should be cut in half,' she whispered, opening a drawer, 'and so should their bills.'

The private phone rang. 'Good morning dear,' she said. 'What, what? Yes. We're doing press at eleven and then we'll talk to Richard. Tell them to wait. Yes, darling, tell them to wait, we've got rehearsals beginning at three and we're in make-up for six. Not a hope darling. Tell them to ring tomorrow and in the meantime do sort out the parking. I'm not having that again. Yes. Jolly good.' While she sat speaking to the office, Marion doodled on a pad; she drew a circle and another circle inside it. 'We're not in the business of booking foreign yet. Lawrence can speak to me directly. No. If we win again tonight we might retire her—go out on a high. That's right. That's the ticket. Well you'll have to make them wait, darling, there's only so much we can do. All right. Now, off you pop, dear, time's running along. Indeed. Goodbye.'

Marion went back to the window and looked down the street again. She sometimes wondered if all the eccentrics were disappearing. You didn't see those people much any more, like Dora Wilner, from Vienna, ancient and full of stories, coming along Chalcot Road in her black gown and headscarf, singing to passers-by and shouting out her news. Coming home from the Criterion the previous night, Marion passed Fred Oaglam, a man with no teeth whom everybody knew; he was a casualty of the war, the only man to survive the bomb attack on the air-raid shelter up on Primrose Hill, and now the only people who could get any sense out of him were squatters and layabouts. For years Oaglam had been walking up and down Regent's Park Road with a mailbag of empty fizzy drink bottles over his shoulder. He used to pick them up from building sites and railway stations and at the Queen's they let him exchange the empties for tobacco. And what changes down there, thought Marion, down in the pub, though she hated pubs, and had no interest in what happened there, her only connection to it being in her concerns as a local conservationist. She rearranged the blind and sneezed politely into a tissue in her hand. The Queen's: they were tearing down the old velvet curtains and replacing that beautiful glass, changing everything. And to think that Lillie Langtry once turned heads in there.

Marion's spectacles hung on a chain, yet she had a habit of holding on to one arm of them as she came down the stairs, passing framed prints of caricatures from the old *Vanity Fair*. Further down, on the second floor landing, she stopped to look at her prize possession. Indeed every morning she stopped to survey the picture, and it was, she had always said, 'soothing'. An odd thing for her to say, everybody knowing that Marion was little inclined to speak of comforts of that kind. Yet she had that ability—common to those who had taken an interest in art at Swiss finishing schools—to look at paintings as if looking into a deep and imperturbable pond, a pond as calm as a mirror.

It was the nicest landing, and the painting was a Bonnard: *Preparation for Girl in a Bath*. The painting was lit from above by a tiny strip-light in a brass fixture. Marion looked at the painting every morning and every morning she felt, having such a thing to look on, that she had survived something immense, as if the painting on the wall was a godsend, a perfect sign of what she'd achieved, of what she deserved, a quiet marker of the person she'd become.

Underneath the picture was a rosewood table; it had a single drawer, and inside the drawer was a piece of paper covered in words Marion had written down from an exhibition catalogue. 'The painter should devote himself entirely to the study of nature,' it said, 'and endeavour to produce pictures that are an education.'

She looked at the Bonnard and smiled. 'Golly,' she said out loud, 'I'm parched.'

Maria Tambini was sitting at the round breakfast table when Marion came into the kitchen. A smell of smoked fish was lingering. 'Hello, my dear,' said Marion. 'How do we feel this morning?'

'Okay,' said Maria, tapping her fingers on the leafy placemat, humming a tune.

'Good, good,' said Marion. 'It was jolly cold last night, didn't you think? Perishing. I sent Mr Gaskell down to put the heating back on. I don't make a habit of all-night heating—bad for the skin—but last night we just had to make an exception.'

Maria found she often wasn't sure what to say in front of Mrs Gaskell, who was very nice and friendly but seemed to be in charge of everything, including what should be talked about and when. It had been nearly two months since Maria came to London. Uncle Alfredo stayed until just after Christmas, then he went back to Rothesay. Mr and Mrs Gaskell and Maria waved him off at the bus station, and Maria was so excited about London by then that she didn't really notice how sad Alfredo's face was at the window when the bus moved off.

'Another big day, my dear,' said Marion. 'It's so exciting—there are people queuing up to have a word with us, but I told the office, just the main ones, I don't want you feeling exhausted for tonight.'

'The people are nice,' said Maria.

'Not as nice as you think,' said Marion. 'I could tell you a few stories my dear. But listen...'

'See one of them asked me if I had a boyfriend?'

'*The Mirror.* Such a ghastly little man. You're thirteen years old. Oh, these hacks. Some of them are just appalling.'

'I like most of them,' said Maria. 'Do I have to take my jotters today?'

'Yes, what a bore. We've got to squeeze in a few hours of homework. I don't know how we'll manage that. I wish they would understand. You've got such a busy schedule now. We can do it in the car. Not to worry: I spoke to my friend Mrs Enterkine, the lady at Italia Conti, and they'll be ready to take you in two weeks. All right? What a blessing. She knows you need to work on your dancing. It's all still too sluggish, dear, but good, good, we're getting ahead slowly but surely. Rehearsals at three.'

Just then a sound of scratching came from the patio doors. 'Oh, sweet, sweet,' said Marion, walking over and turning the key. 'Yes, my babies, hello. Hello. My liddle scruffy ones. Sit. Sit. Oh, how are you today my silly sausages? Yeeees. Silly liddle things. Down. No, down. Handsome. You are. Yes you are. Sit. My liddle friends. Yeeees. Is it treatsie time?'

'Mr Green and the men are nice all the time, aren't they?' said Maria.

'And so they should be. That's their job,' said Marion, rooting in a basket of dog leads and litter-bags. 'If they're doing their job efficiently then everybody feels better.'

'Lights are so hot though.'

'I'll talk to Sid about a fan. It is certainly very hot in that studio.' Marion had bent down and was feeding the dogs a treat while nuzzling between the two heads. She looked over at Maria. 'You're already a big star, dear,' she said. 'Do you know that? Six weeks in a row. You're the biggest star to come out of that show.' Maria smiled, shrugged, and turned in her chair.

'Am I really?'

'No question,' said Marion. 'And what's more you are going to get bigger. The record's coming out soon, and Woolworths have been on to the office—they want you to tour the shops, and there is advertising work, and there was a call from Butlins in Skegness. *The Basil Brush Show* want you as a guest...'

'Basil Brush!'

'Oh yes. And they're talking about *Morecambe and Wise*. Foreign people have rung the office too. People in South Africa want to see you and the BBC want to discuss things. Don't you bother your head about them. I'll talk to Alfredo when we decide, but golly, isn't it exciting, Maria? Lew Grade says you're the new Shirley Temple.'

'Africa,' said Maria.

'But I said, Shirley Temple my foot. She never had a voice like you have, my dear. And you're much more mature for your age if I say so myself.'

'Thank you,' said Maria. 'Mrs Gaskell? Is it all right if I phone my mum? I want to tell them all the new stuff. She said the last time they were all watching on the island. Is it all right?'

'Of course, my dear. Absolutely. We'll call them from the dressing room when things are less hectic.'

'Have I got a new dress to wear tonight?'

'Sandra's found a lovely outfit. Last week's was too much of a costume. This week you're going to look pretty. Sandra's found you a lovely gown.'

'What's a gown?'

'A lovely dress. Now hurry along. Oh how yummy. Mr Gaskell's made kedgeree. What a sweet man.'

Marion lifted a wooden spoon and scooped some food from the pan onto a plate taken down from the rack. 'Now eat up quickly, my dear, we've got to get ahead,' she said.

THERE WERE no traffic lights on Bute. On the bus coming down from Glasgow, the lights outside kept Maria awake. The bus was dark, not everyone slept; up the back there were men smoking and drinking from cans, and a young man with a tartan duffel bag sat across from Maria reading a book. In the middle of the night the bus stopped at a service station and Alfredo woke up and asked her if she needed the toilet. When she said no, he tucked his jacket under his head and went back to sleep.

The man with the book had looked over. 'Are you going on your holidays?' he asked. Maria blushed.

'No.'

'Are you shy?'

'No.'

'Have you ever been to London before?'

'No.'

'Well, have a nice time.'

Maria smiled. 'You have a nice time too,' she said. And soon the man was sleeping on his duffel bag and the bus was moving very fast down the motorway and it seemed as if the whole bus was sleeping now. Outside the window, when she looked into the distance where all the thousands of orange lights were, she felt the whole world must be asleep. She saw a sign that said 'Birmingham'. Lorries and lorries. You could see houses and flats for miles; they were all muddled up with the orange lights, and she wondered what happened in the streets out there, in the houses, in the rooms. I am the only person awake tonight, she thought.

When she woke up it was cold and the signs said 'Finchley' and 'Swiss Cottage'. The light was very white outside and people were sweeping the streets. She looked at the millions of shops and tall houses and felt hungry all of a sudden. At King's Cross they got off the bus under a big clock-tower and took their cases and went to a café nearby where they served drinks in giant mugs. Maria blew on her tea and laughed at the faces Alfredo was making. They were in such a good mood to be in London with all the sleepy people in the café and the noise outside which seemed to grow every minute. She was amazed: some of the men in the café were totally black.

The bus had got in so early and it was so cold outside that they stayed in the café for two hours. The lady didn't mind, so they kept ordering more biscuits and tea. Maria held her uncle's thumbs across the table and they laughed out loud to be in London, and grinned quietly, a bit shy the two of them, when Alfredo ordered rolls and sausage and the lady brought sausagerolls. When he went out to find a phone box to ring Mrs Gaskell, Maria at the table squeezed her elbows into her chest and felt nice. London was like a dream in the daylight. Waiting for Alfredo she put some salt on the end of her finger and pressed it into the tip of her tongue.

LES DAWSON came into the dressing room at LWT. Mrs Gaskell put down her sheaf of papers and stood up. 'Les,' she said.

'Hello darling Marion,' he said, and he pointed at her with both hands and pulled a face. 'Come in to my arms, Maid Marion forsooth!' They kissed each other on both cheeks and held one another by the arms. 'I want to claim ten per cent of that back,' he added, then kissed her on the forehead. Everybody laughed.

'Right,' said Les, 'I want to see the singing sensation. The wee belter. Where is she? Where's the singing pygmy?' He pretended to look quickly from left to right. Everybody laughed again.

'Hello Mr Dawson,' said Maria. She had been sitting in front of the mirror and her face was now made up. There was a new ladylike arch to her eyebrows, and blue eye-shadow was built up from the lashes, stopping just short of the eyebrows, where white took over. Her lips looked much bigger because of the lipstick.

Mr Dawson lifted her hand slowly, bowed, and kissed it. 'Welcome to the lovely business we call show,' he said.

Almost immediately (and to the delight of everyone) he began talking about his years in the business. While he spoke, Maria looked at his clothes—the wide lapels of his suit, the velvet bow tie—and she grinned and laughed without really understanding. Through the smoke and the sound of laughter she heard him say he was born in a suitcase at the back of the theatre. He made a joke about being on the road so long he had tarmac rash. When he spoke of people in the business he just used their first names: Tommy, Eric and Ernie, Cilla, Petula, Mike, Michael, Dave, Danny. He used second names for some others, in a way that made you think they were his best friends: Sykes, Wisdom, Tarbuck, Forsyth. The room was filled with laughter and Mrs Gaskell beamed. 'How's the Grand Order of Water Rats?' she said.

'Wonderful, my dear. Very wonderful. I'm the King Rat as you know and it's an honour and a privilege to take care of business. We're just about to set off on a merry charity appeal indeed, indeed. Rehearsing in a church hall in Lambeth this very afternoon. Not kidding you: a church hall so old the woodworm speak Latin.'

Maria held her chin up as she was supposed to. When she laughed she had learned to tilt her head and bite her bottom lip in a becoming way. In the months she had been in London she had grown into herself. Winning *Opportunity Knocks* for all those weeks had given her poise: she impersonated all the women she'd known, but more so the London ones, the dancers and dressers, the other performers, for whom everything involved a little piece of business—walking, holding a glass of water, laughing at an unheard joke. A great deal of this was instinctive with Maria—she always knew how to place her head, and what to do with her eyes—but that first period in London showed her how to co-ordinate everything about her appearance.

The people around her thought she had all the showbusiness virtues—she had them by heart, and, even better, she had been born with them. Everyone in the room said that to themselves and they said it to one another. She knew how to sing a song about love in a way that would break your heart. And she seemed to know all the rules: how to present herself to an audience, how to clamber up the microphone stand and disappear into a song and give it everything. She had talent. She had personality. That is what Mr Green had said. That is how he put it to the press when asked to explain his new singing sensation from Scotland.

'I once turned up at Buckingham Palace wearing two odd shoes,' said Les Dawson. 'Prince Philip called me over and smiled and said in his rather debonair way, "Mr Dawson, you appear to be wearing two odd shoes." I couldn't resist it. "Yes indeed, sir," I replied, "and I've got a pair just like them at home."' The room erupted. Maria put her hand over her mouth and appeared quite lost in mirth. 'Oh,' said Dawson, looking over, 'my sweet, stunted gladioli. Sit on my knee and tarry a while.' At this he budged her off her stool and put his arm round her back and placed her on the edge of his lap. 'Do you like games?' he asked.

'Sometimes,' said Maria.

'My father and I, we'd play such lovely games,' he said. 'Blind man's buff at Beachy Head; hide-and-seek, where he'd hide, and I'd go seek, in Glasgow, Cardiff, and Middlesbrough.' He made a face: a concertina of his forehead, eyes, nose, mouth, chin and neck. Again, laughter. Maria giggled and placed her head on Mr Dawson's shoulder. 'You'll go far, my dear,' he said in a quite different voice. 'You'll go far.'

Later on she sat on a plastic chair for the dress rehearsals, its legs propped among the cables, and from there she could see the bare un-painted wood at the back of the set, and the ragged wooden struts that held the whole thing in place. 'It's just a big lump of tat isn't it, sweetheart?' said one of the electricians.

'What's tat?'

'Rubbish, sweetheart. It's just a load of old rubbish from over here.'

'It's not very nice,' she said, 'but from the other side you think wow.'

'That's right. It's all twinkles for the cameras, sweetheart, and be-hind it's like Spaghetti Junction. Tell you something, babe. All things being right a cracker the likes of you should come straight down through the ceiling and onto that stage. That's the way they should have it. No messing about in all this rubbish. Just right down the middle there like an angel.'

Maria giggled. 'You're daft,' she said, but she imagined it and giggled even more.

'I'm telling ya,' he said, 'I wouldn't have the star of the show hanging about in all this rubbish. No way. Straight from above. I'll tell you what, sweetheart, I'm speaking to that Sidney upstairs about it.'

'Daft,' said Maria. When the nice electrician walked off she remembered how, just watching the TV at home, she thought *Opportunity Knocks* was filmed in a place that was sparkly and lit up, a place that people lived in or walked around in, a place of real colours. The orchestra was tuning up and she tapped her foot on the metal edge of a generator; the gold shoes she was wearing reminded her of ones her mother had back in Rothesay. She remembered tottering up the back stairs in them although her feet were too small. Over on the stage, the floor manager held onto his earphones and waved a clipboard. He asked for quiet. 'Going for a rehearsal,' he shouted. Then he read some words from the clipboard: Maria could tell they were Mr Green's words, but Mr Green had rehearsed with the cameras earlier in the day, and this was just for the performers. The floor manager read the words quickly as if they were dead, though they were in fact quite lively words, describing the next act, Arthur Field the Musical Muscle Man, who now stood on the stage between two Greek columns, wearing a tiny pair of trunks.

The orchestra played a jerky tune and Arthur Field lifted his arms. Keeping a composed expression on his face, he began to move his muscles, one set at a time, making them dance to the music. First one arm up then the other, the jiggling, oiled flesh seeming to move separately from the rest of him, then his back muscles, then the mounds of flesh on his bottom, they moved too in time to the music. His body parts seemed to have lives of their own, obeying their own rhythm, and then he would strike a pose, curving his arms and clenching his fists. His ribs would show, then he would strike another pose, just as the beat of the music changed, and his stomach would be sucked in to show the shape of his insides.

Maria watched all this from the chair. She had never seen a man with skin so shiny before and she had never seen a man without his clothes. Arthur Field looked down at his stomach as if it were a pet, as if the moving flesh didn't belong to him. She noticed the way his chest moved to the music: it was as if the nipples were eyes inspecting the studio. It was horrible the way the muscles in his thick legs moved too and his privates in his trunks. His body was alive like nothing she'd ever seen, not like a woman's body or the body she had—the colour of the flesh and the shape of it and its movements were strange, and she wondered if all men looked like that under their clothes. She looked at his concave stomach. She looked at his darting eyes and his nipples and his penis and she began to smile behind her hand as if she were watching a cartoon.

Walking along one of the back corridors of the studios, Maria would smile professionally to strangers. Whenever she was out of her Primrose Hill bedroom she assumed people were looking at her, and even in her room alone she looked at herself, and in her bed at night she felt watched from above. The corridor's striplights made the tan on her arms look orange, and as she walked, the skin round her mouth felt tight from lipstick, foundation and powder, and her eyes felt glued open. Barbara in the tea-bar gave her a plastic cup of orange squash. 'You look lovely, darling,' she said as she passed it over.

'You don't think it makes me look silly?'

'Not a bit of it, darling. You look like a right lady tonight.'

'I can't win again,' Maria said.

''Course you can, love.'

'They need a new person.'

'Not at all. We'll all be clapping loudest for you darling. Wouldn't be the same around here without you now would it?'

Maria smiled her own smile at Barbara and continued down the long corridor. There was a smell of disinfectant coming up from the floor as her gold shoes clacked along the tiles. At the end of the corridor the swing doors were open and Marion was staring at her. 'Chop chop,' she said, 'it's showtime, Maria. Come now. We're all waiting for you.'

Maria quickened her pace. She felt as if she had an electric heater inside her stomach. Marion winked and disappeared behind the door but Maria stopped just short of it, feeling warm, distant, the swing door making its rubbery bump and then shushing. The world was quiet under the strip-lights. She put the cup of orange squash to her lips and drew the sweet liquid into her mouth. There was a bin beside the doors. She moved her tongue in the orange squash for a moment then spat what was in her mouth into the bin and threw the cup in after it. She disappeared through the swing doors. In seconds they had swung together and were peaceful, and only the overhead lights, yellow to the core, made a buzzing sound in the empty corridor.

3 · Nutrition

Pink coconut snowballs lay on a plate next to the teapot, and on the rest of the tray, around the sugar bowl, heaped between the milk jug and the spoons, was a pile of loose Quality Street, a half-packet of Rich Tea, an Empire biscuit, two fairy cakes with jelly tots in the middle, a Blue Riband, two chocolate Penguins, a Breakaway, a Turkish Delight, a packet of Toffos and a raisin Club.

Blue light from the TV flashed on the edges of the cups. As Giovanni lifted one of the teaspoons it had a reflection of the TV in its cradle, and so did Lucia's spectacles on the arm of her chair, the contorted image of the screen almost watchable.

'I've sugared and milked them already,' said Rosa from her place in the corner of the sofa.

'Magic,' said Giovanni.

'It's bigger than it seems in real life,' said Alfredo.

'You said that last week,' said Mr Samson, the oldest man, who was sitting on one of the dining chairs they'd brought over for him. He didn't have a television set and Giovanni was now in the habit of bringing him up to the living-room so he could see Maria.

'And the week before,' said Lucia.

'You say it every week,' said Giovanni.

'All right,' said Alfredo, 'I say it every week and every week it's true. The telly makes that place look much bigger than it actually is.'

'Very good, Alfredo,' said his mother.

'I'm just saying.'

The logo for London Weekend Television came together on the TV screen to the sound of trumpets.

'That's the Post Office Tower. You can see that from the top of the hill where she's living,' said Alfredo.

They all laughed. 'Shush now,' said Lucia. Then the livingroom door opened and Kalpana Jagannadham put her head round. 'Has it started?' she asked.

'No, hen, come on in,' said Rosa. 'Sit yourself down, it's just starting. Sit here.'

'I'm okay on the floor, Mrs Tambini.'

'Alfredo, pass the lassie some of that stuff over.'

'No, Mrs Tambini, honest. I've just had my tea. No thanks. I'm fine.'

'On ye go,' said Giovanni.

'Shhhhh,' said Lucia.

Just to keep the peace Kalpana took a cake from the tray and placed it on the carpet at her side.

The screen suddenly filled with the face of Hughie Green. His grey hair was slicked back and he was smiling with one half of his face. 'Good evening and welcome ladies and gents and all the viewers at home. What a terrific show we have for you tonight...'

'He must be some age now,' said Mr Samson. 'I can remember him when he was on the radio. He was good on the radio. They say he's a bit of a ladies' man.'

'Let us hear him,' said Giovanni.

Hughie Green made a joke about Concorde and another one about Denis Healey's eyebrows. 'He's good at his job,' said Giovanni. 'He knows his stuff.'

'He uses big words,' said Alfredo.

'There's nothing the matter with big words if you've got something to say with them,' said Lucia.

'Would yez be quiet?' said Rosa.

Hughie Green straightened out his smile, winked at the camera and did a tiny shuffle. 'Over the last six weeks our first contestant has secured a place in the hearts of the entire nation. She came here as a complete unknown, but since then her vivacious, bubbly personality and beautiful singing voice have proved a winner with people of all ages. From the beautiful Scottish island of Bute, this remarkable little girl has proved to be a breath of fresh air with all of you. I mean that most sincerely, folks. The winner of the last six shows, and competing tonight for her seventh, ladies and gents, it's my great pleasure to introduce the fantastic, the sensational . . . Maria Tambini.'

Lucia could feel the heat of the bar-fire coming through her slippers. She blinked and caught her breath as Maria lifted her eyes and looked right at the camera. She looked into the heart of the living-room itself; and then Lucia remembered she was looking into millions of rooms, and people in each one were taking the girl to themselves. Maria whispered the first lines of the song. '*Let me kiss your lips and say I do before you leave my love for the last time,*' she sang. '*Let me hold you close and promise I will before the light goes out for a lifetime. I won't cry anymore. I can't try anymore. Just hold me once before you go and leave me be with a song I know. The world won't come again that's going now.*'

'Oh look at her,' said Lucia, spreading her fingers under her throat. 'Is she not beautiful?'

On the TV, Maria reached the chorus and her whole face seemed to blur with feeling. Her body shook. She drew her arms across the front of her face with the fingers spread; it looked as if she were tearing the song in two, or ripping open the screen that contained her now, and she dived into the song's chorus with her head thrown back, holding the notes until the breath left her, then staring at the floor with wide eyes, closing them, beginning the verse with something new in her expression, her arms falling open again as the chorus approached, reaching, climbing, throwing her hands to the audience as if to appeal for understanding. There was a storm of music around her and she wrapped herself up in it and was gone.

She is gone, thought Lucia. Never is she coming back to this place or anywhere like it. *I called out your name. Be a good girl now. I looked for you. I did. There's room for all of us if we hurry. There will be room.*

Rosa followed the movement of her daughter's arms. So beautiful the white gloves along her arms. She didn't phone today.

'Go on ya wee cracker,' said Giovanni. 'Go on.'

All the way to London I hope she's got a nice coat down there in London. Mr Samson thought it was all so modern to see the lights behind the wee lassie go from blue to pink and back again as she sang the words. 'Mrs Bone always used to say she was the loveliest thing in a pram,' he said out loud.

Lucia flinched in her chair at the mention of Mrs Bone.

'Oh Maria,' said Kalpana. 'You're so grown up. She looks so grown up.' Nobody, she thought, nobody here, nobody anywhere, knows how much they hated her at school. Nobody knows it. *They're just jealous, Maria, and you and me, we'll go up the meadow and play by ourselves because they just hate us because they're jealous that's all. We had nice times, Maria. Oh Maria.* 'I can't believe it,' she said to the others in the living-room. 'Every week she's even better.'

Alfredo looked at the television and thought of all the things the camera concealed. He thought of the green room and the car waiting in the studio carpark. He thought of the drive through London at night and the look of the skyline from Primrose Hill. He thought of Sidney the director and the nice dancers and Mr Green coming past and always speaking in headlines. Alfredo stared at the screen and thought of the bus journey to London and the smile on Maria as she held on to his thumbs in the greasy spoon by King's Cross.

'They're doing wonders with her hair,' he said.

At the end of her song everyone in the living-room clapped and they clapped on the television as the camera panned across the audience.

The lights went down. Maria Tambini could hear Mr Green talking at the other side of the studio. She could feel that her brow was damp and could hear herself breathing. She knew that no one could see her face now. She stood on the platform hearing her own breathing and she liked the sound of the audience and Mr Green. There was nobody up on the platform but her and later in the show she returned to the stage to face the applause of the audience and the clapometer.

In Rothesay, outside the window of her old bedroom, the wind coming off the Firth was rattling the drainpipes down to the street, past the chip shop and its sticks of pink rock. The pavement was wet and seemed in its own way abandoned. There was no one about; they were all at home in the glow of the television that Monday night. Down Victoria Street and past the harbour there was quietness and shadows, and they crowded the seafront, those shadows, flickering around the old palaces of entertainment, the Pavilion, the Winter Gardens, and round the palm trees, over the putting green, to lurk in the bus shelters and the doorways of shops on the road to Craigmore.

Harris's television shop was especially alive down there: a bank of four rental televisions had been left on for the night to advertise their goodness, and there, behind glass, beaming to the sea, they showed the smiling face of Maria Tambini on her final *Opportunity Knocks*.

4 · *The Evolution of Distance*

12 *Cowal Road,*
Craigmore,
Isle of Bute,
10 *February 1978*
PA20 3TF

Dear Maria,

I've been wanting to write to you and tell you all my news but as you know nothing ever happens in Boring Bute. Senorita Doblas has gone back to Spain and we think Miss Marshall is now getting off with Mr Elder the secretarial teacher with the greasy hair (he plays in a band). It's AMAZING seeing you on the telly. AMAZING AMAZING AMAZING. Everybody in the school is talking about you even the turds up smokers' corner and they're THE END. There was another flood Maria and we got three days off. I'm playing hockey for the school and there's a match in Ardrossan, we have to go in a bus. There's nothing to watch on the telly and my dad says I've got to do homework OR ELSE. One night I might make a tape of me talking to you instead of a letter. I will write to you anyway every week so please, please write to me, I know you're busy. Are you going to dressy-up things? Oh my god. WRITE TO ME. Lots of love and kisses, your NOT FAMOUS friend—
Kalpana

• • •

45 St George's Terrace,
London

Dear Kalp,
    It was grate to hear from you and everything thats going on up there, I have been busy all the time and still have the lucky penny you gave me. Its a big house and they gave me my own room, it's brilliant. I have my own clock radio and am putting posters up. Mrs Gaskell is nice and Richard her husband is nice to, in the house they have a piano for me to play sometimes but only for messing about. I go to the phone box at the bottom and tried to ring you but I didn't get you in. I couldn't believe when they said I won again and its brilliant after the show they gave me a drink of Babycham as well. It is a lot different here, sometimes people don't understand a word you say. I will sign off now and hope you write soon.
    Lots of love,
    Maria Tambini

• • •

12 Cowal Road,
Craigmore,
Isle of Bute,
PA20 3TF

25 May 1978 6.56 p.m.

Dear Maria,
    It is sunny now and dad said they might open the boating pond early. I missed you on Basil Brush (is it a puppet on somebody's hand??) but you were on Mike Yarwood and I saw that and thought your dress and hair are great. You were in the Evening Times *and I liked the way the photograph was on a pier with the big wheel behind you. Did you get to have a shot on it? The only good thing on this island is a guy called Tony he's a 'screw'. I think I'll sell my body to him and buy a couple of bottles of Martini and a few packets of smokes with the money (ha ha). The rest of the talent here is hopeless all the rest of the boys go fishing all day or spend their time wanking.*
    I'm really sorry I missed your show because every time you sing now it's better and better. I'm your number ONE fan. I would love to have heard it on the B.B. show. My dad has banned me from the school disco because a boy Cammie from my class was over in the bus stop the other night (he has spots, I don't even know him) and he shouted for me up at the window and he was totally sozzled to the EYEBALLS.

My dad is now writing an article every week for the Buteman it is so embarrassing. They put his picture on it. Bye bye for now. Love and kisses—

Kalpana

p.s. WRITE SOON. G.L. for Aspel show.

• • •

45 St George's Terrace,
London

Dear Kalpana,

You can go to a café round the corner from here it is called Alla Marinella but it doesn't have a jukebox and you don't get a pokey hat, the ice cream is always on a plate. Yesterday morning before setting off in the car to a place I think called Bogner I went into the café to get something and an old man had a flask of tea, he said he borowed it and he wasen't to happy. He smelled of a lot of lager.

I have my own box it has a ballarina inside that springs up when you unhook the lock and plays Raindrops Keep Falling on My Head and I put whatever letters I get inside it, especially for hiding your cheeky ones, but now there are letters that come from complete strangers, we read them in the car. They are fan letters from people who bought the record at the shops.

One thing thats a bit hard is all the training you have to do if your going to make it big. The manager says, and Mr Green from the programme used to say it as well, that I dont really smile enough so I have to practise smiling in front of the mirror and some nights you do it for that long you start crying with just being tired. But its really really brilliant in the studios and all the nice places to see.

I did a public appearance in a Woolworths shop in a place called Palmers Green, I'm not kidding they were all screaming and they had posters up and I mimed along to the record. They didn't bother if you took anything you wanted from the pick and mix. I signed the single for everybody and I'm not kidding it was like a crush. It was also very tiring and the smell of bubblegum yuk!

Say hello to everyone.

Lots of love,

Maria Tambini

• • •

12 Cowal Road,
Craigmore,
Isle of Bute,
PA20 3TF

19 December, 1978

Dear Maria,

I am typing this in Typing because it is sooooo boring and you have not written for ages, are you travelling with a show or something, I hope my letters have got to you. There is one boy in the class he is across from me and he is a great laugh but Tony says he's a poof and I was telling him about you and he says he doesn't remember meeting you.

Everybody goes down the Amusements on Saturday now and they keep them open until late, they've got a Space Invader machine and I'm getting good at it already. My attempts to lose my V* are to no avail, but you know what they say, once a V always a V. Clare Wishart spends all day trying to convince me that Tony is in love with her and that the only reason he won't go out with her is that he is frightened she will get hurt.

I saw your Uncle Alfredo going on the ferry for a night out in Glasgow, he was wearing a new jacket and he said you were busy and doing better than ever. I hope you get this letter.

Lots of love, Kalpana

•••

Swindon,
Near Wales

Dear Kalpana,

I am sending this postcard to you from a hotel on Swindon, the theatre tonight was full and my name is outside with lights on. I am sorry not to write back, there is an article about me in the TV Times.

Sincerely yours,
Maria Tambini

•••

12 Cowal Road,
Craigmore,
Isle of Bute,
PA20 3TF

12 July 1979

Dear Maria,

I have not heard from you for ages, but I wanted to see if you were keeping well and tell you my news. Fergus sent me a Valentine's card and so I said yes I would go out with him and it has now been six months and two days. He is a good kisser and we made kissing licences where you fill in the name of the person and then you can show it to anyone and kiss them. If you want I can type you one. Clare did one for 'sexual intercourse' but it has now been confiscated by Sister Dominic Savio.

We are doing a book in English, God Maria it is so good. The book is about Anne Frank, a girl who is locked in an attic with her family and she is young but keeps a really good diary and she tells it every-thing. When you read the book it is actually the diary she wrote.

I hope you are keeping well and not working too hard. Please write back to me when you have time.

Yours, Kalpana

●●●

45 St George's Terrace,
London NW1

Dear Kalpana,

I am sorry I haven't had more time to write, in the summer season you work all the time and now Christmas is closer and I have a lot of tele-vision to do. I have been given a lot of new songs and my records are in the hit parade in places like Japan and Portogal. Some of my family came to see me in a show in Scarb... I can't spell it, they said they had a nice time and in the dressing room they got to meet the singer Frankie Vaughan who is a movie star as well. They went home with things I'd got for them like free programmes and a T-shirt each. I have got lots of new make-up, they give it to me for nothing because of the shows, and Mrs Gaskell told all of us at the beginning that a woman without paint is just like a dinner without salt, you have to wear it to show up your eyes and it looks as if you've got no lips or are a ghost or something if you go on stage in none.

Sincerely yours,
Maria Tambini

●●●

12 Cowal Road,
Craigmore,
Isle of Bute,
PA20 3TF

Boxing Day, 1979

Dear Maria,

Have you gone missing? Nowadays I have to switch on the radio or watch TV to find you. Anyway, it's your old friend here, still in good old

Bute, wishing you a Happy Christmas. I hope Santa or whoever was good to you. Dr Jag and my mum don't put up a tree or anything, but they like to give presents, and I was so amazed this year. I got a box-set of novels and a diary with a lock on it (goes for 5 years), and some coloured writing paper (as you can see) with envelopes to match and a silver pen that came in a box. Hurrah!

There's a book called *Titus Groan*, it's so good you read it in the bath and I've asked Mr McCallum if I can do it for the mock exams and he didn't know the book but he said he'd look at it and maybe make up a question. There's different characters in it and it's set in a castle with a girl called Fuschia who always wears a red dress. The doctor's shouting for me I'd better go down. PLEASE WRITE SOON.

Yours,
Kalpana

• • •

45 St George's Terrace,
London NW1

12 January 1980

Dear Kalpana,

When you use Pan-stick you have to watch out and 'blend' it carefully in at the neck, and it helps to use a sponge instead of your fingers. Concealer can hide things like broken blood vessels or even spots. The powder is really important and I prefer to use Max Factor, which is loose and makes it look as if you're just fresh for the day.

Sincerely yours,
Maria Tambini

• • •

12 Cowal Road,
Craigmore,
Isle of Bute,
PA20 3TF

18 January 1980

Dear Maria,

It was great to receive your letter. My mum says soap and water is good enough for a girl's skin, but I have washed it with a scrub and then I like just lip-gloss on.

I have been working hard for exams and there is not much fun just now, but at least there are Saturday nights, and I won't be giving them up.

There is now an underage disco at the Pavilion and a lot of us go just for a carry-on. There are some nice boys too and a lot of ugly ones but you can just ignore the neds if you want. They have got a new ferry so everyone is excited about trying it out. You've been away so long I doubt if you could recognise the island; they have a new tourist information place.

Did you get any of the books I mentioned? The Titus one is part of something called the 'Gormenghast' trilogy and I'm now near the middle of the third one. At the same time I read Wuthering Heights (by Emily Bronte) and I thought it was so sad and couldn't put it down. My dad has found some old Indian stories he wants me to read too. I've decided I might do English and French if I ever go to university. Mr McCallum, the English teacher, and Miss Gaston, French, says I could do it if I stick in. My dad of course thinks I should do zoology or something, but anyway it's not for him I'm doing it, I just think it would be great to be able to sit down and learn about the great books. There's so many of them!!

Well, Maria, I haven't heard any news from you but I know from Granny Tambini you're doing the London Palladium which they say is the highest a performer can reach. Good on you my old pal, you know we'll be rooting for you. I'm sorry this letter has been a bit boring but I just wanted to keep you up to speed on all the stuff.

Love, Kalpana

• • •

c/o Marion Gaskell Associates
Top Floor
71 Denmark Street
London W1

Dear Kalpana,

Some people get it into their heads that they have to keep the same hairstyle for ever, but what you find out is that there are all sorts of different things you can do with hair that is fun and also improves the appearance. No way would I have it spikey or shaved or that, but you can definitely make it blonder or put it up if you want, or sometimes cut it short if what your after is a new look. Different sorts of waves are a good idea and even ringlets but the most important bit is to make sure it suits the shape of your face.

Sincerely yours,
Maria Tambini

···

12 Cowal Road,
Craigmore,
Isle of Bute,
PA20 3TF

8 May 1980

Dear Maria,

I think your hair is nice no matter what style you make it.

You're certainly getting to know a lot about it, anyway, but I suppose that's a big part of life in the Big Smoke.

I wish you'd tell me about your new friends and how everything went at the stage school. It said something about it in the paper and it sounded fantastic. Are the teachers a good laugh or do they just give you loads of work all the time? My dad and me had a jumble sale in the square to raise money for Dr Barnardos. I kept a couple of books for you and I might send them but my mum says you're probably too busy just at the moment.

I have been watching the charts to see if your new single goes in. You are much better than Sheena Easton and Kelly Marie and bloody well Diana Ross, I'm not kidding, so I bet you next week you'll storm in. I don't know if you listen to bands as well, but personally I like The Jam, Police, and Dexy's Midnight Runners.

This is a rubbish pen so I'll sign off now Maria and hope to hear from you soon.

Love Kalpana

···

45 St George's Terrace,
London NW1

Dear Kalpana Jagannadham,

A hint of blusher on the cheekbones, the chin, and the forehead accentuates the bone structure of the face and makes everything stand out. Lip pencil lasts longer than lipstick and you can get it right more times. Eye-shadow will stay on longer if you give your eyelids a dusting of powder first.

Sincerely yours,
Maria Tambini

···

12 Cowal Road,
Craigmore,
Isle of Bute,
PA20 3TF

12 August 1980

Dear Maria,

*I have sent you five letters and heard nothing back. What is wrong?
Are you too busy? Just tell me if you are and I'll stop bugging you. Your
last letter said nothing about what you are up to. Please answer this I
want to tell you about my results and everything. Miss you.*

Love Kalpana

• • •

12 Cowal Road,
Rothesay,
Isle of Bute,
PA20 3TF

28 September 1980

Dear Maria,

*You can't be friends with someone and ignore all their letters. Are
you angry or something? If I have done something to upset you it is
better if you tell me.*

Love Kalpana

• • •

12 Cowal Road,
Craigmore,
Isle of Bute,
PA20 3TF

30 October 1980

Dear Maria,

*I just want to say goodbye. I am sad you can't write to me but un-
derstand you're probably too busy now. I will always remember all the
fun we had together. Please look after yourself.*

Love Kalpana

5 • *Marion*

If you want anything said, ask a man. If you want something done,
ask a woman. That has always been my motto I don't mind telling

you. It may be the cock that crows but it's the hen that lays the eggs. Showbusiness is just like any other business I'm afraid: if you don't work hard and fight for what's yours then you may as well just pack up and go home.

For three years that little girl has worked like the proverbial Trojan. I must say it is quite delightful having her about the house. She is like me: she sees the point of a day's work. When the record came out she did *Top of the Pops* and after that the record was a hit. I'm sure that little girl travelled to every single Woolworths in the country you know. Half the time the poor thing grabbed a handful of pick'n'mix on the way out the door and that was lunch. Jolly hard work. She opened supermarkets and petrol stations. We had her advertising everything from Yamaha organs to jumpsuits. Oh she was in demand all right. If God had given us the power to duplicate people like Maria Tambini we'd never go short.

I retired her from *Opportunity Knocks* after she won it for the seventh time. It was becoming a nonsense. They just couldn't find anybody to challenge her. So we were off. Hughie Green of course was having none of it. Such an argumentative little man. That show was on its last legs anyway, we all said that. But Green, he is an institution no question, don't get me wrong, and he's done a lot for British talent over the years, but disputatious! He caused no end of resentment at LWT, and before that it was the BBC—he took them to court and lost. It's a problem in this business you know, you get every kind of botheration. Some people are never satisfied. But I won't cut the man short. He has been around a long time. When I took Maria off the show he caused a terrible row and we didn't communicate for some time after that. Well, it's a tough business. One can't win them all, and that's just the way it is I'm afraid.

We took Eric Sharples and the Band and did a summer season at Bridlington. Now that is when she really came into her own as a performer. Such confidence. Maria was always full of giggles and she has that outlook money can't buy. If people say we gave her too much work they don't know her. The girl wanted to work. She really did. It is my job to pass on the offers and I have to say she always wanted the job. In Bridlington she sold out every night that first season and there were coaches coming from as far as Southport. One really can't argue with that kind of success. Maria didn't anyway.

I never understand that family. They come down maybe just the once at Christmas or something, we are perfectly happy to see them, but they don't really seem to get the point of Maria, coming down to London with plastic bags full of potato scones and those frightful square sausages and fizzy drinks. I think they always make her feel a little nostalgic, which I agree may be no bad thing for a singer, even a young one, but they all seem a bit, well, pained. Maria and I have a pact: we don't talk about the past, only what is coming next, so I must confess I don't know anything about the life they live up there. Of course, you can never really tell how people live their lives. Far be it from me to say. But as time goes on I notice how Maria gets upset by them. The girl has achieved a certain fame and she travels a lot. You can't pin her down and I suppose it's unfortunate when things kind of stall with a family. It's a shame really. But what can you do? It can't be helped. We always give them their place.

We've had clients staying with us over the years, especially in the early days. The old house in Marylebone was at one time more like an arts club. But nobody stayed the way Maria has; we really wanted her to grow up with us and she loves the business. We have a good arrangement with the parents about her earnings—so much for expenses, so much for keep, and they take care of some, and the rest is put away for Maria.

She understands the seaside mentality, and goes down an absolute storm round the coast, doing her bit with the local newspapers and that sort of thing. In Blackpool she was just like a normal young girl on her holidays. We have Polaroid snaps of her on the dodgem cars and the big wheel. You wouldn't believe it—so guileless—and then that evening she would be tapping and jumping and ripping up the Hollywood songbook. Good old Maria. The word trouper was absolutely invented for her. If you plugged her into the national grid, I swear you'd fuse all the kettles in the country. It really is remarkable to be so innocent and yet so knowing with a great song. It's the time of our lives.

Attention is good for Maria. She is simply one of those remarkable people who deserves all the attention they get. We took her on

Eric and Ernie's show, and God bless the boys but she outperformed the two of them. We put out her second album, *Rockaby*, and it's gone Top Ten in Finland and Japan. They want us to go and do a charity special in Vegas. I've spoken to them at Italia Conti, it's all sorted out for time off, so we are going. Maria has that old-fashioned charm and they're going to just adore her in Vegas. But first there's the London Palladium. Really. I ask you. Is there any more to life once you play the Palladium?

I must say I get irritated with the press. Of course you can't control everything they write, and it's not my job to do so, but they keep harping on about Maria being a child star, and they make too much of the Rothesay business. She is a young performer, as Lulu was, as Petula was, and Judy Garland, but she is totally in command of herself, and more of an adult, frankly, than half the people in this business. They always want to picture her holding some dreadful ice-cream cone. Stuff and nonsense. Maria is a mature star now of the stage and television. She can hold her own in any company. She is not one of those now-you-see-her-now-you-don't light entertainment dunces. As far as I'm concerned Maria is like Streisand. She is a proper star of the television era and that will never change.

The *Daily Mirror* call her 'cuddly'. I won't stand for any of this 'cuddly'. The papers always want to stick people in a pigeonhole, that's their problem. The *Radio Times* called her, what was it—'the moon-faced, diminutive balladeer from Bute'. Where on earth did that one come from? Her look is improving all the time. Everyday she is more in charge of herself, more perfect, and that's what separates the men from the boys in this business, I'm always telling her. Sometimes you have to give things up to gain the best. And that is what Maria is doing every day; she's working all God's hours to be the best in the business.

We had the room redecorated for her. Something a bit younger and more with it. Fearfully bright. She's a young woman now, but she still has that lovely accent and such a bubbly way about her. The other night it was terribly funny. We were having a cigarette outside the BBC theatre at Shepherds Bush Green, Richard and I, and Bernie Winters and some of the dancers from the Cannon & Ball Show, and suddenly Maria leaned out of the top dressing room window with half her make-up still on, a towel around her neck, this little window, and she broke into a soprano version of that song, 'I Don't Like Mondays'. She's just the sweetest thing.

She took a glass of water to her room and closed the door as soon as we got home. So tired. I finished signing some letters up in my study and then looked through the blinds at the city and the West End. It's amazing to look out and see all the city's compartments closing down for the night. But some of us take our time getting to sleep I'm afraid. It's a frightful bore. My husband puts his head on the pillow and in seconds he's out like a light. What a sweet man. Don't know where I'd be without him. I sometimes think we love our husbands most in the hours they're asleep. I'm bloody well thrilled when the day comes to an end, mind you, and the phones go quiet, and tomorrow is another problem. I like a whisky and water in my favourite armchair. Even at that time it can be jolly noisy outside: from the top of the house you can hear the wolves howling half the night over in Regent's Park.

6 · Personality

'Squeeze those lemons,' said Mr Wall the balletmaster, walking up and down the line of girls at the barre, pointing his stick and waving a finger. 'Round and through, round and through,' he said. 'Straighten your supporting leg and bend and hold and up. Louisa. Please maintain turnout on the legs and *développé*, and one, and two, and lift, and arabesque. Hold. Hold. Hold. And arms. And down.'

Mr Wall always wore the same outfit to class, brown cord trousers with frayed bottoms and a blue leotard that revealed a ridge of bones on his chest. On his feet he had wooden clogs sticky with resin, and sometimes, on a warm day in a fit of macho zeal—rare in an English balletmaster and unforgettable in Mr Wall—he would kick one of his clogs out of the open window in order to demonstrate an essential pointedness of the feet. Yet he would only ever raise his leg about half as high as he used to manage, showing in one swift movement that he had passed thirty years old and had no intention of breaking his back for Italia Conti. Mr Wall was all eyes and cheekbones. His feet were ugly, gnarled, and showed every minute of their years.

'*Battement frappé.* And...Beat, beat. Hold. Beat, beat. Hold. Girls: lift out of your waists and rotate your hips. You are sagging. You are sagging! Do you hear me or am I talking to myself? Louisa. Maria! You are like elephants today. Beat, beat. Hold. Chins up. Yes, and yes, and beat, beat, hold. And first position arms. And double-beat, double-beat, *plié*, and up!'

If some of the girls were inattentive, glued to their copies of *The Stage,* Mr Wall was always guaranteed the attention of two women, the pianist Mrs Mimms, who lived in Peckham and played for bus fare, and Miss Thompson, a former Tiller girl who taught modern dance at the school three days a week. 'This is not a fitness class,' Mr Wall often said, 'and it is not for deportment. Even if there are no Lynn Seymours in here you'll learn a bit of discipline if it does me in.'

Miss Thompson came in with a full face of make-up. She carried a pot of Leichner in her handbag, the contents of which were not always blended well on her from jaw to neckline, and she also carried a comb and a packet of kirby-grips, which she used to maintain her hair in a bun. Mr Wall and Miss Thompson would sometimes demonstrate a movement together, and they seemed harmonious enough, though on closer scrutiny you could see that her experienced gold heels had the advantage over his clogs when it came to modern rhythm. Mr Wall was very much the artist at Italia Conti, a fact which made Miss Thompson blush with pleasure under her make-up, but the girls had crushes of their own, and Miss Thompson, besotted, experienced, pzazzy Miss Thompson, was often the main subject of their admiration.

'Five, six, seven, eight,' said Miss Thompson, 'kick-ball-change, kick-ball-change, clap, stretch, turn, clap.'

The room smelled of sweat and resin and extra-curricular cigarettes. The whole of professional London smelled like that to Maria. If you stood on the squeaky floor covered in daylight from the windows, watching yourself in the full-length mirrors, the hours passed in a sort of immense whiteness, and your mind could float any-where: she noticed this, standing that way, her eyes going into the mirror, aware of the music that travelled from faraway rooms to be absorbed in the bleached-out drama of her concentration.

She mixed only slowly with the other girls. Most of them came from places she'd never heard of, and they were in a funny position in relation to her, having more knowledge of life perhaps, but less of the business. In the Maths class she got sent out for ignoring the les-sons. The teacher came up behind her and noticed she was writing something at the back of her jotter. It had nothing to do with Maths. She had spent weeks filling the jotter with the names of all the fa-mous people she could think of.

'You have to do some ordinary work,' said her housemaster, Mr Keening, who almost admired her.

'She's not very clever,' said one of the girls.

'She's been on *Parkinson*,' said another.

'So?'

'You don't have to be clever for what she's doing. She's got an amazing voice. She works.'

Most of the girls envied Maria, and she was treated as a sort of oddity at Italia Conti, an enviable freak, just as she had been at school.

Miss Thompson started taking her after-hours for private les-sons. Sometimes they worked hard all the way to supper-time on routines from musicals. 'I love it when you get to know the moves and then you can just go with the music and forget them,' Maria said.

'That's the goal,' said Miss Thompson. 'Don't think about the moves, just learn them, then dance.'

Mr Wall thought she needed more suppleness.

Mr Keening thought she shouldn't sing with groups.

Mr Epping thought she needed more Maths.

Miss Thompson thought she should relax a bit.

Mrs Gaskell wanted her to work.

'Everybody wants me to listen to them,' Maria said to her mother one afternoon, speaking from a telephone box in Vauxhall. She al-ways used phone boxes; she didn't like speaking to her mother from the house in Primrose Hill.

'You haven't been phoning me,' said her mother. 'You have to phone your mother. I know you.'

'I know,' said Maria.

'You've only got one mother, and she knows how hard you've worked. Ignore them. D'you hear me, Maria? Those people are just doing a job. My God if I was down there I would take a strip off those people.'

'Never mind.'

'How do you think this makes me feel? Hundreds of miles away and there's nothing I can do. You never listen to me, I've said what people are like.'

'It's okay, mum.'

'I only want the best for you, Maria. I know it's all working out down there, but, you know, sometimes I think you're a wee bit selfish.'

Maria stared at the cars. Someone was pointing at her from a car parked at the lights. 'There's just so much . . .'

'And d'you think it's easy up here? Let me tell you, lady, you've got it comfortable.'

'Mum.'

'The bloody way things are here, lady. You don't know the bloody half of it. London. Bloody London. You don't know how lucky you are.'

'Mum.'

'Privileges. Bloody easy time of it. You want to come up here, lady, and work in this café for a week, see—'

'Mum. It's not right. It's not right what you're saying. You started off saying you knew what I was meaning. I'm in rehearsals for the show and I'm working hard. What am I doing wrong?'

'Nothing.' There was silence on the line.

'Mum. Everything's good.'

'Is it, Maria? Is everything good? Is everything in your wee fucking world good?'

'I was just saying it was a wee bit tiring. Everybody wants me to be a bit better.'

'Well, listen you to me, lady. You could be better. These people are paid to know what they're talking about. People can forget you,

you know. Oh aye. You can easily be forgotten. Make no mistake about that. You just go back to that school and decide what you're doing, Maria, and what it is you want out of life, because nobody's got time in this world for moaners.'

'That's the pips going.'

'What?'

'The pips. That's the money ran out.'

'Cheerio then.'

Maria waited for her mother to back-track or say something else. She put another coin in, one she'd held back, and she waited for her mother, and eventually her mother did say something. 'Giovanni's moved in with another woman,' she said.

Maria hung up.

MISS THOMPSON was trying to explain what happens in *West Side Story*. 'The main girl is from Puerto Rico,' she said, 'and these people are immigrants in America.'

'She's called Maria,' said Maria.

'That's right, the same as you. And your name is Tambini, so that means you're what?'

'Italian. My grandparents came to Scotland from Italy.'

'Right. As immigrants. So, you know, this is a story you can relate to. This is a story about people coming from one country to another and trying to make a living.'

'I love the songs,' said Maria.

'But to sing the songs you have to understand what they're about.'

'I do,' said Maria.

'What happened to all the Italians in the war?' asked Miss Thompson. Maria tapped the bottom of her shoe.

'They were on the other side.'

'Yes. Did that involve your own family?'

'No.'

'It must have.'

'No. They ran a café in Scotland. Everybody liked them.' Miss Thompson looked into Maria's eyes, wiped her hands, and stood up.

'Okay,' she said, 'I want you to work as a group on this number.

It has a cha-cha-cha feel. We're going to link up the movement, then Mr Keening will take you for the songs. Sexy number this. Okay.'

Miss Thompson reapplied her lipstick and took two of the other girls into the corner to give them steps. Maria leaned on the barre and arched back, mouthing words, and when she came back up she stared at herself in the mirror. When she looked this closely at her own face she caught something in her eyes that made her feel it was somebody else looking. Her body was apart from her. The person with thoughts was different from the person with arms and legs, a stomach and a face. This was the first time this thought had ever occurred to her, that day in the mirror at Italia Conti.

'She's outgrown the school,' said Mr Keening.

'She had outgrown the school before she arrived,' said Mr Wall.

'She was only here for the school lessons,' said Mr Epping. 'She was here because of the schoolwork quota.'

'She's a much better dancer than when she arrived,' said Miss Thompson.

'She's outgrown it. She's old enough to leave,' said Mr Keening.

'Always was too grown,' said Mr Wall, 'and you can't discipline instincts like hers. She knows what she has to do before she does it. Such energy in such a small body.'

'She's very special,' said Miss Thompson.

'She's really sort of shy,' said Mr Keening.

'Except when it counts,' said Mrs Mimms.

'It always counts,' said Mr Keening.

'I don't know about that, Mr Keening,' she said, 'but when it counts not to be shy I've never seen a girl like Maria Tambini, and I've been coming to this school almost since the day it opened.'

Mrs Mimms put half a custard cream on the rim of her saucer and picked a crumb from the corner of her mouth. 'But, I *do* say,' she said, 'have you ever met a girl so completely devoted to succeeding?'

'She has succeeded,' said Mr Keening.

'All succeed who come here, Mr Keening.'

'In their own way, yes,' he said.

Miss Thompson raked her hair with a perm comb. 'I don't really know how to put it,' she said. 'She follows herself with her eyes.'

'That's the training,' said Mr Wall.

'She doesn't have any small talk.'

'It's the training. Being in showbusiness and all the people around her. It's just the training.'

'She's really something of a performer,' said Mrs Mimms.

Mr Keening could smell his own aftershave. He wondered if he had overdone it that morning. 'There's a problem with jealousy,' he said.

'Oh, most certainly,' said Mrs Mimms.

'I think she's had it a lot tougher than she's ever said.'

'She doesn't speak,' said Mr Wall. 'She smiles and works hard and golly she sings, but everyone else talks. She doesn't speak much to the others.'

'There's jealousy all right,' said Miss Thompson. 'It's always a problem with a girl like that. The others see her getting loads of work and it brings out the worst.'

'It's just in the way of things—here, I mean,' said Mr Wall.

'Has there been bullying?' asked Mr Keening.

'No,' said Miss Thompson. 'Names.'

'Swearing?'

'No,' she said. 'Things about looks. You know what it's like. She's already got a career. They try to take her down a peg or two. They say things about the way she looks.'

'She's tough,' said Mr Wall.

'A tough cookie, as they say,' said Mrs Mimms. 'She would have to be something of the kind.'

'Strange girl,' said Mr Keening. 'Nice, talented. I think we've done all we can do for her now.'

Mr Wall rose from his seat in the staff room. 'It's the training,' he said. 'I don't suppose she's had a very ordinary time of it. She's been singing since she was seven. She's got experience. She knows the game.'

'You never know, do you?' said Miss Thompson. 'Girls like that don't come out of nothing.'

'She doesn't say much,' said Mrs Mimms.

'She sings,' said Mr Keening.

'Everybody speaks for her,' said Miss Thompson.

'So what?' said Mr Wall. 'That's who she is.'

7 · The Palladium

An eye, coming from the Westway, the tower blocks overhead and the diesel fumes behind the walls, and down there the railway tracks silver with use in the early evening as the trains come in to Paddington, and as they leave, ignorant of all motion besides their own, the trains squeal and chug and bellow inside the vapour of London. Slick with rain, the passengers sink behind their *Evening Standards*, their minds glazing over with the day's thoughts; tunnelled in warmth, sleep will ingest them, as their hearts pound softly for home.

An eye, passing this, passing St Mary's Hospital, its yellow windows and damp brick, the unwell captured in their beds and the smell of fruit and stewed tea hanging about the wards. Inside, there is movement in the television rooms, the convalescing, the diseased are wearing out the hour in their carpet slippers, the dinner trays undevoured while London darkens, while ambulances gather at the emergency doors. A man dies to the sound of laughter escaping from *Blankety Blank*. A nurse loses her temper with a bunch of flowers too cumbersome for their vase. A woman goes up in the lift to see the mother she has never met. Porters smoke on the stairwell and remember the worst and the best of Friday night. A Pakistani gentleman says prayers to himself, too old to wait, and ignores the football commentary coming from an adjacent radio. A doctor checks a chart and remembers his wife's birthday, and out in the corridor a confectionery machine jams and keeps the money. A bone is set, and a lady who grew up in Cornwall remembers the long walk to school.

An eye, at speed, passing Marylebone Town Hall where confetti lies in blue-reflecting puddles. An eye, coming along Marylebone Road and crossing Baker Street, reaches the dome of the Planetarium with its countless stars fixed in the dark, and Madame Tussaud's, with its famous unbreathing figures, the wax hands and eyes and nylon hair quite still in the cold rooms, famous names smiling for ever, robes and tiaras perfectly balanced to meet the demands of the paying public, and down in the basement a Victorian Whitechapel of the mind lies in mechanical silence, everything switched off, the air dense with what remains of the day's wonder over those cobbled lanes, as waxwork girls look from the taverns and fear for their lives.

Waxworks: they live here in their strange way, seeming real, famous women, as much looking as looked upon, their startled faces now coated in publicity. Madame Tussaud took a mould of Marie Antoinette's severed head as it lay unattended on the grass of the cemetery on the rue d'Anjou.

An eye hovers at the keyhole of Madame Tussaud's. The museum is silent but for the ghosts of female voices.

'Surely people will soon tire of hearing about my weaknesses?' says Marie Antoinette to the dark.

An eye, brightening, going on, passes the Royal Academy of Music near Ulster Place, where on the third floor a young Japanese lady plays Elgar's Cello Concerto in E Minor. She stops because she is told she is not sitting properly. She stops again because she is still too bent. The bow is bouncing off the strings, she is told, and she blushes; the man's eyes are telling her she will never be great. She is told the traffic outside is more musical. The young woman stares at the window and wonders if the sound in her head will ever stop. She wonders if she will ever honour the music, or honour herself: 'The traffic is more musical,' the man says again.

An eye, the self-same eye, travelling at speed round Park Crescent and through the columns into Portland Place, zooming above taxis and wet branches strewn by the road, black bags of rubbish heaped in the doorways; an eye, the same eye, crossing Weymouth Street and New Cavendish Street, over the statues of proud men, British men in the iron throes of remembrance, Joseph Lister for furthering the use of antiseptics, George Stuart White the hero of Kandahar, and Quintin Hogg, educationalist, founder of the Polytechnic Day School for Boys and author of the first *Boys' Handbook*.

An eye, the breeze oncoming, racing down Portland Place and along the window ledges of Broadcasting House; inside the building a hundred microphones are live, and the world listens, and music plays to distant ears. There are voices thrown back and forth in the studios, yet along the corridors, hung with the heads-and-shoulders of celebrities, there is a strange quietness at the BBC. An eye travels over Oxford Circus. Newspaper sellers shout, 'Late final!' A German couple rehearse their arguments while carrying a load of Hamleys bags, each person balanced with goods, each with his, with her own scales of justice. A girl from Boots, a boy from Westminster School with a bag full of sums. Drivers, shoppers, beggars, laughers. A man with a placard against protein. A woman selling sweet peanuts and dreaming of life in Europe. A policeman with no chance of promotion. A poet with an acceptance letter from a small magazine.

Legislators, truants, accountants, Scots. A beautiful woman who works for Asprey's in Bond Street and used to steal good pens when she worked at Harrods. Men who love their mothers more than their wives. Women who love one child more than another. Children out late, who think their parents are good for a few quid, and grandmothers, fresh from the escalators at John Lewis, who quite enjoy being pitied in their old age and wish it had started with their families years ago. Tourists, seamstresses, barmen, lawyers, an airline pilot, an art historian. An actor who works as a clown for kids' parties. A gentleman who sells Christmas cards in the hall at St James's Church every year but has serious doubts about the existence of God. A librarian from the London Library who pockets her own books. A red-haired plumber who worked on a bathroom that morning in Kensington Gore and knowingly drove a nail into a supply pipe and left it there to leak. A woman from New Zealand with a lump in her breast. A man who despairs of Britain and all it has become. A boy who will die soon in a field at the other side of the world. A girl with blonde hair, from Leicester, who will go home tonight and find that her boyfriend wants her to be his wife. She will cry with happiness before midnight and soon choose her dress and walk down the aisle of a familiar church with a notion the world was ordered for her. A young man from Bethnal Green playing saxophone, the notes drifting over the crowd and into the cold air over Oxford Circus this night and never again.

An eye over Argyll Street. An eye in the melée of everyday things, moving up the street and over it all, past the cafés and the people counting their change, and low down now, next to the pavement where people aren't sure where they are, turning maps over in their hands in the rain. A girl with black nail-polish outside a pub wearing a T-shirt that says 'Victim'. An eye travels up the doors of the theatre;

it climbs up a white column and moves over the bold letters of a word—PALLADIUM—and creeping around the white façade and over the side of the building, it finds an open window.

A distant sound of people shouting and hammering and a tinkling of glasses travels along the backstage corridors of the theatre. Red swirls on the carpet, and the walls smell of gloss paint and further along this smell mingles with that of stale cigarette smoke. A blackboard stands against a stairwell chalked-up with the words 'First Half' and a group of names:

FAITH BROWN
RONNIE BARKER
OLIVIA NEWTON-JOHN
ROGER MOORE
CAROL CHANNING
HOWARD KEEL
THE BRIAN ROGERS DANCERS
ELTON JOHN

An eye inches forward above the old carpet then hovers at a door. The door is part open, and an eye passes into the room and stops before a long mirror surrounded with bulbs, and it fixes at last on the face of a girl, who knew it was coming, an eye like a camera from her childhood. Maria Tambini, staring into the mirror, lost in her own eyes.

SHE FELT dizzy looking at herself. She took sticks out of the makeup box and rubbed more red on her cheeks. She had noticed it before: sometimes, if she stared at her face for long enough, she grew dizzy, and what she saw became distorted, like an image in a dream of avarice. She had been in her dressing-room for hours, her hair was done and she had applied her make-up several times. The first two times she wiped it off with soap and water and started again. Her eyes were large in the mirror.

There was a sink in the corner. She stood up. Carefully, without disturbing the tissues tucked around her neck, she went to the sink and vomited. She ran the cold tap while her head was bent down:

there wasn't a great deal to wash away, but she vomited again, while the tap was still running, and when she straightened up her main worry was whether her teary eyes would make the eyeliner run. Returning to the mirror, she took a tube of toothpaste from the smallest make-up bag and, squeezing an inch onto a finger, rubbed it over her teeth and around the inside of her mouth. She felt very clean now. She felt pure. There was something about the taste of mint.

She had no idea how long Hughie Green had been standing behind her. 'You look just swell sitting there.'

'Thank you very much, Mr Green.'

'That was a pretty terrific rehearsal, Maria.'

'Such a big stage. I've never seen such a stage before.'

'A big stage for mighty big talents, my dear. The first time I walked out there and heard the old rustling of the audience, my God...'

She smiled. She'd heard it before. 'You'd come home.'

He winked. 'How well you know me.'

'Were you frightened?'

'Never. Never scared. I was only scared they wouldn't notice me, or they'd take me off early or something. I came here with a gang show and I did the old soft-shoe shuffle and I got the girl. Easy. It was all easy in those days.'

'Did you see Eric and Ernie's show?'

'You were on it. A great success, Maria. You were terrific, everyone is saying the same.'

'I just laughed all the time.'

'No, but you sang.'

'Aye, I sang.'

'You really sang. You're just like I am, Maria—television was invented for you. You stopped the show.'

'Mrs Gaskell said the phone has rung all day with different sorts of work.'

'You be careful.'

'Good things. Abroad and that.'

'Careful. You just watch yourself. You be careful she doesn't have you overdoing it.'

'Exciting isn't it? It's all fine. Mad though.'

'I said be careful what you do. You think there's freedom to do what you want in this business, but you've got to have good advice. Mrs Gaskell's an old hand. She doesn't tread lightly and you can upset people in this business. People are easily upset.'

'I'm sixteen, Mr Green.'

'You're a baby. We were all babies once.' He paused. 'The Great British Public—all those mums and dads, they know a good turn when they see it all right. An American director I worked with used to say to me, "Hughie, talent conquers everything, and it can eventually conquer the talented as well."'

'It's all experience,' said Maria.

'Is that what Mrs Gaskell told you?'

'Just experience under your belt.'

'Did your mother tell you that?'

Maria turned in her chair. 'Mr Green, why would my mother tell me things? She lives in Rothesay. My mother's not in the business. She lives in Rothesay.'

'You're her daughter.'

'Well spotted.'

'Don't be sarcastic, Maria. It doesn't suit you, kiddo. Give us a smile there.'

Maria shook her head and showed her teeth. Hughie Green walked to the side of the dressing-room and laid down the book he was carrying. A plastic ruler was jammed between the pages of the book, *Flight to Arras*.

'Do you like books?' he asked, sitting on the edge of the dressing-table.

She wondered whether to say a true thing or not. Then quite suddenly she spoke five words. 'I've never read a book.'

'None?'

'Never all the way through,' she said. 'I've never had the time.'

'But you like stories?'

'We did some books at school,' she said, 'but just bits of them, for homework and things, and sometimes the teachers would read something. We had these reading cards. SRA. That's what it was called. You read bits of stories off cards and then answered questions from another card and depending how good you were you got a colour. I think olive was the highest and pink the lowest.'

'How extraordinary,' said Hughie Green, and then he paused. 'But you've been busy. I didn't have much schooling either, but my father loved books.'

'No,' she said, 'I think gold was the highest.'

They sat for a while in silence, Maria thinking of the reading cards in Rothesay, Hughie fingering the book's edges. 'My granny liked fairy stories,' she said, 'and they are the stories I remember. I don't know what my dad liked and my mum only likes real-life stories about people like Dolly Parton.' She smiled at the mirror. 'I loved my granny's stories.'

'Well, you're top of the bill tonight, Maria. I'm telling you, that's worth all the qualifications in the world. Huh? Who would have reckoned on that, huh? Those years ago.'

'I better get ready.'

'You look swell.'

'Ta.'

'Swell. One cute dame is what you're becoming. One cute dame I'm telling you. The old puppy fat is still there mind you, are you taking care of yourself?'

Maria blushed. 'It's not really me,' she said.

'Sorry, honey?' he said. 'Don't worry about any silly thing like that. You're looking good.'

She put down her comb and glanced in the mirror. 'Everybody says I look good, don't they? I look fat.'

'Not at all. You know this famous business of ours. We all have to look our best. You look great. You're growing up and I'm telling you it's one fine dame you're becoming.'

'How many people tonight?' she asked.

'Full house,' he said. 'Over two thousand. Engelbert is here and he's coming along to see you. One fine dame. You just give it the lot tonight, Maria. You're a star, do you hear me. My favourite. My girl, huh?'

Hughie Green had a way of looking round a room as if he wanted to suck out all its oxygen. He used words as if words were all he really had, snapping sentences shut in your face. He left Maria in a state of disorder in her dressing room. Her eyes were full of water and her hands were shaking, and when Mrs Gaskell arrived with a sheet of paper Maria was rubbing more toothpaste around the inside of her mouth.

'All right, dear?' said Mrs Gaskell. 'After the show there are some fans congregating at the stage door. They are armed with photographs and records that want signing. Righty-ho? I'm sure photographers will take the opportunity for snaps down there, so reapply, you know, before coming down. Richard will be there with the car.'

'That's all right,' said Maria.

'Good, good,' said Mrs Gaskell, 'but bear in mind the telephone. They're putting through a call from the *Daily Record* any minute.'

'Do I have to?' said Maria. 'I don't feel like doing interviews right now. I just want to sit.'

'No Maria. Come, come now. It's the *Record* and you know they are good to us, so buck up, please, it will only take a few minutes.'

'I wish I could just sit.'

'That's enough, Maria! Come now, it's a special night and we won't go spoiling everything. It's the *Record.*'

Maria grew unfamiliar to herself in the mirror. She sighed and knocked over a group of lipsticks.

'Now listen young lady.'

'Now listen young lady.'

'Don't start this now.'

'Don't start this now.'

'Stop it, Maria!'

'Stop it, Maria.'

'Stop!'

Maria looked up at Mrs Gaskell and narrowed her eyes. 'Listen lady,' she said.

Mrs Gaskell shook her head and folded a towel. 'I don't appreciate this tonight of all nights,' she said. 'All that's required of you is that you behave professionally. It's no skin off my nose, my dear . . .'

'No skin off my nose.'

'Enough!'

'No skin off my nose.'

The telephone rang. Mrs Gaskell lifted it up and smiled into the receiver. 'Absolutely, Sam. How lovely. Yes it's very exciting and a tremendous buzz down here this evening. Absolutely.'

'A tremendous buzz,' said Maria.

'You're not kidding there,' said Mrs Gaskell, giving Maria a look. 'I'd be delighted. Please do. Jolly good...'

'Jolly good.'

'She's right beside me.'

Maria took the phone and looked down into the table of makeup and scrunched-up tissues. Her voice immediately became soft and more Scottish, she giggled, and in a moment she was giving herself on the phone.

'Are you missing Bute?' asked the journalist.

'I'm missing all my family,' she said. 'There are so many big stars in the Palladium tonight I really can't believe it. But everybody up there in Scotland will be watching I hope.'

'Is London your home now?' he asked.

'Well, I really do miss the seaside,' she said, 'but I have a lot of family now. Millions of them.'

'Is it a big audience tonight?'

'I think it's very big.'

'And how do you feel to have come this far so early in your career, Maria?'

'Well it's such an honour to be sharing a stage with such big names. A thrill, really.'

'Did you listen to them all when you were wee?'

'Oh yes. My mum and I used to play the records at home and I have very fond memories of Scotland.'

Mrs Gaskell folded the towels and left the room.

'And are you rich now, Maria?'

'Well, I don't really need very much money but my manager and all the people look after things.'

'Enough to buy a new dolly?'

'Well, if I wanted one, that would be fine.'

'Hughie Green is the compere. How does it feel to be back working with the man who started your career?'

'Oh, he's a lovely man and very professional. It's always nice to see old faces.'

'And what's next for you after this?'

'Well, there's a lot of work. Abroad, and then a new album is coming out in May and, oh... what else? My manager's arranged a tour and it's all going really well.'

'Any plans to perform in Scotland?'

'I have fond memories of all the people there and hopefully it won't be long before I get the chance to sing for them again in the near future.'

She put down the phone then crossed over to the door and pushed it shut. She put her back against the door and stood for a moment. The room was empty but the surrounding mirrors reflected her back at herself from a dozen angles. Everywhere she looked there was another version of herself.

'You're in charge,' she said.

THE LIFE underground. Caverns and chambers filled with darkness—arches, corridors, greasy pipes carrying gas to the metropolis, cracked sewers, bad air, ancient bones, mud, layers of broken plaster, former shelters, night-gloop, the remnants of the Great Fire, dust, soil and the mash of brick, passageways, vaults, lost merchandise, skin cells, a labyrinth of vanished facts, pavingstones, Victorian whispers, telephone cables, a Saxon cross of powdered sandstone, down there, in London.

And tunnels, the tunnels of London, conveying people towards Cockfosters, Brixton, Walthamstow, Ruislip, the end of things. In a tube carriage, Central Line, stopped just short of Oxford Circus, stands a group of strangers packed together in the narrow train. They stand straight and look at each other's shoes, eyes averted from each other's eyes, and some of them look at their books, not reading.

It is 9.45 p.m.

The tube is stalled in the tunnel. There is heat between the people in the carriage, and close up a fragrance of shampoos on rain-dampened hair, a faint notion of aftershaves, coffees, and never has this happened before, these same people, this exact spot of the world underground, then round them the tube train shudders into motion. They are gone.

Overhead, through the tunnel's roof, a layer of bricks gives way to iron filings, to nubs of wood, to walkways, and on and upwards, to unbroken stones and dreck, compacted earth, and then there are shards of wine bottles embedded in a layer of sand near the surface—remnants of a Victorian wine cellar—and finally the beginning of foundation stones, laid in 1908, and then a thick layer of wooden floorboards.

Through the floor and rising still are basement rooms, dark and ill-attended, with old, painted cloths and screens lying around, and one large room's corners are heaped with dustcovered blankets and painted shoes. A voice comes near, amplified.

'...came to an end after a mightily successful run on both radio and television...'

Up through a layer of plaster ceiling and wooden beams.

'...a little girl who has become one of the most sought-after performers in the business, and a personal success for me...'

Passing a layer of electrical wires.

'...delighting audiences. I mean that most sincerely...'

Through the quiet space of an orchestra pit.

'Your Royal Highness, lords, ladies and gentlemen. Please give a warm Palladium welcome...'

And slowly, at last, slowly, at last, through the wooden boards of a stage and into the air.

The stage was black. A spotlight came on, and standing at the centre was Maria Tambini, her bright, even teeth smiling the long distance. Poreless skin, hair blow-dried into waves, her eyes saying yes, her blue dress sparkling. She held a microphone and as she walked forward the music began. A huge backdrop of coloured butterflies brightened to the rear, the lamps burned, and suddenly, as the music crashed into life, many dancers in black and white trousers and skirts ran from the wings to encircle her. She stretched out her hands. She came to the front and swayed with her palms held out and in an instant there was a whole event crowded around her voice. Up there Maria was the very soul of vigour and good humour, and every note she sang was a declaration of plenty.

> Oh-oh-over and over
> I'll prove my love to you
> Over and over, what more can I do?
> Over and over, my friends say I'm a fool

But oh-oh-over and over
I'll be a fool for you

Cause you've got—
Personality
Walk—
Personality
Talk—
Personality
Smile—
Personality
Charm—
Personality
Love—
cause you got a great big heart
Well over—and over
I'll be a fool for you
Well, well, well over and over
What more can I do?

8 · *America*

Another season, Maria was sitting by the window of a plane flying to America. The month before, her mother and Alfredo had come to London and taken her from a private clinic, where she had spent several weeks, suffering from what the *Daily Mirror* called 'exhaustion'.

'I don't like London,' Rosa had said. 'It's that big, and the people are unfriendly.'

'Well, I'm glad you're here,' Maria said. 'And you Alfredo.'

'It's merely a glitch,' said Mrs Gaskell.

'What's that you're saying?' asked Rosa.

'A glitch,' said Mrs Gaskell, 'nothing to worry about. I think Maria hasn't been eating quite as well as she might.'

'She used to eat just fine,' said Rosa.

'Okay,' said Alfredo, 'she's on the mend. You're on the mend, aren't you darlin'?'

'I'm right as rain,' said Maria.

'Maybe it's time to come back up the road,' Rosa said. Maria frowned, and two spots of red came quickly on her cheeks, lighting her papery complexion.

'No,' she said. 'I want to work again.'

'London's too big,' said Rosa.

'There's plenty of work for her,' said Mrs Gaskell.

'It's not the same down here,' said Rosa. Maria stared into the blankets.

'No mum,' she said, 'it's not the same. This is where I live now and I want to sing again.'

Rosa's mouth twitched. She licked her lips and lifted up her head to show a fierce smile. 'Well,' she said, 'far be it from me . . .'

'Mum.'

'I don't know that you have a say, lady,' she said, 'and I was the one that stood by you when you wanted to go into all this.'

'I'm fine,' Maria said.

'Oh well, *you're* fine,' said Rosa, 'that's the main thing.'

'I think it's time for Maria to get some rest,' said Mrs Gaskell, putting another get-well card on the bedside cabinet and placing her hands on the bedclothes in a gesture of conclusion.

'If you don't mind, I'll decide when it's time to go,' said Rosa. She turned to Maria. 'I see a helluva difference in you, hen. You know the room is there for you if you want to pack this in.'

'No mum. I'm fine, honestly.'

'It's not really a failure or anything,' said Rosa. 'You don't need to see it that way.'

'I live here now,' said Maria.

'You live here now,' said Rosa.

They sat in silence.

'Say hello to the Winter Gardens for me, Uncle Alfredo,' said Maria.

'Of course I will,' he said. He winked. 'And you hurry up and get a few Italian songs into your act,' he said. 'You're giving us a right showing-up, so you are.'

Rosa stood up and closed her bag and wrestled with a drip-dry overcoat. She tightened the belt, leaned over the bed and kissed Maria's forehead. 'We'll away for the train now,' she said. 'It's been a nice few days and you'll be on the phone?'

'Cheerio mum,' said Maria. 'Say cheerio to Granny Lucia,' she said to Alfredo.

'I'll say *hello* to her,' he said. 'You'll be seeing her soon I hope. She's always asking for you.'

'Tell her I miss her.'

'And she misses you,' he said.

On the plane Maria lay back and watched the shapes of the clouds. She was tired. Mrs Gaskell sat next to her reading a programme from an opera she'd seen with her husband. 'I never quite find the time to read these,' she said.

Two men in front were talking in American accents. 'You should never make the mistake of thinking Las Vegas is normal,' one said.

'I know that,' said the other. 'It's a circus. Jesus Jones. It's the biggest friggin' circus in the world. I've never considered it normal even for a second.'

'Do you know what *Newsweek* said about Elvis when he first appeared there?' said the first man. 'They said he was like a jug of corn liquor at a champagne party. I'm serious.'

They both laughed.

'There's worse than that,' said the same one. 'You know that during the 1960s, when the nuclear tests were taking place, some of the big casinos used to run "bomb picnics" into the desert for gamblers and their families.'

'You're shittin' me?'

'Check it out,' he said, 'straight down the line.'

Mrs Gaskell paid no attention to the people in front. She read the programme for *La Bohème*, ate a petit four, and occasionally glanced at Maria's tray and suggested she try something. 'It'll be quite some time before they offer us anything again,' she said. Maria just scraped some cubes of roast potato under the chicken and stared out the window. Much later on, somewhere over Illinois, she pretended to eat a roll and butter. The pieces of bread went down the side of her seat; she rubbed the small pats of butter up her arms, into the skin, into the creases around her elbows, and eventually, as the smears began to dry, she felt somehow content, at one with the pure air outside the window.

THE LIGHTS of Las Vegas were known to her. Looking over the strip—the Sands, the Golden Nugget, the neon hearts and the miles of cars—she began to remember the promising suns and the night-lights of Bute. It was not any Bute that had ever existed in the world, but a place that lived in her mind, where the days were Tupperware-coloured and filled with summer dreams, where children lived as children in a painting, where even the rain was a habit of the emotions, and where imagined waves came rolling into an imagined harbour. Las Vegas—there now, alive, beneath her balcony—was simply a part of those imaginings, and in the full glow of the Nevada evening the city was familiar.

She was there to sing for one night only. The theatre could be found somewhere in the hotel, the MGM Grand; she was part of Dean Martin's Summer Benefit for the Retinitis Pigmentosa Foundation of America, and was staying in the hotel's Emerald Tower, where framed posters hung along the corridors. The posters advertised past concerts featuring the great heroes of song and dance, and that night they made Maria feel she was truly part of a special tribe. Mr Martin held her hand and told her she was 'a great little Italian kid from Scotland, *La Piccolina Signorina Lampadina*'.

Mrs Gaskell seemed almost to grind her teeth with pleasure; she blushed full of pride and professional well-being to be standing there with Dean Martin and the others. 'She's not nearly so young as she appears to be,' she said nervously.

Lucille Ball came over to Maria after rehearsals and said, 'God bless you, honey. You've sure got what it takes.'

'And might you be the fairy godmother?' said Liberace, putting his ringed hand out to Mrs Gaskell.

'I'm simply thrilled to meet you,' she said in return.

'Charmed,' he said. 'I love your English accent.' After a pause, during which Liberace stared at Maria and smiled, he told a story about being a young performer on the Colgate Comedy Hour. 'Now, that wasn't the day before yesterday,' he said.

'If you're ever in London...' said Mrs Gaskell.

'I'm very often in London.'

'How exciting. You must come and see us. If you give a concert...'

'So darling of you,' he said, and he smiled. 'I can't tell you how much a boy can miss the Savoy.'

'Quite,' said Mrs Gaskell.

Maria noticed how thin the gentleman's wrists were and how narrow his face. She felt jealous.

'Are you Catholic?' he asked her.

'Well, I suppose she is,' said Mrs Gaskell. Liberace ignored her and looked at Maria.

'Is that so, dear?' he said.

'Yes,' she said, 'I'm a Catholic.'

'I still say my prayers,' he said. 'I say them every night.' Maria didn't know how to reply. She smiled. He began to turn away and winked at her. 'We Catholics oughta stick together,' he said. 'All this *performance...*' He made the word long and swishy like his coat. 'We invented it, honey-pie.'

He walked off and was joined by the stage manager.

'Well,' said Mrs Gaskell, 'wasn't he just marvellous?'

Later in the day Maria sneaked down to the gaming hall to see the people winning and losing, and it was the circus atmosphere around the slot-machines that gripped her most. It seemed frightening after a while: all those lights, and the fixed look in the people's eyes, their fat hands cupping the coins, their fat arms pulling the lever, the wheels spinning.

Amusements.

She walked down the lanes of one-arm bandits and the sound of crashing coins and bleepers got to her for a moment. The noise was too loud and the people were over-weight and didn't care about losing the coins; they would just put more into the slot and keep staring at the machine.

And what happens if the amount just keeps getting bigger and bigger and the thing is spinning and there's nobody to stop it? The numbers. What if the machines just get so good at taking the money they begin to devour everything and then they devour the people while they're standing there?

Down the street was a Walkway of Fame—golden shoe-prints and hand-prints—made from casts left by many of the great performers who had come to Las Vegas. To get away from the slot machines, Maria walked the length of the strip. It was good exercise, she said to herself, and she was able to stop and try her own hands in the pavement prints. Sammy Davis Junior had small hands but long fingers: Maria's were so small they looked lost inside the brass crevices. Yet she wasn't satisfied to find her hands were smaller. Some of the casts had been taken from the prints at Mann's Chinese Theatre in Hollywood. It said so on a sign. 'Shirley Temple brought America through the Depression with a smile,' it also said. Maria grew excited when she saw Shirley Temple's prints on the ground. When she put her fingers into the brass, she felt the cold of the metal and at the same time realised she was touching something that maybe Shirley Temple had touched. She kept her hands there on the pavement, and her mind filled with old pictures. Around Shirley Temple's hand and tap-shoe prints were other tiny prints, Jackie Coogan, Baby Leroy, Deanna Durbin. Maria wasn't sure about some of them, but she put her hands in theirs anyway, and after a moment she felt sick. Her hands were too big for these prints. She felt faint. Her fingers were horrible.

She walked up and down the strip. She saw her shadow moving along the pavement in front of her, and after an hour she began to feel happy again, passing food places and breathing in the smells of onions and hamburgers. She passed all the places again and again and felt gratified with her shadow on the ground. It was like levitating. She needed nothing. She would eat nothing. She walked down the street and it was as if the whole street and the whole of Las Vegas had been built for Maria Tambini, and the traffic moved in response to her walking, and the people only existed as so many atoms squeezed and channelled by her presence on the street, by her power as she travelled forward, controlling everything, and her body seemed almost nothing, cleansed and empty like the shadow on the pavement, and for her the warm breeze itself was shaped and commandeered by her mood.

The theatre was hot and full of people clapping and laughing. Along with the excitement, feedback squealed from the amplifiers, but the applause covered it, and the stage was quickly a furnace of good cheer. Dean Martin and Maria Tambini are standing there together, smiling into their microphones. Mr Martin puts his arm around her waist. Maria wears a smile too big for her face and a skirt a few years too young.

'How are you, darling?'

'I'm fine.'

'You oughta take a rest cause you really worked hard there. You sing terrific. That's hard work you know.'

'Uh-huh.'

'You belt out a loud sound. That's hard work for a girl. A girl can't do it a lot but you do it enough for eleven girls.'

She giggles.

'You're cute. You're pretty and everything.'

'Thank you.'

'You sing terrific. I couldn't believe it. I thought there was a ventriloquist back there, like a big bear that was going "raaaaa".'

She covers her mouth with her hand.

'Are you thrilled to meet me? You should be.'

The audience laugh.

'Oh.'

'Do you wanna talk about something?'

'Yeh.'

'Like what?'

'Um. Um. Um. Swinging on a Star.'

'"Swinging on a Star". You wanna do that first?'

'All right.'

'You don't look like you mean it, little sister. You wanna do something else?'

'"Rockaby".'

He laughs. 'Don't start causing me trouble, honey. You're super-terrific. Okay boys—hit it.'

The brass section explodes into the song. Dean Martin stands back holding a drink and smiles approval at the audience while Maria gathers up the sound and belts it over the audience. 'Give it hell,' he says.

In her room that night she drank glass after glass of water from the bathroom. Crouching by the bed, with the sound of police sirens outside and the hotel television issuing canned laughter from the corner, she sucked a piece of toast and then spat it back onto the plate. She scraped a line of skin from a nectarine and licked the pulp inside. Her head pounded. She threw all the scraps into the bin and went into the closet where she found a bag with a furry pencil case in it. She counted out twenty laxatives and swallowed them with the water.

THEY CAME into Grand Central Station, the daylight glinting through the compartment, and opening her eyes, smarting, Maria saw the tracks and the other trains, the precise movements outside, and at the opening of the final tunnel they all seemed to pick up speed, the trains, and turned like silverfish into the depths of New York.

Maria loved how the station made her feel so small. The windows up there just cancelled you with beams of light: she walked beside Mrs Gaskell and felt invisible with so many people around her, and yet she was tugged by Mrs Gaskell's officious nature to be both present and correct, so they marched across the concourse and out of the station, Maria edged into occupation while wishing only to fade under the buildings and the glass.

'Will you eat something?' said Mrs Gaskell.

'Not hungry,' said Maria.

'This is a jolly good opportunity for you, Maria, so let's have none of your nonsense while we're here. I'm not your mother and I refuse to follow you around with a teaspoon.'

'Good. Nobody's asking you to.'

Mrs Gaskell stopped short of the line for the taxi. 'You're too bloody thin!' she said.

'I'm not,' said Maria. 'Everybody wants me to walk about like a blob. You just want me to be a blob. I ate my breakfast.'

'You put it in a tissue.'

'I didn't! I ate it! It's in my stomach.'

'Stop it, Maria. This is nonsense.'

'There's nothing the matter. Just leave me.'

'Maria.'

'I won't discuss this any more, okay? I am not standing here talking this kind of rubbish with you. I have eaten my breakfast and I feel very good if you must know.'

A driver with a black cap and a name-card came out of the crowd and helped them with the bags. 'I have such delightful memories of the park,' said Mrs Gaskell. They drove across town and Maria smiled out of the window on her side. Mrs Gaskell reached into her coat pocket and brought out a flapjack. She placed it on the seat between them. 'Please have a piece before the rehearsal,' she whispered. And then: 'I beg you.'

Maria glanced at it then continued to look out at the buildings on 59th Street and the steam coming out of the ground at the corner of 59th and Lexington. 'I don't deserve it,' she whispered.

'Sorry?'

Maria turned and her eyes were wet. She smiled at Mrs Gaskell. 'I'll have it when we get to the hotel,' she said.

THE DONNA WISEMAN SHOW

'On that night a young girl from England stepped out and stole the show from all the big stars. She's a belter in the tradition of Ethel Merman and Judy Garland. She's just signed to Columbia Records here in the States and my God what a voice. She's an old-style star in Europe already and been singing since she was ten. Ladies and gentleman, Maria Tambini.'

Applause.

'Where are you from?'

'The Isle of Bute.'

'Is that Scotland?'

'Yeah.'

'What a loud baby you must have been.'

'Right.'

'Your mum and dad sing?'

'Yeah.'

'Loud?'

'My mother loved Shirley Bassey and I think she's great too. My manager goes for Frank Sinatra.'

'Don't we all. Do you have commercials in Britain?'

'Yes. We do.'

'Like what?'

'Well. For loaves.'

'Loaves?'

'Yes, you know. Bread.'

'My God. Like loaves and fishes. Well, folks, we'll be right back with Maria Tambini after these messages.'

THE TONIGHT SHOW WITH JOHNNY CARSON

'She's the talk of the town. Blows you right out of the theatre. Here she is—Mary Tambini.'

Applause. Whistling.

'So you come from Scotland?'

'Yeah. Scotland, USA.'

'Oh, a comedian too. Do you go back there much?'

'No, things have been busy.'

'Your family's there?'

'I speak to them on the phone when I can.'

'They must be proud of you, huh?'

'I think so.'

'You like haggis?'

'Horrible.'

'You don't like haggis?'

'God no. It's a sheep or something.'

'I love your accent.'

'Thank you.'

'You're cute.'

'Thank you.'

'D'you have a boyfriend?'

'No.'

'Can I have your phone number?'

'Cheeky.'

'*Cheeeeky.* You know I love your accent. I'd like to take you home and sit you on the mantelpiece.'

'They told me about you.'

'You play the bagpipes?'

'You're daft.'

'Stay tuned, folks. I'm *daaaft*. Join us again after this word from our sponsors.'

THE DICK CAVETT SHOW

'You are such a talented little person I want to kill you.'

'Thank you. I think.'

'No, seriously. You're amazing. Do they love you in Britain?'

'They like singers.'

'You sing old songs?'

'People like those old ones. I've always sung them. I don't really know why.'

'You're a skinny girl, Maria. You exercise a lot?'

'It's just being on the road. We work hard but I'm always eating something.'

'That's like what my wife says about me. Well, actually, she says there's always something *eating me*.'

Maria giggles. The audience applauds.

'You have nice teeth, Maria. Did you buy them over here?'

'I brush them.'

'You *brush* them?'

'I clean them, Mr Cavett.'

'Well. Who says that Britain no longer leads the world?'

Maria laughs into her hands.

'Ladies and gentleman, Maria Tambini is going to sing a little song for us. It's called "Paper Roses". Thank you, Maria.'

SHE SANG for President Reagan at the White House. He pinched her cheek and she didn't know whether to laugh or curtsy. She stood at the reception and drank her seventh Diet Pepsi of the day, and it felt awfully nice to her, like a passing shower of rain inside, and harmless, under control, the taste of zero, the buzz of Diet Pepsi. At the dinner, when no one was looking, she got rid of the stuff on her plate. She folded a piece of chicken, two new potatoes, and a heap of julienned carrots in a napkin and passed them into her sparkly handbag.

The President had said, 'I know girls just like you on the West Coast.'

'I'm from the west coast too,' she said. 'The west coast of Scotland.'

'You don't have sunshine there.'

'No.'

'Or oranges. Or Disneyland.'

'I've been in California,' she said.

'You sure don't have that in Scotland,' he said.

Mr Reagan moved on and another man in black tie shook her hand. 'But you have the Loch Ness Monster,' he said.

'Yes,' she said.

'Great to meet you,' said the man. 'I'm Ed Meese. You sing beautifully.'

'Thank you,' she said.

Mrs Reagan had a very weak handshake. 'My word,' said the First Lady, 'you're so terribly thin, my dear.'

'I've always been wee,' said Maria.

'Well, never mind,' said Mrs Reagan drawing close to her ear then drawing quickly away. 'A girl can never be too thin.'

Maria went down in an elevator and asked a security man to order her a car. She felt more and more ill as the car progressed down Pennsylvania Avenue.

From her hotel room that night, Maria could see a white steeple-like thing covered in light outside. She felt very cold. She had a headache and only the crackle of the TV news distracted her from the pain and the thought of how cold the room was. There was a drumming inside her head as she lay down on the floor and snuggled up to the radiator; she turned it up full, and the metal was very hot, but she still felt the cold and for an hour shivered there.

She had sung well tonight. The people at the party liked her. They all seemed so happy, thin, and so good-looking in that ballroom, in their clean shoes, bow ties, long dresses, and what bright teeth they had when they laughed. The President used to be a movie star and so did his wife. She was lovely and thin. And when she smiled it was as if cameras were clicking all over the world. Nobody seemed tired or poor. Nobody seemed to belong in any other place. The people were warm, but the air-conditioning made the room cool.

My father is American. I think my father is like Ronald Reagan and his hair is neat and tidy. He has white teeth. My father has white teeth

*and smiles at people. My father is a famous American person and might
live in California.*

Maria's mind was filled with the room, with tonight, and also
filled with other rooms, other nights. She lay on the carpet and in an
instant felt that the hotel was too big and so was Washington, DC.
The world was encroaching, enormous, country within country, city
within city, so many rooms, she said, and in the middle 'me'.

She climbed up on the pillows and wrapped the bedclothes
around herself, yet she felt the heat passing out from the skin of her
back into the headboard. She was shivering and the hours passed.
Around four o'clock, she dialled a long-distance number and spoke
on the phone for half an hour. The person on the line began to worry
about the cost of the call.

'It's a faraway place,' said Lucia.

'I know, granny,' said Maria. 'Your voice is echoing.'

'Are you dressed for the weather? Are you looking after yourself
now?'

'Aye, granny. I'm doing well.'

'Good and good enough,' said Lucia. 'Just remember you've got
good Italian blood in you Maria, and you're used to the nice weather.'

'Aye.'

'I've been sitting these past afternoons with an old suitcase at my
feet,' said Lucia. 'Would you believe it—a suitcase of stuff from
years ago, from a lot of years. They found it in a store cupboard up
in Glasgow, and they brought it down. It's been here a while now. It's
been in the cupboard in the back bedroom.'

'What is it?' asked Maria.

'Just old bits,' said Lucia, 'stuff of mine, stuff of yours as well.'

Maria could hear a delay of her own breath on the phone line.

'It can't be mine, granny,' she said.

'It's from the war,' said Lucia.

'Well, that's not mine, granny. I wasn't . . .'

'Aye, right enough.'

'Maybe mum's.'

'They are not your mother's,' said Lucia, 'not hers. She was always a difficult one to dress.'

'The clothes are somebody else's.'

'Aye, they can't be yours, right enough.'

'Why do you have them?'

'What?'

'Why didn't you open the suitcase or throw them out?' asked Maria.

'They're here in front of me,' said Lucia.

'I know. Whose are they?'

'From the war.'

'What?'

'They're from the war.'

'Can you mend them?' asked Maria.

'They'll go in the bin,' said Lucia. 'That's where they'll go, in the bin, Sofia.'

'Granny, this is Maria.'

'I know, hen,' she said, 'and you're that far away. You're in a far place but what a miracle to hear you.'

'Did the things belong to Sofia?'

'They did.'

'Did they?'

'They did.'

'You should look after them,' said Maria. 'Those old clothes and things can be valuable.'

'Right you are,' said Lucia. 'You can go through them the next time you're up.'

'I better go, mammo.'

'Right you are, dear. I'll watch out for the steamer. Will you come and see me?'

'Of course, mammo,' said Maria. 'I can't wait to see you and we'll have a nice cup of tea.'

'How right you are. I'll hang up the phone now.'

'Goodnight mammo.'

'Is it night time?'

'It is.'

'Cheerio, my darlin'.'

Maria replaced the receiver and sank into the pillows. How lovely to hear Lucia's voice all those miles away. What a nice person: she was getting old. Maria put out the light. The blankets were heavy, not warm, and by contrast her head was light—so light, she felt that her mind could easily have broken away, rising up to the ceiling to bide for the night, from there to contemplate its sleeping enemy. Before she closed her eyes she looked over at the window. The glass was clear, but just before the darkness of sleep, for the briefest second, she was sure she saw the face of a small girl. The girl looked in, tapped at the glass, and disappeared.

9 · Lucia

My husband Mario took a handsome picture. The one over the fireplace is the best one of him I think. He has all the dignity in the world in that picture, and his eyes are grey, like the grey wall around Lucca we walked along in 1930. We wanted that evening to last all the hours God sends—there it was and there it always will be, despite everything, an evening from heaven, walking together for two hours around the old wall, holding hands and falling in love with each other.

I can still smell the rosemary. I can still see the spires of San Michele and San Martino, and the bicycles passing, and feel the sunshine going strong in the evening like a great blessing, and we were young, Mario, seventeen years old the two of us, children more or less, nothing in the world can bother you at that age, your nice shirt, clean hair, the lovely hands you had, and my God, we had the whole world in front of us.

'I'm not one of those girls who enjoys silly talk,' I said.

You were quiet. I liked that. You walked with me and held my hand and knew how to pass the time. You always knew how to be with a person and not smother them, Mario, or make them tired with too many jokes. I began to love you then. The way I remember it you said nothing for half an hour and just walked with me and shaded your eyes from the sun. There was no nonsense or pretending between us. We were quiet so we were. But I remember the gardens in the city and the promises we made by just walking and then stopping to laugh. I remember the heat on my arms, the tall trees and the look of the hills.

You had a newspaper in your pocket and money from your father because of all your hard work. You took out the paper and read me a story on the front page about the death of Mrs Puccini in that old house at the Torre del Lago. 'She outlived the old man by seven years,' you said. Seven years. The very first time we met we spoke of Puccini and you said he was a hero. You stood in the street when you were only a child and cried with the women when he passed in his hearse. And the story about Mrs Puccini was in the paper the night we walked around the city wall.

You took me into the via Fillungo. We looked in all the shop windows then went into Carli. I still remember the red velvet on the walls and the glass cabinets, Mario. All the silver was polished to hell and you had a cheeky smile for the lady and you made her take the trays out. She told you not to waste her time but you said it was our time not hers. Then you bought me this Miraculous Medal and the gold cross to go with it on a chain and I got it blessed on the Monday but oh that night when you paid for it out of your own pocket I could have clapped my hands together for prayers.

'Let us consider the old man,' he said. 'And let's remember his wife who joins him today.'

That was Mario. He took me to the square beside the pink house where Puccini was born and we sat in a trattoria there and ate ice cream and were happy then, the night was still and calm. You said, 'This is a good place.' '*E un' buon luogo.*'

'Like a painting,' I said. '*Come una pittura.*'

It seems like a thousand years ago now.

These things out of the suitcase, they've been spread over the carpet for days now. I'm counting them. I have never seen them before and yet they are more personal to me than anything in this house. I don't own them in any way, but I was meant to own them, they are relics of some life that failed, Mario, our life, my own, Sofia's. For five years it's been in that back cupboard. Couldn't open it. Couldn't send it back to anywhere. Not now.

I'm counting them, these old things.

Three small cotton dresses. Four pairs of white pants. One pair of boots for a child. A mirror. A hairbrush. Socks. A child's winter coat and knitted hat. Three packets of hose. One embroidered black blouse.

One pair of ladies' pumps. A satin blouse with a small collar. A brown fitted suit. A man's grooming kit. A man's green gabardine suit. A red waistcoat. A panty girdle. Men's drawers. A boxed jigsaw puzzle of Edinburgh Haymarket. Three tin mugs. Two bottles of wine. Assorted musical scores with inscriptions. Letters. Tins of tea. Chocolate.

This suitcase has been in a storeroom full of junk at the main post office in Glasgow since 1940. That is what they told me when they brought it up from the pier. The post office was being knocked down and they decided to deliver these personal belongings if the people were still on the postal register. Mrs L. Tambini, Rothesay, Isle of Bute—said the label, the dangerous words on the label.

Here I am. My married name. When Mario proposed to me that summer in Lucca he already had plans to move to Glasgow to go into business with his cousin. There was a café in Duke Street—the Cosmo Café—and so we came here to Scotland and worked hard and lived in a room over the café. I was quickly pregnant with Sofia and when she was born, Mario and I moved to Rothesay. Sergio gave us the money to open the café and we did so well we paid him back within two years. I'll never forget it—down there in Rothesay, with the bay so nice and bright, we were home.

There were so many holiday-makers then, the pier was heaving with boats. We built that café up from nothing. We had all the new milk drinks and the new sweets. Mario was full of life and so good with the customers. There were musical evenings down there and lots of Italian families would come from Largs and Greenock. It used to be a great community round here; we were never out of *The Bute-man* with charity things and galas and competitions. I would go on stock runs to Glasgow and got friendly with some of the people on the Scottish-Italian newspaper, *La Scozia*. They were good people: they wanted the best for Italy. It always seemed that life was taking new turns in those days: people would come from Italy and start new businesses, and the community looked after itself. What happened? The days were good and busy. Sofia was growing up. I would brush her hair at the window every night. A hundred strokes of the brush every night on her lovely hair.

I could never tell him. We were very young. Mario never wanted a life beyond the café and the counting-up at night. He wanted to write his recipes into the book and paste our memories in beside them. He was a meek man God bless him, a decent, good man, and everything he wanted was right there, his soda fountain and a dozen tables down at the front. *La Scozia* was exciting to a young girl and yes I wanted ideas in my life. Heavens above. Ideas and new ventures in life. My husband was good don't get me wrong, he was proud and worked all the hours, but I'm telling you now I knew I had fallen in love not with a man but with a beautiful evening and a medal from the Villa Fillungo. God forgive me Mario: I fell in love with a walk around the city walls at Lucca and the smell of rosemary and a man's clean hair and all the fine talk of Mrs Puccini.

And to think you loved me for my freedom. You loved me for the interests that you didn't have. My visits to Glasgow were escapes, my dear Mario, they were high times. Then I took a train to London with some of the people I'd met through the paper. You were proud that I met Gigli, and at that time, if you remember, you were not against the great patriots at St Peter's Church. You were proud of the photographs. You wanted to put them up in the café. My dear Mario, life was unkind to you, I met somebody else. I met him in London and he adored me, Mario, and I wanted to run and run to Scotland and go upstairs and forget that terrible chance and be with my husband and Sofia, I promise you.

But I let myself love him. That is what I did. When I began to love him, Mario, I felt so large and so proud inside myself. My God, he was wisdom, Mario, he was beauty, and when he sang he opened the world for better things. Then God forgive me I did not want to run home to Rothesay and I did not want to be upstairs. I only wanted to be with this man: Enrico Colangelo. You told me to beware of Mussolini and stop speaking of him, but it was not Mussolini I loved, Mario, it was not him: I spoke his name because I could not speak another. The man I loved. Enrico Colangelo. I took a petition to Mrs Viccari of the West End Café and you caught me with it and told me how she was a suspicious and conceited woman and asked why was I doing this? Why was I making this petition for Mussolini? We lived in Scotland now. We were not part of the Fasci. Why would I do this? Why would I harm us this way?

It's all so long ago now. Yes I lost myself in this love affair but only because I knew I had found my life. I look at these things lying on the floor now and I am shocked by what they bring to mind just as I was shocked forty years ago. When they say, Mario, that time heals everything they are wrong. My only relief now is that I cannot hurt you any more.

At a house in Clerkenwell in London I slept with Enrico Colangelo and my face was wet with tears. He sang. We spoke of New York and Buenos Aires and Paris; he had sung in these places and our future would lie there, one day when all causes of secrecy and fear had dissolved, and we would be so happy together. I came home to Bute from the London meetings and saw Enrico sometimes with his friends in Edinburgh. We walked in the Botanic Gardens and spoke of the future of Italy. We spoke of our future. We had our lunch at the North British Royal.

This is what happened. The war came. Our customers turned against us and in June they came through Rothesay breaking the windows of the Italian shops. I remember holding Sofia between us in the room of a house down where Alfredo's barbershop is now. The people took us in for that night. We had friends: they read the newspapers and I remember the headline in the *Daily Mail.* 'Act! Act! Act!' It was my fault they took Mario in the night. He was gone and Sofia was crying and the café was destroyed. Many of the Italians were safe and I understood what I had done. My name was among those written down in books at the church in Clerkenwell. I took Sofia to Frances Bone—our neighbour Mrs Bone—and her husband Duncan was in the army, but she took Sofia into her house. I knew they would come for me after Mario had gone. Mrs Bone is the only person on this island today who knows the truth. She knew more of the truth than Mario did—and now, even today, down in the town as I sit here now, she is silent, Frances Bone, and she hates me.

It took no more than a week. I had a letter to tell me my husband had been interned at a camp in Warth Mills, a place near Bury in Lancashire. I thought I would meet you there, Mario, but everything changed with a telephone call to Enrico in London. He told me the authorities had a list of the people who met at St Peter's. He said it was not understood to be a social or musical gathering but a political one—we were dangerous, he said, and they had addresses and would soon come for me.

I never understood Enrico's world. I think he had artistic friends in Rome who gave support to Mussolini. He knew people in London and could make telephone calls. I later found out he paid money to someone so that we would both be detained at the same place. It was a scandal, certainly: Mario in Warth Mills and knowing nothing of this. When I look back now I see that Enrico could arrange so much even in those dark times; in the end he could arrange too much, but what's the use? My own heart was arranged by then to follow his plans. Enrico had sung at Covent Garden and was known at the BBC.

I was taken to the camp at Port Erin on the Isle of Man. A policeman and a member of the Women's Voluntary Service came to Rothesay in the early morning; people from the town were standing at the sea-railings as they took me down to the pier. Some other officers went down to the café and searched through the things upstairs. Standing on the pier I could see them at the other end of the putting green: they were emptying drawers out of the window into Victoria Street. Mrs Bone came down, I remember, and lifted Sofia to kiss her mother. The officers chose not to ask a question about that. 'Are you going to Glasgow mummy?' Sofia said.

'I'm going on a train, darling.'

'A train,' she said, holding Mrs Bone's hand.

'Yes.' And I kissed her again.

'I'll write to you soon, Frances. You might have to bring her to me. I don't know what will happen.'

'Just calm yourself,' said Mrs Bone. 'I'm ready to do whatever needs doing.'

I cried for a moment into the arm of my coat.

'This is all just a mix-up,' said Frances.

'Collar the lot!' shouted a man from the side of the pier.

'That's enough of that,' said the policeman. 'Please move away, the boat is coming in.'

They moved away and after a while I walked onto the boat and we were out in the Bay. I stood on the deck and cried for my wee girl.

I remember looking over and seeing Millport and on the other side the lighthouse and thinking I might never see any of these places again. Later I heard people talking about the bad treatment of Italian prisoners, but they were nothing but nice to me. I wore a fur coat and some good gloves and I carried a gas mask. There was a Black Maria waiting at Wemyss Bay and it took me to Barlinnie Prison in Glasgow. I spent the night there: there were signs on the doors of the cells saying 'Enemy Alien'. It was mostly men who occupied the other cells and I saw a man who had worked in the offices of *La Scozia,* but we said nothing.

After a train journey to Liverpool we boarded a steamer for the Isle of Man, and the crossing was stormy. There were more German people in the group than anything else: I remember some of them singing songs and playing mouth organs. When the noise became too much the officers said they should shut up, didn't they know there was a war on. The talk was that there were real Nazis in the group—rumours of Hitler salutes when no one was watching. On the Isle of Man people lined the streets and they whistled at us and you could see some of them were spitting too. We were taken to Port Erin, a seaside town just like Rothesay, and I cried when we got there, thinking of Sofia, thinking of Mario and myself when we first came to live on Bute. They said our camp wasn't so bad as the men's. The Rushen camp, it was called, and it was cordoned off with barbed wire, but you could move about inside.

All the boarding houses and hotels in Port Erin were paid to take us in. That's how the camp worked: the streets had barbed wire at the ends of them, and the landlords took in prisoners. Many of the women had brought their children with them. At the Palace Hotel there were young girls, domestic servants mostly from London, standing around in thin dresses, and women with crying children, standing in groups, and extra blankets were being given out. Any money you had, you had to give to the commandant, who then doled it out to you at five shillings a week. It was kippers all the time. Manx kippers for breakfast, and dinner, and macaroni sometimes, or stew and that terrible tea. I can still smell the kippers.

Lillie Kermode worked in the tearoom at the Palace Hotel and she was friendly from the very beginning. In the first week she pressed a note into my hand as I approached the samovar. 'It's from a gentleman,' she said. 'My boyfriend, he's read it, and he says the gentleman is a good sort all round. Not as if you're Mata Hari, love.' The note was from Enrico.

My dear Lucia,

I am kept at the Metropole Camp on the other side. I know where you are and will contact you again soon. I may even be able to see you here. Your husband is in Lancashire and is working in the kitchen there. He will be valued in this job and will not be moved. It seems you did not bring your Sofia. Be careful but pass any note you must to the lady. She can be trusted with this.

Ti Amo, Enrico

I bought or gathered as much wool as I could and began knitting at Rushen. It made the days pass quicker. I wrote a letter to Mario and told him that Sofia was with Mrs Bone and we would be happy again after all this had passed. I don't know why I wrote this to Mario: I was not sure then that our lives could be normal after the war. Some of the women taught classes at Rushen and I learned embroidery and even went swimming one day in the sea. We had no bathing costumes and swam in our underclothes. I saw a look on the face of one of the women officers. 'These Europeans are quite disgusting when you think about it,' she said.

Many of the women at Rushen had husbands interned elsewhere on the island. Eventually, it was said they could meet with them for just two hours, some of them at Derby Castle in Onchan, others at the Balaqueeney Hotel in Port St Mary. Lillie Kermode gave me a note which said I should go to Port St Mary to meet with Enrico. I remember the women preparing to meet their husbands after their time apart. They curled their hair and sewed up their hemlines and borrowed lipsticks and shoes and earrings from one another.

'I love you,' said Enrico. We held hands across the table whilst I wept into a handkerchief he gave me.

'This is so terrible. What will happen?' I said.

'I have a plan,' he said. It was a warm day and around that town on the Isle of Man there was a holiday feeling. Children were running past the window with sweets. Enrico went on.

'We can go to Canada. I think we will be able to go to America from there. I have friends. There is a boat to Canada next week.'

'No,' I said. 'There's Sofia.'

'I know,' he said. 'We can do this. Mrs Bone will bring Sofia to us in Liverpool. My friends in Edinburgh will bring clothes and some things that we might need. Lucia, we can do this.'

'This is impossible,' I said.

'No, Lucia,' he said, tightening his hold on my hand, 'we can do this if we think carefully. I have planned it out. Your friend Mrs Bone will bring Sofia to Liverpool and my friends will leave a suitcase for us at the pier. It can be done. They are sending Italians to Canada and we can go there.'

We drank the tea and talked for those two hours.

'Why is this happening?' I said.

'It is war,' he said, 'and there are riots against us in all the cities. You lost the café.' I told him we could start again.

'Not here, Lucia, we must go to Canada. This is the only way for us to—'

'Canada. How will we board the ship?'

'I am being sent on the ship, and I have found a way to bring you and Sofia with me.'

Enrico told me the plan again and again. We wrote a letter together at the table to Mrs Bone. She was to bring Sofia in a cap and trousers to a house in Liverpool. The people there would help us and we would see Sofia again. 'I will write more to Mrs Bone tonight,' I said, 'and then I'll send this tomorrow.'

'No, Lucia,' he said. 'There are many internees' letters stuck in Liverpool. It may not get there, or they may read them. There is a messenger who can get this letter to her. Let us complete the letter here and tell her what to do.'

I remember we read over what was written on the napkin.

'Will she do it?' he asked.

I took the pencil and wrote across the top, 'Please Frances. I beg you. This is for the best.'

He looked at me. 'She will do it,' I said.

This is what happened. It was early on 30 June 1940. Under my bed at the Palace Hotel someone, Lillie I suppose, had left a bundle of clothes: grey woollen trousers and a dark jacket, a cardigan, a blue tie. There was also a pair of shoes, much too big but I stuffed the toes with nylons, and a hat which fitted as if made for me. I put these clothes on and pinched my cheeks in the mirror. There was only a single bulb in the room: I could see my face and remember feeling shaky, but looking at myself in that light I began to feel comfortable. That morning at the Palace Hotel I felt it was all for the best.

Impersonation. I had never imagined it, never thought anything like that would happen in my life. I suppose putting on those clothes made me feel that the person who was about to do this wasn't me, she was another person, frightened by what was happening, and in love with this man. Oh Mario, you never knew me. You never saw me.

There was a knock at the door. I opened it and a man in a kitchen outfit put his finger to his lips. I followed him down the stairs and we crossed the breakfast room and went out of a door into a lane. There was a van there, and another man at the wheel. The first man opened the doors at the back and I climbed inside the van and the man covered me with laundry. I can still smell the soap in that van. We moved away and the van jogged and I heard friendly chatter once when we stopped. I don't know how long it took—it felt like my whole life. When they opened the doors a man in a uniform took me by the arm and I stepped onto gravel and then quickly was taken in the door of something that looked like a church hall. Hundreds of men were crowded into the space; some lay sleeping on the floor on bundles and suitcases. The man who held my arm took me to the corner of the room and I heard him tell someone to put out their cigarette. The man in the uniform left me. Then I saw Enrico. He came over and said 'Keep quiet'.

We were on the boat and no one bothered us and Enrico was put into a berth with me and two others. I immediately lay down in the berth and turned myself to the wall. Enrico seemed to know the men well and they spoke of London and played cards and one of them spoke of a village in Italy. When the other men fell asleep and the boat was tossing Enrico leaned into the berth and whispered to me. 'There are only a dozen or so boys to be taken on the boat,' he said. 'Keep her between us. We have to slip her through. Don't worry,' he said. 'Just follow me. There will be a medical officer—we must get past him.'

The quay at Liverpool was busy and confused. I can hardly remember anything about that place, it was so full of people, and we came off one boat and went into a hangar. It was raining, and Enrico disappeared. I thought I would panic but in a moment I felt her pressing into my leg. I looked down and Sofia was there beside me, Good God when I think of it, and she jumped a little on her feet to see me. I crouched down and we were in a state, but I only said, 'Be good, Sofia. This is a nice game isn't it? Don't say anything to anybody.'

She wore long trousers and a rough waistcoat and her hair was in a crew cut. 'Pull your cap down,' I said.

I whispered to Enrico that I couldn't do it.

'Quiet now,' he said. 'We can only try.'

I told him we were lost. '*Ci siamo persi.*'

'No,' he said. '*Continui.*'

I held on to Sofia's hand and there were people shouting here and there and giving tickets out for belongings. Everything was happening so quickly and we were tired and Enrico seemed so busy with looks and gestures to the men who huddled around us. A giant metal shutter was lifted up beside the hangar and the men jostled forward. 'Try not to say mummy,' I whispered to Sofia as we moved forward. 'We're going to have a lovely journey today and I can tell you all about my time.'

'The suitcase,' said Enrico, 'they haven't brought the suitcase. It was supposed to be in here. '*Porco Dio!*'

The people from Edinburgh would surely have left the suitcase. 'It has clothes and things we need,' he said. One of the men beside him said the case might have the wrong label. They thought it was being sent to me on Bute.

'Forget the suitcase,' Enrico said. The rain was lashing down at the dock and we stepped out and saw the ship for the first time. I heard a Scottish voice behind me. 'They've smashed up every single café in Greenock,' he said.

The giant ship had two funnels and I remember noticing that all the portholes were blocked out with wood. 'Don't worry,' Enrico said in my ear. 'Someone is there to help us on the other side. We'll get things. They won't see us. It's organised. We're not going to another camp all right? Just walk forward. Between us, make her stand between us.' He whispered instructions like this and then as we approached the gangway he fell quiet. We shuffled up and I looked down and I remember seeing cars on a road beside the dock. I thought of Mrs Bone. Two officers stood at the top of the gangplank with lists. I was ready to give up. We would just give up and go back I thought. Maybe the war would be over soon and things could be normal again. I straightened Sofia's shoulders between Enrico's legs and mine. Then we were nearly at the top of the gangway—people pushed from behind—and I saw Enrico press the backs of two Italians in front of him, and they started shouting at each other and one of them hit the other with his fist. The British officers didn't put down their lists but they grabbed the men by their coats. Enrico stepped forward and said something in Italian, and with one hand he reached behind his back and swept us off to the side, in one move we were around the men with the lists, and in that very second they were checking the troublemakers' names and we were in the throng of men on the deck.

Enrico said the medical officer wasn't checking people until the boat had left. I remember the barbed wire at opposite ends of the ship and then we were moved down to a ballroom and blankets were spread out. There was a large sign over a bandstand: 'The Arandora Star'.

Florida. Cuba. Canary Islands. Gold Coast.

The ship was full of noise and seemed to be leaving in such a hurry. When berths were given out, the men shuffled back and forth with suitcases and swapped with each other to be with people they knew. No one supervised any of this and some of the Italian men were shouting at the Germans because they were furious when they heard the ship was flying a flag with a swastika on it. I don't know if this was true about the flag, but the men were at each other's throats.

'Don't be scared,' I said to Sofia, who was hidden between us. An old man was talking to us and we looked up and saw that he understood, but he continued speaking as if everything was normal. His name was Francesco D'Ambrosio. 'This is all for nothing,' he said, 'and they should be ashamed of what they are doing.' Mr D'Ambrosio had lived in Scotland since 1898 and he owned a restaurant in Hamilton. 'I have two sons serving in the British Army,' he said to us. 'All this . . . you would think they could avoid all this. I am sixty-eight years old.' Out of his pocket he took a packet of mixed sweets. 'Here you go, little angel,' he said to Sofia.

In the ballroom the food was served on china plates. There was news. Some of the men said they thought England had been invaded. A man who knew about boats managed to get to the upper decks: I remember him coming back and saying it was now sunset and we were north of Ireland. Some of the people on the boat said they were happy to be heading for Canada. Sofia looked up at me. 'Where's daddy?' she asked.

'He is not far from home,' I said. 'Shall we say a prayer for him?' And so we did—sitting there, the crowd of men moving around us—we said four Hail Marys and under our breaths we sang songs Sofia liked.

'Is this our holidays?' she said, and I said yes, it's like our holidays, and I said keep your singing quiet because these men don't know us.

She was a lovely singer. Her hair was cut and I wanted so much for it to be long like it used to be and to brush it a hundred times. Sofia was a real singer. When she started a song everybody would listen, but there on that boat, on the *Arandora Star,* she sang very quietly to herself and me, and I told her one day she could be a singer on the radio. 'I've moved us to a cabin on the lower deck,' said Enrico. He said we could be together.

'Is it far to where we're going?' I asked him.

'Five days,' he said.

In the cabin we tucked Sofia into her blankets and sat together on the bottom bunk. Enrico stood up and stroked Sofia and I can hear him saying, 'I'm your friend.' Then he sang to her in a way I'll never forget. His voice was made to brush away the world's troubles.

'She's asleep,' he said.

I WOKE in the same clothes. There was a terrible thud and I jumped up. It was dark but I saw Enrico wasn't there. I screamed his name then Mario's name, the door of the cabin was open and the lights were out in the corridor. Sofia was sitting up in her bunk so I stroked her head and kissed her and told her everything was all right. Her eyes were sparkling and she looked so calm. My little girl. She just stared, just stared out in the dark.

I ran into the corridor and a group of officers were walking along with guns. 'Who are you?' one of them said, then they took me by the arms and wrestled me onto the stairs and up to the next deck. 'My child!' I shouted, and one of the officers on the deck said, 'Why is this woman here? Why do we have a woman here? There has been an explosion. Where did you find this woman?'

I shouted at them that my child was down there.

'Hold her,' one of them said.

'In the cabin!' I screamed. 'In the cabin!'

At first silence then shouting from all over the ship and people beginning to run. Smoke belches from the corridor onto the deck and the soldiers take me up more stairs and I am screaming. They bring me round to the front where there is barbed wire and you can see the ship is going to one side. I'm screaming and saying, 'Take me back! I have a child with me. Please I beg you. Oh God in heaven I beg you my child is below!' The men let go of me and run towards each other and words are exchanged. They have forgotten about me so I run back, but it's hard to find the door, oh Mario, God bless us, and the smoke comes and people are running now in the corridors I can't see which way. There is so much glass on the floor and it is cutting my feet but I can't feel anything running down the corridors. Maybe Enrico is there, oh please Enrico where are you?

Not this way! I can't see. This is not the right way oh my God where is this leading? I fall against the metal pipes and the ship lists. I don't know how long I have been running and screaming in the corridors. Oh my God what is happening? I knock on the doors and push them in but the cabins are empty and some have people rushing out.

I thought Enrico would come. I thought he would come out of one of the corridors and have Sofia in his arms. I run onto the deck where many people crowd and an Englishman is shouting orders from the top of a platform. There are noises from a siren. 'My baby is lost!' I scream at some of the men passing, but they only pause for a second to look at my face, then run on. There are men up above me throwing rafts down into the water and already the boat is very low and rolling to one side. Some of the Italian men are praying on the deck on their knees. People are throwing suitcases from the upper decks and now oh my God there are people jumping into the water. It is nothing but dark out there and my child is...oh my God the waves you can see them closer. I try to stop people but they are all struggling with lifejackets or just running.

A man with a rifle tells me to jump. I can't see. I can't see. Oh please show me the way below, I'll just lift her out and we'll get into that boat, oh please. I see a man being knocked into the water by a raft coming from overhead. I grip the railing and sweet Jesus don't make this happen. There are bodies floating down there. The ship rolls further and I see a lifeboat out there and everyone splashing into the water so I let go of the railing and fall in.

I can't breathe. I'm under the water and then oh God of mercy is this the stairs and the corridor, am I near the cabin, is it at the end there? My mouth is full of water and the salt, oh mercy is this the corridor? I can see a light on, is that my little girl in there, oh please come out we've got to hurry. There's nice things down in the café for you and if you sit up there we can hear you singing Sofia, you've lovely hair. Oh Lord be merciful, only give us a minute oh Mario come oh Enrico what is happening come quickly it's terrible why have you gone? And then I'm on top of the water and can see fire on the waves and stuff everywhere. Holy Mary Mother of God the water is burning and the people spread out on it have nowhere to go. The ship is rolling over on its side and you can see hundreds of people falling from the decks.

My girl is there. Please I beg you my wee girl.

A noise comes from the ship and the ship creaks and breaks and slides away and is gone. I saw it with my own eyes. The waves rolled over it as if it had never been there leaving nothing but a terrible mess with people swimming and shouting in the darkness and no-body to save anybody.

Covered in oil, I was dragged into a lifeboat. The people were shivering there in their pyjamas. 'It's a woman,' said an English soldier. 'She's a woman. How did you get into this pickle, love?' I was sobbing and screaming then and my eyes were blinded with the oil and many of the men spoke in German. They held on to me in the boat but I couldn't bear to live and cried for I don't know how long and then I remember just staring out as the daylight came. I knew it then and I know it now as I'm telling you that this day was the end of me. There was nothing I could do. It may have been three hours that passed after that or a hundred years: I remember rockets going over the boat and then arms pulling me up onto a metal ladder.

'We have a woman here, sir.'

'I tried to go back for her,' I said.

'Sorry, miss?'

'I went back for her but it was dark and nobody came.'

'Just drink this, miss.'

Every word echoes in my head as I remember. I tasted hot rum and I drank it down as if it were poison and drinking it I didn't know where to put myself. 'Steady on, miss,' said the man. 'Don't burn yourself now.'

I was freezing as they put blankets round me and I don't remember saying another thing. It was the end. You wouldn't have thought there was a sea passing under us—a war on, a world going round, people happy to be alive, people dead. I remember nothing but the terrible blackness, the disbelief, and the sound of the waves.

THEY SAY I was silent for two weeks. I had no papers: no passport, no medical card, nothing. All the survivors were brought back to Greenock on board a destroyer. I later heard that some of the men went back to the Isle of Man, and others were pressed onto another ship, the *Dunera*, which took them on a journey to Australia that lasted fifty-five days.

They put me into Mearnskirk Emergency Hospital. My memory is far from clear. I sat in the hospital bed with my hands bandaged and of course people came and went but I have no memory of conversations or any procedures, only the coming and going of strangers in the ward. Surely I was waking from a horrible nightmare, a story where I found myself in a succession of rooms and vans and boats and strange clothes. I could see crowds and smashed glass and could feel the heat. Only with the passing of the days did I come to realise it was not a dream: in some swift sequence of events, only days ago, I hadn't thought, I hadn't checked, I hadn't paused, I had smuggled my only child onto the *Arandora Star.*

A doctor and some sort of official were beside the bed. 'The boat was torpedoed,' the official said.

I asked him how many.

'We think one torpedo,' the man said. I was crying again but no one remarked on it. 'The boat went down completely in twenty-five minutes.'

'No,' I said. 'How many were left there?'

'We have a list.'

'How many?'

'Dead? We can't be absolutely certain at this stage.'

'Italians,' I said. I remember the wooden chairs scraping on the floor.

'More than four hundred,' he said. 'I suspect the list is not very accurate at present. The embarkation process was muddled.'

'Four hundred men,' I said.

'Mrs Tambini,' the gentleman continued, 'we know you disappeared from the Rushen camp. Why were you on that boat?'

'I can't remember,' I said.

'But you travelled some distance to be on that ship, and presumably at considerable effort. Would you care to tell me who helped you?'

'I have no memory of it, and I don't know.'

He said this was a very serious matter. This is a time of war. 'Who took you onto that boat?'

I asked him if I could see the list.

'It is incomplete,' he said, 'the list of survivors. There is no guarantee we haven't missed people. This is a list of those who came off the rescue vessel at Greenock. There are names missing—your own, for instance—because we had no idea how to identify you. There were no women on that ship. I mean, it was intended that there be no women there.'

I told him I understood what he was saying.

He said something about the newspapers and something about panic among the Italians and the courage of the officers and the fall of France. They had typed the list in alphabetical order: I remember staring for what seemed like an eternity at the blank space between the names of two men, Guglielmo Sugoni and Roberto Taraborelli. Sofia Tambini was missing. Of course, they never had her name, but I thought her name would be on this list if she had survived. They would have taken her into a lifeboat and asked for her name. The white space glared at me and I cried into the bandages on my fists.

'What name are you looking for madam?' The man said it over and over. 'It is very important you tell us.'

'Nothing. Nothing.' All I said was 'nothing'.

'This is very serious,' he said. I went back through the pages. Andrea Benedetti, Sergio Colpi, Leonardo D'Annuncio.

Again. I read it again.

'Nothing. Nothing,' I said, beyond tears.

Enrico Colangelo was missing.

'Please calm down, Mrs Tambini,' said the doctor.

'I want to die,' I said.

'Please calm down. You are safe now.'

'I want to die.'

'This is not the time,' said the doctor turning to the official. 'We will come back to this.' I don't remember what else they said; they talked among themselves.

'You must get some rest, Mrs Tambini,' said the man. 'This is very mysterious and we will speak again.'

'Try to sleep,' said the doctor.

Sitting in the dayroom at the Mearnskirk Hospital I saw people outside the window in a queue for the mobile library van. The sun was out and there was an awful glow in the fields. I watched the people coming with their books and wondered if there could be any peace to be found in stories. I was in mourning in my brown chair by the window at Mearnskirk: I was dead in myself. What had happened had happened in a blur of accident and disguise, and there was no way back now, none of the hope and none of the love, and nothing to save me from the guilt I have carried with me all the days of my life.

They began releasing interned people that September. I was never sent to another camp; I just gathered myself at the hospital, and I never saw the man from the Home Office again. One day Mario came. We sat in that room by the window and I told him everything. I stared at the carpet and said all I could say and even to me the words coming out were like those of someone mad or confused. 'No,' he said. He just repeated the word no, a hundred times. My poor Mario had to be taken shouting from the ward by the attendants, his face contorted with the horror, my beloved, quiet, hard-working Mario, the man who once took my arm as we walked as young people along the city wall at Lucca, all the blue hills and dignity around us.

'Terrible things happen in war. The cruelty of the German Uboats will always be on our minds. They took away many innocent lives. But there is nothing to be gained in pursuing the matter to our own graves.' These words of Father Monaghan of St Andrew's are etched on my mind. He said, 'Your place is with your husband. That is what he wants.' Mario was terrifying in his forgiveness. After a time he came for me and we returned to Rothesay and put ourselves in the trust of Father Monaghan. On the way over to Bute, Mario and I said almost nothing across the miles.

He asked me who else knew.

'Only Frances Bone.'

'Yes,' he said. 'She will never forgive us.'

'Me,' I said. 'She will never forgive me, and that is how it should be.'

Mario spoke to her and told her that I did it because I was frightened. I told him I should not have involved Mrs Bone.

'It is at an end,' said Mario.

Down at the seafront my husband had already begun to prepare the café for business. He found himself again in his work, the days progressed, and slowly the old customers returned to the shop. Mrs Bone set down the memory of Sofia Tambini with all the tragedies of the war. Her own husband died in Normandy. We have not spoken since.

Three small cotton dresses.
Four pairs of white pants.
One pair of boots for a child.
A mirror.
A hairbrush.

Socks.

A child's winter coat and knitted hat.

Three packets of hose.

One embroidered black blouse.

One pair of ladies' pumps.

A satin blouse with a small collar.

A brown fitted suit.

A man's grooming kit.

A man's green gabardine suit.

A red waistcoat.

A panty girdle.

Men's drawers. A boxed jigsaw puzzle of Edinburgh Haymarket.

Three tin mugs.

Two bottles of wine.

Assorted musical scores with inscriptions.

Letters.

Tins of tea.

Chocolate.

10 · Mirror

CHILD STAR'S SECRET ORDEAL
Exclusive by Showbiz Editor

Scottish singing sensation Maria Tambini is back in her home town of Rothesay today after checking out of the London clinic where she has been battling with the long-term effects of the slimmers' disease anorexia nervosa.

The 21-year-old songbird rocketed to stardom at the age of 13 when she won Hughie Green's talent show *Opportunity Knocks* and has already appeared at the Palladium and starred in her own TV show.

But now Maria, four feet nine inches tall and just five stone in weight, this weekend faces the agony of knowing her career may be over.

Looking pitifully thin and sick, the girl who once sang with Liza Minnelli emerged from the All Saints' Clinic in

Kennington, South London, yesterday, and was driven away by her uncle. She was understood to be heading for her family home on the Isle of Bute in Scotland to recover and take stock.

Tambini's ordeal started at a young age when the pressures of fame and looking good began to tell on her. Last year she spent time in a psychiatric clinic after her weight dropped to a pathetic four stone during her preparations for a summer season at Torquay.

Showbusiness insider Steve Wins comments: 'Maria is a much-loved British performer but her loud, stage-school style of talent is going out of fashion. She's really a product of the 1970s light-entertainment world and the end-of-pier variety shows. Her problems are perhaps a sign that it is now time for her to call it quits. She's been ill for a long time now and the pressures of fame have just been too much.'

Dr Alan Yule of Guy's Hospital in London said anorexia was an increasing problem among young girls. 'We find that many young people show a propensity for this illness when they consider themselves to have little control over their lives,' he said yesterday. 'By controlling their own body-weight, they are in fact achieving, albeit destructively, a feeling of superiority and well-being. There are more and more cases of this. People just stop eating.'

Marion Gaskell, a top London agent who manages Maria's career, denies that the pressures of showbusiness have had any connection with her client's condition. 'Maria is a very wonderful performer and we have been monitoring her health carefully over the last while. She has been suffering from tiredness and has agreed to cancel some shows only at our insistence. We are positive she will be back on form soon and we very much look forward to that.'

An event that shocked the music industry two years ago was the death of American singer Karen Carpenter, who finally succumbed to the killer disease at the age of 32. She had been starving herself for many years. Stephanie Mallard, who shot to fame at the age of eight in the West End production of

Annie, said today she was glad she got out of the industry so soon. 'It gets to you after a while,' she said, 'and I feel so sorry for Maria. She's an amazing singer, but when you start as a kid you've got so much to prove all the time you begin to wonder if you'll ever be allowed to be just a normal person instead of a personality.'

11 · Home

Close to the shore at Bogany Point, Dr Jagannadham could be found walking in the mid-morning sun. His beard had begun to show some whiteness of late, and with it came an improvement in both his general refinement and his good looks. In one hand he carried a black notebook, and in the pockets of his favourite jacket, less pockets than tweed bags, he stored a number of blunt pencils, a pad of pH paper, an old penknife, and some plastic specimen trays. He dabbed at his forehead with a handkerchief and skipped over a wall. Daydreaming, he thought of laughter in Madras, he thought of his father reading out loud from the newspaper, and speaking of great events across the sea.

The doctor had three great interests of his own that season: types of fern on the Isle of Bute, the manufacture of soap in Third World countries, and most of all, most pressing of all, the nature of the sulphurated spring at Bogany Point. Dr Jagannadham surveyed the clear blueness of the sky over the island. He was deep in thought about the mineral content of the water in the spring—sulphate of lime, sulphate of soda, chloride of magnesium, silica, and common salt—and he considered it a shame that nobody bathed there now. He wondered if any of his patients suffering from rheumatism could be persuaded to come.

He checked his watch. Reaching the main road and fumbling for his car keys he made notes about the bracken. 'Unfamiliar height this year. Browner. More persistent like a roll of carpet down to the rocks.' He then got into his car and drove in the wrong direction round the island, the direction away from his surgery.

The doctor prided himself on the simple notion that no spot of earth or sea was too small for him. He said to his wife many times that a slip of land no bigger than the garden was world enough for a lifetime's study and a lifetime's pleasure. Yet his mind was often enough at a great distance, contemplating volcanoes, arguing religion, considering methods of production, converting from fluid ounces, and without this his work at the surgery might have become depressing.

He loved the island. He loved its bizarre Scottishness, its palm trees and mussel-shells: here was Madeira lost and found among the sea-lochs and narrows of the Firth of Clyde; here was another eternity of interesting things and typical sicknesses and pockets of history unexplored or taken for granted. Bute was a place of old habits and new discoveries, all of which saw him emerge in the morning with a special kind of aliveness.

He had the condition of finding nothing boring. His wife had an interest in ornamented beads and in Sigmund Freud: he found all that quite strange, but he would sit down quite happily and discuss them for hours. Dr Jagannadham liked to say the universe was accessed through an infinity of doors; he imagined too that none was truly closed to him, not if he put his eye to the keyhole or fashioned a key to its lock. But those things outside of himself were always the more gripping: he didn't care to read his own mind or question his own motives, and when it came to the study of people, he found the greatest amusement in looking at his wife and daughter. To him they were always fascinating, always true: it was the very basis of his philosophy, their minds, their hearts, the world they breathed, his love of all that.

He was late as usual and the extra distance he drove that morning added half an hour to his lateness, but he considered it worth the trouble. Driving towards Ascog he thought about his interest in trees and this led him to think about graves. As he drove past the churchyard at Ascog he remembered there was a cemetery of one: only one person, an actor, Montague Stanley, who suffered at the hands of the London critics and died in 1844 with a moderate purse and a single wish, that he be buried against the church at Ascog.

Up ahead, on the way to Kerrycroy, the doctor saw two remarkable ash trees, favourites of his, which stood on either side of the road. The locals called them Adam and Eve. The trees were very old with numerous branches, some of which, like tender fingers, reached out and touched one another above the road. He drove further west over the island and stopped for a minute near Kingarth, breathing the air, looking over the water, and considered his closeness to the ruins of St Blane's chapel and further inland the standing stones of the Black Park plantation. He turned and smiled into the sun, remembering that women and men had separate enclosures in that graveyard at St Blane's. There was life in the grass as a breeze came in off the water and ruffled the blades and passed through the leaves overhead; Dr Jagannadham thought of a stone monument hidden in the field, a stone, quite recently chiselled, in memory of Eleanor Watt, 1745, who was taken by the islanders for a witch and a spy. The legend says her tongue was cut out and thrown at midnight into the sea.

Driving the car back to Rothesay, his imagination mingled with the air that came through the open window. He could smell compost and the smell was all over him in seconds. Edmund Kean was another one who would have liked a local grave: the tragedian had kept a cottage on the edge of Loch Fad, and the oak that grew there was once famous, nearly a dozen feet in girth. Kean had asked that his body be buried under that tree. 'It never happened,' said Dr Jagannadham. 'The spot is empty.'

THERE WERE babies crying in the waiting room. 'Hello, Dr Jag,' said several of the women in turn. They sat in two long rows surrounded by scattered leaflets.

'Hello, ladies,' he replied. 'A good drying day.'

'It is that,' said the one by the door.

The receptionist passed some letters through the window and the doctor disappeared into his room. Dr Jagannadham had never enjoyed the air of his room, which smelled strongly of carbolic. He was friendly as well as proficient; he knew them well, his 'customers', and managed to follow with solid interest the progress of Mrs Watt's catarrh and Mr Kelso's lumbago, allowing himself the occasional chuckle at the doorstep of adversity, though he was never known to be under-serious when the moment called for it.

After seeing several patients—a case of infant jaundice, a poison-finger needing lancing, an angina, a productive cough—he had ten minutes to himself. He took out the specimen trays from his pocket and scrutinised them, then put droplets of iodine into two of them, took a smear from another one, put it on a slide, and looked at it under the microscope. Ever since he was a young student it had given him a rush: the universe to be viewed under a microscope, familiar cell structures and microbes hurrying past the viewfinder in the mysterious blaze of their short lives.

There was a knock.

'Can I come in, doctor?'

'Of course. Oh hello, Rosa. Come and sit.'

Mrs Tambini had her hair in a bun and was wearing a raincoat despite the nice day, a raincoat held together by a belt from another coat, the colour of saffron. Dr Jagannadham smiled unobtrusively as he patted the notes into order. Rosa's file of cards was more than usually thick, and written on them, in different pens, was a queue of notes, things she had said, doctor's advice, and details of prescriptions, which he could see at a glance were uniform: powerful sedatives and anti-depressants going back years.

'I'm that upset,' she said, and immediately, quite automatically, she brought out a balled-up tissue.

'Take your time,' he said.

'They haven't even been round to see my new carpet. I got a new carpet put down and you'd think they'd come and see it and how you're getting on but not one of them. You've got no idea the way they carry on. After all I've done. I've said it before it's not people outside that hurt me, it's family. They just walk all over you and they've never got any time just to sit down with you and take a cup of tea. How doing? How you coping with this and that? Half the time they'd walk right past the door and it's weeks at a time. Two weeks is a long time when you're just sitting.'

The doctor clasped his hands on the desk.

'I would fall out with them if I took it into my head. I'd just say don't bother I don't need anything from yous. Half the time you think well if that's the way they want to be, I've never done anything but please them, they can just hang as they grow. I hear other people talk about their families and it's "Steven and thingmy were round last night" or "Angela was in with the weans", and sometimes I just pretend mine have been round because I'm that embarrassed about how long they can let it go without a single thought. It's no as if I'm an interfering woman, doctor. I just wish things were a wee bit normal. It's a lonely life. When you're just by yourself all the time it's lonely and you'd think they'd want a cup of tea or a wee blether. It's all work and you just feel hurted, it's really very very seldom you see any of them now. Oh when they need something that's a different story. Never lift a phone. It's too dark at night now round here and it's not my place always to go over to their houses without them asking. I got the man to come and put the wee bit carpet down but you couldn't ask the likes of them to do a thing for you, I suppose they're all getting on with their own lives. Maybe it's just me. I can't go to them and they've got *cars* doctor, you know.'

'Has Giovanni been there?' asked the doctor.

'You never know if he's coming or going. First he's there and then he's not. Terrible. Even when he's there it's no use, he is one selfish man and I'm supposed to just sit and take it and never complain. I've had it up to here. I'm not kidding it was easier years ago when we had to struggle and he would disappear but at least when he came back there was something. Now half the time I'm just sitting and I don't know if he's in or out and you can't rely on him to do the café and that's always been hard work you know. Nobody realises how much hard work and sometimes you just can't be roasted doing it and it's bound to get to you at times. I think to myself I've made them all welcome but they just go on as if you've not got feelings, as if you're like a brick, and they say oh she'll just get on no matter what, but half the time you think what's the point.'

'Rosa,' he said, 'slow down. You stopped seeing the counsellor.'

'That's not for me doctor, I mean he's talking to me as if I'm half-daft, you don't get anywhere with them people. I've taken the tablets but I thought what the hell and I put the rest of them down the sink.'

'You've done that before. I believe they help you.'

'Well I can see you're right, but sometimes I just wish my family could be normal and I would be fine. I've done more for them than a lot of men and wives and would they lift the phone? What's the reason? It's lonely at times believe you me. It's strange in that house and you don't know where they are and I know they've got their own lives to lead but you don't just forget the people that've helped you get to where you are today. I know my mother and I have never been great ones with each other but you'd think she'd come by. She knows it hurts me and I never see Alfredo, he used to be that good. Giovanni, well, you know he's hopeless. He wouldn't give you daylight in a dark corner. My problem is I was just too close to them and it hurts you, I was too close to them, and I've never asked for half of their bad feeling but that's just life.'

'Calm down. Here, Rosa. Take some water,' said Dr Jagannadham. 'And Maria is home?'

'Her head's in the clouds. She's away with the fairies. You can't talk to her, never could, not since she was a wee lassie when she was a different person altogether. I mean people come into that house and I make them welcome, I say "Take your coat off" and it's a wee cup of tea and them that's got babies can lie them kicking on the floor and I'll go in and make tuna and mayonnaise sandwiches and we have a nice day. But family? I could run a mile. I've needed some papering done for a while now but you'd never ask *them*. I'll get a stranger to do it. I wish to God it wasnae like that and you wonder sometimes what you've done to deserve it.'

'But Rosa, Maria is not well. You know that, don't you?'

'Of course. She's my daughter.'

'Well, don't you think maybe she needs you to be patient?'

'It's not her I'm talking about. It's not her, it's them that are in my life all the time. She's here for a holiday.'

'Not quite a holiday, Rosa.'

'Well, she's never taken much to do with me, doctor. I will do my best and will run here, there and everywhere for her, but I wouldn't hold my breath waiting on her to do the same.'

'Have you spoken to her?'

'You can't speak to that girl. She's always right. You can't say a word to her, it gets to the stage everything you say to people is wrong.'

'I think she's very ill, Rosa.'

'I don't know what she's trying to do. Can she not look around her and see what this eating thing is doing to her family and everybody else? People who have worked hard to put her where she is . . . I wouldny know where to start helping her. I've given her the best years of my life—her and all the rest of them.'

'How's your sleep?'

She paused and looked into the broken tissue.

'Bad. I can't get asleep. I'm up all night and now with Maria here I'm worrying half the time. I have bad thoughts, doctor, and I don't know what to do about them. I wonder half the time if anybody would even notice if I wasn't here.'

'No, come now,' said Dr Jagannadham. 'I'm reluctant to keep giving you this sleeping medication, Rosa. You know that. It is not a long-term solution, I've said that to you. You are depressed. You must try to keep up your sessions with the counsellor and seek to put some balance into your life. Do you understand me, Rosa? I can't keep on writing prescriptions for ever. It is not the answer.'

'I know that, doctor. The tablets are just till I sort things out. It's not as bad as that. It helps me calm down I know that and sometimes if only I can get some sleep I know everything will be okay. I need to sleep.'

The doctor sighed. 'Please tell Maria I will be round to see her this week. She needs to rest.'

'That's what she needs,' said Rosa, wiping her cheeks with the heel of her hand. 'Things have just been a bit too hectic for her. Just getting on top of her a wee bit too much. A person can't work like that and not get tired.'

THE NIGHT Maria came back from London, she didn't go straight home to her mother's; she stayed with Alfredo until after dark. They had travelled from London on the train and Maria had shivered in her coat most of the way. She said she didn't feel like going straight to the café, not yet, so Alfredo took her up to his flat on the Serpentine, and he sat her down and made her drink a glass of water.

Alfredo's flat had always smelled of biscuits. Sitting on the black leather sofa, Maria remembered the smell, and also a day from years before when she and Kalpana had been playing on swings made out of rubber tyres, exhausting themselves, and then had come to Alfredo's to drink tumblers of American Cream Soda. Alfredo's coffee-table was the same one, and Maria noticed it was still covered with many of the same objects. Two packets of Silk Cut, a large calculator, a digital clock, a bottle of Tippex and a pile of the *Hairdressers' Jour-*

nal. Everything was laid out in order, squared off, dusted, as if it had scarcely been moved or touched in years. That was Alfredo's life: efficiently ordered and prepared, full of privacy and small, undeclared luxury, centrally-heated, shag-piled, and sometimes despondent and always mysterious.

He brought her a blanket and switched on the TV. Maria said she just wanted to sleep so Alfredo let her do that for a little while but then woke her with all his talk about what was going on in Rothesay. At ten o'clock he picked up her bags and said they'd have to go down to the café and see Rosa. Maria started to shiver again when they stepped outside and she took Alfredo's arm and held on to a metal railing as they descended the steps of the Serpentine to the seafront.

Inside the door at 120 Victoria Street the café was quiet except for a few children standing around the jukebox. They didn't turn round as Alfredo and Maria came in. Rosa was behind the counter and she nodded over. 'That's us closing now,' she said to the boys. 'Away ye go.' The boys complained for a minute but then went out the door. Rosa came over and turned the sign to 'Closed' and turned the key.

'Hello, mum,' said Maria.

'Heavens above, look at you,' said Rosa.

She quickly rubbed Maria's shoulder and helped Alfredo guide her into the back kitchen. They sat down at the table and Maria saw the table was polished. Rosa immediately started talking about something that was happening on a television soap, and asked for their opinions, but Alfredo said he didn't know it, and Maria just smiled.

Rosa turned. 'What a state you've got yourself into, Maria.'

'I know.'

'But we're gonnae get you back to your old self,' said Alfredo, and he reached over and patted her hand. He stood up. 'I'll see you tomorrow, Rosa,' he said.

'Send me a postcard first,' she said from the sink.

He went out and then Rosa went up the backstairs. The tap was dripping just as it always had. Maria noticed there was new wallpaper over the kitchen and the fridge was new. The room was quiet in a way she never remembered it being. It was as if all sound and life had gone from the house. She sat at the table, scanning the grain for familiarity, but felt she was in a dream, somehow visiting the past in her sleep. She stood up and walked over to the fridge and when she opened it her breathing halted for a second. The fridge was completely empty like the fridge in a cartoon. It wasn't half-empty. The ribs of the white shelving were pristine in the midst of nothing. There wasn't a butter dish or a bottle of milk: it was bare and the light at the back illuminated a hollow space.

She lifted the smaller of her two bags and went through to the stairs. She made her way up slowly and stopped to look at the photograph of her grandmother Lucia and her husband Mario on the stairs. She loved this picture of them in their fine clothes; their nice eyes and their young coupledom.

Maria dropped her bag on the landing. She walked into the living-room and saw it was dark. But her mother was sitting on the sofa looking at the wall, and Maria said 'Mum', and when she reached down to the lamp and fumbled for the switch she felt that the bulb was warm. She pressed the switch.

'Come in,' said Rosa.

'It's changed,' said Maria after a moment. 'You've got a new carpet.'

Her mother paused and picked a thread from the sofa. 'There's been stuff in the papers,' she said.

'I've not read the papers,' said Maria. 'I can't stand the stuff they put in the papers. Did it say I was visiting here?'

'It said that, yes.'

Rosa then spoke for over an hour without a break. There were whole sentences Maria knew by heart, many, many sentences she knew by heart. Eventually she plucked up the courage to say she was tired. 'I have to go to bed,' she said.

'Why are you doing this to us?' said her mother.

'Pardon?'

'Go to bed.'

When Maria washed her face in the bathroom she inspected her neck and found it disgusting. She felt meat had gathered and puffed up under her chin and she panicked while looking at it and remembered a half-sandwich she had eaten on the train to please Alfredo. She travelled into her own eyes for miles, then began to feel everything might be all right in the morning. She knew she could avenge the sandwich and sort things out.

She reached for the towel rail and found nothing. Walking into the hall with her face wet she got to the airing cupboard and pulled the handle but it wouldn't budge. When she looked closer she saw the two handles had been tied together with string. She went back into the living-room and found Rosa sitting in the dark again. 'I need a towel,' she said.

'There's none clean,' said Rosa.

'But there must be a towel.'

'No. There's none clean. You think I've got nothing better to do than clean all day?'

Maria went into her old bedroom. Nothing was different. The bedclothes were the same, and the posters; up on the cupboard were her old teddies and sitting there on the windowsill was her Girl's World. Even pencils and colouring-in books were still piled in the corner under the lamp. Only one thing was new: a Holly Hobby cushion that had been placed on top of her old pillows. She used it to dry her face. Her old duvet felt almost heavy on her legs and chest and she looked out to where the lights of Ardbeg were glowing as they used to do.

The handles of the airing cupboard were no longer tied together the next morning. When Maria pulled open the doors she saw what she knew she would see: piles of towels in all sorts of colours, filling the shelves to the top, each of them washed, dried, ironed and folded.

12 · Shopping

A teenager worked behind the counter most days now, so Rosa had all the time in the world to wander round the shops. Nothing ever occupied her like the shops: the same items would be on display each time she went out, but she never tired of going down Montague Street to see them again. At Bojangles, the knick-knack and gadget shop, her fingerprints would have been traceable on every item, the silver dolphins and novelty telephones, crystal pineapples and ceramic bears, but only now and then would she get out her purse and buy something.

Rosa had a credit card. Something in its hard plastic shape gave her a feeling of overwhelming force; walking down the street with the card in her coat pocket she would scratch at its edge with a fingernail, and in Woolworths, in the quiet lanes in the afternoon, she picked up bumper pads of writing paper and found box-sets of American country singers. She bought them immediately and quite often she never opened them again. Under her bed were cartons of unopened purchases. She bought toasters and heated rollers, bread-bins—and shoes, almost any kind of shoe, and very few of them tried on first. She often had a daydream of shoes, imagining footprints that stretched away for miles on a long beach. A new hat shop opened in Castle Street and she bought six hats at once. She told the woman she had a wedding to go to, but it wasn't true. Still in their hat-boxes, the hats were piled on top of the bedroom cupboard.

She knew every pattern in the carpet shop, every wallpaper sample in the decorators, and she loved the colour cards with the names of paints: Lipstick Pink, Moroccan Blue, Tangerine Orange, Dark Bracken, Telephone Box Red.

You think he'd lift up a phone.

On a normal day, a day when Giovanni had done a Giovanni and was out of the picture, God knows where, she would sit in one of the rival cafés with her fingers gathered around a cup of milky tea. She lost track of time, and often, her eyes fixed at nothing in particular, she would sit there stirring the tea until it was stone cold.

One time she saw an advert in the *Glasgow Herald*. They wanted a new artistic director at the Scottish Opera, and sitting there with her tea on a day when the wind was fierce outside, she imagined the newspaper was sending her a message. She imagined the job was made for her and grew excited at the prospect of what she would do. They need operas of things that have never been done before, she decided. They need to be set in new locations and have different sorts of costume. Out with all that boring stuff, it's as old as tea. What I'll do—she said to herself—is bring in fresh blood and mix everything up and get new composers to do modern-day things. She tore out the Situations Vacant pages and hurried along the street in her old shoes.

'I want you to write me a reference,' she said.

'What for?' asked Maria.

'For this here,' she said, and gave Maria the page and pointed to the job.

'But this is for an experienced person, mum.'

'I'm experienced! I have always loved the opera.'

'Yes, but—'

'You don't want me to get on!'

'Of course I do, mum. It's just that this is a very senior position and the person will need to have directed things and know a lot about music.'

'I know everything about music!' Rosa's crimson face was both determined and defeated. Her eyes blazed in the living-room. Lying on the sofa with a blanket around her, Maria straightened up and looked at her mother. 'Everybody in my family loved opera,' said Rosa, 'and I was brought up listening to the great songs and they need somebody for this job that can shake it up a bit.'

'Okay, mum. What can I do?'

'They'll know who you are.'

'Me?'

'Aye. They'll know who you are and if you write a reference I'll get an interview.'

'Okay. Have you got a piece of paper and a pen?'

'It needs to be on a typewriter!' said Rosa. 'I don't have the strength to work a typewriter to be honest,' said Maria, 'but I'll write it out.'

'You don't want me to get this!'

'Of course I do.' In the few minutes Rosa had been in the livingroom, Maria had undergone a change. Her eyes were bright and her voice was modulated for ease and comfort. Over the last week since she'd come home she realised something—she was performing. It helped her understand much better how to deal with Rosa. She did the very thing she knew they were all good at: she performed.

'I'll write it out,' she said, 'and then you can take it up the library and type it.'

'I'm busy.'

'I'll sit here and write it carefully, and then it can be typed. That'll be fine.'

'On you go then,' said Rosa. 'Remember to tell them I've had a lot of experience of running staff and my father was a great one for songs and even her up the road was knowledgeable on that. Tell them I have secretarial skills and can work overtime.' Rosa brought a pad in from her bedroom and found a pen on the fireplace. 'Don't be long, Maria, 'cause the library shuts half-day.'

'To Whoever It May Concern,' wrote Maria. 'I have been in showbusiness since I was quite young and I know that Mrs Rosa Tambini is an excellent organiser. She is very imaginative and knows how to get people involved in her work. If she was to get this position I know she would give it a hundred per cent. Down in London I often see musical directors and suchlike who have less natural rhythm than Mrs Tambini. She would be an asset to any firm she joined. She is familiar with many kinds of office work and has a typing speed of 80 wpm. She is a team-player and would be happy to work any overtime that came her way. Mrs Tambini comes from a family of opera-lovers and grew up knowing a lot of the Italian ones right off. My agent in London Marion Gaskell would be happy to vouch for Mrs Tambini's abilities and I would be delighted to discuss further her suitability for this post. Sincerely yours, Maria Tambini.'

I DON'T want to eat this it's so disgusting . . . biting it . . . I'm chewing just the end watch yourself and mashing it . . . in the bowl there's another ten bananas just keep chewing oh my God it's sugar inside this banana . . . I'm not swallowing oh Christ watch it's not going down watch watch and shush there's the bowl just spit . . . okay go for it just spit it down . . . that's . . . spit all at once . . . that's so horrible you can't put that inside . . . shush and just chew it I can't feel anything.

Maria's weight dropped below four stone so she had to go to the Southern General Hospital in Glasgow. It was an old place down beside the shipyards, white shiny bricks around the walls of the wards, and full of patients who were unhappy with their treatment and swore at the nurses. Maria said she had never seen a place like it: lying in the bed with a saline drip in her arm (how many calories, she wondered) she began to feel she was far away from London. She missed the freedom of Primrose Hill and her room where nobody ever bothered her. She missed Mrs Gaskell's wooden chairs and her lovely cushions spread across the livingroom and the look of the Post Office Tower from the top of the hill.

'What you in for, hen?' asked an old lady who had wheeled herself up to the door of a fire escape where people could smoke. 'You're only a wee slip of a thing. You must be young.'

'It's colitis,' said Maria.

'Is that to do with the stomach?'

'Mmm.'

'Aye, there's a lot of them's in here for that. You get that thin.'

Maria smiled at the lady and went back to bed. On the first day they brought her in she felt depressed but also superior. She had lain on top of the bed feeling in charge, but today, with the greyness of the ward and people looking at her, she had begun to lose confidence. 'I want to get back to London,' she said to herself. 'I'm looking good.'

Dr Jagannadham had made the trip to the hospital. 'Seeing as you keep avoiding me in Rothesay, I thought I'd track you down,' he said, putting his coat and briefcase on a chair by the bed.

'Dr Jag,' said Maria. 'Are you working here?'

'I had a word with one of the consultants,' he said, 'and now I'm here to see this showbusiness person everybody's been talking about.' Maria slightly flushed and then fidgeted and coughed. In a strange and sudden moment she wanted to take the tips of Dr Jagannahdam's lovely brown fingers and kiss them.

'You sit there like a bird in a cage,' he said.

'Like a scarecrow in a cage,' she said. 'None of my clothes fit me, they are meant for a fat person.'

'Not so, Maria. They are meant for someone who isn't starving,' said the doctor. 'I was speaking to Kalpana on the telephone. She was asking after you.'

'Where is she?'

'She studies at the University of Stirling. Or rather, she has a good time at the University of Stirling and I do her studying for her.'

'Nice.'

'She is the news editor at the student newspaper. Maybe you'll see each other if you are in Rothesay for a while.'

'I have to get back to London,' Maria said.

He reached forward and touched her bottom lip and asked her to open her mouth. He saw that her gums were bleeding. 'Is your mother not patient with you?' he asked.

'Giovanni came back to Rothesay last week,' she said, 'and at first she wouldn't speak to him but later on I heard them laughing and I think she hasn't laughed very much this year.'

'Let me ask you, Maria. Do you think you will be able to go anywhere if you don't gain a little weight?'

'Why does everybody want me to be a different size? I feel nearly the right size.'

'Maria. You are dying.'

Maria started to cry. 'I am not really here,' she said.

'You are here,' said Dr Jagannadham, 'and you are very ill. Maria, I have known you most of your life. This is a very serious problem you have. You will die if you do not eat.'

'But I do eat. I eat all the time.'

'You have stopped menstruating.'

'That's a lie,' she said. 'I can have babies.'

'I am here to talk to you as a doctor and as an old friend. I want to listen to you. But we must start by understanding that you are not well.'

She cried more into the raised blanket. 'How many times do I have to say I am not hungry?' she said. 'I do eat. I do. People just want me to be fatter and they don't know me.'

'Let's take our time, Maria,' said Dr Jagannadham. 'We have all the time in the world.'

Maria pulled herself together. After a while she sat in a wheelchair and the doctor took her down in the lift and along the walkway to the little green at the back of the hospital. She almost forgot herself listening to his talk of Glasgow and funny stories about inventors and people in history. For two hours in the afternoon she grew distant from the sound of herself: on the motorway over the hill, they saw cars passing, and laughing together they counted the red ones until the grass underneath them started to ruffle and the breeze grew cold.

————

BY THE end of that summer, Maria was six and a half stone and the gauntness had gone from her face. She befriended Flora, the dog belonging to Mrs Bone next door, and she would walk Flora up and down the seafront in the hours when she felt disgusting, which was often, but still the hours would pass and sometimes the feeling did too. Down by the pier people would stop her to say how much they loved her singing on the television. They told her she was looking great, but she didn't believe them.

On Alfredo and her mother's birthday, Maria decided to have a dinner party like the ones they had in London, and she set about planning it days in advance. Before she bought what she needed, she wandered around Tesco's to see if they had all the things, and she made notes of new stuff she could include. Rosa had been playing country music all morning as she went about her housework; people standing on the putting green could hear Dolly Parton over their heads and making for the sea.

When Rosa saw Maria's shopping list, she took it, went up the street to photocopy it, and came back smiling. 'You know something, Maria?' she said. 'I'm going to tape this into the *Book of Stuff*!' She took down the crumpled book of recipes from the shelf on the kitchen, cuttings falling out, and placed the folded shopping list in with everything else. 'These are good old recipes,' said Rosa. 'They have stood us in good stead so they have. It's good to look back on.'

Maria leaned into one of the large fridges in Tesco's. The supermarket was empty—so empty, in fact, she thought she could hear the hum of the strip-lights overhead, and leaning into the fridge she paused to let the cold air enclose her. Breathing it was like having mint in your bloodstream. She delayed coming up, and then, with the sound of squeaking wheels behind her, she lifted four tubs of ice cream and took them to her trolley. She needed both hands to accept the parcel she'd ordered at the meat counter, and at the delicatessen she asked for blocks of pâté, packets of smoked salmon, herring roe, olives of several kinds, and a great many cheeses. 'I am in charge of this trolley and I have my own money,' she said to herself.

She bought a brand-new food processor from the electrics aisle and more cutlery. She found a party bag of red napkins and straws and dropped everything into the trolley, after-dinner mints, family-size bags of crisps. She felt more and more elated: the horrible abundance in the shop steadily joined with a great compulsion that drove her forward, but by the time she reached the drinks aisle she was sweating and short of breath. She went to find better soap for the kitchen and paused at the toiletries; she took three boxes of Tampax from the shelf and threw them into the trolley. She found a new tube of toothpaste and two new toothbrushes and bought a packet of plasters for corns and bunions. She felt so nice when she got to the checkout, then very quietly removed the Tampax from her trolley and dropped them in a dumpbin of Wrigley's Spearmint Gum.

WHEN MARIA got home there was a letter from London sitting unopened on the phone table. It was from Marion, written on paper from the Denmark Street office.

Dear Maria,

Hello darling. It was so lovely to speak to you on the phone the other day—you sound quite marvellous, and I know from speaking to Dr Forbes in Kennington that he's spoken to the people in Glasgow and you are firmly on the mend. Bravo! We've been missing you here in NW1! A certain pair of dogs have spent the summer moping around the utility room door waiting for treats and I can tell from the look of them there'll be all sorts of bother if you don't hurry along.

You asked what work has come in. I can't tell you everything—there's been tons—but Butlins in Skegness are extremely keen to have you for two nights in September and Wogan *wants you.* Des O'Connor Tonight *is very keen, as are many of the kiddies' things,* Runaround, Ask Aspel, *and there's a ton of work coming in from Blackpool. Good old Little & Large want you, and Ken Dodd's doing a new variety show at Worthing. I think darling you should do quite a few of these before we think about new recordings. There's also* Songs of Praise, *who want you to come on and sing—Christiany stuff, but that's all right isn't it? They want to film it down in Brighton or thereabouts with a charity called St Clare's (they look after the men blinded in the wars) and the BBC's idea is that you would talk to some of them and sing down there.*

I think this is a perfect thing to bring you back on. There's been a lot of publicity about you being unwell, and this is the right kind of place—gentle—to say you're all right and working again. The money is not fantastic but worth it anyway for the reasons I've said. So don't worry about work dear, there is any amount of work, and we're looking forward to getting started.

By the way, on the Songs of Praise *front, I had a call from a terribly sweet-sounding young man who works for St Clare's. He comes from your island up there and he used to know you. When it was suggested you might be working on the show they're doing he wanted to make contact. His name is Michael Aigas. He says to tell you he used to work in the television shop. He knows your number up there but said he'd leave ringing you until you were feeling better. I thought I'd tell you about him, as he seemed very nice and spoke very kindly about you.*

As I said the dogs are missing you and we can get back to work as soon as you like my dear. We've all been frightfully busy here and the news you're better is the cause of big relief and excitement with all of us. Lots of good wishes have come from people in the business and the Water Rats have made you an honorary member. What about that? Good old Les. Even that old curmudgeon Hughie Green's been on the phone. The Variety Club want you to present an award in January. So much to be going on with, Maria, we'll be up and going again in no time, mark my words.

Let us know when you'll be coming down and we'll arrange a flight and a car to come and get you.

Best wishes,
Marion

Maria folded the letter, put it in the Yellow Pages, and took the bags of shopping to the kitchen.

For a while she contemplated what Marion had said, then she went upstairs and lay on the bed feeling lighter. Blue shadows fell over the walls from the net curtains, making patterns on the worn paper. The shadows grew darker, the light outside failing now, and a dog barked. She stared up at the ceiling with her eyes more alert, with bones that seemed to rise in her chest as she breathed. She had things to do. She got up and stood in front of the full-length mirror and forgot the time as she looked at her naked body. At first she pulled and pressed it, as if it were clay, then she stood back from it and hated it. She saw a stranger in her eyes and sometimes the look of an animal. She was an owl with brown feathers and moving hardly at all, aware of the big-eyed need for prey, an owl in the forest, its feathers quivering, a solitary bird in the black night ready to swoop down from the trees with wings spread and eyes alive. She went into the bathroom and closed the door. There was no window. She looked at the small soaps lined up on the bath-rack. They made her shiver. Out of a plastic bag she took a tube of Aapri Facial Scrub and unscrewed the orange lid.

She licked the brown stuff and it tasted of soap. It was thick as masticated cereal, the Aapri; with trembling fingers, she applied it to her face in quick circular movements. She looked at the packet after it dropped in the sink.

> *Aapri Facial Scrub Cream*
> *with ground apricot kernels*
> *deep-cleanses and stimulates your skin.*
> *It removes the dirt, grease, and dead skin cells*
> *that can make your complexion dull and lifeless.*

With both hands now she rubbed it over her face and her nose too, going under the chin and up to the hairline, and back again. She scrubbed along the cheekbones and kept scrubbing harder and faster as her breathing became heavy, and as she scrubbed, her eyes were owl-like in the bathroom mirror. She could feel the skin growing tighter and the particles in the stuff rubbing away the deadness and going past the surface of the skin to make it raw. She went faster, thinking soon it would all be rubbed out and maybe another person would appear after the cold water, or else nobody at all, just clean air in front of the mirror.

'SO THE dog jumps up and takes the pay packet right out of his fucking hand,' said Giovanni.

'Language!' said Lucia.

'Right out of his hand. And so the dog's chewing away at the wage packet and the notes are turning to mush. What do you think he does? He sticks his hand right down the dog's throat and grabs the wage packet, and the dog's left with a mooth like a bent pair of scissors.'

'The stories he drags in from the pub,' said Rosa.

'All true,' said Giovanni. 'He's a headbanger, that Frankie. Down at the Job Centre they've got this thing where if you've been on the dole for a while and you refuse to take work they can stop your money. Well, they calls him in. He's in a queue waiting to go in with the rest of them. They all know that when you go in there they try and get you onto some training shite. So, Frankie—he's up on all the rules and that—goes in and the idiot says to him, "Well, Mr Drummond, we see you've been unemployed now for sixteen years, that's rather a long time. You do not have a doctor's line but you say you are mentally unreliable." Mentally unreliable—that's what he comes out with. Anyway, the bold Frankie says to him that's right it's a terrible problem, and the guy says, "Well, Mr Drummond, is there a history of insanity in your family?" "Oh, aye," says Frankie, "I've a brother that works."'

'Away ye go!' said Alfredo.

'I'm telling ye,' said Giovanni, 'that's what he said.'

All the table laughed and Lucia looked up at Maria who was busy stirring two pans of white sauce. 'Are you all right, Maria? Can I give you a hand with these things? Are you hot over there, there's a fair heat from that oven?'

'No mammo,' said Maria. 'Just you enjoy yourself.'

'There's too much noise in here,' said Lucia. 'Too many people. I can't hear the half of what they're saying.'

'And that's not the end of it,' said Giovanni. 'Frankie looks at the guy and things are going from bad to worse. The idiot says, "And have you been actively seeking work, Mr Drummond?" "I have that," says Frankie. "Because the rules clearly state, Mr Drummond, that unless there is a specific line of work you are holding out for, and unless you are actively seeking work in that area, then we are obliged to offer you a retraining scheme and you are obliged to accept it." "Aye," says Frankie, "I understand you well enough." "So," says the idiot, "you've been out of work for sixteen years and the last time you worked you were a roofer in the employ of Messrs Brannigan and Lyle of Paisley." "Aye," says the bold Frankie, "they were very unsympathetic employers." "That's as may be," says the guy, "but what line of work are we to understand you have been pursuing since that time?" "Astronaut," says Frankie. "I've always wanted to be an astronaut. I've written away to NASA and everything. I'm passionate about it. Ever since I saw thon fella bouncing up and down in his big helmet. I couldn't take anything else in the meantime. It's my life's ambition." "Well, Mr Drummond, that's very admirable..." "No," says Frankie, "I have been reading books about it for years and it would be distressing to have to consider work in any other area at this time." "But, Mr Drummond, you've chosen a very competitive field. I'm not sure you have the qualifications." "You check, son," says Frankie. "They are willing to accept people from all walks of life." "But Mr Drummond," says he, "in the meantime, might you not consider something a little more... eh... realistic?" "It's as real to me as you sitting there," says Frankie, "and it would break my heart to lose hope of getting into space one day." "Meantime," says the guy about to lose the head, "might you not consider a scheme that will enhance your chances of future employment? There's a very highly regarded metalwork course at the Scotvec training centre at Skelmorlie. Or you could learn typing or perhaps take a course in computer skills. This might prove useful in your future career." "No thank you," says Frankie. "I will keep on trying to get work in the field that suits me. Thank you very much." And that's it. The guy has nowhere to go. He's snookered. "Good day, Mr Drummond," he says.'

Rosa rocked with laughter in the armchair while Alfredo sprayed her hair with Elnett. There are times like that, times when some other part of her reaches out and grabs the moment, and she is great then, laughing her loudest, and when she cries at Giovanni's stories you'd think nothing in life ever had the power to disturb her.

Maria licked a slither of wet carrot and sucked it at the sink while waiting to take the lamb out of the oven, then she put the piece of carrot back in the basin and breathed in: rosemary, garlic, olive oil. The table was already creaking with salmon and chicken, sausages were going cold next to plates of stuff Lucia said she'd never seen before, hummus and pitta bread, parsnips roasted in honey. Everybody was eating and Maria was putting more on the table. Quiche. Toad in the hole. Green beans.

'When did you start to cook all these things?' asked Alfredo, coming over and placing a hand on Maria's waist.

'She's not so keen on Italian food,' says Lucia. 'That's why she's so thin. This is all rabbit food.'

'Sit down and have something yourself,' said Alfredo.

'In a minute,' said Maria. She sipped some red wine as if in salute to him then turned back to the sink.

Giovanni's cigarette bounced in the corner of his mouth as he spoke. He was good at telling stories: whatever the story was about, it came in the telling to seem like a very precise statement about Giovanni himself, about the mad corners of his life and the company he kept. 'Those Gourock pubs are all Irish,' he said. 'In fact...' He searched in his jacket pocket. 'Here,' he said, 'I tore this wee bit out the *Greenock Telegraph*.' He held out a rag of newspaper and spoke in a posh voice. 'An announcement. "McFeelie's Bar, Gourock. Due to the sad death of Desmond, the bar, to all intents and purposes, will remain closed during our grief; but so as not to inconvenience our esteemed customers, the door will remain ajar. 'Tis what Desmond wanted. Thank you. The McFeelie Family."'

'Eccchhhhhhhh,' said Rosa, 'that's what they're all like.'

Lucia stood up to find a water glass.

'Out of the way!' said Rosa. 'Out of the way, mother. I'm trying to take a picture of my wee lassie.'

She was drunk, having fun, but every second her happiness was more encroaching: she would have digs at Lucia or kiss Giovanni with her mouth open. 'Sit down and enjoy yourself, hen,' said Rosa. Maria smiled, opened the oven and brought out the lamb.

'That would feed the Argyll and Sutherland Highlanders,' said Giovanni.

'It would feed the whole of Argyll,' said Alfredo.

Maria put it on the table then sat down at one of the chairs herself and pretended to eat some potato. 'Delicious,' she said, but they were all pouring the red wine and saying they'd had enough. She took up Lucia's plate and put some meat on it. 'There you go, mammo,' she said. 'I like to see you having a nice meal.'

'I'll have to get my coat soon,' said Lucia. 'I can't stay up at my age the way the lot of yous can.'

'Just have a nice bit of pudding first,' said Maria.

'You're getting that big.'

'Big?'

'Well, you're getting bigger and smaller at the same time. It's that nice having you back here. I've missed you, hen.'

Maria slid some potato gratin under her knife and fork, then went to the sink and drank a glass of water. She noticed Alfredo was laughing more. He seemed to laugh whenever anybody said anything. 'This is London food,' he whispered to Rosa.

'Happy birthday the both of you!' shouted Giovanni.

Maria put ice cream and lemon tart and cheese on the table. She looked at Alfredo and gave him one of her professional smiles. 'Where's a kiss for your wee mammy?' said Rosa. Then quite suddenly Maria felt her legs go weak and her head hurt. 'I always said a wee break would do you the world of good, didn't I?' said Rosa. 'A walking holiday.' And she ruffled her hair. 'Let's put on a wee bit of music,' she said.

Lucia had finished eating and her hands were clasped in front of her on the table. The two men were laughing and showed a great interest in one another the way laughing men do. Lucia looked at Giovanni and decided he was losing his looks; one of his white teeth was broken, shadows had begun to appear under his eyes and the shine had gone from his hair. He had a woman in Ardrossan, everybody knew it, and one in Largs; women had always been Giovanni's trouble, he was unable to walk past them, and each one believed in her doomed way that he was put into the world to make her happy. Lucia saw him laughing with Alfredo and returned her eyes to the mesh of her fingers. One thing she couldn't trust was good looks. Men like Giovanni Corso: they went on as if they might laugh their way into heaven, and lived as if sex was a thing you did on the way to thinking nothing of yourself.

Standing with her back to the taps, Maria, in her black pencil skirt, was passing slowly to another place. Lucia saw that there was a layer of soft blonde on Maria's face—that face, so photographed, so lit on, and now, in the upstairs kitchen at Victoria Street, the ordinary bulbs sent out a yellow haze to find her, a poor light that trapped itself in the down on her face, making her glow like a sick angel.

'Are you all right, hen?' asked Lucia.

'Absolutely,' said Maria, and she showed her teeth, which seemed too many, and too wide.

'That was a fine dinner,' said Lucia. 'You could've fed the five thousand out of that.'

'The old songs are always the best!' shouted Rosa from the living-room. 'Always the best! Here, mother. This is one of your old favourites. One of the ones belonging to my daddy.'

It sounded as if the crackles were from history, and the pitter-patter of static added much to the purity of the voice, which came into the room now like rain onto a table of crystal glasses. Carlo Buti singing 'Porta un Bacione a Firenze'—Carlo Buti, olive oil in the grooves of his larynx, his heart a bastion of ancient loves and provinces—and so it came to seem like music that had travelled far to reach the ears of a single girl. Rosa kicked off her slippers and began to dance on the carpet with a tumbler held up. She was on her own. The men continued to laugh and talk together, but Maria and Lucia were listening to Carlo Buti and found themselves quite frozen in one another's eyes. The evening air of Lucca circulated for a second in Lucia's thoughts and she heard this song in one of the squares and the thought gave way to a picture of the music playing at a trattoria in Clerkenwell and in the drift of her stirred memory she heard the sound of ropes unfurling at speed. Lucia stared at the kitchen wall as if an old film were playing there just for her, and she was filled with the charm and innocence of an early enjoyment. She looked at Maria, and distinctly, for everyone at the table to hear, she said the words: 'I came back for you but the corridors were impossible to pass.'

The song came to an end but Rosa soon found another. In the meantime, Maria continued to smile at her grandmother, not under-standing her but offering smiles of consolation. On hearing the words Lucia spoke, Alfredo stood up, took a stiff gulp of wine from his glass, and went into the hall to fetch the coats. Maria pressed a finger into some lamb and rosemary juice and rubbed it round the edge of her tongue, then she drank more water. When Lucia came through with her coat on she hugged Maria at the sink. 'Will you go back to London?' she asked.

'I'm ready, mammo,' said Maria. 'I'm ready to get back to work. I'm better now.'

'Watch yourself,' said Lucia, 'and ring me on the phone. I love it when you ring me on the phone.'

'Cheerio, mammo.'

'You have to watch yourself in London,' said Lucia, showing her age in the way she walked towards the door. 'It's not all fun and games in London.'

WITH SCALDING water Maria scrubbed every plate and surface after they'd gone. Every spoon was washed and rinsed and dried with a towel and put away. All the scraps of food—pounds of cooked meat, uneaten beans, pasta, salads, puddings—were dumped into black bags and carried down to the back of the shop. By the end the kitchen gleamed and Maria stood back and felt tall and superior as she looked into the centre of its cleanness. The music from the living-room was much louder now; she could hear them laughing and thumping about to pop songs.

She stepped into the cold. As usual, the wind was carrying sea-spray over the railings and into the town. She pulled up the collar of her mother's raincoat and walked over to the middle of the putting green. Up there at the window, she could see her mother and Giovanni dancing together and kissing. They were at the window and the light was very red behind them. Her mother and Giovanni were in their element and seemed happy. Maria watched as they swayed and let their hands hang loose over one another's backs. They danced like youngsters, each with a cheek laid down on the other's shoulder.

She walked out of the town. From higher up she could see the oily-looking harbour with the lights of the pier shivering over the water. She felt empty of everything; there was no food inside her and nothing to hinder her breathing, and walking along the pavement she felt she was somehow above everything. She told herself that no one could stand in the way of her and all the perfection in the world.

I am all breathing, all voice, she said to herself. 'Michael Aigas in London now,' she said. Then she thought of something else. 'The Water Rats. I'm not going if they expect me to give any kind of speech.'

The stars shone out as she climbed higher and began to take great gulps of the night air. She saw the meadow and how dark it was at that hour and she felt exhilarated and began to quicken her steps, involving herself with the wind rushing past her, then she began running over the grass and eating air as she moved. The branches were covered in leaves and she could see them floating down and hear the noise of the wind passing through them as she ran, saying to herself the moon was a great lamp, and the dark was falling behind her, past her ears and gone at her heels lifting off the grass. She ran as if the moonlight was something merciful in these non-human hours, the night air opened up and became her, and she could feel it inside as she swallowed more. Up ahead there was every promise, and she ran through the tall trees of the meadow with all her heart.

PART THREE

1 · Michael Aigas

I went to one of those universities where the English course is run by pop sociologists, clever, long-haired, Oxbridge men, the kind whose universe changed for ever the day Bob Dylan went electric, the ones who write unpublishable articles about the aesthetics of the leisure industry, tight-lipped, ambitious, tutorial-dodgers to a man, annoying in their zany socks and faded Nikes. These professors can be found in the corners of Northern pubs, on every side an adoring student desperate for a research assistantship at Rutgers. While the students get the drinks in, the great hero stares through the smoke and boasts of the books he has never read. I spent many a weary hour at those tables.

'*Moby Dick!*'

'That's worth a double brandy.'

'*Titus Andronicus!*'

'Storm the gantry.'

'*Barnaby Rudge!*'

'Bottles of sherry at the Halls!'

And back in some manky kitchen the real stuff would come out with the old punk records. The professor would proceed from single volumes to entire authors.

'Thomas Hardy!'

'Spark up that joint.'

'Flaubert!'

'Has anybody got any acid?'

'Henry James!'

'Is it okay if I crash here for the night?'

It was during one of these sessions that I became an enemy of the people and ruined my chances of a First. (No one comes out of this story at all well, especially me.) 'From a certain point of view,' I said, 'wasn't every form of tactlessness a contribution to Modernism?'

The professor almost froze mid-inhale. 'Holy Christ, man,' he said, coughing a lungful of dope smoke in my direction, 'who invited F. R. fucking Leavis?'

'You should try reading a novel now and then,' I said.

'For why?' he asked.

'For fucking pleasure, if not for instruction,' I said. 'I suppose it would count as a Fascistic act to expect you to avert your eyes from the mysteries of Abba for a nanosecond.'

'Go to sleep, little baby,' he said.

I said, 'Fuck you, Mr Semiotics of Tupperware. You don't have a fucking clue. Those books you mentioned before—I've read them all.'

'Nice one,' said the professor.

'Every one!' I said. 'Some of them twice!'

'Well, you have nice dark eyes,' said the professor.

'Books matter to people,' I shouted.

'An interesting point of view.'

'They do.'

'Dream on, Michael. Books have nothing to do with people's lives. The novel is dead on its feet.'

I didn't get to go to Rutgers.

I came to London after graduation and found a bedsit off Kensington Church Street, a place of antique shops; there was a tree that came up to my window on the top floor and a caged lift down to the street. Early in the mornings I walked across Hyde Park to a swimming-pool at Lancaster Gate. There was no one to talk to and London was a mystery, but I loved those first times in the city, reading newspapers and going to lectures near the Albert Hall. I walked across the park as if it were made for the likes of me, people with nothing to do in the morning but contemplate what they might do next.

In a suitcase on Portobello Road, I found a run of the literary magazine *Horizon*, and the man sold it to me (suitcase included) for twenty-five pounds. I would sit nearly every day eating a bag of apples and smelling of chlorine; my favourite spot was a bench across from the Peter Pan statue in Kensington Gardens, and sitting there I must admit I was more attentive to the innovations of Cyril Connolly than Margaret Thatcher.

I found a job in the *Evening Standard*. It said: 'Assistant Editor Wanted. *St Clare's Review*. Experience required. £8,000 per annum.' My experience was two summers in a television shop back home and a love of jazz: I cheered myself up on the way to the stationery shop by wondering if I was maybe over-qualified for the post of assistant editor. I got a pass and went to the round Reading Room at the British Library. St Clare's had been going since 1915. They used to run a home in Regent's Park and they looked after the war blinded, giving them houses and holidays and things to fill their time.

The office I first came to smelled of lemon tea and carbon paper. I was interviewed by a Wing Commander Philip Rodney. He had maps of Kent and Sussex on the wall of his private office and slipped me a mint imperial during the interview. 'There's not a whole lot to it,' he said, 'though you will have to be good with the old boys. That's a must.'

'I haven't really edited before,' I said.

'Oh, never mind that, it's not *The Times* or anything of that sort. Just a bit of lick and stick.'

'I would give it my best shot.'

'Marvellous,' said the Wing Commander. 'You seem like a good chap. Can you start a week on Monday?'

Before I stepped back into Marylebone Road I was taken around and shown more of the office. Philip was the public relations officer (the place was run like a battalion of the Kent dragoons under heavy bombardment at the Front, and I often told Sheila who came round with the tea-trolley she would soon be mentioned in dispatches) and he did the magazine and looked after publicity and clippings and stuff like that. There was a larger room attached to his office where the smell of carbon paper was at its strongest. This room housed Betty, an old lady with a turned-down mouth and round glasses, a really formidable, quite tiny woman from Hastings, who kept her Cairn terrier, Paul, in a basket under her desk and who was set in her ways to an Olympic gold-medal standard.

Across from her, next to a large oval window, was a rather beautiful-looking woman in her mid-forties, Jennifer, who kept her hair in a wooden Celtic clasp and spike. Jennifer had an Amstrad computer on her desk and kept her files and headed notepaper in perfect order. She was married to Martin, the deputy public relations officer, whose own small office was just behind her desk, and she attended to him alone as if they worked for a different firm. Martin was an ex-para who had been blown up in Derry. He was blind and gentle as the air-conditioning, and he was mostly interested in computers and sailing. All day, he and Jennifer would hold a private confab, only broken when Philip required his attention, which wasn't often. Martin had a talking computer and the office silence was broken by the sound of an Americanised lady's voice which announced the letters on the keyboard as Martin pressed them. Sometimes, unexpectedly, the dog Paul would yap back at the disembodied voice.

On my first day at St Clare's I discovered that Betty and Jennifer hated each other. This was mostly Betty's fault: she guarded her boss with a vengeance, and felt, in her old-age-pensioner way, that the younger woman and her husband were trying to make her redundant. Betty refused to use the photocopier, she wound sweet-smelling carbon paper into her typewriter for every letter, and she typed slowly and used Tippex before filing the second copy in a bank of hanging folders. Edwardian dust would float down to her desk every time they were disturbed. Betty came to work every day in a bad mood. She would open the post in silence and put to one side the things for Martin. By the time the lemon tea and biscuits came round, at eleven, she was sometimes ready to laugh at a joke, but mainly she cleaved entirely to her resentments, and was always on the look-out for trouble from Jennifer.

Philip and Martin were the sort of men who claimed to want nothing to do with their guardians' strife, but in some ways they kept it going, and benefited from it. In my first weeks at the office Philip told me to keep my own counsel. 'They will fight over you and try to persuade you,' he said, 'but just remember your tasks, old chap, and leave them to it.' I took his advice, but it wasn't easy: Betty was nervous of me, I think, and she was always taking work off my desk. She liked to proofread the magazine—she'd been doing it for forty years—and was always inserting commas and consulting Fowler's. She liked to make jokes about Scotland and the way I spoke; that was fine, anything to keep her happy, but some days her relationship with the older St Clareites made it impossible to get anything done. I'd be about to ring Surrey to find out about some anniversary or sporting success for the Happy Events page, and Betty would appear at my desk with a mouth full of pinking shears, saying, 'I'll speak to Tom and Edna. That's one of the things I've always done.'

The magazine was a bit of an absurdity. I would often stay late in the office with the lights of Marylebone glowing outside, and I'd hang over the lay-out desk, sizing photographs, writing captions, forming headlines, for a magazine that nobody except me and Betty was really going to read. It was like one long *Monty Python* sketch, the magazine for the blind, and Betty sniggered like a schoolgirl one morning when I said I was planning to lay out the next issue upside down. *St Clare's Review* went straight onto Braille, which Martin supervised, and it also went onto tape, read every month in a plummy voice by an actor Philip had known in the army.

The other departments were staffed mainly by ex-army officers and women in their sixties. There was an officer-corps mentality in the canteen, and some of the women brought knitting to work, and you half-expected them to shout you out for air-raid drill at the drop of a stitch. I was soon having what appeared to be over-the-desk affairs with all of them. Minnie Hopfield worked in Legacies. She was nearly seventy and she travelled in from Putney every day. To Betty and Jennifer's horror—and Philip's and my delight—she swore like a darts fan and smoked like hell. And yet she was Home Counties posh in the way most of them were: she loved a nice glass of wine, home-made jam, she'd been around the world, and she was ultra-aware of the poison upstairs in our office. 'Jolly well keep your distance from all those nutcases,' she once said. 'They'll drag you into every fucking thing if you're not careful.'

'Why doesn't Philip put a stop to it?' I asked.

'More trouble than it's worth,' she said. 'He's a gentleman, and he just wants to sit in his office with the door shut and read the *Telegraph*.'

Minnie told me the charity was insanely rich. Ex-servicemen had been leaving money to St Clare's since the 1920s, but the generations who were blinded in war were dying out, and the money, which had been brilliantly managed by a series of chief accountants (the real bosses of the organisation), was just growing and growing with nowhere to go. 'It sounds fucking perverse,' said Minnie, 'but the folk upstairs were almost excited when the Falklands happened, I swear. Don't get me wrong, dear: nobody wants a young fellow to lose his eyes, but the charity is dying and it will have to do something. The idea of some new people to benefit did seem, well... it created a bit of excitement. Make no mistake about that.'

I told her she was a terrible person.

'That's as may be, but as Elsa used to say'—Minnie had been friends in the 1940s with the actress Elsa Lanchester, and she thought that Elsa had been through everything, being married to Charles Laughton and all, and would quote her on any subject, no matter how unlikely a preoccupation for a Hollywood actress—'as Elsa used to say, "One can't feed hens if there's no hens to feed."'

However sublimated, this point had been thoroughly absorbed into the mind of the charity by the time I arrived. I would sometimes run into Sir Edmund Noble, Admiral of the Fleet and Chairman of St Clare's, as I walked down to the strong room to find some photograph of the wounded at Passchendaele. He was a tall, lean gentleman, high-toned and watery-eyed, and he would stop in front of you as if waiting for a salute. 'Good afternoon, sir,' I remember saying one of those times.

'Are you civilian?'

'Yes, sir,' I said, feeling a bit of a let-down.

'And Scottish?'

'Indeed, sir. Scottish. But I can't help it.'

'No need to help it, my boy,' he said (he didn't care for jokes). 'Some of the best men I've ever met. Good people. You've a lot to live up to.'

'Well, thank you, sir.'

'Not at all. Well, on your way. We won't win the battle standing here.'

Edmund Noble was the man who told Thatcher he could organise a flotilla of ships for the Falklands in forty-eight hours. He had done so, and was known at St Clare's for being closest to those young men, the few we had, who were blinded at Goose Green and on HMS *Sheffield*. He was always asking us to prepare for future casualties. 'Never go to sleep on the job,' he said. 'There's poison gas out there, and barbarians not afraid to use it.'

Betty wanted to be my friend once she was sure I wasn't going to take sides with Jennifer and Martin. I sometimes took Paul the dog for a run at lunchtime, that won her over, and then she giggled up the sleeve of her cardigan one day when I was sorting out the wallets for the audio tapes and accidentally told Jennifer I didn't much fancy the Welsh. 'Why ever not?' she asked.

'They're always moaning,' I said.

'Well,' she said, turning into her husband's office and closing the door at her back, 'we know you *needn't* be Welsh for that!'

Betty was almost levitating with pleasure. 'You silly sausage,' she said. 'Her mother's Welsh.'

'Oops,' I said.

Later that day, Betty came to my desk with a cake she'd taken from the canteen. 'That report you wrote about the Brighton reunion,' she said, 'it's the first reunion report that wasn't boring in years. I liked the thing about the end of the pier from Trollope.'

'A bit cloggsy,' I said.

'That's okay,' she said. 'I'm sure we can cope with one clever clogs about here. Here's a present for you. Now don't be getting used to it.'

Betty had lost what she called 'my chap' many years before and she would mention him often but never explain. His name was James and they weren't married—not enough leave, I suspect—and by the time I knew her Betty had spent many years both tidy and alone, giving a succession of small dogs the greater part of her love. She had got into the habit of her unhappiness, so you couldn't be surprised at the way she protected her resentments and her old way of doing things, and yet unexpectedly, now and then, she would get the giggles, you'd see a flash of goodwill, and for a second it would refresh her whole face and the atmosphere around her, bringing to mind the girl she must have been with James.

'Do you look like your mother?' she asked.

'I don't know,' I said. 'I was adopted as a baby.'

'I'm sorry.'

'No need. They're great, the parents I've got. I just don't know who the real ones were or what they looked like.'

The years of living too much in her own head had put something coarse into Betty's notion of intimacy. 'Did they abandon you?' she said.

'I've never asked.'

'"Abandon" is such an old-fashioned word. It probably doesn't mean anything much.'

'Well, it means something,' I said. 'It's really what people mind about. It's what music is nearly always about—abandoned by this or that, a woman or a man or your parents or God.'

'I don't know any songs about being abandoned by God,' said Betty.

'Neither do I.' We laughed. 'Shall we write one, then?'

Betty laughed about four weeks' worth of laughter.

'I don't know what happened to my real parents,' I said. 'It's never really bothered me. I suppose they must have their own story.'

Betty frowned then shrugged and the moment passed. 'I'd better get back to these galleys,' she said. 'Those typesetters aren't worth their wages.'

I was also spending time with the St Clareites, walking with them in the countryside, supervising bus runs to here or there, going to re-unions, refereeing blind sports, and I became close to some of them. Most had been young men when they were blinded; the last time they had seen the world it was full of smoke and flying dirt, but now they wanted to be guided to peaceful places. St Clare's had taught them Braille, it had given them work, pensions, holiday homes, communities—but it couldn't return them to English normality, the things they craved most and loved.

My job on those days out was to be the eyes, and there is one day I remember better than the others. I was leading a group of veterans of the old stamp, eight of them, half over eighty-five (veterans of Ypres, the Somme and the Dardanelles), three from Dunkirk, and one younger man, Ronnie, blinded by shrapnel during Suez. All of them loved the South Downs. It was something to do with their sense of England: the loveliness of the Downs themselves existed in their memories, but they were also conscious of the sea beyond the cliffs, and of Europe out there. The men seemed pleased to be with one another in the open air and away from their wives for the day, and it felt strange to be thought of as their leader, aged twenty-four, describing the many shades of blue I could see, picking up stones and grass for them to touch and flowers to sniff.

I had named the group the Rodmell Fusiliers, and devised a system for getting them across the Downs: it was to use a clothes pole, with me holding the front of it, Ronnie at the back, and the veterans of the trenches and Dunkirk between us, holding on to the pole as we marched up the South Downs Way. On each trip with this group, I added more stuff I could say, just to make the afternoon work better. I had passages from *The Old Yarns of Sussex* and pamphlets on botany and I would recite poems to liven up the journey over the fields. One of the older men, Archie, had known some of Rupert Brooke's companymen, and walking one foot in front of the other we would go quiet listening to what he remembered.

This one day stands out above the rest. The Rodmell Fusiliers were in good form; they stood beside the van at Lewes in their dark glasses, their knapsacks of lunch on their backs. They never brought white sticks to the Downs. They were old but they were in good shape, apart from the eyes: each man had lived with blindness so long he had mostly forgotten how to think of it as an affliction. They touched things. They listened. They sniffed the air and made the kinds of joke and said things they knew they could only do in the company of other men.

I drove them first to Charleston. I had been talking about Bloomsbury to some of them—'arty-farty,' they said—and then they decided they wanted to know what it was all about. I parked the van and gathered them at the gate to the house. 'There's a fine pond,' I said, 'and a willow at one side and a stone or flint wall edging the garden part, and a lawn that slopes down there, with formal bushes. Further up there are box hedges and it's all well-ordered.'

'Were they all poofs?' said Simon Gedge.

'More or less,' I said.

'They were COs and poofs,' said Archie. 'The women an' all.'

'Artist folk,' said another.

'Intellectuals,' said Simon. 'Never worked a day their lives. Should shoot the lot of them with the enemy's bullets.'

Inside the house they occasionally stopped complaining while I told them what things looked like. 'Doorknobs in pink and leaf-patterns over the furniture,' I said. 'There's a dresser painted different kinds of green and a fish-carpet. Just under where you're standing.'

'Would give you a sore head,' said Simon.

'Do they have clocks?' said Ronnie from the back.

'No, Ronnie, they weren't that fond of clocks.'

'Were they fond of loos?' asked Archie. 'I'm bursting for a pee.'

Ten minutes later, in the shop, I was trying to describe a Picasso poster. 'I can't imagine it,' said Ronnie.

'Very black eyes,' I said. 'Iberian eyes. Like Picasso's own eyes in fact. So many of his paintings have these very round and very Span-ish black eyes.'

'I'll give him black eyes,' said Simon. 'Let's get the fuck out of here, it's boring.'

'You're an ignoramus, Gedge,' I said. I put his hand on my shoul-der and got the others to file behind. 'Even if you weren't blind as a bat you'd still be blind as a bat.'

'He's proud of it,' said another.

'There isn't much to see here,' said Simon.

We drove on to Alfriston and I parked the van in the grounds of St Andrew's Church. Archie told us how he knew this village before the Great War. 'I remember the look of it very well,' he said, 'and the Long Bridge over the Cuckmere. My sister and I once scraped our names into one of the stones there with a thrupenny bit.' He put his fingers over the front of his dark glasses. 'You can feel right enough it's a warm day today,' he said. 'I wonder if the Cuckmere gets high like it used to. It used to get very high.'

We ate our packed lunches under the trees. I poured the tea from a flask jammed in the spare wheel at the back of the van, and Simon stuck his finger into his cup. 'Don't be stingy,' he said. 'This cup's half empty. I know you're giving that Ronnie more than me just be-cause he's arty-farty.'

'You can't beat Sussex for weather,' said Jim Nelson. Jim was a Scouser; he'd come with his wife several years ago to live at the St Clare's house at Ovingdean. His skin had seen all weathers and was shiny, ever so white, with little scrubs of red on his cheekbones where the vessels had broken. 'You get a different smell in the air down here.'

'You do that,' said Simon. 'Smell of cow's shite.'

'Very good, smartarse,' said Jim. 'It's not that. The place smells green.'

'No. I think it's yellow,' one of the others said.

'No, Jimbo. You're right enough. Green.'

'I would say blue,' said Norman Oakley. 'Blue as the day you were born, sunshine.' Norman was the oldest. He was ninety-one. He wasn't married and insisted he be allowed to come on the walks. After I packed away the tin foil and cups and got the clothes pole from the van we made our way onto the Downs. Norman stood behind me, held the pole tight, and chattered.

'Just say if you want a rest, Norman.'

'Champion, son. Just you lead the way.'

'We've a bit to go today,' I said.

'Step smartly.'

They all liked to talk about being blind. For each of them it was the great subject of their lives. Norman could grow breathless telling you about a mustard gas attack. 'That's the last thing I knew,' he said. 'My eyes were stinging, but not as much as my armpits and my balls. It stings so powerful you wouldn't believe. Then the eyes went out.'

'That's right enough,' said Archie.

'The balls,' said 'Wobble' Gadney. 'I wasn't worried about the eyes. I thought the old knackers would be off.'

Simon and the younger men tended to go quiet when the older veterans spoke like this. They didn't know about gas, but that wasn't why they shut up: it was to let the older men have their say and to respect their seniority. Nobody ever contradicted Norman. He was in charge of his own experience and they left it at that.

I stopped sometimes and laid the pole on the grass. Then I would try to describe the view: the slope of the hills and the sheep scattered about, the occasional butterfly disappearing behind a stone dyke. At one point we found a mound of wild parsley; I picked a bunch and told them to put out their tongues. 'Body of Christ,' I said, and they laughed.

'Born Celtic supporter,' said Simon. 'You're telling us this is parsley. I bet it's shamrock.'

'You'll never know,' I said.

'Definitely parsley,' said Ronnie. 'Our Jeanette could whip up a great sauce for cod out of that.'

'We're not going to have to walk back, are we?' said Simon.

'Just you,' I said.

'Piss off. I'll just hitch a lift back with a sexy woman,' he said.

'I don't doubt it,' I said. 'And she'd need four eyes for your none.'

'You tell him,' said Norman.

'The porter from Ovingdean is collecting us on the other side,' I said. 'Don't worry your poor legs.'

'I could walk from here to the Black Sea,' said Ronnie.

We had a rest beside a rape field and then at Norman's insistence we headed on. The men went on talking about football results and house prices and Ronnie sang a sentimental song about a girl from the Forest of Dean. As we climbed over the Downs the sun seemed to rise alongside us and eventually we could smell the sea. 'Smell that,' said Jim Nelson. 'The Channel.'

I could feel the clothes pole stiffen and the pace was stepped up behind me. 'Steady,' I said. But there was a resolve now to get to the top and I started to tell them how the water looked with the sun making it glimmer for miles.

'Are there boats?' said Archie.

'Nothing,' I said. 'It's clear to the horizon.'

'Very blue?' said Wobble.

'Blue,' I said. 'Changing blues, it's a million wee strokes of paint out there.'

'And you can't see boats?' said Simon.

'Clear,' I said, 'not a single boat to be seen.'

'At one time whole squadrons of RAF would go right over here and that was them off,' said Archie.

We stopped and all listened together as a cricket made its noise beside us in the field. 'Lead on, Mr Aigas,' said Norman.

'Officer Aigas,' said Archie.

'Captain Aigas,' said Jim.

'Herr Kommandant Aigas,' said Simon.

'That's just enough of that,' said Norman.

We were up near Beachy Head. No one else was there at that hour to see the Rodmell Fusiliers marching on the pole, and in an instant the whole scene seemed very dear and quiet.

'Can we sit down for a while?' Archie said. And in that moment I wanted to do better for them.

'We'll go closer,' I said. 'I want you to hear the waves.'

'Yes,' whispered Norman behind me, 'take us closer.'

We went forward and the wind lifted.

'This is a lovely day,' said Norman.

'Sit down here,' I said. 'All of you sit down.' Touching one another's shoulders for guidance they sat on the downland grass.

'Right enough,' said Jim Nelson. 'You can hear the water coming in.' They sat quiet for a moment and they listened for the sound of waves on the beach far below us.

'It's all out there,' said Simon.

'Michael,' said Norman, 'give us some of your words. This is a lovely day. We'll just sit up here for a while. Read something.'

I stood up with my back to the Channel and looked at the old men sitting on the grass.

'In *King Lear*,' I said, 'blind Gloucester is really at the end of his tether...'

'Shakespeare,' said Wobble.

'Yes,' I said, 'and Gloucester's son Edgar, who's in disguise—his father doesn't know who he is—takes him by the hand. His father is blind and he has lost interest in all his hopes and the king has gone mad.'

I paused to think.

'Go on,' said Norman.

'Why is the son in disguise?' said Archie.

'He's in danger,' I said, 'and his mind isn't right.'

'Go on,' said Norman.

'Gloucester wants to end it all,' I said, 'so he persuades Edgar to lead him to a cliff so's he can fall off and die. But Edgar loves his father and only pretends to do it. He keeps him on flat ground but tricks his father into thinking he is indeed on a high cliff and is about to fall. Gloucester can't see the truth.'

The men were quiet. They said nothing for a minute and the sea at my back was calm and almost imaginary, but you could hear the waves coming to wash the chalk cliffs from under us. Each of the veterans stood up and lifted his face to the fresh air—England behind them, eyes closed, they listened to the lapping waves and the words:

> Come on, sir; here's the place: stand still. How fearful
> And dizzy 'tis, to cast one's eye so low!
> The crows and choughs that wing the midway air
> Show scarce so gross as beetles: half way down
> Hangs one that gathers samphire, dreadful trade!
> Methinks he seems no bigger than his head:
> The fishermen, that walk upon the beach,
> Appear like mice, and yond tall anchoring bark,
> Diminish'd to her cock; her cock, a buoy
> Almost too small for sight: the murmuring surge,
> That on the unnumbered idle pebbles chafes,
> Cannot be heard so high: I'll look no more;
> Lest my brain turn, and the deficient sight
> Topple down headlong.

Towards the end of the summer things took a turn for the worse in the Marylebone office. Betty went berserk one afternoon, shouting so much and so loudly that Paul hopped out of his basket and sought refuge under my desk in the corner. There was no surprise at the subject of Betty's fury—it was Jennifer, whom Betty accused of taking a pile of work off her desk, and, furthermore, of bringing lemon teas for everybody in Public Relations except her.

Wing Commander Rodney heard the kerfuffle and made a rare appearance. 'Betty, you're distraught,' he said.

'This . . . this *bitch* is stealing work from me and trying to make me look idle, Philip.'

'You want to be careful there,' said Jennifer, who was younger and less unhappy, more than capable of coming into her own in a crisis.

The deputy public relations officer felt his way out of his office. His eyes were on the ceiling. 'Is something the matter?' he said.

'You and your wife are trying to put me out of a job!' shouted Betty. 'I've been here since 1946!'

'Calm down, Betty,' said the Wing Commander. 'We'll sort this out in a jiffy.'

'Philip,' said Jennifer, straightening up and looking at the boss as if her point was already clear to him, 'we need these anniversary invitations to go out today. I know you gave the job to Betty, but we'll miss the deadline if she goes on refusing to use the photocopier. She's been typing the same letter for the last week and a half.'

'Have you seen *her* letters?' said Betty. 'They are barely literate. Where's my coat? Here, Paul.'

Philip said Betty's name several times and as she put on her coat and blew her nose and unfurled Paul's lead he grew surprisingly red in the face. 'Betty,' he said, 'I forbid you to leave your post. We will all stay here and sort this out!'

'Goodbye, Michael,' she said, looking over, and with that she went home and took to her bed for a week.

'Blast!' said Philip.

While Betty was away we got all the anniversary stuff organised and into envelopes and continued to include her in all our plans. I have to say the office was dull without Betty; it was true, she was probably the cause of most of the problems, but she was more interesting than Jennifer and Martin, who were simply laying plans to take over the show when Philip retired.

The seventieth anniversary of St Clare's. What a job. They had special services and parties, reunions all over the place and a thing at Buckingham Palace. 'Have you got a hat?' I said to Betty the day before the do, when she was back at her desk.

'Same one as the fiftieth,' she said. 'I doubt the Royals'll remember it. You should come.'

'No,' I said, 'there's too much to do at Ovingdean. You go, Betty, and have a nice time with your friends. They'll all be there.'

'I could give you some money if you're skint and need to buy something.' She was facing her antique filing system when she said this and I could see the dust descending to the back of her cardigan.

'You're lovely,' I said, 'but I've got to be in Ovingdean to sort out the reunion. It's mainly the TV people. The *Songs of Praise* people. They're doing a whole bit there and I've got to stop them all from crashing into one another. But it was really lovely of you to offer, Betty.'

'Nothing ventured nothing gained,' she said.

It was my main job that month. I was talking to the BBC researcher every day and on one of them he said they wanted to book a singer to do a hymn at Ovingdean. They would have St Clareites talking about their lives and some stuff down at the sports field and a bit of the reunion. Then the singer would come on and do a big number with the choir. 'It has to be someone they would all know,' said the researcher, 'someone who can do it with a bit of feeling.'

'It's always Vera Lynn,' I said.

'We've been talking about her,' said the researcher, 'and we've had her on so many times before. We were hoping for someone younger and with a less obvious connection to these things. We thought we would try for Maria Tambini.'

I remember pausing and standing up at my desk.

'What a good idea,' I said. 'Is she working?'

'She's trying to get back,' he said. 'You know she's been ill for a while.'

'Yes.'

'She's better. She's looking to work again.'

'Good. That's a brilliant idea.' We spoke for a bit about vehicle access and electricity points.

'Let's just hope for the weather,' he said.

'I used to know Maria Tambini,' I said. 'We grew up in the same place in Scotland. I know her.'

'Really?' said the guy. 'Before she was famous on that Hughie Green thing? Before she had her own show?'

'Yeah,' I said, 'before all that. She's just a few years younger than me. We grew up on the Isle of Bute.'

'Amazing,' he said.

'She used to sing in the pubs and at local talent shows and all that kind of thing.'

'Yeah?'

'And you could tell she was good,' I said. 'You could tell something was going to happen to her.'

'How amazing. Well, that's who we want for this. I'll keep you posted.'

After that—when everything was sorted up—I asked him for the number of her manager or whatever. I suddenly wanted to see her before the show, to talk to her again. I just wanted to see her. Her manager was called Marion something, they put me through to her. She said Maria was in Scotland. I told her who I was and that I worked for St Clare's and just rambled a bit. The manager said she would pass on my message.

Maria Tambini. When I thought of her I saw that wee lassie with a voice that lifted the roof. She had a way of singing that stopped you right where you stood; my pals and I were full of America at that time, jazz and bebop, yet Maria Tambini was above and beyond the everyday thing in Rothesay. Even as a girl there was an atmosphere around her. Over these last years you'd always see her on television. Made for TV. I can see her racing to the camera from the middle of a group of tall dancers, this bundle of energy, or stepping up to the microphone to sing one of those great big onion ballads. She would tremble singing the song. She felt the words, you could tell that and she got more beautiful over time, before she got too thin. You'd see these articles in the paper about her being in clinics and stuff about the perils of being famous too young, and Maria was always there.

A letter came to St Clare's. 'Dear Michael,' it said, 'Marion Gaskell told me you are involved in the *Songs of Praise* recording next week. What a surprise after all these years. Well, not that many years, but it feels like a long time. I'll be at the Metropole Hotel. Please come and see me, I want to hear all your news.' And it was signed, 'Sincerely yours, Maria Tambini.'

I folded the letter into my wallet and got on with the plans for Ovingdean, but every so often I would look up, and it wasn't Betty I saw there, or Paul the dog, or Jennifer plotting the future of the office or the Wing Commander vanishing again, but the face of Maria Tambini and an old feeling as familiar as milk.

'Penny for your thoughts,' said Betty.

'I only work in tenners,' I said.

2 · Wogan

MARIA: Well thank you. It's nice to be back.

WOGAN: That was a terrific song. Beautifully sung. Nothing wrong with the old vocal cords then.

MARIA: Thank you.

WOGAN: You're a bit shy aren't you? A girl like you. You've sung with Dean Martin in Vegas... what?... come away. You've topped the bill at the Palladium. You've had your own TV show. Come on my girl. You're not shy are you?

MARIA: Thing is Terry, I'm a bit shy because I've heard from my showbusiness friends what a thrill it is to touch your knee.

WOGAN: Oh, not that again. People are willing to pay good money for that. Oh, go on then, seeing as it's you. It's a bit better than your average knee isn't it?

MARIA: My mother will be so jealous.

WOGAN: Enough of the mother. I'm younger than I look. Doing this show has put years on me. Now, enough of this tomfoolery. You're very much back and to hear you sing it's like you've never been away at all. You were very young when you first came to everybody's attention. Do you think that's hard for a performer? When you see some of the younger ones coming through...

MARIA: No, not really. I just loved singing.

WOGAN: But it's the pressure isn't it?

MARIA: That's right. Some of the things that were happening, I don't think I even realised how big it was. You just turned up and somebody gave you a costume. It was just so brilliant and exciting for a young girl.

WOGAN: But pretty daunting. Here you were—what, twelve, thirteen years old—away from your family and down in London. You're busy, so you don't have the time for normal things, do you? You wouldn't call it a normal childhood.

MARIA: Such a new place. I mean, I had never seen traffic lights before coming down. Things like that.

WOGAN: Is that right?

MARIA: Yeah, and double-decker buses. It was amazing really. But my manager was always showing me the ropes. I've always had my own room and everything.

WOGAN: Not normal though, the normal things children do with themselves.

MARIA: Well, it was normal to me. I loved singing and the performance bit was always in me, I suppose. We used to sing at my mother's parties and we'd put a curtain up at the door and they were just really, really good times. There's pressure, but when you're new to the business you only see the bright lights and you think wow.

WOGAN: I know you don't want to go into this too much, but you've been ill a lot over the last couple of years. You recently admitted in an interview that it was the slimmers' disease, anorexia nervosa. How did you cope with that?

MARIA: I don't know really. I suppose you just get caught up in wanting to look your best and at stage school you see the other dancers and you think, 'It's not fair, they look better than me.' And you don't realise you're losing that much weight. I don't know really. You just want to be the best you can.

WOGAN: You've been very brave to talk about it. And you're over it now. You've got the new show in Blackpool. You're fighting fit, and food isn't a problem, is that right?

MARIA: Definitely. I just want to sing again and do what I do best.

WOGAN: Your family are all Italians, aren't they? You've got the café and the old fish'n'chips up there in Scotland. You'll be able to join in with all that again?

MARIA: Uh-huh. It's nice to do the normal things and be with your family.

WOGAN: The illness must have put pressure on them. Have they been supportive in seeing you through?

MARIA: Oh definitely. They're always there to help me if I need them. You can always rely on your family.

WOGAN: That's terrific. What about this celebrity business? People like you who come from normal backgrounds and then make it as a singer, it's a fascinating business for people, isn't it? I mean, when you go through a bad patch it's all in the magazines and everybody's interested.

MARIA: I don't know. It's easy to criticise people for liking all that but if you go to work every day it's probably quite nice to hear a singer you like or see someone doing well or buying a nice house or whatever. I don't know. It can become a bit much I suppose. You've just got to ignore some of the stuff that's written and remember who you are.

WOGAN: I've got to ask you. How's the old love life?

MARIA: People are always asking me that! The truth is I'm too busy at the moment for a relationship like that. There's always so much work to do.

WOGAN: Well, you've got all the time in the world for that. I must say it's been a tremendous pleasure having you on the show, and looking so well. We wish you the best of luck. You're going to do another number for us, what is it?

MARIA: It's a lovely song called 'One Day at a Time'.

WOGAN: Ladies and gentleman, back on form again, and appearing up and down the country from now until Christmas and we hope for a long time after that, please put your hands together again, for the lovely Maria Tambini.

3 · They

'I've been waiting to talk to you for a long time,' he said, 'and sometimes I've looked for you when I looked at other people. I only realised that at the Metropole last month. I only knew that when you walked over to the table and sat down.'

She felt nervous in her fingertips, but she lifted a hand from the table and brushed the hair from his eyes.

4 · Light Entertainment

A bus was hired to take Maria and the band and the dancers up for the Blackpool Christmas Special. Maria sat at the back looking out of the window; the speed England passed the window made her unsettled and she bit her nails to the quick.

Stop the bus. I want to go back. He is working now at his desk and he is inside his shirt. I want to go back.

As the bus moved up the motorway, Maria imagined the houses and the electricity pylons were blurring into fuzz. Marion came up to the back and told her there was no reason to look so sullen. 'The show's a sell-out,' she said.

'I don't want to do the show,' said Maria.

'Well that's a lovely attitude, Maria. Just perfect. We're trying to get you back to work, dear. Can you look at me when I'm talking to you?' Maria turned round; her eyes were damp and for a moment she wanted to slap her manager in the face.

'How long will it be before I'm back home?'

'In Rothesay? There's no plan to go—'

'In London!'

'This is a fearfully good three-week engagement.'

'How many...?'

'Eight shows a week.'

Marion's face seemed blurred and there appeared to be static around her head and over the window. Maria blinked and tried to pull herself together. 'It's a good arrangement, Maria. Are you feeling weak? You've always loved working. What is the matter, dear?'

Maria kept as much of her life secret as she could. That had been her habit; it was now her character. She liked to think of Marion knowing nothing about her; she took comfort in the notion that she was able to make herself a stranger to her family. Marion shook her head and walked back to the front of the bus, and Maria, feeling at once elated and hungry and weepy, looked out at the crackling and fizzing grey of the motorway.

He showed me the blind place at Ovingdean, with the glass place that overlooks the water and you can nearly see all the way across to the Continent. The men used to be soldiers and they are his friends now and when we walked up the hill we all sat on the grass and the men were chatting. We walked off and stood on our own and he held my hand and gave me an apple. My stomach was turning and it was just us standing there and I began to cry in front of him. 'I don't deserve this,' I said. And what he did, he kissed the apple and he put it in my hand. 'It's me that doesn't deserve you,' he said.

Maria fell asleep in confusion as the bus moved and her head was elsewhere and strange to her. Months ago, before she met Michael, she had started having 'static', that's what she called it: she would be walking down the street and suddenly it became like a television at night after all the programmes have finished. The greyness seemed to pour into everything she looked at. At times, talking to one of the dancers or trying to learn the words of a new song, she would be aware of the world moving away from her, growing unfocused, and her insides would flutter as she stepped into this far-away place. All the while, she would smile more, giggle more, trying to present a lively girl to the people in front of her, yet for all her words, for all her songs and show-business gestures, she experienced herself, more and more, as entirely removed from reality, at first pawing the static around her to find her bearings, but then, as the minutes passed, as the hours and the days passed, becoming inseparable from it and seeing only greyness.

When she opened her eyes her head was against the window. It was dark outside, reindeer glowed by the road, the Seven Dwarves showed their different faces, and Little Red Riding Hood was shadowed by a purple wolf. Pinocchio was in conversation with Jimminy Cricket. The Darling children flew over some cardboard London. Dorothy glowed in her ruby slippers and Cinderella was separated from an elegant shoe, left by accident at the base of a neon staircase. With her head on the window, Maria stared out unblinkingly, and the Blackpool Illuminations reflected on the wetness of her eyes. She could see clouds of colour, rotating, flashing, travelling over the glass towards her. It took seconds for her to realise she was looking at the Blackpool lights. A *Star Wars* tableau hovered into view: Princess Leia with a small robot.

'Have you woken up?' said Marion. 'We're almost at the hotel, dear. Aren't the illuminations beautiful this year? They get more and more amazing every time. Can you see them?'

'Yes,' said Maria.

At the Winter Gardens there is a wooden board in the ticket hall which commemorates the legends of British Variety. After playing for a fortnight, Maria went down there one afternoon before her show, with nobody about, and looked up at the board. She had been talking to Michael every night on the phone and she dreaded that he was bored with her already and it made her panic a little as she looked at the names on the board. 'Arthur Askey,' it said. 'Danny La Rue.'

During the Blackpool run Maria was mostly on her own. She wasn't joining in with anything and never ate with anyone. 'Don't you start' is all she would say to people who asked how she was feeling and what was she going to eat. But she had good showbusiness manners: she would always go and shake hands with any new act that came into the show. Albert Gay, a ventriloquist from Lancashire, was supposed to be on the bill for the whole run, but he was drunk on whisky all the time, and finally they fired him. The night before he went, Maria turned up at his dressing-room and found him slumped in a chair in the corner. 'Aren't you going to do your make-up?' Maria asked.

'No, little girl,' he said, 'I'm colourful enough.' He sat thinking for a second and opened his mouth. 'I am sorry,' he said. The sound was clear though he hardly moved his lips.

'Let me tell you something, Albert. I couldn't care less about this show or about any of it. Make-up. No make-up. I couldn't care less. I'm not the boss here, you can say what you like.'

'You'll go far,' he said.

'Can I have a drink?'

'You what?'

'I'd like to have a drink.'

Albert Gay took a bottle of Bell's out of the drawer and shaking his head just the once he went for two glasses.

'You know what this place smells like?' said Albert. 'It smells of chips and orange peel and sweat, and it's been like that for as long as I can remember.' Maria smiled and then winced as she drained the glass. She held it out. They drank two more.

'I'm enjoying myself,' she said.

'We all are,' he said.

'I wish I could just leave here.'

'Shhhhhhhh,' he said. He put a yellow-stained finger to her lips and shook his head. Then he drank the last of the Bell's and spoke about years ago. He closed his eyes at one point and went on speaking. Maria slipped out of Mr Gay's dressing-room and went back to her own, where she locked the door and was sick.

There was too much weight on her face and she couldn't stand her chin. Growing tearful, she dabbed her blusher-brush into a tray of ruby-coloured powder and stroked it up her cheekbones. She saw a bunch of carnations standing against the mirror with a note. 'I've seen your show every night Maria and think you're great,' the note said. 'Please keep on singing and remember the old ones are always the best. God bless you. Kevin Goss.'

THERE WERE people whose interest in Maria Tambini seemed to rise with her decline. Over the years she had uncovered an audience who were attracted to her suffering: she could disappear into her illnesses for a year or two, and during this time letters and cards would arrive, written by people who only saw her perform once, in Blackpool perhaps, or in Bridlington, or who remembered her big smile on *Opportunity Knocks*. They wondered, these people, as they said in their letters, what had happened to Maria Tambini and how she was getting on. Some of them had found one of her old LPs at a jumble sale: it made them think of how much she had given and how sick she had become and that they needed to reach out to her. At the office, Marion Gaskell had a giant file of these letters and a few more would be added to it every week.

The summer after the Blackpool season, Maria went to perform at Butlins in Skegness. She did the first evening with Cannon and Ball and it turned out to be fun: she and the dancers had good memories of working on the television show, and the two men teased her and made her feel stronger somehow. She was given a large chalet at Butlins. She felt it was damp but she didn't complain; at night, though, after the show was over, she would lie in the bed listening to the sound of drunk people laughing outside, and she felt the cold in her bones.

He kissed me on the stairs to the rooms at Ovingdean. He made me steady on his arm and I could feel his fingers move over my shoulders and into my hair and breathing quick and the feel of his jaw was scratchy and bending down to my mouth he put his tongue into my mouth and right then I wanted to bite his tongue and suck it and there was water in my mouth and I could feel my breasts. I wanted him to put his tongue there so I said to him all I want is a cuddle that's all I want if you don't mind is a kiss and a cuddle.

Michael came up from London one weekend. They went on the boating pond and went into Skegness where he bought her a gold bracelet. 'Can we put our names inside?' she asked. The man in the shop engraved their names while they waited, and Michael took her hand so easily, and she promised herself she would come and buy him a watch one day. Sometimes he would just put his lips high up on her cheek and whisper to her. On the monorail going round Butlins he drummed out a rhythm against the window and made a voice like Louis Armstrong's and when she giggled he leaned over and clasped her knees and kissed her head. They looked down at the Ferris wheel, the rows of chalets, the fountains, the outdoor swimming-pools and the factory dininghalls. 'It's like a concentration camp down there,' Michael said.

'I want to move away from Marion's house.'

'Live with me,' he said.

'I'm not ready,' she said. 'It's too big a jump. Do you think I could find a flat close by?'

'Definitely.'

'Will you help me?'

'Definitely.'

'I won't always be asking for help, Michael,' she said. 'It won't always be me needing help. I hope not.' He leaned in and held her ears and widened his eyes and she laughed into his mouth.

'I love you,' he said. And there on the monorail—so high over Butlins, close to the first real sun of the British summer—Maria kissed Michael as if to lose herself in that small act, or gain him for good, and they went on kissing and Michael soon tasted salt in his mouth from her tears running down. 'I'm going to look after you,' he said.

'No,' she said, 'I will.'

'We both will,' he said.

The train started moving again and they had a view of the sea outside the fences of Butlins, the beaches going out of Skegness. 'It's dead nice, the water today,' said Michael.

Maria looked out. The sea was a great slab of dark grey card with a million dots of white and silver appearing and vanishing. 'Michael,' she said, 'I'm not well.'

'You've lost weight again,' he said.

'Not that,' she said. 'I can't be normal. I always feel I'm falling backwards into somewhere. The noise, the greyness: it's like static. It's like the crackling and interference you get on a radio or something.'

'We're going to work this out, Maria.'

'No,' she said. 'I'm frightened it's going to get me.'

'Come on,' he said, 'we'll work it out.'

They climbed down the steps onto the pavement. Both could feel the heat and Maria noticed their shadows on the ground; his seemed so massive beside hers, and she looked up at him and saw he was not a giant, merely taller, and his short hair was neat and dark like his eyes. 'You are my handsome man,' she said out of nowhere. He squeezed her hand.

'I have to get going for the train,' he said.

'I hate it,' she said.

'I'm going to find you a lovely flat.'

'I hate singing.'

'It's not for long. But if you really want to leave I'll take you out of here right now.'

'I hate them looking at me.'

A family walked past and stopped near them at the ice-cream kiosk. The woman's hair was peroxide blonde, she wore a dab of pink lipstick, she held her purse in her hand, and the man wore a cardigan and suit trousers despite the heat. Beside them two small boys were dressed identically in sky-blue shorts. The man and woman argued about whether they should go to the bingo or ball-room dancing. The smaller of the two boys looked round at Maria and Michael and stared at them. He came over with a book and a pen; the book said 'Autographs' and was filled with the Redcoats' signatures. 'Could you be in my book?' said the boy.

'Of course sweetheart,' said Maria. She wrote her name in a swirl of loops and crossings.

'Thanks,' he said.

'Do you think they were twins?' Maria said to Michael as they moved away.

'No,' he said, 'I wouldn't have said so. They were just dressed the same.'

'My mother's a twin,' said Maria.

That night she brought the house down at the cabaret. She did four encores, and the entertainments manager said he had never seen her perform so well. Over the course of the day she had taken over forty laxatives, and while standing on the stage for her final applause, she had stomach pains, but the more her stomach convulsed the more she smiled. After the show, some of the Redcoats gathered backstage. They opened a bottle of Asti Spumante and gave Maria a glassful. She drank it carefully and told stories about television shows. Ready to leave, she walked outside and was stopped beside the fountains by a man asking her to sign his book. 'That was brilliant,' he said. 'You were absolutely brilliant tonight.'

'Thank you,' she said. 'Can I write your name here?'

'Just put "to Kevin",' he said. 'That's lovely. Slike really summer tonight.'

She looked up as she handed it back and realised her stomach was worse and she had to go.

'Can I just talk to you for a minute?' the man said.

'I'm sorry...Kevin,' she said, 'I'm awfully tired tonight. I'm really really glad you enjoyed the show.'

'Do you not want to speak to me?' he said. She looked at him. 'You can't even spare me a minute?' he said.

There was a blue light on the man's face. It came from a neon sign that shone above the entertainment centre. 'Our True Intent is All for Your Delight,' it said.

Maria bit her lip and tried to smile at him. She walked forward and the entertainments manager appeared and said there was a car waiting. She looked round shyly one last time at the man, hoping he would understand, but he didn't understand. His eyes narrowed, the book flapped open at the end of his arm, and the man gritted his teeth.

'Fucking slut,' he said.

MARIA SAID she would miss the dogs most.

'Never mind,' said Marion. 'You'll be ever so near to the BBC. You know, dear, you can come here and visit any time you like. We shall expect it. Remember there will always be space for you here. The dogs and you are like brothers and sisters.'

Michael had found a house in Shepherds Bush and Maria had the funds to buy it outright. 'I've been working since I was thirteen,' she said, 'and I got some of the money two years ago. I can have the flat. It will be mine, won't it?'

'It will certainly be yours,' Michael said.

He borrowed a St Clare's van and came round to St George's Terrace to move her things. He was amazed to see her bedroom: it was filled with soft toys, on the bookshelves, the bed, the cupboards, the dressing-table.

'Did fans send you these?' he asked, picking up a handful of teddies.

'Some of them,' she said.

Michael stood looking at a painting above a table on the landing. It showed a naked girl lying in a green bath. 'I'm leaving most of these clothes,' Maria shouted from the bedroom. 'I don't like the style of them any more.'

'Good,' Michael said. 'You can pick new ones.'

When she went down to the linen cupboard, he walked into her room again and sighed looking at the posters. Everything was ten years out of date. A portable television sat on the dresser. He slid open one of the drawers underneath; a smell of perfume and talcum powder came from it. He looked inside, and there, several layers deep, were dozens of balled-up tissues and chocolate wrappers.

'Come out of there,' said Maria at his back. 'All of this is going in the bin. Everything.'

'What can I take down?'

'Take these records, will you? And this pillow—that bag, Michael, if you can. There's memories in that.'

'This?' he said.

'Yeah,' said Maria. 'We might dump it in the canal.'

She opened her wardrobe and in seconds was throwing dresses up in the air. 'Take it easy, Maria,' he said.

She put her head on his chest. 'I just want to get out of here,' she said.

When he went down to the kitchen the dogs licked his hands. Marion was standing by the cooker smoking a cigarette and drinking a brandy. 'I didn't know you smoked,' he said.

'Just the occasional.'

'Have you got any more carrier bags, Marion?' he asked.

'I'm afraid we've none left,' she said. She rifled through one of the drawers. 'Here's a couple of black bags. Most of that stuff is old junk anyhow.'

Michael looked at her. 'Charmed,' he said. She drew up to him and kicked the kitchen door closed with her foot. 'Well, young man,' she began, 'we haven't had a great deal of time to speak to one another. But I feel it would be irresponsible of me not to ask you: are you aware of what you are taking on?'

'Taking on?' he said.

'Maria,' she said. 'She is not a well girl. Not too bad at present, as it happens, but she can be very difficult. My husband and I have, quite frankly, been through the mill with her. I only hope you have the . . . the resources to cope.'

'We'll cope,' he said.

'You think it was easy?'

'Mrs Gaskell, I'm sure Maria appreciates everything you have done for her. It is not my job to tell you so. She is a woman now and she wants to—'

'—turn her back—'

'—get on with her life!'

'—on what she's achieved.'

'Are you afraid that she's leaving you?'

'She's not leaving me. We have lots of work to get on with, but she's leaving this house and I worry for her.'

'Have you asked her what she wants?'

'Young man, I am very familiar with Maria's wants. I require no lessons in the matter. We understand each other very well.'

'Do you?'

Marion paused and stubbed out her cigarette. 'She is a very sensitive girl, and my only concern is for her welfare. Her own family are too preoccupied to help her.'

'Mrs Gaskell, I love Maria. If she wants to move into her own place I will help her. This business . . .'

'And what do you know about this business?'

'Not much. I'm only interested in what Maria needs—'

Marion raised her voice. 'Maria needs! Maria needs! What would you know about what she needs? I have fed her and clothed her. I brought her into this house. She has always needed looking after. She is nothing but a child!'

'She is not a child,' he said, 'not anymore.'

'Yes—more,' she said. 'You cannot just uproot a girl from a place where she's secure and expect her to cope. Not a girl like her. She needs to be looked after.'

'Is that what concerns you, Marion? I'll help Maria look after herself. Maybe you should think about . . . yourself.'

The air between them was thick with what had been said but thicker still with what hadn't. Marion looked at him with hate but then it quickly became a kind of pain. Michael was sorry to have risen to this; lifting the refuse bags he made the decision to go easier with Marion. 'Look, Marion,' he said, 'we shouldn't be enemies.'

'You have said enough. Please go now and help Maria with her things.' Michael stepped forward and put a hand on one of the chopping boards. 'Marion,' he whispered.

She looked at his hand. She could hardly believe Maria was going from the house in the company of a man. It seemed unreasonable to her, unbelievable, this man in her kitchen, the look of his hand, his fingernails, the hair on his arm and the confidence he showed. One of the dogs came in from the patio and nudged against Marion's leg. She bent down and kissed it between the ears. 'She's not a normal girl,' said Marion, looking up at him. 'She's special. That little girl who came into our lives is not just anyone.'

'She's a person, Marion. She's a grown-up person.'

'She won't work again.'

'That's something only you and she can decide,' he said, 'and I've got nothing to say on that score.'

She came to her feet. 'Just let her make up her own mind, Michael,' she said.

'That's all I mean to do.'

'Well, let us be civilised and shake hands,' she said.

She was aware of the heat in his hand as it held her own, and suddenly she was afraid of him and wanted to run, but her training made her stand her ground. She looked with pity into his dark eyes. 'You think you can save her,' she said to herself, 'and you call that love and you don't have a clue.'

5 · Mr Green

I once said to that little girl, I said: 'Honey, this business isn't worth a nickel you can spend if you don't have your health. You have a great talent and you can't argue with that, no siree, but you have to take care of yourself I'm telling you or the talent bombs and you're back where you started.' Years ago I was in Reno, Nevada, and they showed me onto the set of a John Huston picture—what do you call it? *The Misfits.* Marilyn Monroe and Clark Gable, good God, a whole world of talent, and that poor girl, God Almighty, she was so far gone they couldn't even focus her eyes for the shot. She said to me, 'You think I'm beautiful, huh?' I said: 'Honey, the whole world thinks you're beautiful, but the question is what do you think?'

That Tambini girl spent half her childhood hiding in dressing-grooms and starving herself. No wonder she breaks down now and again. People said, 'You should've left that girl where she was', but I said, 'Where was she?' I'm telling you a girl like that is travelling under her own steam. We just made it a bit easier for her by bringing her to the attention of the Great British Public. If it hadn't been *Opportunity Knocks* it would've been *New Faces* or she would be ripping up the nightclubs in Glasgow and Newcastle. Believe you me, you don't invent talent. Talent invents you. It changes your mind and brings you up short. Jesus. The girl wanted a life and she got a life. She spent a little too long in costume, I'll say that: a baby has to grow up eventually and face the music as an adult performer. Don't get me wrong, you have to be honest, people like a bit of suffering, Jesus yes, it adds to a performance no doubt about it, but you got to get a grip on it for Chrissakes before you end up in the drink.

The Variety Club of Great Britain had a tribute for me a few months ago—Lordy Lord, a roast they'd say in New York—and they gave me the works, bags of talent onstage, the speeches, handshakes, the bloody gold watch, all the best acts from the shows I've done over the years, and there we were, down at a theatre in Bridlington with the lovely Princess of Wales in the audience, and all in a good cause, all in a cracking good cause indeed, not me I mean but the National Youth Theatre, all those kids and bless them there's talent in there somewhere.

I came to the theatre early. I know I was supposed to turn up in a car like some la-di-da but Jesus I had to come and see what's what, that's my style you see, and turning up later I'd miss the greasepaint and all that palaver, the stuff I like. They weren't too pleased of course, but hell, I've been out of the business now these last years, and you don't often get a chance to do the rounds and turn a few door handles. I found that nice Tambini girl chucking hangers around her dressing-room. 'What you doing there, stranger-o'-mine?' I said.

'I'm counting my dresses.'

'You're what?'

'I'm counting my blessings. Come in here.'

And she welcomed me into her room the wee thing. Oh my what a change in a person I have to say. Thin. Not an inch of gristle on her. The skin was stretched across her face but Jesus there's no use denying it the girl was lovely and her eyes glittered just the same as they did when she was barely as much as a teenager. 'This is your big night, Mr Green,' she said.

'Hughie,' I said. 'Call me that.'

'What are you doing here?' she said. 'You should be away having a meal or something.'

'So should you,' I said.

'Oh, don't start,' she said. And the smile I'm not kidding you would have upset a chandelier. I said, 'Are you looking after yourself, Maria?'

'I am,' she said, 'I am that.'

Well good enough, and what do you make of her, she goes and gets me a wee dram and I'm saying to myself this girl has all the class now that we spotted in her years ago. 'The older you get, Mr Green, the more Scottish you sound.'

'Hughie, call me Hughie. My father was Scottish. You know he was the Fishmonger General. Well, I always had affection—cheers!— I always loved the Isle of Bute, and you've no idea how lovely a place it is from the air. You fly over there and it's like New Zealand or better than that.'

I drank a malt whisky in front of her and promised myself a few glasses of wine, but you want to look after yourself on a night like that so I kept it down. 'Affection demands a hug from you,' I said to her, and she smiled at me, Jesus, the girl is not your run-of-the-mill, and I said to her I really hoped she was enjoying her career despite everything.

'I am,' she said, and there was no two wits about it. She said, 'I am.'

'Because I get worried for you,' I said, 'and people say we brought you into the business too young.'

'That's nonsense,' she said. She said it herself and I'm not worrying to contradict her, I think she's right enough.

I'm old now and you don't sit down to sup tea with all the pains-in-the-ass, good God, we gave it our best shot to make people's lives a bit easier in our own way. I looked into the face of that wee lassie Maria Tambini and I knew we did honour to who she was and who she will be for years to come if she works hard.

Later on, they sat me in a box. Lord Jesus. Her Royal Highness Princess Diana was two chairs over from me and there is another girl who knows how to fix a room with her eyes and everything. As long as I live I'll remember that lovely occasion, the pink dress the princess wore, believe you me, it seemed to float about her in slow motion. The Tambini girl came on in the first half and I was proud of her. I really was proud: she came from nothing that girl and no-body in her family had ever been outside a chip shop and the way she sang that night it was as if to confirm every notion you could ever have about talent and what it means. A thing happened, Her Royal Highness leaned over, you know the way she blushes, and she says to me, 'Is that woman unwell?'

'She's a trouper,' I said.

'No, Mr Green. Is she eating?'

I just told her what had been in the magazines and the papers and that she was on the mend. You have to hand it to that Princess all the same: she takes an interest in people, and I watched her out the corner of my eye, looking down at the stage and her blonde hair was all swept round in that lovely way and she had such a care for that Tambini girl you could really tell, although some of the acts that night were better acts you'd have to admit.

The TV cameras were fairly swinging from one end of the place to the other and Les Dawson had us in stitches. After Maria's big number—the way she held those notes!—she came out and her and Les did 'Be a Clown', you know the old Donald O'Connor number, and good Lord, the two of them threw in every joke and every ounce of talent they had between them, I'm telling you, and the energy down there, it's hard to believe. And then they did a scene, you know, where he is supposed to be the reprobate and she's the nagging wife. 'Aw wifey,' he says, 'come and sit upon my knee. Here's a wee seat, my bonnie dwarf,' and all that stuff. The audience are killing themselves. The Tambini girl climbs on his knee and the audience are loving it but she is supposed to put her arms around his neck and just pretend to cry for a second.

'She's not pretending.' The lady two chairs up was waving her programme like a fan and said it again: 'She's not pretending.' I thought the Tambini girl had missed her cue but it turns out she was holding on to Les's neck, and I must say that is not at all professional even if you're tired or whatever, you know how it is in this business, you have to just dust yourself off and we certainly didn't train people to lose the place onstage. But good old Les he can always save the day—what a turn—he just lifts her up and makes a joke to the audience about her being in a coma from too much Scottish mince and tatties and he carries her right off the stage to loud applause.

6 · The Hunger Artist

'I don't know a single thing about history,' said Maria. 'Not even any of the proper dates for things. I don't know when the war was really or what it was about. Couldn't tell you who fought who in the Hundred Years War.'

'At least you know there was a Hundred Years War.'

'I heard them speak about it on *The Krypton Factor*.'

'You know a lot more than you think you do.'

'Well, yes,' she said. 'I know when Elvis died.'

They were standing together in the observation lounge of the St Clare's building at Ovingdean. The lounge had large windows facing the English Channel a few hundred yards down the hill, the miles of water going from green to grey in the evening. Maria was good with the old soldiers: she found it easy to help them, and though she never mentioned as much to Michael, it gave her comfort to know that the men couldn't see her.

She stood behind him and hooked her fingers in his belt and put her head on his shoulder. He always smelled clean, like fabric softener, like a warm iron over washed cotton, and his own smell, the smell of his skin, was to her mind like biscuits and polished wood. She wondered sometimes where all his confidence came from, the ease of his laughter and the way he used his voice, she could marvel at the way he spoke on the phone or just shrugged when comments seemed wrong. He was always shaping facts to make her feel stronger, or presenting the world to suit themselves, and he was someone who lived easily with what he knew and what he didn't know. He took lines from the books and poems he loved, to clarify things, to elevate them, but it never seemed oppressive to her or taxing to anyone, it merely seemed characteristic of this person Michael, who could laugh at himself in advance of others.

'Hard to believe Paris and Rome are somewhere out there,' he said.

'You've said about Rome before.'

'Aye,' he said, 'there's a kind of sister organisation to St Clare's over there, so I've gone once or twice. I don't know. I think I love the idea of it. As a place to live. It seems . . .'

She leaned her back against the window.

'Old and modern at the same time,' he said.

She smiled up at him and said, 'I don't know if that's a good or a bad thing.'

He made a face and she laughed.

'Just free somehow,' he said.

She looked into the buttons of his shirt. 'I'd like that,' she said quietly. He loved the life in her eyes. He loved her skin and her quiet way of saying things indirectly. Her capacity for wonder, eyelashes dark and beating in time to her thoughts. He loved her mouth. He kissed it.

'You're going to be all right,' he said. 'Time is what you've never had.'

The sea ran out of light and they went downstairs to collect their bags from the bedroom. Some of the wives were in the corridor next to the dining-hall. 'Hello, you pair,' one of them said. 'It's the Sussex reunion soon, Maria, and we'll be expecting a song from you.'

'I'll do my best,' Maria said.

'You'll do great,' said the woman.

WHEN MARIA was feeling up to it—on her good weekends— Michael would show her places around London she'd never seen before. He took her to small places in Soho where you could have a drink, hidden bars, and he took her round the Egyptian rooms of the British Museum. They went to look at the stuff you could buy in John Lewis and she felt dizzy going up the escalators, then round to Ronnie Scott's to listen to the latest thing on saxophone. Michael loved to watch the way Maria would glide into those places and take it all in with her eyes. He would encourage her gently to eat something here and there and to drink water; they both knew she was trying her best, and they held to the notion that patience might allow her to recover in her own way.

'Is this boring?' he asked in the jazz club.

'Yes,' she said, and she laughed into an empty glass.

'Good,' he said. 'That obviously means you're beginning to like it.'

He tapped the rhythm out on his jeans and she got a picture of him then as he had been years ago in Rothesay. She found it hard to imagine they were still in any way young: he sat there listening, he played with the wristband of his watch, and sometimes he looked over at her and winked. He had been interested in listening to her speak as well as sing years ago, as if taking real notice of her living and breathing. And he had winked at her back then too.

'I'm happy,' she said to him.

He lifted one of her fingers across the table and kissed it as if to silence himself. 'You're so beautiful,' he said.

Her health was up and down, but he would appear out of her terrors like a calmative. He made her laugh when he could, slipping into the American slang he had used as a teenager, and he made way for her confusions, not solving her head but caressing it, and walking around what she couldn't say. She began slowly to eat and they got to know one another, favourite films and styles of shoe, admired buildings, perfumes, matters of taste and personal choice. She noticed that when he made tea he put the sugar and the milk and the bag in before the hot water. When he drove the car he liked to lay his hand on the gear stick and feel the vibrations. He noticed that she liked the smell of diesel and hated the sound of polystyrene. She liked to ask questions: Why does toffee go white if you stretch it? And so did he: What is your favourite month and why? Their love wasn't a choice, it was a recognition, as much for her as for him, and so they seemed to enjoy something new yet something familiar, while fearing the worst the world had to offer.

They went one day to the South Bank to see paintings. Maria was vulnerable and Michael held her hand as they walked up the steps. 'It's grey today,' she said.

'Take it easy.'

On the second floor of the gallery the walls were red and the thock of heels on the wooden floor could be heard as Michael and Maria walked between paintings by Otto Dix. The room was empty, the security man slumped in his chair by the fire escape, his eyes opening and closing, gratefully oblivious to the entertainments around him. The pair loosened hands and separated and went off to look at the pictures in their own way. Michael stood close to them: he leaned in to examine the paint, and noting something livid in the eyes of the subjects, he recalled an essay he had read in *Horizon* one of those afternoons before the job at St Clare's, an article about the Germans and charisma.

A rumble of heavy shoes quickly filled the space as children entered. They carried clipboards and some of the girls had linked arms and one flicked her fringe and another pulled chewing-gum from the end of her tongue. There was pushing and bursts of laughter, and the children jostled together behind the information officer, a woman in a blue suit. 'It's important to remember,' she said, 'that he actually volunteered. He spent much of the war as part of a machine-gun unit, so he saw a great deal of active service, and experienced the full horror of the war. He was at the Somme in the summer of 1916 and witnessed many deaths and terrible injuries. This had a deep impact on his imagination. He was badly injured himself.'

The painting was called *Trench Warfare*. Some of the girls were still giggling and there was a smack of chewing-gum. 'Now,' said the woman, 'by the end of the war Dix had won the Iron Cross. After-wards, he quickly became disillusioned with the war however, and in paintings like this one, his disgust was given artistic expression. These paintings became important anti-war statements.' She looked from the painting to the girls. 'What can you see in this painting? Yes?'

'Tons of dead bodies,' one girl said.

'Yes.'

'They look like they've just been thrown in,' said another.

'Yes. The bodies are decomposed. Many of them are crooked and almost indistinguishable from each other and from the roots and the trees around them.'

'It's gross,' a boy said.

'Yes,' said the woman. 'I think the artist wanted it to appear that way. He wants to represent the waste of human lives and his depic-tions of the dead men are uncompromising. Would you say the painting looks ugly?'

'Totally,' said the same boy.

'Not ugly,' said someone else. 'You can see from the red on the sky and it's like maybe you can get out of this horrible place.'

'The sky is mostly dark.'

'But there's this pink bit.'

'Yes,' said the woman, 'like red sky at night. What do you think the artist means by that?'

'It's like a fire going on in the distance,' said one of the boys.

'Maybe,' said the teacher, 'but what else?'

'As if hell or somethink is there. Like hell.'

'Possibly,' said the teacher. 'Anything else?'

The girl with the chewing-gum took her finger down from her

lips and tilted her head. 'It might be that the next day it will be better and the war will finish,' she said.

'Good,' said the woman. 'I agree with that. I think that in all the devastation and horror the picture depicts, there is a note of hopefulness in the use of colour. Human degradation has perhaps reached its lowest point, and tomorrow, or soon, there might be an end to this kind of madness and suffering.'

Michael stood in front of the painting called *War Wounded*. He was listening to the woman and the pupils. 'Dix was upset by the way crippled ex-soldiers were being treated in Germany,' she said, 'and his work is often a kind of protest. Like many people, he believed the world the soldiers returned to would be a better one, but in fact it was worse. Dix was viewing it from the German side. But some English artists were interested in the same thing. They wondered what kind of country would exist after such horrific fighting. Dix had hoped there would be freedom and beauty, but instead there was more ugliness, and in one of his paintings he shows himself returning from the war as a wounded officer and being greeted in Berlin by a group of prostitutes.'

Some of the boys sniggered into their collars.

As the woman spoke of German decadence a fly came into the room; it went over their heads, buzzing into the air of dispelled words, private thoughts and small breaths.

Maria had been standing in front of one painting for some time and when the children and the teacher approached she didn't move. She stood between the painting and the group and Michael stood at the very back watching this arrangement, and thought to himself that the painting was like a stone dropped into the pool of their thoughts, Maria, then the girls, then the teacher, then the boys, then himself at the back.

'This is called *The Hunger Artist*,' said the teacher. Everyone looked. Men sat at tables in a restaurant with green wallpaper. They had round faces and bowler hats, and spittle came from some of their mouths. Some had moustaches and they seemed aggressive with their knives and forks. The plates were piled with food. Women with red faces and blue eye-shadow grabbed at pork chops with their fat fingers. And there at the far end of the restaurant, high on a wooden table, a small girl sat cross-legged in a bell-shaped glass case, her large, black eyes staring out at the crowd, her body emaciated. The bones stood out on her face, her ribs protruded and her hair was sparse and thin.

'We see here how Dix set out to provide a moral portrait of his time,' said the teacher. Maria didn't move: she stood still in front of the painting and her shadow affected its colours. 'But he was also reflecting many everyday realities. Hunger artists were people who starved themselves as part of a public entertainment. In 1926, when this was painted, there were six hunger-artists performing in Berlin. These artists, as they were called, were often young women, and, as you see depicted here, they would be placed inside glass booths while the diners enjoyed their meal. The diners are eating sausages and fried potatoes. The girls would exist on water and many of them smoked cigarettes behind the glass. There was a restaurant in Berlin at this time called Zum Goldenen Hahn, and it is believed that Dix ate here, and he became fascinated with the hunger artist as a grotesque symbol of what was happening in Germany with the rise of Nazism. Only he painted this picture much later.'

'Was the girl really starving?' asked one of the pupils.

'Yes, very often,' said the teacher. 'See to the side of the picture a blackboard. It would be usual for the restaurant owner to write on this board the number of days the hunger artist had gone without food. No one quite knew who these performers were, or what their story was; they would seldom speak for themselves.'

'Were they not allowed to talk?'

'Nobody knows. People mostly spoke for them. Or about them. That was the story of their lives.'

'Did they get money for it?'

'Oh yes. They were paid. Restaurants where they appeared would always be full. It proved extremely fascinating to the people of Berlin at the time and Otto Dix believed this gave a shocking insight into modern culture.'

The teacher then spoke of the way the faces had been painted and the style of the eyes. She made reference to other painters of the period and pointed to certain features in the work's execution—blur-rings, estrangements—which, she told them, were evidence of the way the painter had adapted his technique to the subject. The pupils were chit-chatting among themselves; the tour was getting a bit boring for them.

Maria still stood in front of the picture. Before going up and putting his hand on her arm, Michael paused: she seemed so private and untouchable, and the few steps to take her arm seemed like miles. She turned to him then and smiled in a careful way. She kissed the back of his hand. 'Clever, those children, weren't they?' she said.

'Yes,' he said.

'Let's get out of here.'

Maria didn't want anything from the bookshop and the daylight outside was glaring. As they went along the walkway, she took a lungful of air and thought it was like fresh wind from the Thames. A man was leaning against the wall. She had seen him briefly in the gallery and the sight of him had registered with her and made her anxious. Now he was looking at them, and as they were about to pass he stepped forward and Maria suddenly shrank inside her coat. Almost unnoticeably, she tightened her hands around Michael's arm. The man had two shirts on under a lumber jacket, he was very white-faced, dirty-looking, and he wore a wet smile on his lips. 'Miss Tambini,' he said, 'it's grand to see you out and about. Would you sign my programme?'

Michael could feel Maria shiver. 'Not just now, mate,' he said. 'Thanks anyway.'

'I'm not asking you,' the man said. 'Maria. Would you just sign this for me?'

Maria tried to take a step forward.

'It's only a fucking name on a bit of paper,' the man said.

Michael put his hand out and kept the man back. 'Just leave it,' he said. 'Get out the way.'

The man went to take a further step forward and his face was animated with fear and hurt. 'Fuck off,' said Michael, looking right into the man's eyes, and as he said it he swept the man out of the way with one strong swipe of the arm.

'Don't look back,' Michael said as they went down the steps and made for the tunnels of the South Bank, and later, after they had laughed about other things and Michael had kissed her in the ticket hall, Maria felt glamorous. Going down the escalator, the sound of a saxophone at the bottom, the moving steps conveying her at speed past faces and coloured posters, and Michael somewhere behind her, she filled up with a sense of soaring strings and advancing audience. The audience that loved and needed her. The audience that lifted her over the chaos of things. She opened her eyes wide as the escalator took her down the long staircase; she smiled and heard applause, the orchestra swelling with pride, the world waiting.

7 · *Skin*

A vase of white tulips stood on a table beside the window. The tulips were the room's central event: the green stems alive as grass snakes, and the white flowers, closed-mouthed, sedative, were awkward in themselves, ashamed to need the sun.

It was the beginning of April, and they lay together on the bed asleep, Maria and Michael, a year or more after her last TV appearance, two days after her twenty-third birthday. Michael still had his own flat in Kensington: it sat there pristine and hardly used, a memoir of his first days in London, full of books and forgotten T-shirts, a place to return to in those hours when Maria needed to loosen him from her attention.

They lay together in the soft-breathing aftermath of the night before, its whispers, kisses and tears; the light came through the wooden blinds and lay over them in stripes. She dreamed a familiar dream: she and her grandmother were playing noughts and crosses on the flagstones of an old cemetery and laughing and dancing together in a rainstorm of boiled sweets. When she opened her eyes she reached out and touched a bare arm. 'Michael,' she said, 'don't leave.'

'I'm right here, lovely,' he said.

Maria fell back to sleep as he sat propped against the headboard smoking a cigarette and carefully watching the bluish trails of the ascending smoke. She turned and snuggled into his legs. Her mouth was against his stomach and she began, still halfasleep, to lick him there, and then she began to bite his flesh and his cock became hard and her hands plucked at the waistband of his pyjamas and tugged them down, then her hand travelled over his arse and came round. She held on to his cock and she stroked it with her hand up and down.

'Maria,' he said. His head was back and he exhaled deeply into the pillows. She was awake now and shivered with nerves but at the same time in the dryness of the morning she thirsted to suck his lips and in the growing heat all her hatreds became tenderness for him. But she felt too fat.

'Maria,' he said. 'You're the only one I've ever loved.'

He was naked now lying next to her; she could feel the smoothness and roughness of his chest and she buried her head into his neck and bit him again. She wanted to bite him and break the skin and eat what was inside. She could taste his smell and licked the salt from his neck and drew her tongue along the line of his jaw and could feel his hard cock against her. She imagined the blankets were waves and sank under bringing her arms against his body for balance and she swallowed a mouthful of her own saliva.

She dug into the mattress, as if to escape or climb further inside the warmth around him, and her fear was made odd by the excitement she felt at the words he spoke and the way his hands were undressing her. 'I want to be inside you and stay inside you, Maria,' he said. 'I want to lick and fuck you and make you come.'

She was naked now against him, wanting to cry. Her skin was white and her nipples brown and he licked them in circles and sucked the raised nipple and grazed it with his teeth. He could feel her ribs against his arms as he leaned up and kissed her forehead and licked her eyes. 'Don't hurt me,' she said.

'Wouldn't hurt you,' he said. 'I love you.'

It was not terrifying so much as blurred. He sucked at her wrists then chewed her earlobes and caressed the sides of her body until she felt she had completely opened and was lost in him and not sad. He lifted her round in the bed and sucked her breasts and kissed her stomach and put her fingers on his face and made her touch his cheeks and eyes, then he put all her fingers in his mouth at once and he moved his warm tongue over and between them.

Her legs were thin and he felt afraid and choked as he stroked them. He had tears in his eyes. 'You are so beautiful,' he said. She looked up at him and felt like somebody else as she reached up and kissed his mouth and put her tongue inside his mouth to suck his saliva and it felt familiar the feeling in his mouth and he loved her for doing it.

'Don't stop,' she said. 'I want to be with you.'

His fingers became light as he paused between her legs and re-alised how hard he was and that she was wet. He sighed into her mouth and drew his tongue over her teeth feeling the warm fold at the opening of her and wanting to scoop the wetness from her and smear it on his chest and mouth and rub it over his tongue and drink her. She moaned into his ear and kissed the inside and drove her fingers through his hair as he probed and stroked her cunt and loved her. He raised himself and licked her throat and she bit hard into his shoulder and harder again and still wanted to eat through him and become full of him and the sound of his breathing excited her more.

Michael lapped at her arms, kissed her eyes again, and his fingers went inside her and his cock was covered in wetness at her opening. She was moaning now and weeping too and she opened her eyes to him. 'Can we just kiss and cuddle?' she said.

'I'm doing that, sweetheart,' he said, 'kissing and cuddling all of you with myself. Is that not all right?'

There were tears in her eyes and she said yes and don't stop and he slid his cock into her and she said his name and grabbed his neck with both hands. The warmth inside her made him want to come but he held himself back and looked down at her and saw her mouth the words 'You are me.' He pushed forward and licked her breasts and felt his cock ease its way into her and she moved her hips for him and breathed in sharply and ran her hands up and down his chest as he began to fuck her. Then he raised her legs and came in and out of her gently and slowly until she lay relaxed, being fucked on the bed.

'Oh, please,' he said.

He could feel the length of his cock sliding against her clitoris and he licked her open mouth and fucked harder. Sweat was soon running down his back and he stroked each of her legs around his waist, sliding his tongue into her mouth with each thrust and listen-ing to her breathing and her words and loving her skin. Her hands and eyes were closed, and the words she spoke pushed into him like her cunt moving against him making him harder.

She felt he was going all the way inside her, could feel him in her stomach and in her fingertips and on her scalp, her buttocks grinding forward. At first she thought she would have to stop him: everything is pain, she thought for a moment, but she saw the way he licked her wrists and even her fingernails, and as he moved forward in her wet cunt she wanted him to pin her to the bed and loved his heaviness and with every stroke she began to feel her body was good and wanted to speak out and cry. She bit him wherever she could and lifted her head off the pillows to find new places to bite and she caught her breath, she wanted him.

He turned her over on her side and kissed the skin between her shoulder-blades and licked her back. He leaned round the side of her head and kissed her soft cheeks and dragged his tongue over her ear. At that moment he loved her beautiful feet and the soft hair on the back of her neck and he grew harder looking at her red lips open on the pillow showing her glistening top teeth, and when he put his hand down again she was swollen and open for him so he drew himself close to her and positioned his cock again and pushed into her.

'I want us to stay like this,' he said.

'Don't leave,' she said.

He caressed her thigh and rode her with his cock and pressed his chest into her damp back and at the same time he put his hand over and stroked the top of her cunt. He revolved his hips to let the movement be free and she put her hand over and dug her ragged nails into him. He became even stiffer as he fucked her and looked at the beauty of her face and smelled her and felt the endless warmth of being inside her. She was crying into the pillow and he was afraid he might be hurting her so he slowed down but she said 'Don't stop' and they felt each of them like one person for those seconds as she moaned his name and he fucked her and tried to spread her thighs, and she said his name out loud and he came inside her and opened his mouth and said her name and she put kisses on the palms of his open hands.

8 · Kevin Goss

Dear Miss Tambini,

I always wondered what happened to the little girl with the loud voice who was on Opportunity Knocks. *I remember she wore socks right up to her knees. She seemed like a person you could have a nice conversation with. I wrote to the magazines* Jackie *and* Bunty *to find out more about you but never heard a thing. You were probably too busy. The magazines were rubbish and not worth the money unless you were in.*

My name is Kevin. I am not famous but showbusiness is very special to me and I like your songs. I saw you on the Royal Variety and thought you were the best. I'm sorry this notepaper is not nice I will be getting more at W. H. Smiths. If you could send me back a signed picture it would make my day. I can send a postal order for whatever it costs to send. But if you have not got any photographs an autograph will do.

Yours faithfully,

Kevin Goss

· · ·

Dear Maria,

Thank you very much for the photograph. It is one of the nice ones of you. I like your hair you should always wear it down. The dress in the photograph suits you as well. I have been finding out more about you. I knew already you are Scottish but have now found the right island on the map.

You are probably wanting to know some things about me. I am 42 years young and am presently employed as a kitchen assistant in a restaurant. It is in Leamington Spa. When I left school I wanted to be a cook. This is a difficult job and not very suited to me. I now would like to be in television or the radio. I think you need qualifications but I have written off anyway. Maybe you could give me some advice. I was listening tonight to one of your best songs. The one 'I'll be Seeing You'. In my opinion yours is better than Liberace singing it. I saw you on Morecambe and Wise *and don't think you did yourself justice. They are not funny them two.*

Yours,

Kevin

Dear Maria,

They are not very nice to people at your office. The one where I am sending this. I went there to ask if there was any more records coming out. They just said to write to the fan club. Well the fan club is bloody useless I don't mind telling you. The girl there takes ages to answer anything you send her. If I was you I would get somebody else to do it.

I am not working at the restaurant now. They want people to work all hours for slave wages. You wouldn't work all night for two quid an hour would you? Of course that is not something people in your position have to think about. I don't know what to do now. I might move to Scotland. That's home sweet home for you isn't it? Some people think they can just use you that's the problem. It said in the Daily Mirror you had to go to hospital. I am not surprised you don't want to eat the food they hand out nowadays. I hope you get better soon. I am sending a card to the hospital as well. If you ever want someone to sit you down to a nice dinner remember your friend Kevin. Get back to your singing soon darling. Your number one fan.

Kevin

•••

WHEN YOU'RE DOWN, REMEMBER FRIENDSHIP'S THE GREATEST TONIC IN THE WORLD.

Get well soon Maria. You are the greatest. Love Kevin.

•••

Dear Maria,

I saw you singing in De Montfort Hall in Leicester tonight. My head is still swirling. Maria you are the greatest. I was clapping so much my hands are still sore from it. The people sitting next to me were talking when you were singing 'Memories'. I told them to shush. You were so lovely looking. I made out you were singing the song to me about all we've been through. Most people don't understand all the hard times you've had like I do. When I saw you on Wogan the other night I rushed to put a tape in. I have watched it now I don't know how many times. You are not so thin again. I don't mind you whatever size you are. To me you are the best star in the business. It was great to see you smiling again. If there is a tape-recording of tonight could you *let me know? I am writing this in a hurry and will post it tomorrow. I love you.*

    Kevin

• • •

TO MISS MARIA TAMBINI. FOR HER EYES ONLY
My Lovely Maria. These flowers are for you because you are wonderful. Break a leg. Love Kevin.

• • •

Slike there's somebody behind you and when you turn round they're gone. Slike that. I'm keeping a taped scrapbook to record my favourites and then so's I can talk like this when I miss you at night time. No point just thinking about you and not doing anything about it, that slike a waste. There's an old wardrobe here my father left me and it's really old and has old wallpaper inside the drawers. It smells of dead people's stuff and everything and there's so many moths. Slike great to get the vacuum cleaner out and suck them up and some of them are big as well and you can still hear them flying about in the Hoover bag. They're trapped in the machine man it's fucking great, you know it's dark in there.

• • •

Maria,

    I'm leaving this with the porter because I know that's what you would want. These letters are private anyhow. Those bitches at your manager's office open the mail I know they do. That's why you're not writing back. I know you're busy being beautiful and thinking of me all the same. I always think about you when I write my music and poems. That was a cheap-looking show you did with that fat comedian the other night. You are too good for them and I've told you before you should take my advice. You are too good to be on with those people. I saw you last night at the Langham Hotel you were not able to speak to me but it's okay because I know you wanted to. After you left I took a stirrer from the glass you were drinking. I have it beside my bed. It tastes of you and you left it for me like a kiss I know that. I am going to see you at Butlins in Skegness it's the only thing to look forward to.

    Love,
    Kevin

• • •

I drew round one of my hands and then round the other one on a piece of paper and sent it to her, slike touching her. Those old men on television shows are smutty and they try to make her fancy them but she's not interested in the likes of that. They don't deserve to breathe the same air as the God of Gods. I might put these tapes in one of them safe deposit boxes at a posh bank and one day when we're old we can listen to them. You and Lady Diana are the only people who will ever hear them. The television people try to change you with their dirty talk. They write lines for you to say and you have not been well so you say them and it makes me want to cry and put a bandage on your mouth.

• • •

You fucking bitch,

All I wanted was to speak to you for one minute and you had to walk away with some bastard. They don't even know you and are using you, if you weren't so fucking thick you would see all they want to do is exploit you for money. I come home at night and don't expect you to have my dinner ready or anything. How quickly you forget I have allowed you to have your career and be away from me and who else would have done that? You cunt I'll fucking forget you and who will be left to look after you? Not those pricks who come to your shows they don't even know you. They don't even like you. Every fucking record and telly thing you've ever done it's been me standing by you and you can't stop and speak to me for one second. It cost me a fortune to get the train to that place and stay there and everything. At least now I know you are the same as all the rest a selfish bastard who is not worth bothering about.

Kevin

• • •

I've moved address so you can call the police all you like I'm not worried you fucking bitch.

• • •

Slike out of hundreds of celebrities I know only two or three who are properly good people and deserve success. You don't want to smother those women or smoth those women or moth them or mother them, slike good to just help them. She's the God of Gods because she can sing up on a stage or into a television camera and you know it's just for you. That is the be-all and end-all when it comes to being a star and she can't be perfect all the time because there's all those pricks telling her what to do and wasting her a little bit. Happens. Crappy business if you don't watch out. But those people don't know our secret language and she does and I do so everything's fine. Sgood. I will look after her because I'm the only one that gives a monkey's. Kindness. Got to be done, for goodness sake. Don't mess with the best cause the best don't mess with the rest. You need to look after your health properly if you're going to go on being successful and good on stage and all that and you need the right people around you. Seasy if you know there's somebody you love watching out for you. Seasy then. Seasy as pie.

• • •

My Dear Maria,

On Des O'Connor you were the loveliest person in the world tonight and I am proud of you. Never stop singing and remember your number one fan will always be here for you in good times and bad. I don't always see the celebrity things in the magazines but I saw one which said you were happy and moving to a new house. This is just to say you deserve all the happiness in the world. I think your new short hair is very becoming and it has the official approval. Don't put on or lose any weight you are just fine now as you are. You are one of life's special people Maria and don't forget I told you so.

Love and kisses,

Kevin

9 · Static

Every other day Maria went to Shepherds Bush Market. She was always on the hunt for domestic equipment, and her kitchen had every kind of floor cleaner and every kind of spoon. Mugs and place mats and a pedal-bin: she wanted them pink and cherrypatterned if possible.

Michael could never really fathom her afternoons: he would be at his desk in St Clare's and would ring her, but often enough, though he couldn't know it, the phone would ring beside her and she would sit by the window or stand motionless on a spot of carpet in the hall, and sometimes she did this for days at a time, not answering the phone, drinking water in her nightie.

Journalists would sometimes turn up on the doorstep. Once or twice they took a picture as she walked down the path to go shopping. She hated it—always a story about child stars or slimming or recluses. Sometimes when they rang the bell she would just sit at the top of the stairs biting her nails. 'I'm not here,' she would say to herself looking down at the oval glass on the door. 'I'm not here. I'm invisible.'

She went to W. H. Smiths one afternoon and bought dozens of newspapers and magazines. As she made her way home down Goldhawk Road she felt the cold, felt it in her bones, while the two newsagent bags swung heavy at her sides. She spread the publications out on the kitchen table and her mouth became watery as she looked through the pages. A knitting pattern for cardigans made her salivate—pink wool, red buttons—and so did the recipes for cod, salsa verde and chicken salad. She turned the pages fast and grabbed another magazine. She saw pictures of celebrities stepping out of cars or holding glasses of champagne at parties and laughing. Make-up hints. Horoscopes. Gardening news and advertisements for stair-lifts and foot-spas and commemorative ornaments. She looked at the faces of the people in the interviews and knew the lines on their faces had been smoothed away, the whites of their eyes had been whitened and their teeth painted and their chins invented.

She began to tear the pages out of the magazines, then strip the photographs away and pile up the text. On the sideboard she plugged in the blender and poured some water into it then added a load of the ripped-up paper to the water. She flicked the switch and watched the words and the pictures swirl round at great speed and disappear as they turned. She added more shredded pages and whizzed them and put more water in and loved to see the people and their made-up faces and lives disappearing and the words vanishing into mush. It looked like porridge. She kept adding more pages and more water and whizzed it faster and faster until all the pages on the table had gone though the blender and the mush was lying in a giant heap in the sink. She put her fingers into the basin and squeezed the paste through them; lifting it to her mouth, she ate a little and cried when she found it tasted of nothing.

Days she would just stand at the kitchen window looking into the garden for hours. There were no birds. She watched the washing line with empty dresses moving in the wind. The grass was neatly cropped and the paving stones cleaned. In the daytime, standing there, framed by the window, she imagined someone was looking at her from the bushes at the back of the garden, beside the shed. She imagined he was watching her perform in the square of the kitchen window as if she were appearing on television, reading the news, or singing, and she stood there for hours, looking into the silence of the garden and feeling watched. As it grew dark, the kitchen window would become a mirror; she would see that she was looking at her own face, still she felt she was being watched, not only by herself.

Some days she woke up exhilarated. She would be up and about dressing carefully and playing records; she'd put on makeup and blow-dry her hair with her favourite vent brush, then go out to the shops to buy food and ring Michael to say she had been very busy today and would he like his dinner? Michael had got used to watching her from a distance when she was in a bad way: that was all she would tolerate. He would come round on such a night and she would cover him in kisses at the door and there would be food all over the kitchen. She always made too much.

He was frustrated that things had taken such a step back. They had been so close the previous year, now his journey up Holland Park Avenue was made in a state of apprehension. He began to lose his carefulness and to sound to her like other people she knew. 'I won't eat unless you do,' he said.

'There's no fucking point in making all this food for somebody who's ungrateful,' she'd say. Then she would throw every bit of food into the bin and scrub the plates. Sometimes, in this mood, she would come to bed and grow delirious as she tried to bite into him, and he would take her by the shoulders and shake her and she would grind her teeth in the bedroom in the dark.

She would make up stories to suit herself. 'I've got an illness like my Auntie Sofia,' she said. 'She's my mother's older sister. She died very young from leukaemia and I read something in one of the magazines about leukaemia, it said it's a family illness.'

'You don't have leukaemia,' Michael said. 'You have anorexia nervosa and sometimes bulimia.'

'You're a pig like the others.'

'Stop it, Maria.'

'Get out! You're a useless pig like the others and you don't know me.'

'Maria, you need help!'

She would scream the most terrible scream and run to another room. 'Who am I? Who am I?'

Michael lost his temper and smashed a red teapot off the wall one day. 'Who are you when you're in bed with me?' he said. 'Is that a performance like everything else?'

'When you're raping me,' she said quietly.

'When I'm *what*?'

'Raping me. You all want to use me. You all want to use me for something.'

'Who's *we*, Maria?'

'All of you.'

'I'll tell you what, Maria. You're fucked up. *Rape,* you say. *Rape.* When somebody loves you it's rape? And here you are in your little world, getting skinnier by the day. The place is covered in sick bags and all the suitcases in the cupboard are full of diet pills and there are laxatives under the beds. But it's all *us* loving it and causing it and wanting more, that's what you think, isn't it, Maria? It's all just something that's happening to *you*. Of course. Yes. We all just stand by and enjoy the show!'

'You and him! You and him!'

'Who's *him*?'

'You're the same person. You want to hurt me and make me fat and put me in a dress and make me go out there looking terrible.'

'Who's *him*, Maria? What are you talking about?'

'All you want is to ruin my career.' She stabbed herself with her finger. 'Me! I built this—me, and none of you have anything to do with this. I am in charge of this. Me! I'm a singer and you all want me to get so's everybody hates me. I'm a singer! They love me out there and all of you can't stand it!'

Michael looked at her raging eyes.

'I want to love you,' he said.

'You don't know a thing about it. Goodbye you. Goodbye all of you. I can sing you know. I can sing a song.'

'Maria.'

'Goodbye. I have won. You can't kill me ha ha. You can't do it. Go and rape somebody else. Goodbye and goodbye and fucking goodbye.'

'That's it, isn't it, Maria? Goodbye. All your songs are goodbyes. It's always been goodbye.'

She let out a long scream in the kitchen that travelled all the way through the house and all the way through his own life and hers too.

Michael was due to take some of the St Clareites to France the week after that argument with Maria. He phoned Marion Gaskell at her office and he sounded shaky on the phone.

'This has been a long year for you,' she said.

'Longer than that,' he said. 'Longer.'

'You're not to blame,' she said. 'You mustn't think that, dear.'

'We're all to blame. Everybody's to blame.'

'That's enough of that,' she said. 'You were right to ring me. She won't answer my messages and it's a job to keep the press back from her. She's never out of the women's magazines. They're always after new pictures.'

'I love her,' he said quietly.

'You can't do it, dear heart,' she said. 'You can't protect her any more than you have.'

Michael didn't have a key: Maria was always at home when he arrived, and they hadn't got round to cutting him a key, but he knew a neighbour had one for emergencies.

He spoke through the letterbox. He knew she was there. He said he would be back for her but she needed better help than he was giving her. Maria just sat on the stairs and cried into the bottom of her skirt; all over the walls and flowing up the stairs and over the carpet there was static and greyness. She could hear Michael's voice echoing beneath the static somewhere and she thought of kissing his naked shoulder, but she covered her ears and only heard bits of tune and old song-words and she rocked into her knees until long after he was gone.

Songs marched in twos through her mind.

> *You Made Me Love You. New York, New York.*
> *If They Could See Me Now. Rockaby.*
> *What I Did for Love. Maybe This Time.*
> *Love Me Tender. Personality.*
> *The Man I Love. Happy Days Are Here Again.*

The static was all around her, engulfing her, and she grew helpless, baby-like, blurred, tumbling in static, the pupils of her eyes like pin-heads, and she curled up on the top stair and looking into the wall sang the same lines over and over.

She was asleep on the stairs when Michael and Marion used the emergency key to get into the house and take her to the Kennington Clinic. She stood up and let them pack a bag and barely murmured or lifted her head when he carried her out in his arms and they drove her away in the car. The house was silent except for the tick of a clock in the living-room. The white tiles in the bathroom were gleaming; a washing-up cloth was folded in two over the silver taps. A Hoover stood next to the stairs in the hall, and on the carpet, under the let-terbox, lay a piece of paper with a single word written in pencil.

'Bitch,' it said.

10 · Alfredo

Honest to God the things that were in that cupboard. Right at the back I found stuff you could never buy now for love nor money: a record player with the record still sitting on the turntable, dusty, mind you, dusty as all get out, but nothing wrong with it, an heir-loom by the looks of it, the very first record player in Scotland or at least Argyll. I got a screwdriver and changed the plug and when I plugged it in the record started playing no bother, I swear to God, as if the singer had just paused for a second in the middle of a verse.

Dresses from donkey's years ago, coats with fur collars, nice things: you don't like to chuck them. All kinds of stuff in a brown suitcase; it must be the one she mentioned to me years ago, the suitcase that came on the boat from Wemyss Bay. Two brilliant bottles of red wine. Mammo was never really one for wine. You can't just ask her, though. There's no way to ask her now about a bottle of red wine. Nineteen-forty it says on the label, good God I bet you that's worth something. It must have been kept over from a big night out or a special occasion years ago. Old-fashioned chocolate, personal stuff, men's shaving gear. Clearing it all out, I sat on the bed at one point just looking at the things in the open suitcase, gloves, those nice combs you used to get, the Langdale, the Bela, the gloves were good ones too, and I'm telling you I just knew the men's stuff had never belonged to my father, don't ask me why, but it seemed obvious that the suitcase and those dresses were part of some other life my mother had lived, a life we didn't discuss.

Too late for that now. My mother was just getting more forgetful and it was time, and as for this house, it was always too big for her and houses don't last for ever. The police found her one night wandering down the pier in her nightdress. When they stopped her she said it was time for her work. She thought it was time to go down and open the café. I hate to bring her down from here, I said to my friends, and so I do: it was always nice to think of mammo up here on the hill looking down on us. She just wasn't safe any more and that's that. It comes to us all I suppose. She wasn't recognising people the same way as before, and you wouldn't want to leave her, not up here, not on her own with hot water and fires.

She's in Nazareth House. I go and see her every day. She's one of the better ones up there: she'll sit and talk some days no bother, and she'll say, God bless her, 'I'm fine in here, just nice and warm. Bring down any washing and ironing you need done and I'll get going on it.' She still likes a wee joke and that, you see her sitting there happy as Larry, and you don't need to worry—she's up there with nice people looking after her, and sometimes everything's for the best.

They say some people take a long time to lose themselves with that disease but with other people once they start, it goes quickly after that. My mother has slowed down, the last ten years she's been slowing down, but maybe we didn't notice what was happening to her, until suddenly one day she just couldn't cope up here in the house. Never mind. She's safe now where she is and that's the main thing. But it's quiet here without her. It's very quiet.

It was a mercy, really. She didn't understand what happened. The whole business passed her by and that really was a mercy, you had to thank God. I don't know: they didn't always see eye-to-eye but I know it would have broken her heart, the terrible business with Rosa. Poor Rosa. You can't stop thinking about it. You can't get over it.

I hadn't seen her for weeks. I knew Giovanni had fucked off altogether; first it was the oil rigs then some woman in Aberdeen and he was out of it by then and it was good riddance to bad rubbish as far as I was concerned. But Rosa wasn't well. We're always trying to speak for one another but you can't always speak for people: she was devastated that he wasn't coming back, she just couldn't cope and that's that. You know, years ago I always thought it would be him; I thought he'd be the one to be left on his arse, nothing to show for all the work, all the love that was spent on him. But he had the charm. He had the gift to be able to reconcile himself to any sort of life, and it was poor Rosa, the home-maker, the ambitious one, our Rosa who gets left without a leg to stand on. 'That's the old style,' she said to me one afternoon in the café. 'They're all away now.'

'Women don't put up with that nowadays,' I said.

'Don't they?' she said.

People make out the world is all what happens tomorrow and the day after that. But I remember my sister. I remember us sitting at the window when we were young counting the bumps on the Cowal Hills and making lists of the colours from here to the lochs. Rosa always found more colours than I did and she would always laugh and write them down or store them up in her head.

My sister chose a clear day to die on. It was Hogmanay, and it should have been cold: usually you can't see two feet in front of you at that time of year. In the afternoon I took mammo a walk down the seafront and people were out buying carry-outs for the Bells. Mammo took my arm and we walked slowly beside the railing and even the water was calm. I saw as we passed on the other side that the café was closed, so we stopped at the telephone box and I rang. 'Hello Rosa,' I said to the answering machine, 'just wanted to see what you're doing for the Bells. I'm going up to Nazareth House to sit and bring them in with mammo and Maria is singing on the *Hogmanay Show.* Give me a ring.' That's all I said.

They had a poster up outside the Esplanade Hotel for Lesley Presley, Scotland's Greatest Elvis Impersonator. Mammo and I were just walking and a man came along in a kilt. Mammo chuckled to herself and yawned like a lion. 'The Fyfe and Fyfe entertainers,' she said, 'and a man on the pier selling canaries.' She stopped next to the sea wall and looked up at me. 'The man selling canaries was just selling sparrows painted yellow so don't be fooled,' she said, then we walked to the tea-room at the old pier at Craigmore and had our tea and strawberry tarts.

The television room was full at 11.45. The nurses at Nazareth House had put the tired ones to bed, and there was steak pie and peas being dished out, mainly to the families of the residents, you know, all of them around their mother or father or whoever in the chairs. I brought mammo over a glass of sherry and she took it no problem. The room had streamers and balloons and that, and some of the families had brought their weans and they were quite happy playing on the carpet. So all the families just watched the TV. Scottish country dancers whirling about as usual to the Alexander Brothers.

Mammo sipped her drink and told me I should mind and say my prayers. I'd never noticed it before in Nazareth House, but every family speaks on behalf of the old ones in their chairs. The old ones sit there staring at the telly or into space, and their family says what the old person might say if she or he wasn't ill. Every family does it, and they put questions to the old ones but answer the questions themselves.

THE O'NEILLS: Oh there's Moira Anderson, mother. You always loved Moira Anderson didn't you? She loved Moira Anderson. Of all the singers it was always Moira Anderson you loved the best, sure it was? Aye it was.

THE MCDAIDS: You're the same, aren't you faither? Aye. Look at all the people enjoying themselves. He's happy wi' his drink. You enjoying your wee drink faither? Aye, he's happy. Sharon what time is it? How long have we got to the Bells? Oh fine. You don't like to miss the Bells. He always liked Hogmanay in his ain hoose. Eh, faither, in yer ain hoose? Aye, he says, nae bother. Nae bother at a'. He wouldny step outside the door on Hogmanay. Never in his life. He's that happy sitting there.

THE O'NEILLS: He looks that happy right enough, his nice shirt and tie. Mother, she's been looking forward to the night, haven't you mother? Oh, aye, she's brand new sitting here. You're glad we're a' the gither. Oor party's as good as anybody's, intit mother? Aye, she says—this is the place to be.

THE BOYCES: Drink up your drink. She likes a wee lager.

THE MCDAIDS: Everybody likes a wee dram at ne'erday. Faither. So you do, don't you? He liked a wee lager at ne'erday.

THE DUFFS: Maw. Wake up noo. Wake up. She wants to be awake for the Bells. You don't want to sleep through the Bells. Here's a wee bit shortbread, you love your shortbread maw. Aye, she loves her shortbread. There's Andy Stewart. She always said Andy Stewart was that handsome. Andy Stewart's on the telly maw. There maw. Aye. She loves him. She says I wouldny mind taking the pin oot ma knickers for that Andy Stewart.

THE MCDAIDS: He's steamin'.

THE O'NEILLS: Blootered.

THE DUFFS: Sozzled.

THE O'NEILLS: Oot his tree. I bet he's put a few drams away. Eh, maw? He's put a few drams away the night that Andy Stewart. Aye. Maw says he's probably got a half-bottle in his sporran. Ha!

THE BOYCES: She's sitting there in a wee world of her own. Eh, mother? Aye. You're wondering how long it is to the Bells. She's wonderin'. Drink your lager. There's a few songs to come up. Mrs Tambini's granddaughter is coming on. You remember her? Mother. You remember Maria Tambini? She always loved Maria singing on the telly. Didn't you mother? That's right. She loves Maria Tambini. Mother. That's Mrs Tambini's granddaughter. She's coming on to sing.

THE MCDAIDS: Nobody like her. That's what you always said, eh faither? Scotland's greatest export. He loves her. Look at the telly, faither, Maria Tambini's coming on. What a singer. You always said that didn't you faither. Aye. He loves her.

THE DUFFS: Oh, she'll no be wanting anything to eat. Do you maw? No, nothing to eat. She's just happy sitting there and looking about. Tap your wee feet to the music, that's right maw, oh she's enjoying herself.

THE O'NEILLS: Fill your glasses. That's Hinge and Bracket. Look up. Aye, you like them, she likes them. It cannae be long noo tae the Bells. Is your glasses full?

THE MCDAIDS: Hard to believe that's two men. They're that funny the two of them. You would never know that was two men. You cannae be bothered wi' them can you faither? No. He hates all that don't you? He hates a' that. Men dressing up as women. No his style is it, no your style is it faither? No. Oh, you're sitting there laughing a' the same, aye you are so, you are, and widyecallit, the two o' them on the telly... look at him, he's wondering when that Hinge and Bracket are gonnae finish. You waiting for one of their wigs to slip, is that it faither? Aye. Aye. He's waiting for one of their wigs to slip off on the telly.

THE O'NEILLS: The clock. That's the clock now. Sit up straight mother. Okay. Sit up straight that's the clock. Nine...

THE DUFFS: Seven. Six... There y'are maw.

THE BOYCES: Five. Four.

THE MCDAIDS: You're laughing away faither. Three. Two. One.

Happy New Year. The Bells rang out as usual. All the families cuddled the old ones in the chairs and went round kissing each other, kissing us, and the old ones just sat there bewildered, spilling drink, and the families were quiet at long last and having a wee greet. I leaned over and kissed mammo on the cheek and she smiled and kept her eyes on the TV. Big Ben faded out a bit and there was Maria sitting in an old wicker chair. Her hair was permed. She looked that thin and right away, seeing her, a sob caught in the middle of my throat.

'There she is,' said the McDaids, shaking the arm of the old one and pointing at the screen.

Maria sat with a glass of champagne on a side-table and her eyes were bright and she just sat there and sang 'Auld Lang Syne'. 'Oh, she's that lovely. That's your wee niece,' said the Duffs.

'Mammo,' I said, 'it's Maria.' And my mother just smiled at the television and her foot was tapping the carpet just like that.

ROSA NEVER called me back that day. I rang and rang her number. Then I thought, maybe, with one thing and another, she just didn't fancy going through a Hogmanay party. On the way back down from Nazareth House I looked up at her windows and the lights were out so I went home to bed.

I didn't sleep well the first of January. You know that way? I felt anxious, as if I was waiting out the night. Maybe that's just me looking back, but definitely, I rolled this way and that way on the pillows: it might be time to turn on a heater I remember thinking; despite the nice day it had been earlier, there was frost on the windows.

It's murder not to sleep. Maria's face kept floating in front of me, all the colours strange, like on television, people milling around her lifting glasses of drink and drinking out of them and laughing. She was a woman now and that was hard to believe. Ages since I'd been in London, you just don't go, Maria wants to live her own life, she's with a nice fella who used to live round here, and they say he's looking after her. Not easy. I thought she'd given up showbusiness but then the phone rings and she says she's doing that Hogmanay thing and they're only up in Glasgow for one night.

I must have been dozing but at seven o'clock I heard a car passing outside and then the seagulls. I got dressed quietly. Rosa had asked me for her spare key back a while ago, so I couldn't go straight up, but I thought I would chap Mrs Bone's door, she was always up early.

She said, 'Goodness, Alfredo,' standing at the door in her housecoat with her rollers in. 'Happy new year, Mrs Bone,' I said.

I asked her if she'd seen Rosa and said I was worried and had she got a key for the café. 'A minute,' she said. When she came back Mrs Bone was wearing a raincoat and a scarf over her rollers and she came down with me. The café was dark. Strange the things you notice at a time like that. The stock was low in the cabinets, I noticed that, and most of the crisps boxes were down and the sweetie jars were sitting empty. Through the back the kitchen was all scrubbed. Up the back stairs you could hear a radio playing. Rosa was lying in the bath and as soon as I looked I knew she was dead. Floating in the bath around about her and lying on her chest were brown pill bottles and a vodka bottle was in the water. 'No,' I said.

Mrs Bone came in at my back. 'Jesus, Mary and Joseph,' she said. 'Oh Rosa. Alfredo. Oh my God.'

The radio was playing on the floor. I put my hand into the water and it was freezing and Rosa's eyes were closed and I thought she's wearing a shower cap, of course that's right she wouldn't want her hair to get wet, and I just kept saying, 'Rosa, it's okay, it's okay Rosa.'

I don't remember what else. I know that all the lights in the house went on and people came and I was sitting on the toilet seat talking to Rosa and that was that. Dr Jag appeared. He put his hands here and there and checked Rosa in the bath and he lifted some of the bottles and shook his head and he was chalk-white. I remember saying, 'Dr Jagannadham, let me sit here a minute.'

They all went downstairs and I could hear talking and the telephone ringing, but I shut the bathroom door and just stroked my sister's forehead for I don't know how long, and later on I remember leaning down beside the bath and switching the radio off.

Just sitting here with mammo's boxes. Once this is all over I'll go and see my wee niece. She can't make it home just now and I'd like to see her. Maybe she would like some of the things from this house, I didn't think of that. This morning I took mammo out and we stopped for a mug of tea. As we walked up the seafront she pulled her coat in at her throat the way she always does and she told me how men used to come up the front years ago with rolled-up towels under their arms for the swimming.

I thought she hadn't really understood what happened to Rosa, but this morning we bumped into Mrs Bone outside the Pavilion, and normally my mother and Mrs Bone would just pass each other, but this morning mammo stopped stone dead. Mrs Bone looked nervous at first, then a sad look came over her face. They hadn't spoken to each other for years. 'Here, Lucia,' said Mrs Bone, and she put her arms around mammo and mammo lifted her hands onto Mrs Bone's shoulders. When the two of them stood back they were crying. They cried quietly and the seagulls picked at the stones in the road.

'Cold,' said mammo.

'Aye, it is that,' said Mrs Bone. 'This weather would put years on you.'

Half the pots in mammo's kitchen have money in them. We're going to put it to good use, get a wee car: by the spring me and Bill will be able to take her for days out to Loch Lomond and round to Dunoon, just the three of us. If you're lucky and the roads are clear you can get a straight run all the way to Fort William.

11 · *This Is Your Life*

Maria left the *Hogmanay Show* and collapsed in the hotel. Everyone knew she wasn't fit enough.

'I want to sing,' she had said to Michael.

'Give it to the summer,' he said.

'No, I'm ringing Marion. I know she could get me a booking if she wanted to.'

They argued. Maria said she was ready for a comeback but Michael said she was kidding herself. 'You just want me to lie in this bed like a fucking baby for ever,' she said.

'No, Maria,' he said, 'I want you to weigh more than six stone. I want you to build up your strength. If you take a booking you know you'll just starve yourself for it.'

'You want me to fail,' she said.

'It's not a failure. I want you to stop fighting yourself.'

'This is my life,' she screamed.

He drew his hand through his hair. 'Is it?' he asked. 'Is this your life, Maria?'

'I just want to sing, that's all,' she said.

'Your life,' he said.

Marion said the booking was in Glasgow and she'd make sure it wouldn't be tough: just one song at the Bells.

Michael couldn't deny how replenished she seemed at the thought of facing an audience. The first two months after coming out of hospital were great: she allowed him to cook things for her, and she ate them, some of them, and her face filled out and she said she was ready to strike out into the world. She told everybody she was in love, but after those first months she began to lose weight again. She wouldn't eat with him, she was taking laxatives, the doctor said she could die.

Michael was upset at his desk one day. 'No use crying over girls,' said Betty, blowing on her tea. Over in the other office Martin's talking computer was spelling out a document; the android female voice had Paul the dog spinning in his basket.

'Fuck off,' Michael said.

He went into his boss's office and sat there for a while. He spoke to Philip about the possibility of a posting with St Clare's in Rome; they discussed apartments and logistics. When he came out he went up to Betty's desk. With her tiny aggrieved nose twitching over her typewriter, her glasses low, she was winding two sheets of A4 and a sheet of carbon paper under the roller. 'I'm sorry to swear at you, Betty,' he said. 'It's not your fault.'

'Never mind,' she said. 'I heard much worse in the war.'

Michael tried to back Maria up as best he could. When the day came for the trip to Glasgow she agreed to drink some Bovril; she ate some grapes and a mint at the airport. A car picked them up in Glasgow and took her to a hair appointment. She fell asleep in the chair, and Michael told the stylist to leave her there for a while, and when she woke she loved her hair and they went to the rehearsals at Queen Margaret Drive.

She collapsed in the room after the show. The ambulance took her to the Southern General Hospital. Michael spoke to the consultant on his own. 'I'm so weak to have allowed this.'

'We're all weak when it comes to this,' the man said.

Maria knew the ward when she woke up and she immediately noticed the feed bag; Michael was sleeping in a chair by the bed. 'I'm so sorry,' she said. 'Do you hate me?'

'Don't be silly,' he said.

'Was last night good?'

'Everybody said you were fantastic.'

'I don't need it any more,' she said.

'We'll see.'

'I'm not giving any concerts,' she said after a long pause.

'You don't give concerts, Maria,' he said, 'you give yourself.'

MICHAEL BANNED newspapers from her room. He had spoken to Alfredo and they had both decided not to tell her yet. 'I don't know what to say,' he said to Alfredo.

'Say a prayer.'

When the day came, he sat smoking cigarettes in the corridor next to the lifts, the sound of the electric ropes screeching and toiling above and below him. She was looking better and was sat up in bed reading old magazines and eating toast. He didn't want her to know: out there, in the corridor, with the lift-noises and people going past in their slippers, he wished to God for once they could be free of other people's stories.

She was pretty in bed. Hair in a bun. She put down the magazine when he came in. *Woman*. He saw the headline lying on the bed. 'I Had My Throat Stapled and Lost Eighteen Stone'. She looked from the magazine to his face. 'It's all rubbish in those things,' she said. He closed the door.

'You look so beautiful,' he said. She put out her hand to him. 'No matter what,' he said, 'we'll get through this.' Her mouth grew thin and her fingers stiffened.

'What is it?' she asked.

'I'd do anything not to tell you this,' he said. 'It's terrible news. Your mother died.'

Maria drew a breath and it seemed then as if she would never stop breathing in, as if she were drawing water into her lungs instead of air. She gasped, and all breath seemed inadequate, thick and un-manageable, then she sobbed, and her tears ran onto the bedclothes. 'I'm so sorry,' he said, holding on to her, and for almost an hour she knocked her head gently against his shoulder and cried.

At last she looked up at him. 'Did someone kill her?' she asked.

'No,' he said, stunned by the question. 'She took her own life.'

'Is that true? Is that what my mum did, she killed herself?'

'Yes. I love you, Maria. I'm so sorry.'

When she fell asleep that night, he went to the telephone and rang his parents. As he dialled the number he pictured them sitting by the fire on the farm at Scalpsie Bay. 'Hello stranger,' said his father, his adoptive father. 'We were just talking about you. A big frigate is moored over towards Arran.'

'Dad,' said Michael, 'did you know about Maria's mother?'

'We read it in the *Herald*,' he said. 'There's been no answer on your phone.'

'I'm in Glasgow with Maria. She's back in hospital.'

'It's a sorry business, son. Remember we're here. Your mother wants to speak to you.'

'Poor Maria,' his mother said. 'Poor the lot of you.'

'Come and see us for your holidays some time,' Michael said.

'Of course,' she said, 'we'll do that.'

'Somewhere sunny, maybe.'

'Wherever you say. Just let us know.'

'Somewhere sunny.'

'That's right.'

'Apart from you, Michael,' Maria said next morning, 'everything is like a black hole and I'm going further and further in.'

She left Scotland for the residential clinic in Kennington. She complained that her static was worse: the street is grey, she said, there's a wall of static between me and the world. One week there was a break-in at her house in Shepherds Bush and a great horde of showbusiness memorabilia was stolen. 'Nothing means anything,' she said to the counsellor. 'I feel dead inside.'

Michael had to go to work but his mind was elsewhere. The Queen came to Rottingdean to open a new swimming-pool. 'I might not have good eyes,' a St Clareite said, 'but I can tell that you're not yourself, Michael.'

'Just stuff, Simon. There's your queen coming now. Do you want me to describe what she's wearing?'

'Bugger off,' he said. 'Just describe the way to the nearest pub.'

Those months, Michael came back to the clinic in the evening and Maria was folded up in herself, dark-minded, starving in a big jersey. He climbed up on the bed. 'Wish I could live inside you,' she said one night, 'just here.' She placed a fist on his stomach and Michael looked at the soft downy hair along her jawline and above her lip. She was five stone. After she was washed and tucked in the bed he looked at her as she slept for hour after hour, her bony arms outside the blankets in two straight lines, her delicate neck, the jaw so tight that her mouth seemed wider and her eyes retreated back from her face. She opened them and stared unblinking into the lamp overhead. Her eyes had never appeared so green, her blonde hair spread out on the pillow. Lying there she was finally like a doll. She was motionless. Then like some unblinking personage in a fairy story, she would move her large eyes and say something. 'Michael. Are you there? Is there a glass of water?'

'It's a story of ups and downs,' said the doctor. 'Losses and gains. But it can't go on for ever.'

Michael took her home for a week. She told him one day he couldn't watch over her all the time. 'Go to work,' she said, 'and I'll lie down on the sofa and later maybe I'll cook you something.'

'Don't cook,' he said.

'Don't worry. Go to work.'

She was drawn in by the afternoon TV shows. They made her rock with wakefulness and think of recipes, and there was some long segment about women who cheat and hours of this seemed to pass in minutes. She spoke to the television, imagined she was being interviewed about her years in the business, and then the programme was finished and it was horse racing but still she stared at the arm of the sofa and spoke to the interviewer about being famous.

She pulled on jogging pants and a coat of Michael's and Wellington boots and the clothes drowned her. Her face seemed pinched and strained as the wind blew in her face and she took small steps down the road feeling everything was fuzzy. She walked to the mini-supermarket on the green. Hanging from the ceiling in the aisle where you found the cans of beans and soup was a picture of a woman's smiling face, a woman with her clean teeth bared in front of a spoon with steam rising from the spoon and her nostrils open and her eyes closed but happy.

The rows of coloured tins and packets seemed alive. Under the fluorescent strip-lights the rows moved as germs do under a microscope and spread and fell over each other. Maria walked under the lights and heard tunes with no words and saw a great spillage of milk and thought it was blood on the floor of the minimarket. She wandered through several aisles and near the end she turned and lifted a box of Quivers jelly and put it in the pocket of the coat and walked straight out the door.

'Empty your pockets, madam.'

She was arrested for stealing an item worth forty-nine pence.

She would wake in the night. Michael was there. 'Your skin,' she said, 'your skin is only yours and nobody else's.'

'Sweetheart,' he said, 'try and sleep until the morning.'

But she couldn't always sleep. Some nights she went around the house emptying bins and ashtrays. She smoked instead of eating. In the hours she couldn't sleep she would do her private rants then sit very quietly in front of the living-room window, the shadow of net curtains falling over her and the wall beside her. She would smoke one cigarette after another, staring out, listening to her thoughts, her face lit up by the beams from a car often parked across the way, lamps on, lamps off.

I'm all right. Don't panic.

The static settled down and she felt all right smoking cigarettes there and feeling watched.

Trained for this. Settle down now. Shhhhh.

One night by the window she imagined a scene. She'd thought about it before, the scene, but it had never been so complete, and as it began to occupy her head the light flashing into the room became steady, and the room brightened. Waves of applause fall from all the tiers of the Palladium; she feels high and clear-headed from singing. She stands still in front of the microphone and is almost see-through with the emotion of the songs and the endless applause coming down. Feeling the scratch of the sequins, she hitches up her dress and curtsies, then flowers and toys fall around her. She walks from the stage and takes a glass of water in the wings and walks back onstage to take another bow. A man approaches from behind with a red book.

A roar comes from the crowd. He touches her shoulder and when she turns his eyes are smiling. She covers her mouth and he waits for the applause to die down and says, 'Maria Tambini. Singer and great star of British light entertainment. I'm Eamon Andrews and I'm here to say, This is your life.' The theatre is filled to the high ceiling with noise and there's a rumble of feet. She cries with happiness and is led offstage. It cuts to a studio where swirling music plays around her and she is led by Eamon Andrews onto a sound stage where people are waiting for her and a studio audience is clapping.

There's an empty chair on its own and she is led to sit down. She reaches out beside her and her mother is sitting smiling and wiping tears away. 'I'm so proud.' Her mother mouths the words. Giovanni is sitting next to Rosa with his black hair slicked back and his smile glowing. Alfredo is laughing beside them, smiling in a new suit; further along is Lucia, like her photograph when she was young, with Mario, her husband and Maria's grandfather, who folds away his pocket-watch and blows a kiss. Mrs Bone waves a hand and sniffles into a tissue. Dr Jagannadham and his wife are smiling in the back row surrounded by teachers and the priest from Rothesay and entertainers from the Winter Gardens. Maria sits in her chair and looks round as if she can't believe it.

Her hair is beautifully waved and sleek, her eyelids are frosted blue, skin clear, lips glossy. She is wearing jewels and as Eamon Andrews opens the red book she looks up at him and the studio lights pick out her dress and her eyes and jewels dazzle together. 'You are joined tonight,' says Mr Andrews, 'by a great crowd of family and friends, but there's one or two people missing...'

A voice came over the air. 'We were queens for a day once upon a time, Maria, and I'm still your number one fan.'

'You haven't seen each other since you were young girls together. Now working as an executive officer with a Glasgow health trust, she has flown down to be with you tonight. Your best friend, Kalpana Jagannadham!'

The doors swing apart and the music sounds and Kalpana comes out wearing a dark-blue suit. Maria's eyes fill up again and she throws open her arms. Kalpana is taller than Maria and when they stand apart Maria points to her short hair. They hold hands and wipe away tears and the camera flashes to Dr Jagannadham clapping and nodding.

'What are your early memories of our star?' asks Mr Andrews.

'She was just such a great friend to have,' says Kalpana. 'It was dead obvious from a young age that she was going to make it. We used to put on wee shows of our own in her mother's kitchen. I couldny sing for toffee but Maria used to just blow people away with her great voice and her personality. Even before she was a star she was a star to us and it was such a privilege to be her friend.'

The audience applaud and Maria stands up and they hug each other before Kalpana walks over to the seats. A screen at the side of the studio set comes to life. 'Here's a message from sunny California,' says Mr Andrews. A man appears on the screen: he looks like Dean Martin and has a suntan and to Maria he seems instantly kind and familiar.

'Hello, Maria,' he says. 'It's always been a regret of mine that we didn't get to spend as much time together as I would have liked, but rest assured, honey, I've followed your wonderful career with such pride and admiration all these years. You're a wonderful person and a real star. Everywhere I go I'm pleased to say you're top of the world.'

'He's here tonight, flown in all the way from Beverly Hills. Your father and what a fan of yours.'

The doors swing apart and the man comes walking down with his arms open and a big American grin. He looks like a movie star and when he arrives in front of Maria he kisses her hand. She feels enfolded by him and he blows a kiss to Rosa and as he walks to his seat Maria's hand is covering her mouth.

'Maria Tambini,' says Mr Andrews, 'you were born in the town of Rothesay on the bonnie Scottish island of Bute on 10 April 1964. You grew up in the family café among Scottish-Italians and holiday-makers and at an early stage you showed a unique talent for singing. Even at school you stood apart. While your friends were following childish pursuits you were already rehearsing with your mother Rosa and attending dance classes. Was she a hard worker, mum?'

Rosa looks up and is smiling like someone who knows she belongs in this moment. 'She always had great discipline,' she says, 'and she did without things just so's she could improve as a performer. She always kept herself clean and tidy and up in her room at night she would sing herself to sleep. Our relationship was always the greatest: I knew that no matter what happened to Maria she would turn out to be a great person.'

The audience applaud. 'There was always music in your child-hood,' says Mr Andrews, 'and Italian songs and all the wonderful sweets that every child loves. You had a great friend in your Uncle Alfredo, whose barber shop was an early haunt of yours, and it was Alfredo who sent off your details to the great television talent show of the day, *Opportunity Knocks*.'

A voice came over. 'And she exuded talent I tell you the way other kids breathe oxygen, and I mean that most sincerely, folks!'

'The man who gave you your big break in showbusiness. Here he is: Mr Wonderful himself—Hughie Green!'

The music blares and Mr Green walks through with a lopsided grin and he does a little dance move as he walks towards Maria. He kisses her on both cheeks and winks at Mr Andrews before address-ing the audience directly. 'This lovely girl,' he says, 'was a power-house of talent from the minute I saw her. Just phenomenal. To think all that wonderful sound was coming out of that little girl. You know, I'd been around child performers all my career—I was one myself—but this girl has that special something you can't quite put your fin-ger on. And chatterbox! At the auditions, I remember her coming up after doing her number and she said, "Mr Green"—her wee Scottish voice—"is it okay if I go and speak to the other acts?" "Sweetie," I said, "after singing like that, I think you should maybe just sit down and give your tonsils a rest." But I mean this...'

Mr Green puts up his hand to encourage the audience.

'MOST SINCERELY, FOLKS!' they shout back.

'... she is a credit to showbusiness and everyone in the industry admires and respects the young lady of talent that she has become. You deserve this, honey. Have a wonderful, wonderful evening.'

Mrs Gaskell comes on and speaks of the joy of having Maria to live with her in the early days. 'She has always worked jolly hard,' she says, 'and it's been such a tremendous delight to play a part in the ca-reer of someone so dedicated to the pursuit of excellence. I must say the industry thrives on what Maria has got, and so does the country! She's very special. I only wish we had more of her to go round.'

Maria sits back in her chair and the evening becomes hazy with strange and reliable comforts. Morecambe and Wise appear and hold her up between them. Les Dawson comes on. The teachers from Italia

Conti tell funny stories about her training. On the screen, Johnny Carson speaks from America and Billy Butlin comes out to talk about Maria's wonderful summertime specials. Laughing and looking scrubbed, hair combed, wearing a T-shirt from one of Maria's concerts, is Kevin Goss. 'I'm really her official number one fan,' he says, 'and it's great to love somebody like Maria and know that she really loves you.'

All the seats are filled on both sides of the studio. 'You were the nation's favourite for seven weeks on *Opportunity Knocks*,' says Mr Andrews. 'You had your own show and were a star in America before you were out of your teens. You have made records and television shows that have captured the imagination of millions of people who know that dreams can and will come true.'

Maria is a thousand points of light. The music is swelling and familiar and they all smile at her and soon the audience begin to clap and the cameras shift across the floor. Maria looks up at Mr Andrews and her eyes fill with tears. 'I've been loved,' she says.

'Maria Tambini—This Is Your Life.'

He holds out the red book and everyone stands. Maria looks behind her at the swishing doors. Panic enters her eyes as she takes the red book from Mr Andrews but he can't hear her. 'I've been loved,' she says. 'Where is Michael?'

She looks again at the doors and they are open but no one is there, just emptiness filled with studio light. The theme music of *This Is Your Life* is playing and she is guided out of her chair and she holds on to the red book, but over her shoulder she can see that no one else is coming through the doors. The camera closes in and she holds the book tightly and all the people come round her, they touch her and laugh and speak to her and she can see their faces looming but her voice is gone as she walks forward to the camera.

'Maria.'

There is only white light in the room.

'Maria! Maria. Come to bed.'

She was sitting at the window but now the living-room light was on and Michael was standing in pyjama bottoms at the door. 'Come to bed, darling,' he said. He came over and crouched down behind her and put his arms over her shoulders. She could smell the toothpaste from him; his skin was warm and soothing against her. 'Michael,' she said, 'don't leave me.'

There was nothing much of her sitting there. 'Come on, lovely,' he said, and kissed her neck, put his arms under her legs, and lifted her out of the chair. She lay her head under his chin as he carried her up to sleep. On the stairs, he stopped for a moment; her breathing was quiet, the hall was full of shadows, and outside he could hear a car's engine starting up and he held Maria as the car disappeared up the road.

12 · Michael

I thought she was gone that time. The bedroom upstairs had mirrors on every wall, and I lay her down on the bed; strange how incomprehension can gather at that time of night, Maria lying under the white sheets and me full of fear. I placed a chair in the middle of the room and sat watching. How had it come to this? Why? Maria lay there and all the words that usually surrounded her, all the voices, my own words too, were finally stilled by her silence. She slept, she slept all night, my heart breaking, no mercy in the wallpaper or the cups and books by the bed, only the hours of the night growing terrible, my own mind defeated and full of thoughts about the past, and Maria asleep, down to her bones, my only love, and blind with victory.

The next morning was Sunday and the ambulance came and took her to Guy's. The doctor said she was under five stone and beginning to hallucinate; she needed constant care, and they wanted to try a programme of treatment they run at Guy's. I must admit, that morning I was nearly out of it with self-pity—why me? why this?— and the medical smells were disgusting. When the nurses were rigging up the drips and stuff, I went walking round and round the corridors and up and down stairs; one of the stairwells had a fire exit and I stared at the bar. I stared at it and Christ knows what I was thinking, but it was all too much that morning. All I ever wanted was her. All I really wanted. Near Eastbourne one day there was a burn with stones across it; she was laughing and her eyes were lovely I swear and one foot slipped into the water and her shoe was wet. We were both laughing so loud. I leaned back towards her over the stones and when I took her hand her skin was soft. She laughed at my crappy trainers. We could hear voices coming from across the grass so we got out of the burn and ran towards them, and no day was ordinary or lost when I was with her.

Tiny pieces of banana, inches of toast: that's what it took. For weeks she drank wee sips of water, then I'd feed her, with no one coming or going to disturb us, the days just stretching into one another. We talked of things we'd never got to before: family things, current affairs, my time at university; it was a slow time but you felt walls were coming down, Maria began to reveal herself, getting over sadness and panic. She reached into herself over that time and saved her own life.

'You are the half of me,' she said.

I gave her a glass of water to keep her throat from becoming dry and said nothing. For so long she had looked like a woman in a wind-tunnel, her face wizened beyond her years, and now, day by day, her face emerged as the face of someone released from a terrible dream, and she was tired but also relaxed as I hadn't seen her since I first knew her. 'She was at her lowest point,' the doctor said. 'She can't go back to that again.'

'We're not going back,' I said.

She asked the nurse if she could have her own knife, fork and spoon, and put them in a drawer by the bed. 'Trying,' she said.

One of the days she asked me if people had really liked the songs she sang. 'I think they did,' I said.

'They were all goodbye songs.'

'Yes.'

'From the beginning. Every one of them.'

She took the food too quickly in the first weeks and couldn't keep it down. But then she forged a routine: cornflakes, semolina, banana, egg. She began to drink tea with a half-spoon of sugar in it. From the side of her bed at Guy's you could look across the roofs to the Thames.

Egg, chicken, beef soup. She kept a few books by the bed and read them to suit herself. *The Friendship Book* by Francis Gay, Fodor's *Beginner's Guide to Italian*. 'My mouth tastes of ink,' she said.

She asked me to read to her in the evening and we read the same poems and things over and over. She said she liked my voice, and it was good, eventually, because she came to know the words herself and when I read the poems her lips would move. One night, I began to say the words and then reduced the sound of my voice, and Maria's own voice came up in my place: she was saying the words herself.

She was cursing one day—she hated the food, or hated the need for it, yet she lifted the spoon. Her weight became more and more normal; her face filled out and her eyes glowed and filled their sockets at last. She said the static in her head was becoming less by the day; she was full of plans.

One large suitcase and a bag of books: that was all we needed and all we would take. We discussed everything in detail and I made plans in the daytime and we got excited the healthier she became and the more the doctor said 'Soon'. She wanted to get rid of all her old dresses and shoes. 'Nothing fits me and nothing is nice anyway,' she said.

'Come back to Shepherds Bush and see,' I said.

'No,' she said. 'I'll never be in that house again.'

The bedsit in Kensington was gone. I slept in Maria's house and every night threw more of her things away. Sparkly tops and dresses covered in beads, painted shoes, and tons of make-up—half-squeezed tubes and trays of powder lying in plastic bags or wrapped in towels from seaside hotels. There were a few belongings I thought she must surely want: small frocks, dozens of pairs of children's gloves. 'Chuck them,' she said. 'All the things I would've kept are gone anyway.'

I think some of the local kids came round during the day and took stuff from the bins. The bins outside would be sitting differently from the way I'd left them, as if they'd been raked through, and when I looked properly, I noticed some of the black bags had gone altogether. 'Doesn't matter,' I thought, but when I mentioned it to Maria she started crying and said she wasn't feeling well. I stayed with her late that night. She was sleeping so I went down to the machine to get a coffee, but when I came back up she was standing in her nightdress at the window with her palms on the glass.

I took her back to bed. 'Michael,' she said, 'I can't wait to be out and I can't wait to be away.'

'The house is nearly empty,' I said. 'I bought a big suitcase. Just our essential stuff. Let me know if there's anything else to pack.'

'Nothing,' she said.

I told her Alfredo sent his love and we'd speak to him soon.

'Mrs Gaskell is arranging the rental of the house,' I said. 'She'll put the money into your account.'

'Did you tell her goodbye?' she asked.

'I did.'

'Goodbye from me?'

'Yes,' I said. I told her everything would be fine. 'The office will handle whatever comes up. I gave Marion my work address. She said to tell you she was happy for you.'

Maria licked her lips and her eyes filled when I said that. She looked straight at me and her mouth was trembling. 'Last night I had a dream about statues and lemons,' she said. I told her to try and get some sleep. She leaned up, kissed me, and wiped her face. 'Tomorrow,' she said.

'Tomorrow,' I said.

I sat by the bed and looked out the window. I'm telling you, I would have made her better but I wouldn't have changed any of these days. There wasn't much for me in the world out there without her, and I realised it and still do: some of us only ever have one destination, to love someone, and the nights and difficult days can make you certain of it.

She kept some pain to herself. I know that. I asked her to explain some things but she shrugged it off and I let it go. But I remember that last night at Guy's: while she was asleep, I put the last of her things into a bag, hair clasps, bracelets, stuff she might want. I opened a drawer of the bedside cabinet and found a pile of get-well cards, thirty or more, and I remember deciding to say nothing about them. I was always too much like that with Maria. I suppose I trusted we'd be leaving it all behind. I can still see the cards, each one with the same sort of picture, flowers or animals, and inside, scrawled in big letters, the same words. 'Love Kevin'. 'Love Kevin'. 'Love Kevin'.

13 · Kevin

Slike some people need you for life. They use nice soap and get their hair done all the time and then people just want to go and mess them up and get in their road. Every day some person comes out and tries to spoil them and seasy for me to just make sure they're okay and that. Nine times out of ten a famous person is not being looked after properly and that's a total liberty you know. People forget how hard it is for a girl to look like her photograph.

She was bigger than the lights at Blackpool. Always smiling she was and always happy to be looked at. I've got tons of these photos but they've been left out in the sun or something and half of them are all faded now and I want to leave this dump and go. People can refuse to speak to you but slike I've worked it out and if they live in your heart they can only really die when you die. Salright that way.

Good weather outside. Snice night and you wouldn't believe all the daffodils are up in the park already. It makes all the difference you know. Slike summer already. Nights like this we used to have sandwiches and cans of shandy for our dinner and the window would be open with people out laughing and playing rounders in the square. The telly would be on in that house and they would come through the kitchen and everybody was welcome. The ice-cream van outside, I can still hear the jingle. It was just like a nice family those times and the telly was good. Sall changed. Sall different. There's nothing on the telly any more, sall rubbish and the thing just sits there gathering dust.

14 · Tomorrow

'You're strong,' said the doctor.

'I feel I could run the marathon.'

'Take your time. Is that not always the rule?'

'But thank you. I feel good today.'

The nurse came along with a smile. 'Early this morning there was a call for you, Maria. You were in the shower. Your uncle—Fred. Is that right?'

'Alfredo.'

'Yes. Quite a young man. He sounded nice. A bit confused. He asked when you were getting out and I think he was a bit surprised.'

Maria stiffened on the spot but in those seconds her fear began to change into anger. 'Did he say anything else?'

'No,' said the nurse, 'he was off the phone before I had a chance to say much, but I expect he'll reach you at home anyway.'

Maria sat on the bed. Her body did feel strong and her mind was full of distances: thoughts of the journey ahead had begun to revolve with pictures of the past. Now she was ready in her raincoat and shoes, her hair shiny and fair, held in a short pony-tail, just as she had liked to have it when she was young and practising hand-stands against the wall of the gym hall.

Michael stood on the path outside the house that morning and thought of it as the house of a missing person, not the kind people hear about on the news or see on posters, but another kind altogether, the sort who disappear into public view, who lose themselves in recognition and are never heard of again. All the personal belongings had gone from the house. He locked the door and stood for a moment and the street was quiet with its drawn curtains and the wheely-bins out on the paving stones. He walked across the street to the postbox, dropped the keys into a Jiffy bag, then felt its weight and looked at the stamps and the address written out, Marion Gaskell Associates, Top Floor, 71 Denmark Street, London W1. Lifting up the suitcase and the rucksack he walked back over the road and noticed as he walked that pigeons were flying over the houses and some were perched on the television aerials. The noise of the black cab pulling away made the birds scatter in the air.

KEVIN GOSS was parked outside the Old Operating Theatre Museum in St Thomas Street. In the middle of the morning he saw them coming. Maria was hardly recognisable, filled-out, fatter-faced, with a raincoat over her arm and wearing a pretty dress, the boyfriend in a suit and laughing with bags in his hands. To Kevin's eyes the boyfriend faded away and it was just her at the gates. He reached to open the door; he saw her face smiling, looking shy, normal, not as he remembered it on television or when he'd seen her before in the street. Kevin had one foot on the road then a cab stopped on the opposite side. He watched her climbing into the back and he shook with nerves and closed the car door.

Maria sat back and Michael stroked her hand as the cab moved down Southwark Street; the people outside stood at bus stops or crowded the pavement looking enraptured at nothing. Michael was checking the tickets and he said the word 'Domodossola.'

'So that's the end of the train?' she asked.

'I've rented a car from there,' he said. 'That way we can take it slowly through the countryside.'

'That's great,' she said. 'You know something? This woman, someone my mother knew, has a delicatessen in Edinburgh, her father walked all the way from Tuscany to Scotland in the 1920s, just to get work and he started his own shop.'

'You're kidding?' Michael said.

'No. He walked all the way.'

'Well,' he said, 'I'm wearing my good driving shoes so don't start getting any ideas.' Maria smiled then and cosied into his arm, blowing air out of her lungs, pursing and unpursing her lips as the cab moved on.

Kevin stalled the car coming out of Stamford Street onto the roundabout at Waterloo, he kept looking ahead and turned the key, cursing himself, and quickly he was moving again and could see he hadn't lost much ground, the cab was just turning into York Road and not far in front. As the car moved forward his frustration became more like excitement so he pushed a tape in: Maria's powerful singing voice from ten years before ripped through the car and Kevin kept his head down and drummed the steering wheel in time to the music he loved.

> Oh-oh-over and over
> I'll prove my love to you
> Over and over, what more can I do?
> Over and over, my friends say I'm a fool
> But oh-oh-over and over
> I'll be a fool for you.

Michael was looking out of the window on his own side. 'Before long people won't go to Victoria,' he said. 'The train through the Tunnel's going to leave from here.'

'Waterloo?'

'Yep. No getting off on the way. Straight through to Paris.'

'I don't think I could do it,' she said.

'So fast though, and they say it'll be smart. You can have a drink and everything.'

'If I can't fly nowadays I can't see me going into a tunnel,' she said.

'That's not going to be for ever.'

'No. Probably not. I hope not.'

'A lot of Italians used to live round here, a really big community,' said Michael as the cab reached the end of York Road. 'Your uncle Alfredo told me Waterloo and Clerkenwell were full of Italian shops at one time.'

Maria looked out of the cab window. 'I didn't know that,' she said.

> *Love—*
> *Cause you got a great big heart*
> *Well over—and over*
> *I'll be a fool for you*
> *Well, well, well over and over*
> *What more can I do?*

Kevin spun onto Westminster Bridge and nearly bumped a red bus. He could see the water sparkling under the bridge and his eyes were screwed up against the light. There seemed to be hundreds of people walking along the pavements at each side of the bridge. He became sick of looking at people and the traffic was getting bad. He started swearing louder and twisting the volume control back and forward so the song became distorted.

They passed the Houses of Parliament and Maria looked up at the windows and realised she had never seen them before. Michael whistled to himself and the cab moved into Victoria Street. They hadn't noticed any of the other cars in front or behind them, but Maria got lost for a second looking at a row of people on one of the buses, and she was truly solitary in that instant, as she imagined the people were too, with their own stories and their own lives, and she was aware suddenly of the great many people on the bus, and the many buses on the road, and the roads going out in all directions. She knew she was now one of a horde of people, travelling, moving, standing or sitting still, and it began to appeal to her, the thought that she and Michael and the cab driver were being drawn further into the unconscious actions of a crowd.

Kevin by then was in a panic about losing them. He strained his eyes and turned the steering wheel next to the Apollo Victoria Theatre, then he stopped, scanning the black cabs that were dropping off in front of the station, his breathing wild, clouding his rear-view mirror. The cars behind were beeping and he banged the dashboard with his fist, tears welling up, then he climbed out the car leaving the keys in the ignition. The door wasn't closed and the cord of his seatbelt trailed out of the door onto the road.

He walked quickly and wept, which made him angry because it meant he couldn't see properly. Wasn't that the back of her head gone through the arch? He pushed past the people going into the Underground, almost slipping when he stepped onto the station concourse. He looked over the crowd, blinked rapidly, and turned his head from side to side as if taking snapshots, but it was hopeless, nothing was still and nothing was entirely itself, the crowd hid everything except its own sweep and noise, colour seemed to blaze and retire, starlings swept past in one black movement overhead, and the only voice was the one falling from the air announcing the departures of trains.

Kevin saw everything freeze to a whiteness. His hands pressed deep in the pockets of his coat, he wandered forward and staggered and was short of breath, and he fell into people, noise rushing into his ears, then he stopped against the window of the Wimpy. At some great distance he heard music in the burger bar, saw colours passing, laughter, and up ahead the terrible flicker of the passenger information boards. Dropping his eyes he saw Michael Aigas standing on his own under the board.

It was as if the field had cleared. Everyone else in the station vanished now and the starlings moved slowly from beam to beam. The concourse was polished and Kevin walked forward and saw the person up ahead as a version of himself, and digging his hands in his pockets again he believed there was something terrible and familiar about Michael Aigas, this man with clean hair and a blue suit so smart as he looked up at the board and down at tickets. Kevin stood a few yards behind Michael and said to himself he could walk straight through the man and absorb everything. Four steps and he could replace him in his black shoes. But no. Noise flooded into Kevin's ears again and turning his head he found what he was looking for: 'Ladies'.

Going down the stairs, Maria had walked under a hot-air vent, and she felt just then a luxurious apprehension, as if she were about to step into a warm bath. The tiles at the bottom were shiny; a smell of pine rose from the newly cleaned floor and made her think of fresh Argyll days she had known once upon a time, days in her childhood when the wind tasted of trees. A wet mop stood under the towel dispenser. She smiled at a woman who was applying lipstick, then she ran some cold water over her own fingers and smoothed back her hair. Drying her hands with a paper towel, she felt her wrist and realised she was still wearing her hospital name-tag. She squeezed it off and looked at her face in the mirror. Her eyes were clear and steady with only a little worry at the centre, the irises calm and green, the pupils black as full stops.

Kevin came into the Ladies but it was empty. He went to the sinks and ran some water and reached out for the soap. He was weeping to himself and looked around but she was nowhere to be seen. Then he saw the plastic name-tag two sinks up and he took it in his wet hand. His heart froze over, he gasped: 'Maria Tambini'. He tried to pull the name-tag over his hand—it wouldn't go very far, just onto his knuckles—and then he put the hand into his pocket and stepped to look at himself in the mirror. There she was, behind him, looking into his eyes.

'Such a talented wee thing,' he said.

Maria, in one intake of breath, drew all the moments of her life together, and reaching over pain, over doubt, she became perfect in that fraction of a second as the knife's silver glinted and rose with his fist. She pushed forward with all the force of love's opposite, the pressure of decades flying into the motion to protect herself from the brutal lie of his affection and his grip on the knife. Her soul bounded forward in that moment, she pushed hard, and his feet slipped apart on the wet tiles. He fell back among the sinks with a thud and hit the floor, and he lay there, the knife with his hand clasped around it stuck in his throat.

He tried to say something but the words poured out as blood. Maria was shaking against the door of a cubicle but she felt alert to the urgency of the moment. She stepped forward and pulled a paper towel from the dispenser, then without delay or reflection loosened her name-tag from around Kevin's hand and scrunched it in the paper towel and put it in the pocket of her raincoat.

'What is it?' Michael asked.

She cried into his shoulder and shook.

'You're chalk-white, Maria, what's the matter?'

'Just got a bit frightened,' she said. Her voice was trembling, but she was unbreakable in those minutes, as if at some level of herself, out on the concourse, she knew this might be the last and most decisive performance of her old life.

Michael lifted the bags. 'Come on, love,' he said. 'You'll be all right once you're on the train.'

15 · Maria

I always liked the trips over to Wemyss Bay and the way the seagulls followed the boat. It was so lovely to see the foam going back to the place you had left. Every time they threw the ropes from the pier I said goodbye as if it was the last time, and we had so much to look forward to, our bags packed for the next big thing, and the island got smaller behind us until it was gone.

The Dover cliffs are something else again and Michael is leaning over the side to get a good look. It's nice up here, you can taste the sea-salt in your mouth, and there are children laughing and running on the deck. Just now Michael kissed me and I could smell something great like lemon on his hands and he looked back, what a distance now to the white cliffs. He closed me in next to him and I'm here now and calm. I dropped a ball of paper from my pocket over the side and it was there on the waves for a second then it opened up and was washed away.

'Hey, litterbug,' he said.

There will always be the words to other people's songs, but Michael is here now, and I am here, and the fresh air my God you wouldn't believe it. When I look up I think of all the miles the air has come to reach us, I think of it passing stars and planets, falling through clouds, and blowing over the English Channel, our mouths open to catch the air and to say what we want to say, to speak now, to speak out loud, and before long the land begins to appear over there, another coast. The day is beautiful, we are far from home, and the boat moves like a prayer over the water.

Acknowledgements

A number of publications were helpful to me in the writing of this novel. There are many, and I mention the main ones here. At several points in the narrative I draw on these sources, or import words from them, without reference being given in the text itself. I would like to express my thanks to the authors.

Peter Ackroyd, *London: A Biography*
J. J. Audubon, *The Birds of America*
Françoise Cachin et al, *Cézanne* (exhibition catalogue: Grand Palais, Tate Gallery, Philadelphia Museum of Art)
Italo Calvino, *Italian Folktales* (trans. George Martin)
David Cesarini and Tony Kushner, eds., *The Internment of Italians in 20th-Century Britain* (Miriam Kochan's study of women in the camps was invaluable)
Terri Colpi, *Italians Forward*
Errol Fuller, *Extinct Birds*
Hughie Green, *Opportunity Knocked*
Compton MacKenzie, *Life and Times: Octave Eight*
George Martineau, *Sugar*
Susie Orbach, *Hunger Strike*
Doreen Orion, *I Know You Really Love Me*
Wilhelm Hermann Solf, unpublished memoir
Walter Vandereycken and Ron van Deth, *From Fasting Saints to Anorexic Girls*

The Buteman newspaper
The Rothesay Academy Magazine, 1951–9